Wrong as Two Left Shoes

TEDDY HAYES

The X Press

Published by
The X Press
PO Box 25694
London, N17 6FP
Tel: 020 8801 2100
Fax: 020 8885 1322
E-mail: vibes@xpress.co.uk
Web site: www.xpress.co.uk

Printed by Cox & Wyman, Reading, UK

Distributed in UK by Turnaround Distribution
Unit 3, Olympia Trading Estate, Coburg Road, London N22 6TZ
Tel: 020 8829 3000
Fax: 020 8881 5088

ISBN 1-902934-21-0

This book is dedicated to my daughter Kai

Acknowledgements

Special thanks to Jennie Rosenthal whose loving good vibrations and hard work went into helping me prepare this book and to Bob Silverstein for his support and encouragement of Devil Barnett over many years.

The uniqueness of this book is made possible by the superb talents of the music writers and producers Roly Diaz, Anthony Laird, Gui Tavares, Siraj al Hasan, Curtis Lugay and Alessandra D'Agostino. All those hours in the studio were like magic.
Thank you.

ABOUT THE AUTHOR

Teddy Hayes, a native of Cleveland, Ohio began writing short plays during his first year at Cleveland State University. He has written four stage plays (*Hondo Gothic, The Holding Pen, Breakaway Angel*, and *Mammi Dance Salsa*). He has also produced and directed *I Remember Marvin* a stage show celebrating the musical career of Marvin Gaye and produced and directed the feature film *Case No. 603*. Presently Teddy is living and working in London, England.

Wrong as Two Left Shoes is the third novel in the Devil Barnett detective series. The others are *Blood Red Blues* and *Dead By Popular Demand*.

A special limited edition of this novel comes with a music CD soundtrack. The text is marked to show where the music appears within the story.

CD MUSIC TRACKS

1. **Devil Barnett- intro: Love Everlasting** ~ ~ ~(T. Hayes. Siraj al Hasan)
2. **Love Come Rainin Down*** (T. Hayes, R. Diaz)
3. **Body Flow*** (T. Hayes, R. Diaz)
4. **On and On and On****(T. Hayes, G. Tavares)
5. **I Don't Blame You***(T. Hayes, R. Diaz, E Estruch)
6. **Messin' Wid Me** (T. Hayes, R. Diaz)
7. **Stupid***(T. Hayes, R. Diaz)
8. **Wonderful Light*****(T. Hayes)
9. **Never Walk Out***(T. Hayes, R. Diaz)

Additional songs from: WOODHENRY'S Notebook

10. **Touchin' You in The Morning^^**(T. Hayes, A. D'Agostino, A. Corlis, L. Calamandrei)
11. **Been Good To You*****(T. Hayes)
12. **Your Healer*****(T. Hayes)
13. **Next To You***(T. Hayes R. Diaz)
14. **Obsession****(T. Hayes G. Tavares)

* Produced by Roly Diaz and Anthony Laird for Red Smoke Family

** Produced by Gui Tavares

*** Produced by Curtis Lugay

^^ Produced by Alessandra D'Agostino, Lorenza Calamandrei, Antoinette Corlis for Sevensensis ~ ~ ~ Produced by Siraj al Hasan

All lead vocals performed by Teddy Hayes

Roly Diaz - Body Flow, all other backing vocals T. Hayes, Violins Ernersto Estruch - Your Healer, I Don't Blame You, Never Walk Out, Backing Vocals: East London Gospel Community Choir - Wonderful Light

Castro –(Rap) Next To You/ Greg Harrison- (Dancehall Rap) Never Walk Out

Live Bass: Anthony Laird-Love Come Rainin' Down /I Don't Blame You/ Messin' Wid Me

"HAH HAH...GOOD ain't it you dirty bitch..?" The man's thick gravelly voice growled deep inside his throat like some wild and primitive animal as the sweat of passion covered his body.

"Ooohhh..." was the only sound that the woman was able to manage as the energy in her slim body seemed to melt away under his power. She was on her knees in the doggy style position. "Ooohhhh shit", the woman moaned in ecstasy as the naked man behind her shoved his penis deep inside her as hard as he could. She could feel his sperm shooting out in short quick explosive bursts as her body responded in uncontrollable orgasm. His strong, rough hands held her slender hips vice-like against his swivelling pelvis. He slowed his grinding motion to a halt as his body shuddered from the force of ejaculation.

The woman's head was filling with thoughts of how this encounter had been unexpectedly enjoyable when suddenly like a shot from a Colt .44 pistol she was propelled forward. The motion was so violent that when her small moon-shaped face hit the top of the hard plastic headboard on the bed she saw a sudden flash of stars. The blow broke open her lipstick-covered mouth and sent fresh blood spewing against the wall in a spatter. Like a striking snake she turned in shock, with her eyes flashing fire at the naked man..

"What the fuck you......" she almost said.

But before she could get the rest of the sentence out, he

leaned forward and slapped her hard across the mouth with such force that it sent her hundred and twenty pound frame flying damn near to the other side of the room. Though the man was big and muscular weighing over two hundred and eighty pounds, the movement and agility of his body had the grace and purpose of a well-tuned athlete on his way to victory. The fear in her eyes excited him all the more as he manoeuvred towards her grinning through two rows of large yellow-stained teeth that resembled a fighter's mouthpiece.

Rhonda had been a prostitute for three years and she had had her share of freaks. The ones who liked to be shitted and pissed on, ones who wanted to be spanked with whips and hair brushes, even men who liked to dress up as women and be fucked in the ass with dildos, but she had never before been confronted with this kind of beast.. She tried to find her feet but instead only discovered legs made of limp spaghetti. Rhonda looked up at him through dazed eyes as the big man shifted from one foot to another in a dancing motion. He punched the air and beat his hairy chest like a cross between King Kong and a heavyweight pugilist. Suddenly and miraculously she found enough adrenaline to stagger upright. But as she did, he bent over and hit her in the ribs. An ocean of pain took her breath away as another fist blasted her face like a ton of bricks.

Anguish and confusion exploded like a grenade inside her head, creating a huge white blank space in her brain where thought once existed. She crashed into the wall losing consciousness. The man was laughing like a maniac as Rhonda lay at his feet in a crumpled heap.

The door to the room opened and an angular head belonging to a slim black face man poked inside. Behind the tinted glasses, his eyes registered shock at the scene before him. The bespectacled man searched his mind for some justification, but there was none. The brutalization of defenseless women was not in his mental vocabulary.

"Fuck" was all that came out in a disapproving tone. He didn't dare say more. Adrenaline pushed his body back out of the room

The man-beast inside the room had paid the bespectacled man no more attention than if he had been a dead roach, as he reached down and grabbed the woman and lifted her with one massive paw. Still grinning he brought her face close to his own and opened his mouth like a bull mastiff on the attack. With one savage motion he sank his massive teeth into the woman's delicate nose and succeeded in almost tearing it from her face. The scream of the hooker was all in her eyes because her voice was lost in the agony and horror of the moment. Then the man's hands closed tighter and tighter around her throat. With her last bit of life force she tried to struggle to but to no avail. She was dead in two seconds.

The other man standing just beyond the doorway physically jumped at the sound of the woman's neck snapping in the big man's hands. Bobby Jones automatically took a step back further into the other room. His body felt sick and strained as he started to tremble and pace the floor. Brutality and violence had always unnerved him. But long ago he had accepted that brutality and Brax were as intertwined as the chicken and the egg.

"Fuckin' lunatic bastard " Bobby thought. He took a deep swig from the bottle of Wild Turkey that rested on the glass coffee table. He wanted to run away but he had nowhere to go. Damn. He was as much a prisoner out of the joint as he was when he was inside, maybe even more so.

He could hear Brax laughing and snorting like a wild boar as he continued to rain blows upon the corpse of the woman with his meaty fists. A few minutes later a noise at the bedroom door brought Bobby's eyes up to see Brax standing naked with blood running from his lips and spattered on his face and chest as he held the limp woman in his right hand by the throat like a lion on the African plain dragging its kill. Her once pretty young face with it's sparkling green eyes and ready smile was now just a dull blank mask with a bloody gash in the centre. Brax walked to the middle of the room still grinning and dropped the dead woman in the middle of the floor. He took up the half empty bottle of whiskey from the table and took two long gulps.

"Ahhh..." Brax patted his stomach and grinned at Bobby whose face looked as if he had just bitten into a lemon.

"Bitch thought she was gon' play me but look who got played," Brax laughed and finished off the whiskey with one long swallow.

Bobby didn't want to look at the woman but couldn't help it. Brax went into the bathroom and turned on the shower. From the living room Bobby could hear Brax singing "Give me a home where the buffalo roam where the deer and the antelope play, where seldom is heard a discouraging word and the sky is not cloudy all day."

"Fuckin' lunatic bastard" Bobby Jones said again to himself.

It was 8:45 in the morning and already Brax had killed someone. The thought of murder before breakfast was incongruent with Bobby's sense of good manners.

"I can't fucking believe this shit" Bobby said to himself in a voice low enough not to be overheard even by the dead woman. But what could he do? He might as well have been back in Sing Sing with Brax, in that funky little cell for all the good his being on the outside had done him. His luck was shit. At the moment he was a long way out in the middle of the fucking woods in a cabin, in the middle of upstate New York with a homicidal maniac in the next room In prison it all made sense, it was a case of survival. Brax was a psychopath who had taken a liking to him because they had attended the same high school and had played for the same football team. As a result Brax had offered Bobby protection in return for writing letters to the prison parole board on his behalf, listening to his bullshit stories and pretending like he was the king of the world. In prison a man will do what he has to in order to stop from getting killed or raped, or both. But outside where a man had more choices it didn't make any sense at all that he was still paired with Brax. But he was, and that was that. If he tried to leave, he knew that Brax wouldn't hesitate to kill him as easily as he had the poor unfortunate hooker that lay dead on the carpet.

After leaving the joint Bobby had drifted around and did a whole lot of nothing until Brax walked free on parole three months later. By that time he had gotten the inside word on the operation of a young successful crack dealer in Brooklyn. Within a week of Brax's release, he and Brax walked into the crack dealer's house in the middle of the day disguised as gas company workers checking a reported gas leak. Once inside Brax beat the dope man and his wife to within an inch of their lives with a lead pipe, raped the woman and then made the man open his safe which contained fifty thousand dollars. Brax then stabbed the man to death with a kitchen knife and broke the woman's neck. They split the money fifty-fifty, and their partnership outside of prison had been cemented.

Brax was a dangerous, sadistic homicidal imbecile and

Bobby was a bullshit coward con-man drug dealer, the perfect combination for the white man who now paid them regularly for pulling jobs together. The very thought of the white man made Bobby's skin crawl as he pushed the thought as far away as he could and sneaked another look at the lifeless hooker who lay stretch limply on the rustic cabin floor. His insides almost gave way but Brax coming out of the bathroom took his attention away just long enough to stop him from vomiting.

"I'm hungry, lets eat" Brax said wiping himself dry with a giant green and blue beach towel.

'Man we gotta' do somethin' about her, she...".Bobby was saying when Brax cut him off.

"Fuck dat bitch, time to eat." The words were not a suggestion but rather a command.

Bobby obeyed meekly and headed towards the kitchen with Brax in tow like a hungry kid full of innocent anticipation. Both of them liked eating the same thing everyday, so making breakfast had been an easy thing to ritualise. Brax would make the toast and coffee and Bobby would fry the eggs and bacon.

As Bobby looked down into his plate and saw the two sunny side eggs looking up at him he was reminded of the whore's lifeless eyes staring blankly into nothingness from the next room. Normally he wasn't the squeamish type, but for some reason the thought seemed to overwhelm him and he pushed his full plate away.

"What's wrong with you Lil nigga?" Brax mumbled through a huge mouthful of eggs and toast.

"Man we got to do somethin' about her," Bobby finally got up the nerve to say.

"Man that bitch dead, dead is dead ain't it? What she got to do with us? We did what we was supposed to do," he laughed and crammed his mouth full again.

"We gonna' have to do somethin'," Bobby chimed back blankly.

"I am," Brax laughed, "I'm eatin',". He guffawed at his own dumb joke and went back to chomping down his breakfast like a hungry pig at the trough. Brax's bulk and muscle came from continuous years of lifting jailhouse weights. His light tan skin stretched taught and smooth against his stone hard physique. He was what some black people would call a "yellow nigger "or "redbone." His skin colour and wavy hair reflected the features of his mother who was a poor white trash hooker from Florida while his thick lips and broad nose mirrored his father who had been a black stickup man from Alabama.

Brax was five years old, when one Saturday morning as he sat watching "Tom and Jerry" cartoons, his father walked through the front door carrying a policeman's night stick. Brax stood in the bedroom door and watched his father use the stick to beat his mother and the man she was in bed with to death. Melvin Braxton the father got the electric chair and Melvin Braxton the son got sent to a series of foster homes until he was eighteen years old. By the time Brax was nineteen, he was already serving his first penitentiary sentence for rape and attempted murder. During the few years he had been out of jail Brax had worked as a bouncer, a wrestler, a bare-knuckle boxing hustler, and a strong armed robber, so violence was as natural to him as leaves on a tree.

The doorbell rang just as Brax was finishing his coffee. Bobby felt a cold shiver run down his leg and Brax suddenly looked serious, they both knew who it was.

The man who stood before Bobby as he opened the door was short and ugly with features that seemed to have been haphazardly carved by a drunken sculptor. His smell was rank and overpowering, like he had just bathed in the cheapest perfume on earth. But his clothes were just the opposite. He wore a grey pinstriped tailor-made wool suit that fitted his ill-shaped form so perfectly that it could have been made by an angel. The oddest thing about him, even odder than how he looked or smelled were his hands. They were small, slender and delicate, like a little girl's. The white man's cloudy, dull blue eyes alighted on the dead woman as he crossed the threshold into the room. Bobby quickly closed the door behind him looking unsettled. He glanced over at Brax who stood in the kitchen doorway looking as deferential as a caught mouse.

"You find out anything?" the white man said in a voice so low it was barely audible.

"Not really but I recorded everything just like you said Mr. Nicolli," Brax responded obsequiously.

"Um," was all the white man said and took a seat at the end of the sofa, slowly crossed his legs one over the other and lit a cigarette with a Bic lighter. Every motion was deliberate like he had to think about it before he did it.

"Let me hear it," he said.

Bobby disappeared into the bedroom. A minute later he came back with the voice-activated mini tape recorder that had been fixed to the bedpost the previous night about an hour before the prostitute arrived.

Nicolli listened and smoked while Bobby and Brax sat in silence sneaking glances at the ugly little man and then at each other. With the woman still lying in the middle of the floor it looked like some kind of bizarre wake.

The voice on the recorder was mostly hers telling Brax that she didn't know where some man was. Brax's instructions were to say as little as possible and let the woman talk to find out how much she knew. Nicolli had somehow found out that she had been an ex-girlfriend of the man he was looking for and he had hatched the plan with the rigged tape recorder. The hooker was a dead woman before she ever walked through the front door.

"So you let our bird fly out of the cage Mr. Jones," the white man said turning his ice cold blue eyes towards Bobby.

Bobby bolted ramrod straight up in the chair with fear in his eyes..

"Naw Mr. Nicolli, I didn't lose him, he was just there one minute and...but when I went back he wasn't there. I didn't lose him," Bobby stammered. His frightened pathetic mind searched for more appeasing words but found none.

Nicolli looked over at Brax who sat like a coiled cobra on a chair in the far corner of the room. Brax looked back impassively. Over the years, Bobby had seen Brax in lots of violent and dangerous situations but he had never seen fear in him until he saw Brax with Nicolli. Though the small ugly white man was no physical match for the giant, he was easily and thoroughly a hundred times more evil. So much so that even Brax physically recoiled under Nicolli's disapproving stare.

Nicolli's presence was a like a seeping poisonous mist that permeated the atmosphere adding to the smell of death that already claimed the room. Bobby could feel his scalp tingling. Sweat popped out on his brow and rolled down his face as if there were a sprinkler system operating in the top of his head. He was petrified that Nicolli might say the word and in the next minute there would be two dead bodies laying on the floor, one of them his.

"Bury her," Nicolli said.

Brax wrapped the body in a sheet and flung it over his shoulder. He and Bobby loaded it into the back of the Lincoln Town Car that they had rented and drove to a deserted site deep in the woods that they had selected the day before.

As the two men dug the prostitute's grave Brax bragged jubilantly about how he had fucked the shit out of the dead woman and how he had forced her to let him fuck her in the ass even when she had protested. He liked the idea of forcing sex on people. Like some men are born to play music or sports or to be scientists or doctors, Brax seemed born to violence, with rape being his speciality. Even in jail he had gained a reputation among the homosexuals as a feared rapist. It took them thirty minutes to bury her..

Nicolli looked up at the pair as they walked back through the door and then back at his watch. 11:16am. They had been gone exactly one hour and four minutes. Both Bobby and Brax's eyes fell on the coffee table where a clear plastic bag filled with green currency rested along with a bottle of Jack Daniels and three empty glasses. They both knew the envelope contained two thousand dollars.

Nicolli motioned for them to sit down as he lit another cigarette. Bobby saw from the ashtray that while they had been gone Nicolli had smoked five cigarettes.

"Getting back to our missing golden goose," Nicolli said flatly looking in Bobby's direction.

Suddenly Bobby was nervous again.

"We're all friends here gentlemen, unfortunate things can happen, that's part of our business, part of life," Nicolli said pouring out drinks all round.

"Like I said Mr. Nicolli," Bobby jumped in defensively, "I didn't know he had plans to run, otherwise I would have told you, he must have gotten spooked by something."

"How is it exactly that you knew him again?" Nicolli asked in a dry whisper.

"I knew his family. My ex-wife and his wife were real good friends till she died. He used to spend time at our place cause he missed his wife. Him and my son got along real well. He used to take him to baseball games, sometimes."

"You think he could be in touch with your ex-wife now?" asked Nicolli lowering his eyelids into two glinting slits.

"I don't honestly know but maybe he could have been, I'm not sure"

"This ex-wife of yours, you still in contact with her?"

"No sir, she divorced me when I was in the joint and I haven't heard from her since. That's been a few years ago now," Bobby said.

"But you mentioned your son, do you still see him?"

"Not really, he's at college so I write to him but he don't write back much, you know how kids are," Bobby informed.

"No I don't, never had any," Nicolli replied, "but I do know people, and I know people usually go to places they are familiar with when they are scared or in trouble."

"Yes sir," Bobby said.

"This boy's ass is hot as fire," Brax chimed in.

"That's right Mr. Braxton," Nicolli said in a condescending tone as if he were talking to a two year old.

"You're a smart young fella' Mr. Jones, so I'd like to hear it from you. If you were me where would you start looking for our flown golden goose?" Nicolli said.

Bobby didn't want to say it, but he had no choice. Even before he said the words he hated himself for saying them.

"I guess I should try contacting my ex-wife and see if she's heard from him."

"I knew he was a smart young fella, didn't you Mr. Braxton?" Nicolli smiled towards Brax.

"Yeah, be nice to see that pretty little wife of yours again. I remember seeing her when she came to visit you a coupla' times in the joint, fine as a motherfucka', I'd like to put my big dick to her myself," Brax heckled.

Bobby felt his insides turning over at the thought and wanted another drink to wash away the ugly words that Brax had used to assault him.

"Now now, Mr. Braxton, lets be respectful," Nicolli retorted without conviction. "Mr. Jones is going to contact his wife and we are going to find this young man, after all it was Mr. Jones who lost him so I think the pleasure of finding him should also be his."

Bobby shifted in his chair again and swallowed hard.

"Don't worry I'll find him," Bobby reassured weakly.

"I have taken the liberty to seek out some information that you might find useful, I hope you don't mind," Nicolli measured each word carefully.

"No, no" Bobby said..

"Correct me if any of the details are not accurate," Nicolli continued as he took a small leather bound notebook from the inside of his jacket pocket. "Your ex-wife lives and works in Harlem as manager for a night club called the 'Tease Me Club. She was born in Detroit Michigan to a Henry and Ellen Lavelle, married you in New York. Together you have one son, Harold who is 21 years old and presently a junior at the University of Connecticut studying computer science. Let's see, you were convicted of selling narcotics and sentenced to serve ten to twenty at Sing Sing. She divorced you two years later. You served seven years, two months and thirteen days. Does all of the information I have sound factual to you Mr. Jones?" asked Nicolli and shot a sly glance at Bobby..

Bobby was tight again and his mouth was as dry as the desert but he did barely manage to get out the words.

"Yes sir."

"That's good then, so since we all know where we stand, there shouldn't be a lot of trouble getting this thing sorted out, I should think," Nicolli stated and smiled at Bobby. Nicolli was using the iron fist in the velvet glove approach and it was working like a charm. Bobby felt the bile from his stomach coming up into his mouth.

"So when we get started?" Brax wanted to know.

"As soon as possible, and don't worry about money, as you know you gentlemen are entitled to twenty five percent of the take, so I feel it only right that in addition to the two thousand dollars for the work you've already done that I advance you say five thousand for expenses. How's that?" Nicolli said.

The grin came so quickly to Brax's face that it looked as if his teeth would jump right out of his mouth.

"Fine Mr. Nicolli, that's just fine." Brax nodded happily in the white man's direction then he turned quickly to his partner in crime. "Where you think she at tonight then Lil nigga'?"

"Huh...what?" Bobby answered.

The abruptness of Brax's words startled Bobby

"What?"

"Where she at tonight, your wife?" Brax repeated.

"My ex-wife." Bobby corrected, "How should I know, I ain't seen her in years," Bobby quipped trying to keep the irritability out of his voice.

"Oh not to worry gentlemen, finding her won't be a problem. On Saturday nights she performs as a singer at a jazz bar in Harlem called the Be-Bop Tavern," said Nicolli.

"Fuck," thought Bobby. This slimy asshole had his whole life at his fingertips.

"The Be-Bop Tavern huh, I think I heard of that place before" Brax said.

"Yes" Nicolli said, "it seems to be quite a popular place among the locals. By the way, she performs under her maiden name Honey Lavelle, and it's owned by a friend of hers, a man called Devil Barnett."

CHAPTER 2

Music Track # 1
DEVIL BARNETT Intro: LOVE EVERLASTING

My name is Devil Barnett and I was born and raised in Harlem New York, Even though I'm here now for a long time I was away from Harlem. You see I was working. Yeah, working for the CIA. The official title on my personnel folder said that I was employed as a liquidator. In reality that meant I was an assassin. But that's all behind me now. Since quitting the agency, I'm back in Harlem running my own business. It's a jazz bar and restaurant located up on Lenox Avenue called the be-Bop tavern. When I'm not there you can find me around Harlem doing other things….things ike..well…like a private detective might do. In fact I guess you might even say that these days I spend a lot of my time as a private detective. Yeah Harlem USA, it's good to be back home.
Love Everlasting, Sets my spirit free.
Harlem on my Mind
Keep on movin, Harlem is the sight,
From 110th Street on the westside all the way up to Washington Heights.
You can see us the brothers and the sisters twenty four seven permeating the atmosphere with our existence
Tall tenements dressed in shades of brown and grey concrete acting as a holding pen for our hopes dreams and sorrows. We're making it the best way we can. Day to day, hour by hour minute by minute. Some will make a change and make it out, maybe to Long Island or Jersey, but as for me, I ain't goin nowhere. This is my piece of the rock. My piece of the universe, my mirror, my reflection.
Because I am Harlem one of the crowd of black faces families and friends up from the jaws of mint julip land. Places like Alabama, Arkansas, Carolina, Mississippi and Georgia too, not to mention Africa and the Caribbean. Every wearing big innocent Koolaide smiles, with eyes as shiny as newly minted dimes as the train

arrives into Grand Central Station.
Welcome to the Big Apple brothers and sisters, have we got a surprise for you.
Looking forward to a place we could call our own even if it did mean living in a brick box.
Keep on movin keep on prayin, keep on keep on workin, keep on sayin tomorrow is another day and each new dawning brings a brand new chance, a different vision, a genius idea, a new life. Forget about the toil and the strife.
We are separate but inseparable like fingers on a hand grabbing for the gold.
We're going to get there. We're going to make it work too. Because you are me and I am you. Harlem Love Everlasting, Harlem on my mind. Keep on movin.
Uptown in Harlem, my spirit flies free unburdened by downtown skyscrapers full of people unconnected with me. As my spirit breezes down 125th Street past the world famous Apollo Theatre visions of Malcolm X, Langston Hughes and Adam Clayton Powell call out to me, moving me, grooving me, making my spirit stronger than ever before. Stronger than the pain and poverty that surrounds me, stronger than the slaves of slavery that used to bound me, stronger than the drug dealers than the drug dealers who walk hand in hand with the devil, telling lies as smooth as glass tabletops. I am of a spirit stronger and more powerful than anything conceivable by the human mind. The same spirit that moved through my people gave the world inventions like the traffic light, the refrigerated truck, the ironing board and jazz music is still alive and in full effect in Harlem USA. My people's spirit even performed the first open heart surgery, dig it. Harlem on my mind. My spirit keeps on movin higher beyond all constraints and barriers like an eagle soaring towards heaven, higher and higher and higher and higher. Love Everlasting, Harlem on my mind.

"WHAT DO YOU think boss?" Christine said, placing an orange leaflet with black letters on the table. I was nursing a coffee and reading the sports section of the New York Times. The leaflet announced a Sunday Brunch at the BeBop Tavern featuring local musicians, wines, cheeses, couscous, olives, vegetarian lasagna, and a few other treats Christine had dreamt up. I gazed down at the leaflet and then back up at her. She was working hard to look nonchalant. This was her baby: She had organised the talent, the food, as well as managed to get an article printed in local newspaper with a photograph of the front of the bar.

"I know if anybody can make it work, you can," I said.

"Thanks boss" she beamed back, showing a set of even white teeth that radiated against a smooth brown complexion. Since Christine had come on the job as manager, I had been able to relax and not worry about the day to day running of the bar restaurant. She was honest, organized and worked hard. More you couldn't want or ask for. Though she was a single parent with two children, she always went beyond the call of duty to make the place into a smooth running operation.

"Any suggestions?" she asked.

"No, you seem to have everything under control."

"OK, I'm going to the printer's now. I'll be back in about an hour," she said turning to leave.

I went back to reading the paper but got occasionally interrupted with thoughts of Sonia running through my head. Sonia and I had been seeing each other on and off for almost two years. At the moment it was off. She said she couldn't cope any longer with me being what she called "the neighborhood gun for hire." She was always nervous that one day she would get a call from someone saying that I had been found with a bullet in my head. True I had been in a couple of scraps but I had come out OK. Still, the woman had a valid point. But what I did, I did for my own reasons and we both knew that I wasn't about to change my way of living any time soon, so thereby was the reason for our present Mexican standoff. Sonia decided that we should take a break from seeing each other until she could figure things out. Fair enough. My years as a CIA agent had planted something deep inside me that was impossible to erase. That's why I did what I did. Not that I needed to hurt people or even work behind the scenes fixing things that the police couldn't or weren't interested in dealing with, but that's just somehow the way it seemed to work out. Anyway the Mets were winning and the weather was warm and my CD set of Charlie Mingus had just arrived in the morning mail, so I figured life could be worse.

"Hey Sugargirl" the voice belonged to my daytime bartender Duke Rodgers. Without turning around I could almost see the grin on his face as wide as an eight lane highway. That tone was reserved for one woman and one woman only.

"What's happening" a female voice returned as rich and sweet as cane syrup.

"Everythings everything" Duke said as his aging eyes checked out the merchandise that belonged to Honey Lavelle as she walked past him towards the back of the bar where the booths were located. By the time she reached me I had folded my newspaper and was thinking of who I might lure into a sucker bet against the Mets.

"How're you doin' Youngblood? she quipped in her relaxed Midwestern accent.

"It's all good," I said as she sat down.

The afternoon sun glinted through the window pane and highlighted the glow on her caramel-coloured skin and smooth features consisting of high cheek bones, a full mouth and the kind of soft brown eyes that were able to go straight into your heart like a laser beam sent by Cupid himself. Honey was somewhere between 43 and 46, but looked fifteen years younger. The regular fitness workshops and the yoga and dance classes saw to that. She was quality, make no mistake about it. Kind of a cross between Halle Berry and Pam Grier if you can image that. But most importantly, she was one of my best friends. More like a sister really. At least it was safer for me to think of her in that way.

"She ain't playin' is she?" Honey said eyeing the leaflet Christine had left on the table.

"Not at all."

Honey ordered a coffee, then fell silent and started playing with the underside of her fingertips in a gentle circular motion. Her eyes rested on a blank space between my coffee cup and the folded Times. The vibes between us were strong and right now her silence was screaming loud enough to wake the dead.

"So you gonna tell me now or make me wait?" I wanted to know, hoping the direct approach was the best one.

She looked up and me and smiled.

"I got a strange call today" she began, "from my ex-husband Bobby. He wanted to know if I had recently seen a mutual friend of ours, well more of a friend of mine really, a man named WoodHenry Taylor. He tried to make it sound casual enough but I could tell he wanted to know badly, a lot worse that he wanted me to realize. Know what I mean?"

"So what did you tell him?"

"The truth. I haven't seen WoodHenry for over a year. But what really bothered me was why he wanted to find WoodHenry. I asked him and he made up some weak ass excuse about a business opportunity involving foreign bank funds because WoodHenry works for a Wall Street brokerage firm as a messenger, but that was bullshit. The other thing that bothers me is that I know Bobby inside out, and I could tell from his voice that he was under some kind of pressure to find WoodHenry."

"Pressure?" I repeated.

"Bobby has always had a tendency to get in over his head, and whenever he is, he tries to turn on the charm, but beneath the charm I sensed desperation."

"A desperate man is often a dangerous man" I said looking directly into her eyes.

"I was thinking the same thing, and it bothers me that WoodHenry might be mixed up in something with Bobby. Bobby is evil and conniving and if he got his hooks into WoodHenry anything could happen. WoodHenry is a sweet man but he's got about as much brainpower as a bullfrog in heat. And I know for a fact that Bobby is the type of person who wouldn't be above putting WoodHenry's life in danger if he thought he could make a quick buck."

We sat in silence for a few moments.

"When I was young and dumb," she continued, "I thought Bobby Jones walked on water"

I looked up at her.

"OK we all make mistakes," Honey said defensively

"I didn't say a word" I smiled.

"You didn't have to, I heard what you were thinking by that look you gave me"

"What look?" I defended trying to keep the smile off my lips.

"That look on your face that said you just walked into the room and found Mary Poppins giving a blow job to Jabba The Hut" she said.

The imagery of her description made me laugh out loud.

"I never gave you that kind of look".

"Yes you did, poor little Mary Poppins, how could she, so bright, so innocent, so sweet," Honey said.

"OK" I conceded. "Maybe I was a little surprised, I'm sorry"

"You don't have to be sorry, I know you only looked at me like that because you care about me, but we all have to grow up"

"Don't we though" I agreed.

I definitely had. Until three years ago I was a walking time bomb for the CIA. Ready to kill anything and anyone that my old Uncle Sam told me needed killing. But now thank God all that was behind me. Like a strange kind of dream that had dried up and blew away. At least I hope it had.

"I got worried so I called WoodHenry's," Honey continued, "but I kept getting the answering machine with a woman's voice on it."

"Maybe he's away on vacation," I said hoping to lighten her thoughts just a little.

"No, I called his job and they said he definitely wasn't on vacation but that he hadn't been in to work all week. The woman I spoke to sounded concerned. Said that he hadn't even called in. She also said that in the ten years that he has worked there she can never remember him not calling in if he was sick. She's even called the hospitals looking for him because she thought he could be too ill to phone or had hit his head and was walking around with amnesia or something. Then she said that everybody seemed to be looking for him including his wife."

Honey started playing with her fingertips again.

"Is this WoodHenry a very good friend of yours or just someone that you know casually?" I wanted to know.

"Yes he is a good friend. WoodHenry was married to my best friend Paulette who grew up with me in Detroit. After graduation from college she got this big job in a Wall Street firm as an analyst, so they moved here from Detroit. I moved here about two months after she did and I met Bobby and had my baby . But Paulette died of cancer about three years later and since then WoodHenry seems to have been at loose ends. Over the years he would often show at my house and just sit and sit and watch TV, then sleep on my couch so he wouldn't have to go home and be alone. Then for a while it was one fast woman after another. I felt sorry for him because I'd known him for a long time, ever since he and Paulette started going together in high school back in Detroit. When they were married she was always as much like his mother as his wife. She took care of all the business and made all of the important decisions. She was real brainy and he was...well not exactly slow but kinda' simple-minded and childish in a lot of ways. I remember when Paulette was going to Wayne State University for her degree WoodHenry was working with horses at the racetrack. He was just as happy as he could be hanging out with his racetrack friends during the week and playing music and singing in small clubs on the weekends. But whenever Paulette hit the door after work WoodHenry would be there waiting with the house all cleaned and dinner cooked. We always got along well together because he loved music so well. Sometimes we would play old jazz tunes hour after hour on his old beatup piano. A lot of times he would just make up songs and the three of us would sing them for hours on end. He has a real talent for music, especially at writing songs. Paulette and I always believed that he could have been a real success in music if he had wanted to, but for some reason he never pursued it professionally. WoodHenry is a real sweet man and I wouldn't want to see him get involved with a snake like Bobby."

"Tell me the name of the place where this WoodHenry Taylor works and I'll see what I can find out" I said.

CHAPTER 3

THE MAN ASKED if I didn't mind meeting him at his home rather than his office. I didn't mind because the cool drive up the Henry Hudson Parkway to a rich section of Greenwich Connecticut was preferable to a hot sweaty subway ride down to Wall Street where his office was located. I announced my name to the metal box at the electronic gate that guarded the property. A few seconds later, a buzzer sounded and the gates crawled back allowing onto the property that belonged to Tom Jerrod, chief executive officer of Fidelity Trust Brokerage. The same brokerage company where WoodHenry Taylor had worked for ten years as a messenger.

I drove along a tree-lined road that snaked through a beautifully landscaped area for about two minutes until I came to a clearing decorated with a three-storey white mansion. I could make out two white women playing tennis on a court built to one side of the house as I pulled my car into the semi circular cobble-stoned driveway. By the time I had switched off the engine, an elderly Asian man who looked to be in his sixties and wearing a white servant's jacket was walking from the house in my direction.

"Mr. Barnett, my name is Oscar, Mr. Jerrod is expecting you. Please follow me."

I was ushered through the house filled with modern looking furniture made of light sand-colored wood. The three rooms I passed through were decorated in pale yellows, pastel blues, light oranges and whites. At any moment I wouldn't have been surprised to see a fairy flying out of one of the rooms with gossamer wings. We turned down a corridor, passed through a door and came to a study decorated in dark mahogany wood, straight backed chairs, bookshelves and a Louis XVI desk. The smell of fresh flowers wafted in from a nearby garden through the French windows.

"Can I get you something to drink, coffee, tea, juice, a cocktail perhaps?" Oscar offered.

"Juice will be fine"

"The peach is very nice this time of year" he assured me.

"Yes thank you" I nodded, accepting his recommendation.

"Please have a seat, Mr. Jerrod will be with you in a few moments, he's just finishing a phone call," Oscar said and left the room.

I sank down in an overstuffed maroon colored armchair at the side of the desk and continued taking in the room. By the look of things, the man liked horses. In addition to two large sculptures of horses in the corners of the room, there were four paintings of a polo match that adorned the walls that looked like Leroy Neimans.

"Sorry to have kept you waiting Mr. Barnett" the man said as the voice entered the room from the doorway followed by a portly man with dark Mediterranean features who stood about five eleven and weighed about 195 pounds. He carried a small pot belly that had started to show under his white cotton polo shirt, but otherwise he looked perfectly fit. I put him at between 55 and 60 years old. He sat behind the Louis the XVI and propped his bare legs up on the desk's corner to show that he was wearing dark blue shorts and matching blue espadrilles.

"I'm very glad you phoned Mr. Barnett. Frankly it was a godsend," he said as he took a cigar from the humidor on the desk.

"Cigar?" he offered.

"No thank you. Why is that?" I asked sitting nearer to the edge of the chair.

"Because there's a bit more to things than meets the eye and I was wondering how I was going to handle it."

"Really." I was all ears.

"You see when WoodHenry went missing he did so with a very valuable package," Jerrod said lighting the cigar with what looked like a gold plated lighter that had a horse head carved into its side.

"To be exact, a four million dollar package," Jerrod said. He raised his eyes from the end of the cigar in his hand and looked over at me.

"You're right that is a valuable package. What did the police say?"

"Nothing, because I never reported it to them" he said drawing on the cigar until it glowed at the end.

"That's a lot of money not to report, but I'm sure you had your reasons."

"You're right. I didn't name WoodHenry because he was doing me a favor when he disappeared," Jerrod said.

"The kind of favor the police wouldn't be willing to look the other way for if they found out about?" I asked.

"Strictly speaking, nothing I did was illegal, but a police investigation most probably would mean publicity, and that would put me in a very precarious position within my company. And as I said WoodHenry was doing me a favour and if I went to the police I'd have to name him which wouldn't be fair to him. Aside from the money which is insured, I'm worried about WoodHenry."

"A four million dollar favour huh?" I said.

His face changed slightly, but not so much that you could tell it if you weren't watching with a trained eye.

"I know this might seem very odd but I'm telling you the truth," Jerrod said, then leaned back against the corner of his desk and eyed me over the smoke drifting up towards his face from the cigar. He was playing it cagey to see what kind of person he was talking to. He wanted to see if I someone who would cut and run at the first sign of a sticky situation or if I was someone who wanted to put my hand into his pocket and see how much of that four million I could fish out for myself.

"In my business," he continued, "I make trades worth millions of dollars every day. On any given day we may move a half billion dollars around through various accounts, buying and selling. In the case I'm speaking of I took a position in the stock market. I put up some bearer bonds to secure the trade and that's what WoodHenry disappeared with."

"A four million dollar position?"

"Actually it was a twenty million dollar position but I put up four million as security for the trade."

"Why didn't you secure it through the electronic system like most trades are done these days?" I inquired.

"Because quite simply I didn't want the trade going through the books in the regular way because I bought stock in a company called Amalgamated Bio-products, a company that our Board of Directors used to own and forced me to get rid of. So you can see that if it went through the books in the regular way then I would have been at the mercy of those people on my

Board who would have used that knowledge to try and hurt my position in the company."

"Aren't you a major shareholder in your company?"

"Yes, I am one of them, but presently I only control 30 percent of my company's shares. Quite frankly there are two or three other people who own more shares collectively, and were they to decide that they wanted to get together and vote against my 30 percent then I would be on my way out. You see I happened to receive information on the day previous to making the buy of their stock options that there was going to be an announcement that Amalgamated Bio-products was going to be bought by a large German conglomerate, that's why I collateralized the four million in bearer bonds to secure the position."

"So you decided to do an end run, do yourself a little insider trading, behind the scenes, trading with the company's money in hopes that things would go well with their shares when the buy-out was announced" I said.

"Yes. And when the bottom line showed the profit then I would have been considered a genius and in line for a bonus that would have amounted to about seven million."

"But instead you're looking at an insurance claim amounting to four million, and the exposure that will provide your fellow shareholders with the ammunition to get rid of you as CEO."

"Yes unless you're able to help me find out what happened to WoodHenry and the money."

"You say he was doing you a favor, exactly why was he doing this favor for you?"

"I could give you a lot of bullshit Mr. Barnett, but I won't. In short I agreed to pay him one thousand in cash if he delivered the package without signing the delivery into the ledger book which all the messengers are supposed to sign upon going in or out with any deliveries. I happened to know that he could use the money so I figured that it was a way to solve both our problems."

"How did he get the money out without being noticed?"

"I prepared the package myself and had it ready for him when he arrived at work that day."

"You mean to say you guys just have four million lying around in a safe somewhere not earning any interest?"

"The bonds came directly from an emergency fund that we set up years ago. The arrangement with the bank is we still get the interest on the bonds as long as they know that the bonds are safely locked in our vault. They don't need to hold the bonds physically but only need to know that they are safe."

"And no doubt you paid for this special arrangement also."

"My company is a fifteen percent shareholder in the bank and through our clearing business that we have with them, they make a few million with us every year guaranteed, so the kind of deal that we had with them would not have been so much out of the question."

"So how long have you got before somebody figures out what's happened and you have to report the money missing?" I asked.

"Maybe ninety days when our quarterly auditors come in."

"So the long and short of it is, if I'm able to find the money before the auditors find it missing then you'll be out of the woods and squeaky clean again."

"Exactly."

"I hear what you're saying but I'm seeing it slightly different if you don't mind my saying" I said

Oscar interrupted the exchange by bringing in a tray with two glasses, peach juice for me and what looked like a martini for Jerrod.

"Thank you Oscar, make sure we're not disturbed," Jerrod said as he took the drinks from the servant's tray.

Oscar nodded, turned and left as Jerrod stood up and walked to the centre of the room.

"Go on Mr. Barnett" he said.

"I'm hearing what you're saying about WoodHenry needing the money and how you were such a benevolent soul, but I the way I see it is WoodHenry happened to be the right man at the right time. One because he was simple minded and two because a thousand was a lot of money to WoodHenry just for forgetting to write his name in a book and three, because if you got caught with your pants down he would make the perfect fall guy and you could worm your way out of things and leave him holding the bag and maybe a jail sentence to go along with it."

Jerrod looked at me hard and long then took half of his martini down in one gulp.

"Mr. Barnett, I'm not going to say that you're not right. I'm the first one to admit I'm what you call a real bastard. But I have to say if anything had gone wrong WoodHenry's name would have never come up, because I'm the only one other than him who knew what he was doing. In fact he didn't even know what was in the package he was carrying."

"He was getting a thousand for taking a package across the street. He would have been a three way idiot not to know that the package contained either classified government documents, drugs or illegal cash. By the way how did you pay him?" I said coolly.

"I gave him half the money when he left with the package. As you know he is not the brightest guy. I had hoped that the cash in his pocket and the promise of more would take his mind off of everything else."

"But it didn't quite work out like that because either WoodHenry wasn't as dumb as he looked or maybe he took a little peek inside the bag," I said.

"I honestly don't know, but that's what I want you to find out," Jerrod said.

"What makes you think he's not dead somewhere or maybe lying in a villa in the south of France and living under a phony name with your four mil?"

"I've known WoodHenry for about four years, and from time to time I've had the occasion to talk to him. No that wouldn't be his style."

"You're the top man, why would you even be close enough to a messenger to ask him that kind of favour?"

"We're both lovers of horses. When I found out he loved and knew about horses, I would invite him in and we would talk about horses sometimes. Then a little while after that he would come up to my place and help out in the stables. I keep a couple of thoroughbreds."

I didn't respond. What was there to say?

"Mr. Barnett, you want to find WoodHenry and so do I, albeit for different reasons but nevertheless our goal is the same," Jerrod said.

"Let's put it this way, If I can help WoodHenry and it helps you at the same time, it's no skin off my back, but my priority is finding him."

"Mr. Barnett, excuse my saying this, but how do I know your motives for finding him are any purer than mine ? On the phone you said you were looking for him on behalf of a friend. What if it turns out that your friend somehow found out about the money and is using you to find the money for them?"

"That's a big 'what if ' that I guess you're going to have to live with" I told him.

"For finding him you want to name a price?" Jerrod asked.

"I might , but not just yet"

"Well at least will you take money for expenses? " he countered finishing off his martini and walked back to the desk.

"OK."

"This should help you find him" he said pushing over a wad of cash along with a sheaf of papers he took from the desk.

Looking through the papers, there was a photo of WoodHenry taken within the past six months for his security badge. Reading through his job application, according to his affidavit, he had never been in trouble with the law when he was bonded. Also in the file was his address and social security number.

"Interesting" I said, taking the money from Jerrod and straightening the papers into a neat pile on my lap.

"Needless to say, if you find out anything I'll be the first to know" he said.

"No doubt" I answered.

I thanked Jerrod for his time and got up to leave. Oscar magically appeared and escorted me back through the pastel labyrinth of rooms. Just before I reached the door to exit, a middle-aged white lady entered.

"Oh hello" she said, taking me in quickly with pale green eyes. She looked to be about fifty, had short blond hair and was wearing a white pants suit. Her skin looked tanned but not a healthy natural tan. More like the kind of artificial red-tinted burned-on tan people get from baking under a tanning machine.

"Hi, I'm Greta Jerrod," she said. Her voice was much smaller than I expected.

"Hello I'm Marcus Barnett" I said.

"Are you one of the musicians that's going to play for our charity jazz concert? Tom said that he would arrange the band."

"No I'm sorry I'm not."

"Oh what a shame. Well have a nice day," she smiled and bouncily disappeared into the house.

I started up the car thinking that Jerrod must have thought either I was a 14 carat fool or that he was the smartest guy in the world but most probably the latter because I had seen lots of guys like him who were so full themselves that they believed their own bullshit. I knew there was more to the story than he was telling, but just how much I didn't know.

As I drove my Jaguar slowly back down along the tree-lined road toward the gate taking in the smell and feel of the place along with the memory of Jerrod, I thought about how evil Honey said Bobby was. It was obvious now why he wanted to find WoodHenry. Now that I knew that four million bucks were at stake, I figured WoodHenry was as good as dead if I didn't find him before Bobby did.

CHAPTER 4

THE ADDRESS IN WoodHenry's employment file was in a red brick four storey walk-up over an Italian restaurant called Fagino West, in Greenwich village at Hudson and Bank Street. On the directory outside there was a bell marked Taylor on the third floor. I rang it once, then waited for a few moments and rang again. Still no answer. 12:15 pm. Most people were at work anyway. I rang another bell and waited until I heard a voice through the intercom.

"Who?" was all the voice said. "A special delivery for Mr. Taylor" I said.

The buzzer rang allowing me to enter the building. I walked up to the third floor and rang the door that matched the WoodHenry's Taylor's bell downstairs. Apartment 3B. I knocked and waited for five minutes. Still nothing. When I turned to leave, the door from across the hall opened and a white man who looked to be in his seventies with a shock of platinum blond hair entered onto the landing with a brown and white cocker spaniel on a leash

"Looking for Elvira?" he wanted to know in a thick wheezing voice as he looked me over from head to toe.

"Yes, but she doesn't seem to be home."

"I heard her go out about an hour ago, but if you want to wait she'll be back by 1:30" he said.

"Yeah?"

"She gives the old lady downstairs her lunch at 1:45 on the dot six days a week."

"Thanks, maybe I'll come back" I said moving down the staircase behind the man and his dog.

"Who are you, somebody selling something?" he asked turning his head over his shoulder.

"Just a guy making a delivery. Nice dog" I said.

"Spoiled rotten. You know she won't eat anything that isn't cooked. I have to cook for her like I cook for myself. Spoiled rotten," he repeated.

When we reached the bottom of the stairs the old man looked at me and squinted.

"You don't look like the other trash she has in and out of there all times of night."

"This is my first time ever coming here" I said.

"Make enough damned noise over there to wake the dead. I called the police at least a half dozen times but they but they don't give a shit. They only come if another cop is being attacked" he scowled.

"Do you know her husband WoodHenry?" I asked.

"Yes why, you a friend of his?"

"No, but we've got friends in common"

"I know him, not too well, but I know him. When he's around it's quiet. He's a decent guy. I knew his wife before she died. But he's not been around much lately. When he's not around that's when you hear the shit. Rap music. She plays it so loud I can hear it through my bedroom walls. Keeps both me and the dog awake at night. Once I wake up, I can't get back to sleep. I hate rap music. If I see WoodHenry I'll tell him you're looking for him. What's your name" he asked.

"Barnett".

"Come on Katie, it's a nice day we'll enjoy the park today. Beanie will be there to play with you." The old man said to the dog who appeared to understand by the enthusiastic way it wagged it's tail as the pair moved down the street.

I decided to sit in the small park across the street until Elvira arrived. I had her description from Honey who had seen her with WoodHenry once. She was one of WoodHenry's many fast women that Honey had mentioned.

It was still early September so the summer heat hadn't relinquished it's hold on the city. Young mothers and nannies with baby carriages filled the park enjoying the stretch of Indian summer by soaking up the last of the sun and allowing the children to play on the kiddie sliding board and in a sprinkler system that was going in the middle of the play area.

This area with all it's yuppie types and boutique shops was a section of The Village where even a small studio apartment rented for between $1,500 and $2,000 per month unless the tenants were on rent control or stabilization program. The next question running through my head was, how much would WoodHenry have to earn per month to afford a place in this area? But I already knew the answer. More than he could earn as a messenger. I sat watching the world go by, as two drunks sat down on a nearby bench to share a can of beer and a pretty Latino woman wearing a red shirt and matching red sandals ate her lunch from a brown bag while the pink-faced cherub-looking baby she cared for slept peacefully in it's stroller.

At 1:10 pm, I walked back across the street and took up a position against the wall near the entrance of the building. I wasn't disappointed. Elvira showed up at 1:23 pm. She was in her early thirties with a good shape, hawk-like features and light brown skin.

"Hello my name is Barnett, " I said as she stepped towards the doorway carrying two huge bags filled with groceries.

She halted and looked at me with vacant, nervous, light gray eyes that would have looked at home in the face of fortune teller peering into a crystal ball.

"Let me help you" I said relieving her of the bags as she pinned me for a long moment with suspicion .

"Who the hell are you anyway?"

"I've been asked by a friend of mine to try and locate your husband."

She peered at me awkwardly as I handed her my business card.

"I'm kind of a private investigator. I can show you my I.D."

"By my husband, you mean WoodHenry?"

"Yes, WoodHenry Taylor, you are Mrs. Taylor aren't you?" I asked.

"Shit, I ain't seen that nigga', he could be in China for all I know, heh heh," she laughed, then fished into her pocket for the door key and opened the door.

As I followed her into the building l could smell remnants of stale whiskey breath lingering behind her.

"Why you want him anyway?" she called over he shoulder as she climbed the stairs.

"Like I said, a friend is looking for him. A friend whose got some money for him. He loaned it to her and she just wants to pay it back. She called him at his job but the people there said that he hadn't been going to work," I said.

"If anybody would probably know where he is, his boss Mr. Jerrod would, a lot of time WoodHenry spends time up at his house tending his horses and tomming and shit," Elvira said as she fitted her door key into the lock of her apartment door. "Horses and music the only two damn things he know anything or care anything about." Then she added "but since I'm closer to him than anybody you can give the money to me. How much is it?"

"A fair amount" I said and followed her inside the apartment into the kitchen which was a small dingy affair that looked like it hadn't had a good cleaning in months. From where I stood I could see old cooking grease caked around the gas rings on the stove and a pile of plastic bags that stood about three feet high in one corner that had turned from white to yellow with age. The room's saving grace were the purple curtains at the windows, the mustard colored walls and the hardwood flooring that gave it a feeling of character somehow. I put the packages on the small kitchen table and took a seat.

"You can give it to me, I'm the closest thing he got to any kind of family" she said.

"I was told I have to see him. He's got to sign a paper releasing her from the loan collateral," I said. Even though it was a lie, it sounded plausible.

"That's WoodHenry for you. He so stupid I'm surprised he got any collateral at all from anybody" she said busily taking the food from the paper bags and placing it inside the fridge.

"Well, I appreciate you taking the time to talk to me."

"Sorry I can't offer you a cup of coffee or something but I gotta' get this old lady's lunch ready. If I'm just five minutes late she'll start bitchin'"

"Don't worry about it. When was the last time you saw WoodHenry?"

Without answering, Elvira took a can of tuna from a cabinet and used a metal mechanical hand to open it. A few quick movements and her hands were busy deftly cutting celery, dicing boiled potatoes and opening a jar of mayonnaise.

I decided that there was a reason she wasn't responding to my question. I was thinking of how to play it a different way when the doorbell rang.

"Would you get that for me Mr? That'll be Spongey" Elvira said.

The doorbell rang again impatiently as I walked towards the door. I opened it and a smallish rat-faced man stood on the other side of the threshold looking agitated. He walked in past me and headed straight for the bathroom which was down the hallway in the opposite direction of the kitchen. At the sound of the bathroom door slamming, Elvira looked up from her task.

"Whenever he come here he gotta' run straight to the bathroom, like this place got a funny effect on his bladder or something," she laughed.

"When is the last time you saw your husband?" I asked again.

"Do I look like his keeper? All I know is he better turn his sorry ass up by the first of the month when the bills start coming in here," she said as she poured milk from a container into a glass and placed it on a serving tray.

"You don't seem too worried."

"Me and WoodHenry have an understanding, as long as he shows up with the maintenance payment on this apartment, we don't bother each other about what we do in each others personal lives. He do his thing and I do mine. See we ain't married legal, just common law."

She pulled a new bottle of vodka from one of the bags and poured herself a stiff drink which she swallowed in two gulps. If I had served that same drink at the BeBop it would have been a triple double.

"Drink Mr. uh..was it Barnett?"

"Yes it was, no thank you."

She chased the vodka with a dash of water from the tap then started mixing the tuna fish together with the potatoes and mayonnaise into a salad.

"When was the last time you say you saw him?" I said again trying to sound as nonchalant as possible.

"I didn't say," she quipped with a mischievous glint in her eye, "but anyway it's been four days."

Just then the rat-faced man appeared in the doorway.

"This is Spongey, he a friend of mine. This is Mr. Barnett, he's looking for WoodHenry" Elvira said without looking up.

"Hey brother what's up" Spongey said looking me up and down the way street hustlers have a tendency to do. He was trying to figure out who I was: the new man in Elvira's life, some trick Elvira was setting up for the sucker play or maybe even a bill collector or a cop.

"Do you know WoodHenry? I asked him.

"Me, oh yeah, he a friend of mine, in fact he my main man,

ain't he Vira?" Spongey smiled showing a set of dental work that boasted a gold tooth in front.

"Have you seen him lately?"

"Why, you the man or sumpthin'?"

"No, a friend of mine asked me to check on him. He was supposed to contact her a few days ago but never did."

"Her?" Elvira said a tinge of jealousy in her voice.

"Is this information worth anything to you?" Spongey asked deadpanning me.

"Not really, I'm just doing somebody a favor," I said.

"I haven't seen him since last Thursday" Spongey said dismissively as he pointed a hungry eye in the direction of the tuna fish Elvira had finished mixing.

"Damn that's smelling good" Spongey said then sniffed the air twice like a mouse on the trail of a scrap of garbage

"What you got good?" Spongey asked stepping across the room and opening the fridge.

"Nothing, just cottage cheese and shit. Old folks food," Elvira told him.

"Why your friend looking for him?" Spongey spoke in my direction then bent down and peered inside the fridge.

"I've got something for him," I said.

"If I see him, how does he get in touch with you" Spongey wanted to know with a cagey edge in his tone. "I bet you must be some kind of lawyer or something, huh, dressed all nice and everything, this must be very important information, like money information for a smooth cat like you to be looking for a bumpkin like WoodHenry."

"I'm no lawyer, like I said before, I'm a private investigator," I said.

"Private investigator" Spongey said slowly looking over at me as if he were trying the words out in his mouth for the first time.

"If you see him, give me a call, there may be something in it for you," I said fishing my card from my jacket pocket.

At the mention of the words "something in it" Elvira stopped what she was doing in mid-stroke and jerked her head upright as if a puppet master had her head attached to a string.

"How much of a something?" she inquired.

"Cash on the barrelhead right?" Spongey wanted to know.

"Enough to make it worth your while, believe me," I said to

both of them, thinking about Jerrod and all his money.

"I may know where he is..."Spongey almost blurted out.

Elvira shot him a disapproving glance but right now Spongey was paying her about as much attention as a nickle's worth of nothing. His sights were on trying to pry a payday out of me. I handed Spongey my card and thanked them both for their time and left without so much as another word.

"How much money we talkin about?" Elvira called from the top of the stairs after me as I walked through the door of the building door back onto the street.

At least I had left them with something to think about. I walked over to 4th and 6th and took the A train Uptown. I got off at 110 Street and Cathedral Parkway then crossed the street and went into a barbershop with a sign that read "Ray's Hair Palace" to see if Johnny Ray Slim was in. Johnny Ray Slim was a man in Harlem who knew people that knew other people. Even though WoodHenry lived in the Village, he was known to hang out in Harlem so I figured that it was at least worth a shot to get Johnny Ray to put his feelers out. Johnny Ray wasn't in, so I left my name with one of the assistant barbers and caught the M7 bus west back towards Lenox Avenue. After riding for three stops a young white couple mounted the bus. A well dressed elderly black woman sitting next to me frowned a little and leaned in my direction.

"They all over the place now," she said in a lowered voice.

"Excuse me?" I said, not sure what she was getting at.

"Them. White folks," she said yanking her head in the direction of the white couple.

"Never seen nothin' like it, in the fifty five years I been living up here. All over Harlem now, they coming and driving the rent up sky high. I live in a rent controlled apartment with two bedrooms. And because of them, some people in my building paying fifteen hundred a month for the same thing I'm paying three hundred for. It's scary. Next thing you know we ain't going to have nowhere to live. Where they expect us all to go...Jersey? Yeah I've seen a lots of 'em up here," she said cutting her eyes towards the white couple again as she stood up and prepared to make her exit at the next stop.

When I walked through the door of the BeBop Tavern the first thing I noticed was the voice of Al Jarreau was filling up the room with... "Last night, I thought about you. Last night I thought about you, you you..."

Cowboy one of my regular customers was leaning against the wall watching a checker game between Goose and Po Boy while Duke was cleaning glasses and serving customers.

"Where's Christine?" I called in general direction of the bar.

"Gone to the suppliers, said she'd be back around six o 'clock" Benny SweetMeat who was busy making sandwiches behind the steam table called back in my direction.

"I think I could get with a ham on rye with lettuce and tomatoes" I told him.

"Yeah, lettuce and tomatoes, that sounds good. Comin' up" Benny smiled at me as he started cutting thick slices of ham with the meat slicer.

"Hey Doctor, how's it goin'" came a deep voice from behind me.

I turned to see Hummingbird Moses sitting at one of the tables. He was feasting on a deluxe corned beef sandwich with all the trimmings, a side of fries, and a tall glass of draft beer.

"Hey what's going on?" I said.

"Ain't nothin' going on but the rent, and I ain't paying that" he laughed wiping his mouth with the back of his hand. And he was right too, because he lived in one room basement apartment in a brownstone down the street where he looked after the boiler for the super in exchange for a place to sleep.

Moses was both a man of distinction and contradiction. After being educated at private schools and having graduated from a prestigious eastern university with a degree in mechanical engineering he joined the army where he was then decorated with the purple heart in Vietnam. But somewhere along the line he just decided that the way most people lived life, with their daily concerns, possessions and problems was not for him anymore. So he dropped out of society. Now he made money as a street poet and errand boy. For him one thing seemed just as good as the other. On any given day he could be seen hustling along whistling to himself as he ran errands from one place to another or on a corner with a coffee cup reciting a Shakespeare sonnet, a children's rhyme, a Langston Hughes poem or even his own rendition of bible verses that included rhyming passages. By the kind of lunch he was having business must have been good lately. When things weren't, he would grab a packet of baloney from the supermarket and wash it down with a bottle of cheap wine. But no matter what, rain or shine, sleet or snow, he was always on the scene. One of Harlem's own.

I ate lunch inside my office listening to Cassandra Wilson sing "Drunk as a Cooter Brown" with my mind dancing around the whys and maybes of WoodHenry's disappearance. The energy of my thoughts must have been magnetic because not two minutes later the phone rang.

"Hello Mr. Barnett."

"Yes"

"It's me, Elvira, I just got the strangest call."

"Yeah?"

"All she said was, 'your husband is dead'. Then she hung up. I think it was one of WoodHenry's women. I recognized her voice because she called here before asking for him. Remember I told you we had an understanding like that?"

"I remember."

"Anyway she caught me off guard, so I didn't think to ask any questions before she hung up. I even used my caller I.D., but after I had called back three times, somebody answered and told me that I was calling a phone booth."

"Did they say where the phone booth was?" I asked her.

"I didn't think to ask," she said. I could almost see the look of bewilderment on her hawk-like face.

"Do you think the caller was telling the truth?" I asked.

"Honestly I don't know. Maybe. I'm just scared now."

"Scared of what?"

"Scared that he might be dead for real. Then what's going to happen to me? This place I'm living in, is in his name. His wife left it to him when she died. I'm just his common law wife. The truth is I don't know if he's dead or not but I know somebody who might know where he is, that is if he still is alive," she said.

"You told me earlier that you had no idea of who might know his whereabouts," I reminded her.

"Yeah I know, but I didn't know you or nothing so I just said that."

"But now since you think that maybe your ass may be in a sling your amnesia suddenly cleared up?" I remarked.

"No..well... I, well Mr. Barnett, lets be friends OK?. We don't have to fight do we. I just want to find WoodHenry just like you, so lets try to help each other, O.K?" she said trying hard to inject a kind of sexual helplessness into her voice.

"Yeah OK" I said.

"See I got his cousin's number, and if anybody knows where he is, his cousin Foster Penniford would."

She gave me Foster's number and I told her I'd be in touch if and when I found out anything. I thought about Elvira's words, then about a possible approach. Three minutes later I made the call.

"Hello, my name is Barnett. Could 1 speak with Mr. Foster Penniford please."

"He not here now," a woman's voice informed me. She sounded in her fifties or sixties with a slight southern accent.

"When would be the best time to reach him?"

"Who are you?" she wanted to know.

"I'm someone who has money for him."

"Money?"

"Yes."

"Money from where? What has he been doing, playing the ponies again?"

"I'm sorry Ma'am but I can only speak to Mr. Penniford."

"I'm his wife, Bertha Penniford, you can talk to me cause I take care of all his business anyway. All his business except his gambling business which I don't want no parts of"

"No this is not about any gambling business, but I must talk to him directly. When would be the best time to find him at home?"

"Around five o'clock."

"Can I come by at that time?" I asked her. There was silence at the other end for a few seconds.

"I guess so, but don't come today. If you can wait till tomorrow I'll make sure he's here. You got the address?"

"No."

"350 Riverside Drive," she said. "Hey," her sudden enthusiasm almost jumped through the phone. "You ain't with the lottery, don't tell me he's hit the lottery?" she asked.

"No Ma'am, I'm not with the lottery, but I wish I were."

"I wish you were too," she said and hung up the phone.

I went out to the bar area to get another cup of coffee when Moses who had been nursing a beer and watching ESPN walked over to me.

"Hey Doctor, you got a minute? I want to rap to you about a little something in private."

"Sure," I said and lead him back into my office and closed the door.

"You got it fixed up nice back here doctor," Moses said looking around at the decor of the room. "Listen," he said looking me directly in the eye and taking a deep breath. "You know I usually be around, so I see things?"

"I know".

"Well yesterday when that pretty lady came to see you, I don't know her name but man is she fine..." he said and trailed off. I searched my mind for a moment and came up with the picture of Honey Lavelle.

"Yeah she's a friend of mine," I said.

"Anyway I was out front doing some poetry when she left at around two o'clock and I noticed when she was walking out down towards the train. I swear there was some dude standing across the street who followed her down into the subway," he said.

"What makes you think he was following her?"

"By the way he kept hanging out over by KFC watching your place," Moses informed me.

"How did he look?"

"Thin dude, about forty five maybe, brown skinned, wore glasses about five eleven maybe six feet."

"Good looking out," I said reaching down into my pocket and came up with a ten dollar bill.

"Thanks a lot," Moses said. He folded the bill neatly and placed it into the watch pocket of his faded jeans, nodded and left the room. I sat down behind my desk and let my mind replay his words. Suddenly, I felt the hair standing up on the back of my neck.

CHAPTER 5

WOODHENRY TAYLOR STEPPED nervously onto the street and adjusted his phony hairpiece for the fifth time in as many minutes. It was as if he thought the constant adjustment of the rug would cement his disguise. He wiped sweat from his face as it poured into his eyes from under the wig. He wasn't used to ducking and dodging and trying not to be recognised. He checked his wristwatch. It was 7:30 pm. The sun was starting to set, which was a good thing. At least the darkness of night would help him to hide. The place he was going to wasn't far away. He looked at his reflection in the plate glass window and felt a little better. He was almost unrecognizable, even to himself. The black suit, the white shirt , the blue and black striped tie along with the clear thick-framed eyeglasses and briefcase certainly gave him the appearance of another person. Maybe even someone of substance. He stood in the shadows of a building between 8th and 9th Avenue on 42nd Street as people passed him. He would have much rather stayed in the comfort and safety of the small room he had rented in Hell's Kitchen but he had little choice. For some reason he thought of the song "If Loving You Is Wrong I Don't Want To Be Right" and started to hum it. It somehow made him feel a little better and braver about things.

He walked around the same area looking in various store windows to kill time for another ten minutes before he purposely started walking east with an enthusiastic bounce in his step. He walked until he reached the new movie theatre where a Wesley Snipes film was playing, then stopped and looked up and down the new 42nd Street. New that is, since big companies like Disney decided to clean it up and build 42nd back into a entertainment center rather than the cesspool of seedy porno houses it had been for the past 25 years. He saw the B.B. King Theatre just down the street and thought to himself that he might go there later after the movie and order some ham hocks and stringbeans at the restaurant which was a part of the theatre. In the sky he saw a few clouds gathering in the distance and the thought of rain came into his head. Then suddenly his muse whispered something that connected with the melody bank that was ever-ready in his naturally musical brain.. WoodHenry loved his muse as much as he did his lady love. In some way even more, if such a thing were possible. His muse was all-knowing and all-feeling and whenever he felt something deeply in his soul his muse would wake up and give melody and words to those feelings. It had been that way between him and his muse since he was a child. He never knew where it came from but one day it just did. He was still a young boy about seven or eight years old back in Alabama on his Uncle's horse farm. He was playing around and trying to beat out little pieces of melodies on his Uncle's upright piano when the muse suddenly came out of hiding and started sending snatches of tunes and thoughts into his fertile musical mind. Now the muse was as much a part of him as his own skin. And he knew with all his heart and beyond any shadow of a doubt that his muse would never leave him or let him down. He couldn't even imagine life without his muse. To catalogue what the muse gave to him, WoodHenry kept a series of spiral notebooks in which he always wrote down the songs he created. To date he had written at least a thousand songs in those notebooks which he kept in a safe place at his good friend's house in a big metal trunk.

As WoodHenry continued walking along the avenue listening to his muse and thinking about the rain clouds forming in the sky, and thinking about Missy Free he effortlessly started to connect the words and melody pouring from his soul.

Music Track # 2
LOVE COME RAININ DOWN

Ooh baby.. Listen here..
I'm here waiting for you,
So tell me what you wanna do.
Don't be shy, let me come on by
I'll do what I do to make you feel like you can fly
Touch you in all the right places,
Fill up all the right spaces
Like a detective workin on cases

Like a shadow in the night I'll leave no traces.

I know... you know.. what I'm talkin about
I got what you like, but dontcha wear it out.
I love it ..when you dance the tango
Sweeter than a mango, baby let your brain go.

LET YOUR LOVE COME RAININ DOWN
LET YOUR LOVE COME RAININ DOWN

I can guess what you been thinkin.
The stone cold truth Ruth, dontcha be blinkin,
Or play yourself like an old Nintendo,
Cause I'm top shelf, and I'm good to go.

I'm an under the cover, lover demon,
I'll have you steamin, screamin and wet dreamin...
Love abandoned, breakin hearts at random,
Stand em up so I can knock em down,
Yeah girl I got what you need
And I got it by the pound
I guarantee I won't mess you around

Whenever I touch you, yeah it's the right time,
The morning, the middle of the day or the night time.
Makin love to you will be my specialty,
I got a love black belt... 25th degree.

You know me, I got what you need,
I got the body heat that turns bitter to sweet.
I got the recipe to make our love complete
You are the sauce and the butter, I'm the bread and meat.

LET YOUR LOVE COME RAININ DOWN
LET YOUR LOVE COME RAININ DOWN

It's five o clock in the mornin,
The rain is hittin on the window pane,
You still screamin callin out my name
Cause your body is one big flame, (Yeah)
The bed is shaken, the dawn is breakin,

You know I'm the real deal cause I don't be fakin,
You drink some water to catch your breath,
Then you say that you need a few minutes to rest,
Then you keep tellin me I'm the very best
And then we start makin love again.

Your body is sweet girl so do not waste it,
Let me be the only one to taste it,
Let me appreciate you, let me initiate you,
Let me demonstrate and I will fascinate you.
The love I got is a love supreme,
Make you flow and glow like water from a mountain stream.

LET YOUR LOVE COME RAININ DOWN
LET YOUR LOVE COME RAININ DOWN

WoodHenry was just about to walk over to the box office and buy his ticket to see the Wesley Snipes film when two young men crossed in front of him halting his progress. They looked to be in their early twenties. One was black, tall and lanky wearing a tan business suit and the other was white, medium height in a dark suit. They quickly walked towards two elderly white women who were just ahead of them. The tall black man bumped the shorter of the two women with his body as he walked past her. The woman turned around and looking annoyed.

"Excuse me," the black man said and smiled, while the white man made his move. He reached his hand from beneath the folded newspaper he was carrying and dipped his hand down inside the woman's jacket pocket and lifted her purse. The action was smooth and rehearsed like a magician's trick. Almost undetectable to the untrained eye. As the white man turned and started to move away, the taller of the two old women suddenly became twenty years younger and ran forward pulling a revolver from under her clothes.

"Hold it" she said in an authoritarian voice. "Police."

When people saw the woman running with a gun in her hand they started to scatter in all directions. The black man looked around in surprise and ducked his head as his eyes darted around for a place to run. But before he could make a move, another man in a sports jacket ran forward and rammed him. The black man flew straight into the side of the nearest building and bumped his head so hard that he almost passed out.

"Shit" the tall pickpocket cried as he watched his white partner being forced to lay face down on the sidewalk with the policewoman's revolver pointed at his head.

In all of the confusion WoodHenry felt a surge of panic. Though he wasn't a part of the pickpocket operation, when he heard the words "Police" blinding fear shot through him like a bolt of lightning Before he knew it, he was running full speed in the opposite direction towards 9th Avenue. He picked up speed as he headed north and rounded the corner of 44th Street almost running over a young mother who was pushing her baby in a pram. Half way up the block to 10th Avenue he bumped into a middle aged man carrying a bag of groceries He slowed down a little when he felt the fire in his chest that made his lungs gasp for more air, but only just a little. Like a frightened animal in a stampede, his thoughts were running wild through his head, a mile a minute. Why was he running? He somehow blanked out the pain and found the strength to keep moving. Had the police spotted him?, did anyone recognize him?, was the pickpocket bust just a set up to trap him?. Damn...Damn...Damn... Not only was he now dog tired but the pressure from running had seemed to loosen his bowels. By the time he stopped running he had made it all the way to the Hudson River. There he leaned up against a wall and started to catch his breath in great gulps and shake from exhaustion.. He felt if he didn't find a place to relieve himself soon, there was going to be one helluva' smell walking along the Westside Highway. He still had the briefcase in his hand. He figured maybe he could duck between two of the buildings and use the briefcase as a toilet. Luckily he spotted one of those fancy waterfront restaurants in the next block. Holding his butt cheeks together with his hand, he ran into the restaurant right past the head waiter into the bathroom. Just in time.

When WoodHenry had finished he checked himself in the mirror. His face was dripping wet and his new black suit was limp from perspiration. His fake eyeglasses were missing and his normally smooth brown skin had turned a sickly ashen color. His eyes looked puffy and seemed to have sunk deeper inside his skull. He desperately clutched the inside of his jacket to feel his songwriting notebook.. It wasn't there. He begin searching every pocket furiously. His notebook was like a part of him. It mirrored his inner-most hopes and dreams, the personal and intimate longings which his muse was able to help him express only through his songs. The notebook was like a good friend to whom you could tell all your secrets and never fear betrayal. He turned and ran back out to the street. As he did so he patted his pockets again and breathed faster and faster from anxiety. On the sidewalk, he touched something familiar. It was the spiral spine of his notebook deep in the bottom of his jacket. It had fallen through a broken seam on the inside pocket of his suit coat. Whew.

He walked quickly along the Westside Highway until he came to a small convenience store where he bought a small bottle of Evian water. He quickly drank it down which seemed to help calm his thoughts. Guilt. Yeah maybe that was what had set him off. Guilt and pressure. Maybe it was the same guilt that made him abruptly leave that bar, the night he accidentally ran into Bobby Jones. Bobby wanted to talk about some kind of horse scam involving Mr. Jerrod's race horses. At first he thought he could go along with it. But then he became guilty just thinking about doing something that might be dishonest, especially if it involved a man like Mr. Jerrod who trusted him. Normally he had never been a man to succumb to guilt or pressure but now the stakes were higher than they had ever been. The burden of carrying around his thoughts seemed as heavy as a two ton weight pressing on his brain. The only thing that could lighten his load was love.

These days love was his strength, his reason for being, his courage, his salvation. With love he felt even more salvation than he did on Sundays at the Bethel AME church on Malcolm X Blvd. where he played the piano and sang in the senior choir. Last year despair had closed in and almost suffocated him and he had started a quick downward spiral. At 45 years old he had actually contemplated suicide. But that was then and this was now. Now he was born again. Born again through the power of a woman's love. Love thoughts always brought his musical muse to life sending words and melodies that wrapped themselves around his emotions.

Folks said there was no heaven here on earth but since he

had met Missy Free, you couldn't convince him of that. He figured with her he had gotten pretty much as close to heaven as he was ever likely to get. That's why now he was willing to put it all on the line. He would do anything so that he could continue to be with Missy Free, even stay in a little rented room alone and feeling abandoned until she could find time to visit him. At least with Missy he had somebody to love, even if she did leave him for days without so much as a single word.

Anything was better than going back to the loneliness and to Elvira whom he hated the sight of and back to a life without love that was as dull and drab as a pan of dirty dishwater. As he walked back towards 8th Ave and 42nd Street, he suddenly seem to realize that without his fake glasses and hairpiece he was more recognizable. So along the way he stopped into a Korean souvenir shop and bought a pair of sunglasses and a baseball cap with NYC printed on it. He took off the suit jacket and folded it into the briefcase and hoped that now he looked like a tourist.

When he reached back to the movie-theatre where the Wesley Snipes film was being shown, the film had already been playing for fifteen minutes. He bought a ticket and went inside. He chose the last row on the left hand side and took the seat by the wall. On the screen, Wesley looked as cool as WoodHenry felt when he was in Missy Free's arms. A few minutes later a pretty woman walked to the row where he was seated and took a place at the end of the row next to him.

"Hey, Baby Sweets," Missy Free whispered in his ear and rubbed her hand against his thigh.

WoodHenry looked at her smiling and beaming with love.

"Hey Baby" he said leaning over towards the woman. He puckered his lips for a kiss and she didn't disappoint him. It was a languid hot tongue kiss.

"I brought the money," she whispered and fished something from her purse. It was a thick envelope containing a thousand dollars. He moved his thick fingers over her smooth dainty hand. She squeezed his hand in return and he felt a tingle in his scrotum.

"Can we go back to my place tonight?" he whispered sheepishly.

"Sure, if you want to" Missy Free said in a voice that was sultry yet somehow innocent.

She let her head fall onto his shoulder as she placed a few kernels of popcorn lovingly into his mouth. He smiled and chewed and thought. Thought about how lucky he was to have Missy Free. Thought about how even a big movie star like Wesley Snipes didn't have nothing on him.

Later that night after WoodHenry and Missy Free had made love. After he had done everything he knew to do on top of the bed they rolled off onto the floor still locked in passion. To his surprise she didn't resist. As her body pumped in unison with his own, the muse woke up and started to mix a tuneful phrase into WoodHenry's soul that kept perfect rhythm with their passionate lovemaking.

Music Track #3
BODY FLOW

I WANNA FEEL HOW YOUR BODY FLOWS,
SO BABY LET'S LIE DOWN ON THE FLOOR,
WE'RE MAKIN SWEET LOVE BABY.

The first time you came around my way,
I figured she's the girl, I wanted you to stay,
Now I know I was right you're the girl who rearranged my life,
No more drama, no more trouble
Can I get a witness,

So you know that I know that you're ready
(That you're ready baby).
I WANNA FEEL HOW YOUR BODY FLOWS,
SO BABY LET'S LIE DOWN ON THE FLOOR,
WE'RE MAKIN SWEET LOVE BABY.

You brought about a change in me,
It was obvious, the whole world could see
Love made me a different man,
Some people just don't understand

So you know that I know that you're ready
(I know that you are ready baby.)
I WANNA FEEL HOW YOUR BODY FLOWS,

SO BABY LET'S LIE DOWN ON THE FLOOR,
WE'RE MAKIN SWEET LOVE BABY.
Make some love to me, make some love to me

You gotta make sweet love to me ,
You gotta make sweet love to me
You gotta make sweet love to me
Sweet as sugar baby, let me taste you, I wanna feel you

I WANNA FEEL HOW YOUR BODY FLOWS,
BABY LET'S LIE DOWN ON THE FLOOR,
WE'RE MAKIN SWEET LOVE BABY

Later that night after she had left, he lay on his single bed in the room he rented by the week and thought about the future. For the hundredth or maybe even hundred and tenth time, he opened the dresser drawer and took out the travel brochures from the Escape Travel Agency which told him that it was 'Better In The Bahamas'. Sea, sand, fresh fish and sunshine every day, all year long. "Man, oh man, oh man." He smiled at the thought that he was about to make all his dreams come true.

"Hey." The voice was like a shot into his brain. It came from outside his door.

Instinct made WoodHenry roll from his bed onto the floor. His hand reached under the mattress until it quickly closed around the stock of a six shot revolver. He dared not breathe.

"Hey man, WoodHenry, it's me, Spongey," the voice called in an anxious whisper.

WoodHenry eased up to his feet and looked at the door.

"Shit," he said. Now he wished he had never told anyone where he was hiding.

He hadn't planned to tell anybody where he had disappeared to. He only told Spongey because he figured he might need somebody to help clean up the odds and ends of his previous life. Since Spongey was his best friend, WoodHenry had figured that he was probably his best bet for the task. WoodHenry opened the door carefully still holding his finger on the trigger and stepped back just in case. He felt that he had already been too close to the graveyard once today so he wasn't taking any chances.

Spongey stepped into the room wearing a red baseball cap, yellow t-shirt and matching yellow pants. His face registered surprise when he saw his friend ready to shoot.

"What's wrong with you fool, it's only me" Spongey said quiet and nervously..

"Just come in and close the door man. And I told you 'bout using my name. That ain't my name no more, my new name is Mickey" WoodHenry told Spongey.

"Mickey is OK for other people but I been knowing you as WoodHenry, how am I supposed to quit calling you one thing and start calling you another just like that?"

"Practice" WoodHenry said matter of factly.

Spongey looked around the small dingy room with it's single bed, faded green wall paper, beige moldy curtains and worn dark brown carpet stained with white patches and cigarette burns. He wondered when his friend would tell him more about what was really going on.

WoodHenry hadn't confided in him much except to say that he would be needed to take care of some odds and ends now that he was living under the name of Mickey.

"When you getting out of this dump?" Spongey asked as he sat down in the single straight backed wooden chair in the corner of the room and turned his baseball cap around backwards.

"Why?" WoodHenry shot back and pinned Spongey with the suspicious stare of a farmer who had just discovered a stranger hanging around his chicken coup.

"You getting paid good money to do things for me and not to ask questions" WoodHenry reminded Spongey.

"No problem, just wonderin' that's all" Spongey said still aware of the gun in WoodHenry's hand and decided not to push his luck.

"Man you dangerous, you gon' hurt somebody with that thing" Spongey cautioned.

WoodHenry smiled at the thought that Spongey saw him as a dangerous man. He had never been called that before. WoodHenry put two glasses on the card table and opened a pint of Bacardi rum. He poured both glasses half full and handed one to his friend. Spongey accepted with a nod, lit up a camel cigarette and raised his glass in a salute.

"Lissen man, I got a little problem" WoodHenry said and

took a gulp of the rum.

"Problem?" Spongey echoed squinting his eyes.

"Yeah" WoodHenry said looking at Spongey and hoping that he still looked dangerous enough that Spongey wouldn't give him too much flack about what he was about to say.

"Whenever somebody tell me, it's just a little problem, the problem ain't never little. First of all is it dangerous?"

"Hell naw" spouted WoodHenry, "it's just that when I left home, I left so quick that I forgot my heirlooms."

"Your hair what?"

"heirlooms, you know, stuff that people pass down from one generation to the other."

"That what they call them huh?" Spongey said and held his half empty glass up to the light.

"Help yourself to some more rum man, there's plenty more where that came from" WoodHenry smiled and topped up Spongey's glass.

"What's the catch here?" Spongey asked.

"What do you mean?" WoodHenry replied defensively.

"Everybody know you so cheap you would give a man two nickels for a dime. Why you being so generous all of a sudden?"

"I want my Momma's wedding ring and my Daddy's gold watch chain. I thought I had taken them when I left, but I must have forgotten em'. I want you to go back and get em' for me."

"Me?"

"Yeah, you and Elvira still friends ain't you?"

"Yeah but what I'm I supposed to say. Your missing man sent me to come get his Momma's ring and Daddy's chain?"

"I've only been gone a few days. Besides you don't have to say nothing to Elvira. All you have to do is wait for the right time and go in and get it. I know exactly where they are. They're hidden under the loose floor boards in the bedroom. Just wait till she gets drunk and go to sleep," WoodHenry said.

"Supposin' she wake up and catch me? That's how people get shot you know."

"How you gon get shot? Elvira ain't got no gun."

"Well stabbed then."

"You just scared," WoodHenry said throwing down the gauntlet and twisting his mouth into a tight ball of frustration.

"Scared my ass" Spongey said puffing out his bird chest, "it's just that I'm taking a risk, and anybody who take any kind of risk deserves to be compensated extra."

"So it's down to money is it. I guess friendship don't count for much now huh?"

"Sure it does, but as my friend you gotta' understand, I could get hurt. Just cause you think it's safe, don't mean it is. You don't know what's around the next corner"

"How much?" WoodHenry grimaced.

"You say you know exactly where the stuff is?"

"Zactly."

"And you say Elvira is a sound sleeper?"

"Man when's she gets into one of her drunk sleeps, you could dig up the whole damn building and move it from one side of the street to the other and she wouldn't wake up," WoodHenry assured him.

"A bill," Spongey said and winced a bit without meaning to.

"What! Man you supposed to be my friend, how you gon fix your mouth to charge me a hundred dollars for going to get my heirlooms."

"If it's so easy why don't you do it then?" Spongey asked and took another sip of rum.

"Cause anything could happen, plus people in that neighborhood might recognize me." WoodHenry didn't tell Spongey about his disguise that would have probably fooled most people including him, but that was one of the things he had decided he would keep just between him and Missy Free.

"Just like anything could happen with you, anything could happen with me too,." Spongey said.

"I ain't sayin' something bad gonna happen I say anything could happen," WoodHenry said.

"Supposin' for example if she woke and saw you looking under the floorboards, you could say your ring came off and rolled into a crack in the floor. But if she saw me, she might go crazy and I might have to hurt he,." WoodHenry explained.

Spongey wasn't buying WoodHenry's story but he figured that he wasn't getting any closer to filling his pocket with WoodHenry's money by talking either.

"OK, seventy five" Spongey said and held up his glass to the light again.

"Fifty" WoodHenry countered.

"Sixty."

"OK, sixty" WoodHenry agreed and went over to the closet

and reached into the inside pocket of the black suit where he had put the money that Missy Free had given him earlier. Because the rum had dulled his senses he didn't see Spongey's eyes almost pop out when he peeled off three twenty dollar bills from his thousand dollar bank roll.

Spongey pocketed the money without saying a word. The two men continued drinking in silence as the moon shone through the open window and carried the sounds of Hell's Kitchen into the room. The noise of traffic, people talking, Salsa music and the night wind all combined like instruments giving arrangement to their symphony of mutual silence and suspicious minds.

CHAPTER 6

ELVIRA'S PHONE CALL irritated me like a stone stuck inside my shoe. Whether or not the call was for real about WoodHenry being dead wasn't what really bothered me. What bothered me more, was who would go to the trouble to let Elvira think or know he was dead? Or more pointedly, to whose benefit was it, since in my experience people didn't usually go out of their way to let someone know about a corpse unless that information served their purpose in some way. It could have been WoodHenry himself who had set up the call. If I had a cool four million I sure as hell would want to get away from Elvira, why wouldn't he? At least that would be one way to stop her looking for him. Or was there someone else who wanted her to stop looking for him? When I talked to her, she hadn't seem too concerned whether WoodHenry was living or dead, but now she did. Why now, all of a sudden? Or to look at it another way, did she really get a call or was her call to me just a lie designed to get me either to step up my vigilance or to discourage me altogether? All this was going through my mind as I drove towards 154th Street on a warm September afternoon at 4:30pm to talk with WoodHenry's cousin Mr. Foster Penniford.

The building he lived in had ten floors. A group of two men, three women and two teenager girls were hanging out at the front of the building capturing the rays of the sun and talking about the latest episode of Oz.

"My brother was in the joint for four years and he says that shit they show on Oz is just like the real thing" one of the men was saying.

One of the teenagers was braiding one of the women's hair into an intricate cornrow pattern.

"Is this where Foster Penniford lives?" I asked directing my words to one of the women. She looked at me for a couple seconds before replying.

"Upstairs".

"Gimme a dollar Bro," one of the men called as I started up

the stairs.

A boy of about seven years old wearing an oversized Nike baseball cap answered the door.

"I looking for Foster Penniford."

The boy yelled "Grandad" at the top of his voice while holding the door half open. Within seconds an elderly black woman wearing a faded purple house dress, a towel hung over her shoulder and pair of beat up Nike sneakers arrived to stand behind the boy.

"Boy, go on and get your supper now before it gets cold," she said and the boy disappeared.

"Yes?" she said checking me out and wiping wet hands on the towel.

"I'm Marcus Barnett, you told me to come by today to speak with your husband" I said. Slowly the suddenly memory of our conversation sprang into her eyes.

"Oh yeah, sorry I had forgotten, so many things going on" she said as she backed away from the door so I could enter.

As I stepped into the room I could hear from somewhere at the back of the apartment sounds of children playing and arguing. Suddenly a little girl who looked about three years old wearing only a huge unruly afro and underpants ran into the room holding a spoon in her right hand.

"Gandma they took my bread" she reported to the old woman.

"Who?" Mrs. Penniford answered looking into the child's wide eyes.

"Monty and Beaver" the child said in a small sad voice on the edge of tears.

"Excuse me, Mr. uh Barrett, have a seat," the old woman said and began towards the back of the apartment with her granddaughter in tow.

The room matched the appearance of the old woman, worn and poor but clean and tidy. My eyes perused the room with its decorations of plastic flowers, knick-knacks and photographs of family members crowded on the mantelpiece.

"Y'all better sit yourselves down and eat your dinner before I git my belt" I could hear the old lady saying.

"I ain't take her bread" someone's small voice protested.

"You heard what I said" the grandmother responded.

Her threats reminded me of my own grandmother and made

me smile.

Another young girl, a little older than the first child came out. Before she spoke she stood in the doorway and looked me up and down taking in my every feature with a pair of wide dark eyes mounted in a small round intelligent face.

"My Grandma said come on back" the little girl uttered then smiled quickly showing the spaces where her baby teeth had fallen out.

In the kitchen Mrs. Penniford was busy dishing out franks and pork and beans to the three girls and four boys seated around the large wooden dinner table. It looked like a small classroom with the ages ranging from about three to ten.

As Mrs. Penniford worked between the stove and table, two of the boys teased the girls by making faces.

"Gandma he messing wid me again," the little bare-chested girl with the big afro complained.

"Beaver you better quit it now" the old lady said without turning around from her work at the stovetop.

"I ain't do nothing to Shekeena" Beaver defended adjusting his oversized baseball cap. "She just trying to get somebody in trouble".

The other boy snickered while Beaver continued to torture Shekeena by using his fork to sling a bean across the table towards her. When the bean stuck in her afro, Beaver laughed and turned his attentions towards one of the older girls. He raised his fork to sling another bean but she was too fast for him. Before Beaver could get his shot off she splashed him in the face with her glass of water. All of the children at the table burst out laughing, except Beaver who was too surprised. Mrs. Penniford turned around and pinned all the children with a deadly stare that would have stopped a hurricane. Then without another word, she walked out of the room. The two older girls picked up on the silent message first. The boys didn't get it until they saw their grandmother return to the room with a belt in her hand. She laid the belt on the back of the chair where Beaver sat and returned to her task. All of the levity at the table suddenly died away and the faces of the children became solemn as they turned all attention to their beans and franks. Beaver looked nervous. He didn't dare speak out loud, but his eyes darted around the table where they were met with silent smiles by the other boys.

"Mr. Barrett, these are my grandchildren, I takes care of them while their parents work. They showing out now, but in a minute I'm going to start showing out right along with 'em," Mrs. Penniford said as she worked at the stove.

"Want some coffee Mr. Barrett?"

"Barnett" I corrected her.

"Oh sorry, Mr. Barnett. My son Rodney gets this coffee from his job at one of them StarBus coffee places, it's from Africa."

"That's my Daddy, Rodney" beamed Shekeena.

"It's Starbucks Grandma, not StarBus," corrected the girl with the round intelligent face.

"Thank you Tasha, Starbucks it is" her grandmother conceded as she continued stirring her pots.

Mrs. Penniford looked and saw that one of the girls had finished eating.

"Netty go tell your Grandpa and uncle that the food is almost ready."

The girl child who had not spoken stood up, took her empty plate to the sink then walked down the hallway into another part of the apartment.

Grandma" one of the smaller boys called out. The old woman looked around.

"What?"

"You said you gon buy us a Nintendo."

Mrs. Penniford looked at him. "Walter, with the kind of grades you bringing in here from school, you need to spend more time on your homework and forget about Nintendo for a while."

Walter grimaced and shot a glance at Beaver who looked back blankly, shrugged his shoulders and went back to his dinner. Netty returned to the kitchen took two school books off a shelf then disappeared into another room along with the bare-chested Shakeena in tow. Within minutes a large man in his sixties with a scruffy beard and a lumbering walk ambled into the room. He strained his neck in the direction of the stove, sniffed the aroma of the food screwed up his face then looked over at me.

"Foster, this here is Mr. Barrett. He come to talk to you about something," she said.

"Something like what?" the old man said looking straight at me.

"About your cousin WoodHenry Taylor" I said.

"I thought you said on the phone that it was about some money" said Mrs. Penniford.

"Money, I like the sound of that" Foster said.

"It is about money, but it also involves his cousin WoodHenry" I told her.

"WoodHenry" the old man said and wrinkled his brow, wiped his mouth with the back of his hand then hitched his pants up over a fat paunch.

All the children looked up at their grandfather in unison.

"Hurry up and finish, then put them plates in the sink and go on into the other room, grown folks talking in here," Mrs. Penniford said to her grandchildren.

The children heard but they just kept eating in silence. The expression on their faces showed that they wanted to draw this meal out as long as possible so they could be in on what was about to be said. Mrs. Penniford placed a plate on the table overflowing with steaming porkchops, french fries and green peas.

"I'm hungry" Foster said and lumbered on down the hallway towards the bathroom. There was the sound of the door closing and of the toilet flushing. A few seconds later came the sound of two knocks from inside the bathroom.

"Take it to him" Mrs. Penniford instructed Tasha.

Mrs. Penniford placed the plate of porkchops on a red plastic tray along with a fork and knife and napkins and handed it to her granddaughter. Tasha carried the tray past me and stopped at the bathroom door. From where I sat, I saw her pass the tray inside and walk back. The look on my face must have been telling because the children started to snicker.

"He don't like the grandkids bothering him while he eating," Mrs Penniford explained. "He'll be ready to talk when he finished" she added and went back to her pots on the stove.

"Monty, go help your uncle" she then called to her grandson.

The boy slid off his chair and went down the hall in a half skipping motion.

The other children slowly finished, then one by one went to the sink where they placed their empty plates and then filed out of the room.

"Momma I can't get this hair right for nothin'." The voice belonged to a woman in her early twenties who walked into the kitchen wearing a skin-tight bodysuit with her hair wrapped in a towel. When she saw me she hesitated.

"This is Mr. Barrett, he come to talk to your Daddy 'bout WoodHenry" Mrs. Penniford informed the young woman.

"Mr. Barrett this is my youngest daughter Marilyn."

"Hi" she said checking me out.

"Hi"

"WoodHenry, what he do?" Marilyn asked me.

"Nothin', I don't guess."

"He ain't in no kinda trouble is he?" Mrs. Penniford asked, looking in my direction.

"No I don't think so."

"Hold those fries Ma, I'm watching my diet" the young woman said as her mother dished up food on a plate. She sat down at the table as her mother placed a porkchop and a few peas before her.

"Marilyn, on the little that you eat, I don't see how you keep up your strength" the mother commented.

Just then the little boy came back into the room walking slowly. Leaning on the boy's shoulder for support was another old man. This one looked as if he were in his eighties or nineties. When the couple reached the table the old man let go of the boy and managed to ease down into a seat.

He peered at me through cloudy eyes and nodded in my direction.

"Les this is our visitor Mr. Barrett," Mrs. Penniford said.

"Afternoon, O.B. Lester is my name. Jus call me Les, everybody do" he said extending a wrinkled hand.

"I'm Marcus Barnett" I said as we shook hands.

"Ma I thought you said his name was Barrett, he said Barnett" Marilyn said to her mother.

"I thought I did say Barnett, you know how bad I am with names" she apologised.

"Bertha I'm plenty hungry today, and I don't know why" the old man said.

"Just hold your horses Les, it's coming right now" Mrs. Penniford said.

The shouts of the children drifted in from the other room as the old woman placed a plate of food in front of Les. Without a word Les started in on the pork chops. Then there was the sound of the toilet flushing, water running and then the bathroom door opening. Foster Penniford lumbered back into the room, placed his tray on the table and stared directly at me. He looked wild and dishevelled with bits of food still clinging to his untidy beard.

"Sit down Foster and talk to the man. He wants to talk about WoodHenry remember," Bertha counselled her husband.

"I don't know nothing 'bout WoodHenry" Foster Penniford said.

"When did you see him last?" I asked.

"Last time he was here" Foster blurted

"When was that?" I wanted to know

His face seemed to suddenly go blank as if he had drifted into another world. His eyes found a place above my head and stayed there for at least a full minute. O.B. Lester was watching Foster as he slowly chewed on pieces of pork chop.

"The man waiting for an answer Daddy" Marilyn said to her father. But Foster didn't act as if he had heard her.

"Gimme a drink" Foster said and averted his eyes to the old man at the table who just kept chewing and watching. Foster's wife reached into a cupboard and took out a whiskey bottle. She poured a drink from the bottle that read Old Crow into a water glass until it was about a third of the way full.

"The man asked you 'bout WoodHenry, when did you last see him? O.B. Lester said to Foster between mouthfuls.

"I ain't seen him since...since last time I seen him," Foster said and downed half the glass of whiskey his wife handed him. "WoodHenry owe me money, he give me the wrong horse to play and I lost."

Foster grimaced then took another gulp of the whiskey.

"Said he had dreamt which horse was gonna win, but he was wrong. I told him he gotta' pay me for being wrong and costing me money, but he said he wasn't paying. Shit," Foster said looking at the old man then back to me.

Foster downed the rest of the whiskey then sat down to the table and begin to play with his fingers and laugh.

"I told him when he told me about it, a horse with a name like Green Fields, don't sound like it could win, but he said it would. I played and I lost, that's why he owe me money. I'm gone get my money too. I don't and it's gon' be bloodshed round here. Same way it was back when I caught that boy trying to break into the house" Foster said and looked up at me blankly then went back to laughing and playing with his fingers. He started whistling and stomping his feet then stood up and lumbered back into the hallway. The sound of the bathroom door closing echoed.

"You can bet that's all she wrote today Mr. He could be in there for hours." Les said shaking his head in a slow sad motion.

"He goes off like that all the time, mind messed up. But if I can be of help just let me know," Marilyn smiled flirtatiously.

"His mind ain't messed up, he just forget sometime. He'll be alright in a minute or two, just give him a little time," Bertha added.

"He need to stop that drinkin' cause that's what's doing it," Marilyn said.

"Hush your mouth you don't know what you talkin' bout. That ain't got nothin' to do with it. Doctor said that it was something wrong with him" her mother scolded.

"That bottle is what's wrong" Marilyn said in a muted tone and rolled her eyes towards the ceiling.

Suddenly the bathroom door flew open and Foster walked out into the hallway and back into the kitchen. He was butt naked and was huffing and puffing like he had just ran a long distance.

"What you want honey. Something I can get you?" Bertha asked sympathetically.

Foster ignored her and lumbered back into the hallway. His wife followed. In mid step she halted and turned back toward me.

"He don't feel too well today, Mr. Barnett, you got to come back another time OK?"

"I gotta' get outta' this damn house, that's what I got to do" I could hear Foster bellow from the back of the house.

"Marilyn come here and help me with him" Bertha called as she disappeared down the hallway.

Marilyn sighed and dutifully followed her mother into the corridor.

"Nice to make your acquaintance Mr. Lester" I said as I got up to leave.

Old man O.B. Lester didn't miss a beat, he just kept on chewing his pork chop and nodded his farewell as I left the room.

I walked back into the Be Bop Tavern around 6:30 pm.

"What's up Bossman?" Po Boy who was one of my regular customers chimed as I passed him sitting on his perch. I stopped and looked twice. To see him sitting alone was highly unusual. He was never without his partner and bosom buddy Goose.

"Flying solo tonight?" I asked.

"Goose took sick," he said shaking his head sadly. "I don't know what's going on, I went by to pick him up like I usually do and his old lady said he left me a message that he went to the doctor. Funny thing is I been knowing Goose for fifty years, and I ain't never known him to go to no doctor before, except when he broke his toe down at the job that time." There was worry in his voice .

In my office I popped Joe Sample into my CD player and started going over the bills that had come in during the week. For some reason when I worked on things that had nothing to do with investigations, oftentimes insight about a case became clearer. I was hoping that this was one of those times. Crazy ass Foster Penniford hadn't been any help, so the question of WoodHenry being dead or alive was still hanging in the air. After I filed all of the bills in their appropriate places, I looked at my watch which read 8:06pm, then called Honey Lavelle's home number.

"Hey Baby Girl it's me with the evening report" I joked when she answered.

"Youngblood, you must have read my mind, I was just about to call you " she replied.

"I was hoping that if you weren't busy I might stop by later for a drink" I told her.

"Since when did you start drinking in the evening? If I didn't know better I would think you were checking up on me. Either that or you got some bad news that you want to ease me into" she said.

"No bad goods, but no good news either"

"What time were you thinking of?

"Is ten too late?"

"See you then"

"By the way, if you happen to go out tonight before I get there, just be extra careful. Take a cab, don't go on the subway."

"What's gotten into you Youngblood, you been taking mother hen pills or what?" she laughed.

"See you at ten" I said and hung up.

I called a cell phone number and a rough male voice answered.

"It's me, Devil"

"Hey Doctor" Moses answered.

"How is it going, anything new? "

"Everything's everything," Moses returned.

"See anybody else or anything out of the ordinary?"

"Nothing"

"OK, I'll be coming through at ten, so you can go home" I said.

"I can stay here all night, it's warm, no problem for me at all"

"It should be cool, but just in case I'll call you later," I answered.

He hung up and I focused on LaLa Hathaway and Joe Sample doing their version of Little Willie John's classic tune "Fever ".

I had hired Hummingbird Moses to keep a watch on Honey since he had told me he had seen someone following her. I decided to keep that part of it from Honey because I didn't want to panic her if there was no reason.

I worked until 9:33 pm, and was closing down my computer in preparation to

go meet Honey when the phone rang.

"BeBop Tavern " I answered.

"Mr. Barnett," the male voice at the other end of the phone responded.

"Yes"

"If you keep poking your nose into places it don't belong you could find it missing from your face. Stop looking for WoodHenry Taylor if you want to keep breathing."

Then the phone went dead. I sat still for a moment as thoughts and instincts from the past came rushing back into my mind and body. It was an old and all too familiar feeling. Those sleeping ghosts inside of me that I had consciously struggled to keep in hibernation was now stirring. I opened the top drawer of my desk and removed the Baretta. Then I removed the hunting knife from the bottom of the filing cabinet along with the scabbard which I wore strapped to my calf.

The man's voice on the phone had initiated the call of the wild, and the beast inside me had answered. The time for rest was over, now was the time to go to war.

CHAPTER 7

"LISSEN LIL NIGGA, we agreed that whichever one she went for would be the one to take her home, and she went for me didn't she?" Brax said pushing his face so close that Bobby could smell the whiskey on his breath. Bobby thought it ironic that even though Brax was a rapist, he still liked to see himself as a lady's man.

"Yeah OK" Bobby conceded and finished taking his pee.

Though it was a lie, to have said otherwise would have created a delicate situation for Bobby. Both Brax and Bobby had bought drinks for the woman at the bar and she had spoken and flirted with both of them. But to be honest she had turned her back on Brax in favour of conversing with Bobby more than once, but to Brax that didn't matter. He wanted to take her home and that was that.

"Just remember to go easy," Bobby said.

"What the fuck that supposed to mean?" Brax responded irritably .

"Just that, we don't know if she knows anything, and we need to, that's all"

"Nigga I know all what we need," Brax interjected cutting him off. "We need to find her man. If she know where he is, don't worry I'll find out."

"OK"

Bobby had a lot more to say, but he knew that when Brax was drinking and got his feeble brain fixed on something, there was little chance of changing his mind. He'd just have to play it out.

Bobby finished washing his hands and the two men went back out into the bar area. At a table near the middle of the room of the Penny Bar, Elvira sat nursing her fifth sloe gin fizz. When she saw the two men walking towards her she smiled drunkenly and waved, then held out both arms in a greeting as the pair approached. Brax hugged her as she giggled flirtatiously and kissed him on the cheek.

"My buddy here got to get home to his wife, but me and you

going to keep drinking baby" Brax told Elvira.

"Whatever you say Curly, you the boss of the applesauce" Elvira said rubbing the palm of her hand over the top of Brax's slicked back hair.

"I always did like a man with curly hair" she cooed.

Bobby said goodnight and Brax called out to the bartender for another round of drinks.

Spongey sat in the darkest corner of the Penny Bar careful to stay well out of sight of Elvira and the two men she had picked up. From where he sat he could easily check out Elvira and the big muscular man at the table. He was thinking that maybe now was a good time to go up to Elvira's house to get WoodHenry's heirlooms. WoodHenry had given him the key.

This bar was Elvira's regular hangout and he just wanted to make sure that she was drunk enough before he made his move. Only problem now was the big yellow dude she was hanging with. While he was doing his thing, he didn't want her to walk in on him, especially not if she walked in with that overgrown gorilla who could knock him into next week. Spongey decided the best thing would be to just wait and see which way the cat jumped.

Bobby was outside the Penny Bar sitting in the rented Lincoln Town car feeling uncomfortable. Mostly because he was still thinking about his ex-wife Honey. She had been a good wife. She had been young and impressionable, kind of country when they had met.. He had charmed her with his city-slick hip talk and cool manner. But that was a long time ago; too long ago. If only he hadn't got caught up in the drug game. Or if he had just stuck to his plan of selling to top end clients and avoiding the street corner world of small time bullshit, he would have been on top and Honey would be somewhere safe in a nice home with the finest of everything instead of being in danger from psychopaths like Brax and Nicolli. Bobby had no illusions, he knew Brax and Nicolli would kill Honey without giving it a second thought if they believed she had information that could help them find WoodHenry Taylor. This thought was jarring his mind like a battering ram when he saw Brax and Elvira walk out of the bar. Walking unsteadily as she held his arm around her waist for support. Kissing and laughing they made their way along the street towards her apartment which was just two blocks away.

The plan was that Bobby would wait outside on the street in the car in front of her place until Brax came down. Bobby parked the car in a place where he could see the entrance to Elvira's building and lit up a joint. He hoped that this woman would have the information Brax wanted. That way the pressure would be off him for losing contact with WoodHenry and Honey would be out of danger. He didn't believe much in religion but he wondered if he offered up a prayer tonight, did it have even the slimmest chance of getting through. With his past, he decided that it didn't.

Spongey was being extra careful. That's why he had left the bar by the back entrance and walked around the block, rather than approaching Elvira's building from the front. And it's a good thing he did too. Because just as he turned the corner he saw the guy who was with the big yellow dude with Elvira in the bar. A guy he recognised. His old pal Bobby Jones . Spongey backed away into the shadows and then went to sit in the small park directly across the street from Elvira's building. That way he could keep an eye on what was happening with the guy in the car as he listened to a small pocket sized walkman radio he always carried. Even in an age of television, video, DVD and the internet, Spongey still loved the radio best of all. As he watched the window of Elvira's apartment, he smoked a Camel and listened to an oldies station playing old soul classics by The Temptations and The O'Jays and Aretha Franklin. As time passed he began to think about where in the hell would somebody as dumb as WoodHenry get a bankroll big enough to choke a horse and also why was a private investigator looking for him. The thought occurred to him that maybe WoodHenry had stolen the bankroll. But then he quickly dismissed that notion because for as long as he had known WoodHenry he had always been a square. He played the horses sometimes but he wasn't the kind of dude who knew the ins and outs of the ways of the street. Besides WoodHenry was a church-going man who didn't believe in stealing. And WoodHenry was just too much of a coward to take the chance. So where had the money come from? And what was the reason for WoodHenry's strange behaviour and his hiding out? WoodHenry's story to him had been that his change in behaviour had to do with another woman with whom he was starting a new life; and that in order to make a clean break from Elvira, he had to go underground until he could get his lawyers to evict her from the apartment that his dead wife had owned and left to him. After evicting Elvira, WoodHenry said he had plans to sell the place. Spongey hadn't bought the whole story but he figured some of it was probably true because it would be just like WoodHenry to run away rather than stand up like a man and put Elvira's drunk ass back out in the street where he had found her. But that still didn't answer where he had gotten all that cash, especially since just two weeks before when they had gone to the race track, WoodHenry had been crying broke and placing two dollar bets.

Maybe he had hit the lottery and was keeping it quiet. He had heard of things like that happening before. And it always seemed to happen to squares like WoodHenry. Never to anyone like himself. Life had always handed him nothing but shit. As he played the scenario through his head of WoodHenry with all of that undeserved cash in his room, Spongey became more and more angry. Why should a square-assed fool like WoodHenry have all the breaks, he thought.

After about forty minutes Spongey saw the big light-skinned dude come out of Elvira's building and get into a black Lincoln Town Car that was parked down the street. The same Lincoln Town Car that Bobby Jones was driving.

Bobby breathed a sigh of relief when Brax opened the door and slid in beside him.

"Well?" Bobby said expectantly. He was hoping to hear an answer that would let him off the hook.

"Well what?" Brax smiled.

"Did she tell you where he was?"

"She didn't know. She said he might be dead," Brax said.

For a moment Bobby lost the power of speech.

"Dead?" Bobby finally managed to utter.

"Yeah, she said somebody called her and said that he was dead," Brax said.

"Dead," Bobby said again his mind drawing a blank.

"Start the car," Brax said.

Bobby turned the key in the ignition and the engine came to life.

"Think she could've been lying?" Bobby inquired.

"Oh naw, she was telling the truth, I'm sure of that"

"What makes you so sure?"

"That woman was under my charm, she wouldn't have lied"

Brax said

"Did you fuck her?"

"What the hell you think I was doing up there all that time? It was good too," Brax laughed.

Bobby's face was showing his every confused emotion. Brax patted him on the shoulder.

"Don't worry Lil Nigga, I'll get you off the hook with the man. Dead or alive, we'll find him. Lets drive."

Bobby didn't know what more to say or think, so he just slipped the car into gear and pulled the Lincoln into the flow of traffic.

Spongey waited fifteen minutes after the Lincoln had pulled away before he started for Elvira's apartment. He fingered the key inside his pocket that WoodHenry has given him and hoped that Elvira would be drunk and sleeping. According to his Timex watch, it was 12:46am. To be on the safe side he knocked softly at the door and waited. While listening to the radio in the park, he had thought up the lie he could use just in case Elvira woke up. He would say that he had had a dream about WoodHenry being buried under the floorboards and got so worried about him that he had to check it out. He would also say that the door had been unlatched. As he entered the front room all of the lights were off. He couldn't see shit. Cautiously he moved further into the room looking around and called out in a soft whisper.

"Vira…Vira"

He stopped and listened but there was no sound other than the muffled barking of a small dog coming from another apartment and the grumbling of the hot water pipes which meant somebody in the building was taking a shower. Then suddenly from out of nowhere the thought of sex popped into Spongey's mind. What if old drunk ass Elvira was passed out on the sofa with her legs wide open, and nothing on. He wondered if he would take advantage of the situation. What a crazy fucking thought. In all the time he had known Elvira, he had never thought about doing it to her. Not because she wasn't attractive in a bird-like sort of way but mostly because she was a lush. He didn't like women who got drunk. That's why he never understand what WoodHenry, with all of his squareness and churchiness, saw in a chick like that, especially after having a nice wife like Paulette. "Different strokes for different folks," he thought and moved like a cat on padded feet towards Elvira's bedroom. His eyes were adjusting to the darkness.

Fuck. The sight of Elvira's figure sitting upright in a straight backed chair, caused him to freeze and took his breath away. The drapes were closed and there wasn't enough light in the room to see anything but her outline in the darkness.

"What the hell..." he almost said out loud. "Vira,...Vira" he called softly in her direction. But she didn't move. WoodHenry was right. "This bitch don't hear nothing when she sleep," Spongey muttered to himself. He stood waiting. For what he didn't know, just waiting. Eventually he couldn't stand the suspense any longer and curiosity pushed his feet forward. He leaned toward her and smelled something odd.

Instinct moved him forward and guided his hand towards the small lamp on a table near the bed. When the dim light hit Elvira, Spongey almost swallowed his tongue. She was butt naked and tied to the chair with her hands behind her . Two ugly clots of dried blood started at her breasts and trailed down her legs then collected in a small puddle on the floor at the bottom of the chair. Her mouth was gagged with pantyhose and her neck was twisted so badly that her head was looking over her own shoulder. Elvira was as dead as a doorknob.

"Shit" Spongey said out loud, screwing up his bony face at the horrible sight. He forgot all about what he had come for and bolted straight for the door. Halfway down the stairs he thought about fingerprints. What if the police found his fingerprints in her place, on the lamp? They could, because they had his prints on record from a couple of burglary beefs a few years back. Hell they might even try to blame him. This is what he got for trying to help that cheap-ass WoodHenry. Outside the building he made a conscious decision not to run. A black man running like a scared fool through Greenwich Village in the middle of the night would surely attract attention. By the time he got his bearings he was at 4th Street and 6th Avenue. He swiped his metro card and went onto the platform to take the E train up to Hell's Kitchen and tell WoodHenry. But at 23rd Street he suddenly changed his mind. He started thinking: what if WoodHenry was in on Elvira's killing? Suppose he had set the whole thing up? Maybe he was down with the big lightskinned dude who had killed her. Shit. He got off at the 7th Avenue stop and walked upstairs. A few tourists were still out walking but the cars on the street had thinned out. It's was 1:57am.

Thoughts were racing around in his head like cars on the Indy 500. Then he remembered something. Digging inside his jacket pocket he pulled out a business card. There was a phone booth across the street. He dialled the number on the card and inhaled deeply on another Camel.

"BeBop Tavern" the voice at the other end of the phone answered.

"Mr. Barnett" Spongey. said into the phone.

"This is Barnett" the voice replied.

"Mr. Barnett, this is Spongey, we met yesterday at Elvira's place down in the Village, remember?

"I remember" Devil Barnett answered.

"I called to tell you what just happened. I think it might be worth a few bucks to you."

CHAPTER 8

"I DIDN'T KNOW what else to do," Brax said. His eyes were popping and his neck was corded. He was irritated but fighting to keep his tone from sounding belligerent. Because even though Brax was a psychopath, he was a living psychopath and for as long as he could he wanted to keep it that way. So he was careful not to sound as if he was telling the man off, but rather that he was just having a conversation.

Nicolli sat across the room on the couch watching Brax sweat as he smiled sweetly and gently rubbed his girl-like hands

"But what if you left fingerprints?" Nicolli said softly. "Your prints are on file with the police. What if an investigation showed that you had been associated with me? I visited you a number of times in prison remember."

"I forgot Mr. Nicolli, I'm sorry" Brax said.

"Sometimes you're as dumb as an ox Mr. Braxton" Nicolli said calmly. His edge over Brax was not his willingness to do things that Brax wouldn't, but rather that Brax killed and maimed out of a need and passion to feed an anger inside his soul. Nicolli on the other hand carried out his murderous rampages without either the aid of passion or need. In Nicolli there was no place for passion or anger to dwell, but rather just a dark decayed empty space where a soul was supposed to be.

Upon hiring Brax, Nicolli had made it plain that he would kill Brax or arrange to have him murdered without so much as blinking an eye if he ever double crossed or moved against him in any way. Nicole also explained to him that Brax's name, photograph and social security number were already on a slip of paper sitting in a safe deposit box and in the event of his untimely death, the box would be opened and a hit on him would automatically be carried out.

He also explained that prepayment for this assassination service had already been arranged through a law firm and a Swiss bank account. It was just a routine precaution that he took with certain people he hired. Nicolli was a man who didn't like taking chances or having things go badly. That's why Brax was sweating bullets and walking around the room trying to control the shortness of breath churning in his chest. Bobby sat in the corner fingering the arm of his eye glasses frame and watching the scene almost feeling sorry for his partner in crime.

"Sit down, I have to think" Nicolli said to Brax. The ugly pink-faced man leaned against the back of the couch, closed his eyes and placed his dainty hands into his lap. The only sound in the room was that of a raven screeching in the distance and the wind rustling the leaves outside the isolated rural cabin. Brax looked at his partner sheepishly. Bobby adjusted is glasses on his face and tried to look as concerned and sympathetic as possible. But in reality Bobby was thinking that if something did happen to Brax whether he would get a bigger piece of the pie.

He had been thinking for a while how nice it would be to get Brax out of his life. In fact after this job he had planned to make a move. He would have enough money to go somewhere else and set himself up properly. But that was all conjecture. For the moment he was knee deep in shit along with Brax because he hadn't come up with the goods on WoodHenry Taylor. Bobby and Brax watched Nicolli as if some magical smoke would pour forth from the top of his head with the answer to their dilemma. Nicolli was a patient man as well as a diabolical man. That's why he was so valued in certain circles. Many people had used his services all over the world. At any given time he had worked for the Palestinian terrorists, as well as for the IRA. In Africa he had been responsible for the killing of thousands when called in by Idi Amin to give him some ideas on how to torture and exterminate his enemies. In Columbia, he had been the brain behind the deaths of several judges who had been prosecuting drug dealers. On occasion he had even worked for the CIA. His speciality was creative torture. Nicolli kept of list of over 265 ways to inflict pain and terror on different parts of the human body. His latest invention was to a have a man's stomach cut open and then force the man to eat his own intestines as he was kept alive on an IV. As the man ate his own intestines, a video camera was set up to film the event so that the man could watch as he ate himself alive. It was his idea of humour. In terrorist circles, Nicolli was known as a fixer. If someone had a problem, he could make it go away without many questions being asked. That included business as well as political problems, all aided by his arsenal of tricks, lies, blackmail and murder.

Like any one else he didn't start life as a murderer. In fact he didn't even start life as Mr. Nicolli, but rather as Backtash Nihad, born to a Kurdish family in small village in eastern Turkey. When he was ten years old, things went badly and his father was assassinated for being named as sympathiser to one of the Kurdish rebel leaders fighting for a separate country. As a result the family was forced to leave their village and take to the hills. At the tender age of eleven Backtash was working and training with the Kurdish rebels. At twelve he was raiding villages and killing the enemy. By his fifteenth year, he was an expert in the maiming and torture of men and was made an officer in the rebel army. In this role, the physical torture of the enemy was his responsibility. As time went by, Backtash discovered that blackmail and lies could be equally as effective as the castration knife or fire shoved into the mouth of the enemy's child as the parents watched. In retaliation, the Turkish army searched for and caught his entire family. Twenty seven people were tortured and killed. His wife, mother and seventy-nine year old grandmother were raped, butchered and fed to the wild dogs in front of his eyes. Backtash was spared only because the Turks were planning something special for him. But fate stepped in when the part of the prison he resided in collapsed during an earthquake, which allowed him to dig his way out of the rubble to freedom. After living a hermitic life in the mountains for over a year he eventually managed to get a false passport and make his way to Germany where he quickly made contacts with Kurdish rebels in exile. These like-minded Kurds knew of his reputation, and once again Backtash found himself at the center of mayhem and terror. There he recruited men and began his business of being a fixer.

Nicolli opened his eyes slowly, leaned forward and focused on Brax and Bobby across the room. The gorilla and the weasel. To his mind they were stupid but useful. What he needed now was another approach that would maximise the limited talents he had before him.

"Mr. Braxton," Nicolli began reaching for a cigarette on the cocktail table. "Can you be sure that what she told you was all there was to tell?"

Brax was quick to respond. "I can't see her holding nothing back, not after I cut her nipples off the way you showed me."

Bobby Jones felt a bitter taste in his mouth.

"Okay, since we don't have her to hand, we have to assume that we know everything she knew, which is that WoodHenry was last seen by her on the morning of last Saturday. But what we also know is that Mr. Jones saw him on the previous Friday night. At that time you agreed to meet the following day, but something happened. What we must ask ourselves gentlemen is what happened on Friday night that caused him to change his plans. What about this man that led you to him?" Nicolli asked.

"Spongey, I could find him," Bobby said. "I don't have an address for him but I could find him through the network of hustlers in the street. He's a small timer so people know him."

"I can get him off somewhere and make him tell us what he knows," Brax suggested.

"I don't think so, we don't need no more killings" Bobby blurted out before he realised it.

"We got to find out some kinda way and it was your fault that we lost him in the first damn place. You was supposed to be clocking him and you let him get away. At least if I get to him we got a chance" Brax said.

"Mr. Braxton does make a point Mr. Jones....but suppose we did find him and then discovered that he didn't know anything. Then that would be another body for the police to poke around. Another body that may lead someone back here. No....no gentlemen, I think we need to focus a bit on something that the dead lady mentioned. Something about a man who came to her house asking about WoodHenry Taylor" Nicolli said.

"You mean Barnett?" added Brax.

"Precisely" said Nicolli. "What do we know about him and why is he involved in looking for this man?"

"I know that people come to him to help straighten things out. He's some kind of half assed private investigator" said Bobby trying to get in a piece of useful information.

"And let's not forget he's the same man who owns the bar where your ex-wife sings. Let's find more out about this Mr. Barnett, perhaps if we can find out what he knows, then our search might be made a little easier," Nicolli said.

"What should we do then?" asked Brax

"For the moment nothing," said Nicolli smiling self-assuredly and leaning back into the sofa. "I have my own way of going about it." Nicolli flicked on the television to the baseball game and poured out drinks all round from the new bottle of Jack Daniels on the table.

Bobby's insides were twisting into a knot. Even though he pretended to be calm, his heart thumped inside his chest like a mechanical drum whose timing mechanism had gone berserk. He was worried. It was obvious that both of them still blamed him for WoodHenry's disappearance and it was just a matter of time before he would have to pay for his mistake. But he was worried about whether the payment would come in the form of a slap on the wrist, with the result being that he would get less than the full financial share he had originally been promised, or would he have to pay with his life. Maybe even with Honey's life. How could he ever explain that to their son? Either way it didn't look good. Bobby pretended to be interested in the baseball game, but all he could really focus on was how he was going to stop what could be the next killing. His.

CHAPTER 9

THE BEER TRUCK driver pushed the sheet of printed paper across the bar for me to sign.

"Damn, Cedric" I complained, "you would think that they'd realise that upping the prices on the domestic is going to make people start looking in other directions," I said frowning down at the Budweiser invoice.

"I don't make the prices, I just deliver the beer" he smiled back at me.

"Yeah same old story right, the company raise the prices and the people complain to you," I said writing my signature.

"Don't worry about it, just human nature, see you next week," he laughed and walked out the front door back to where his truck was parked.

Duke was in the basement setting up another keg while I handled the customers. It was still early, so only a few regulars like Po Boy, Goose, and Betty Logan were around. I was checking the latest newscast on CNN when I saw Duke staggering up from the basement holding his back.

"What's up?" I asked him.

"I must have twisted something when I picked up that keg," he said and went to the nearest chair. Po Boy looked at Duke wincing in pain.

"You gotta be careful lifting shit like that at your age man, you ain't 22 no more," Po Boy said looking over his glasses and sipping his beer.

Duke didn't comment. But his expression spoke loud enough. The last thing he needed to hear was an "I told you so" from Po Boy.

"I'll get you some ice," I offered.

"Just give me a minute, it'll be alright" Duke said waving me off and relaxing back into the chair.

"I remember when my back used to give out lifting too much stuff when I worked on the railroad. After I got to be fifty-five I told my foreman, hey no more lifting baby, doctor's orders. I had a letter too," Po Boy said.

"Pay 'em enough money, and doctors will say anything you want 'em to say. For a hundred dollars that old quack doctor you had would've written a letter that said you was about to give birth," Goose said laughing at his own joke.

Betty Logan who had been watching from the across the room saw an opportunity to turn a lemon into lemonade.

"Duke honey, what you need is a liniment rub down," Betty said crossing the room. She moved over closer to Duke as he rubbed his lower back. What he didn't realise was that Betty was watching him with bedroom eyes.

"Oh Lord," Po Boy snickered under his breath as he nudged Goose in the ribs.

Logan was the kind of woman who would jump with two feet into any conversation within earshot without being invited. Worse still her comments seldom if ever made sense. She was especially acerbic towards men when they refused to buy her drinks. In short, most people considered Betty Logan one big-mouthed, bad breathed, pain in the ass who should be muzzled and living in a dog kennel.

Since Duke's wife Mildred had died of cancer three months ago, Betty had been making passes at Duke like she was a quarterback. Only problem was everything she threw in his direction had come up incomplete.

"Let me help you" she said placing one hand on Duke's massive chest and the other gently on his shoulder.

Duke suddenly became aware of her presence and bolted to his feet like he had received a jolt of electricity.

"No, no, I'm fine thanks," Duke said making his way back to the bar. Betty looked disappointed, and frowned in Duke's direction then started towards the lady's room.

"Old Duke jump up from there like old Lazarus waking up from the dead" Po Boy grinned.

Everyone in the bar including Duke was moved to laughter.

"A woman that ugly touch me and I think I'd have to go home and take a bath" Goose said.

"How you feeling?" I asked Duke as he hobbled past me.

"Still hurtin'."

"When Christine gets here in another twenty minutes or so, we'll run down to the Clinic, let em check you out," I said.

"No, I'll be there all day, I ain't got no time for that" Duke said.

"I know a doctor down there owes me a favor, who will arrange to get you checked out right away," I told him.

Duke hesitated and started to shake his head.

"Better get yourself seen to man" Goose said. "Back's a funny thing. You pull something in your back and next thing you know, you ain't got no more sex life."

"And he know about that first hand" Po Boy quipped.

Duke suddenly seemed more concerned.

"Yeah OK," Duke relented. "Maybe I better get things checked out, if it ain't gonna take too long."

The clinic where Dr. Jerry Coleman worked was only about ten minutes away by car. It was a geriatrics clinic. Jerry got Duke into X-ray right away while I waited in the lobby of the residents section.

"Come on now," a fat lady with a food cart called out to members of the live-in residents section of the clinic. The elderly people ambled up to her cart as she took their money in return for hot biscuits, donuts, and coffee. In a nearby corridor, a nurse was dispensing medicines to a group of seniors who had lined up with their mouths open like children as she meted out their daily dosage. Jerry had told me during some of our conversations that a lot of the people who lived in the resident clinic had families who had dumped and forgotten about them. The state picked up the tab for most of them. I wandered down to the end of the hallway and took a seat by the window.

I was looking out at Harlem's skyline thinking about my last conversation with Tom Jerrod in his big mansion and what connection that might have to Spongey's discovery of Elvira's murder when a voice pulled at me.

"Hey don't I know you?" The voice belonged to an old man. I turned around and was surprised to see O.B. Lester, the same old man who I had met at Foster Penniford's house the previous day.

"Hey young fella, I'm Les, remember me?" he said.

"Of course, are you living here?" I asked.

"Me, no, I live at Foster's or rather Foster lives at my place."

I must have looked confused.

"I'm just visiting here, I own that building where Foster lives. I just live in a room in his place cause Bertha takes care of me. Where you from? You don't sound like you from around here" he asked.

"Yes I am. Harlem, born and raised," I said.

"What did you say your name was again?"

"Barnett, Marcus Barnett."

A far off look came into his eyes and he went still for a few seconds.

"You know that's funny," Les said and began a small chewing motion.

"Why's that?"

"I knew a Marcus once, Marcus Harper my best friend. Everybody called him Buck"

"Really?"

"Yeah, back in Georgia." he said

"Not Waycross Georgia?"

O.B. Lester frowned and his jaw fell open slightly.

"How do you know about Waycross Georgia?"

"That's where my grandfather on my mother's side was from and his name was Marcus Harper too."

"Naw," Les said looking directly into my face. "What was your grandmother's name?"

"Lena Mae" I said

"Lena Mae Harding?"

"That's her alright" I confirmed.

"Well I'll be damned" was all Les said and kept looking at me for a long moment.

"So I take it you knew them both?" I said

"Knew 'em like they was my own kin" Les cackled.

"I was with your granddaddy Buck, the night he got hit by that train. You must have heard about that, right?"

"My grandmother told me about it. It happened when my mother was still a young girl."

"That's right, that's right," Les said nodding his head.

"We was working up in Savannah in them days. We moved up there for the work you see. That night me and Buck was walking back from work cause we was both working in the grain mill. In them days the money for the coloreds was good so we was working as much as we could. We had pulled double shifts for two weeks straight and we was bone tired. We got off work and was walking back home. I was walking behind cause I had gotten too tired to put one foot in front of the other and told Buck I had to sit down awhile to rest. I sat down by a tree to rest but your granddaddy Buck said he was going home to get some peach pie that Lena Mae had made. He said I'll see you in the morning and left me sitting under the tree. That was the last I time I ever saw him alive. I guess he was so tired, he never heard that train coming. I cried like a baby when old Buck died. And you mean to sit here and tell me that you Buck's grandson, well I'll be damned. Boy I remember the times me and Buck would go possum- hunting, we would sit up half the night sometimes cooking possum and drinkin' whiskey and tellin lies. I'd tell a lie and then he'd try to top mine with a bigger lie and we would go on like that most of the night many a times," Les smiled. "I didn't move up here until 'bout five or six years after Lena Mae did. I saw her once or twice but you know how people get busy and get outta' touch. Next thing I know about ten or so years back somebody told me Lena had passed away," Les explained sadly.

"It's been thirteen years now since she died."

"Well I'll be damned," Les said again as he sat quietly and seemed to go inside himself. "You know life is a funny thing, I bet I ain't thought about Buck in thirty years and then you turn up. How is your Momma?" Les asked

"She died when I was in my early teens," I told him.

"And your Daddy?"

"Dead too. He got shot in a hold-up about a year and a half ago in a bar he owned up here."

"Tough."

"Yep" I responded and joined in the silence of reflection for a moment.

"How was that you happened to be at my house looking for Foster again?"

"I got kind of a private investigative business going, so I wanted to talk to Foster to see if he knew where his cousin WoodHenry might be."

"WoodHenry?"

"You know him?" I asked.

"Know him? Since before he was born. WoodHenry is my sister Jewel's baby boy."

"I was told by the woman he was living with that Foster might know where he is. He seems to have disappeared" I said, deciding not to mention the part of about Elvira's murder or Jerrod's accusation that he had disappeared with four million dollars.

"Foster, humph. He's lucky if he knows where his own damn self is. He used to be OK, but now that boy's mind is all messed up. He ain't much good now for nothing except acting a fool and making everybody upset," Les said shaking his head sadly.

"Then Foster is related to you too?"

"Yeah, he my brother Roy's boy. Him and WoodHenry are first cousins," Les informed me. "But if you looking for WoodHenry you ain't going to get much help from Foster the way his mind comes and goes."

"What happened to him" I asked.

"Hoodoo," the old man said matter of factly.

"What?"

"Hoodoo, black magic, you heard tell of that haven't you?"

"I've heard people talk about it but...."

"Well it's more than talk. You can't see it, but it's real, just like you can't see the wind or you can't see a scent in the air, but it's real and it's there, same way Hoodoo is real," Les said.

"Hoodoo." I repeated the word to get my mouth used to the feel of it.

"Um hum. Tell you something you might think is strange but I believe in angels too. I ain't seen 'um as such but I felt them more than once and I didn't get as old as I got to be, by not knowing that there is something more to know in life besides what I can see with my eyes. I learnt that long time ago back in Georgia when I was still a boy. I had this friend named Pink. We used to play around together everyday. Then one day a white man come up into Miss Sally Mo's yard where we was playing. Sally Mo was Pink's auntie. She lived close to the swamp. Pink's parents died in a fire and she raised him. I guess we was round 'bout eleven or twelve. Anyway a white man named Mr. Barnhill accused Pink of stealing one of his chickens. Say he had seen Pink playing round his hen house the day before. But that was a lie cause me and Pink was together. We was fishing the day before. Anyway this white man took his belt off his trousers and gave Pink a whippin' just like he was his daddy right in Miss Sally Mo's front yard. When he had finished and was putting back on his belt Miss Sally Mo walked up to him, and looked at him straight in his eyes. Then she said something in a language I never heard before and crooked her fingers in front of his face and spit on the ground. That part of it, I saw with my own eyes. Now I admit I didn't see the next part, but from what Pink told me, Miss Sally Mo started watching Mr Barnhill. She watched and she waited until he went to get a haircut. And on the day he went inside the barbershop, she paid a colored man who worked sweeping up hair in the barbershop a whole dollar for some of Mr. Barnhill's hair. According to Pink she mixed that hair with some herbs and made a poultice and then said some more funny words over the poultice and buried it in the swamp. A week later that white man had broken out in welts and lumps all over his body just like somebody had bullwhipped him. Within a week, these welts and lumps had grown up to the size of walnuts. They was everywhere, top of his head, face, neck, even under the bottom of his feets. He had to take to his bed. Doctor couldn't find a cure, and after about three months of suffering he died. He died for sure, that much I do know cause I saw the undertaker carrying his coffin through town.

"Damn" I said.

"And that's the God's honest truth," Les said.

Then an old lady walked up to us.

"Mr. Lester, I hear you just about to have your ninety-fifth birthday. You must have forgot I told you I would make you a cake, but I didn't hear from you," she said sweetly.

"Naw I just been busy, but don't worry, I didn't forget. Next time I come to see James, I'll stop by Francis" Les said.

"Don't you forget now Les" the old woman said and moved on.

"Shit, folks keep telling me how old I am like I forget my age. Shit I know how old I am, I may not be no spring chicken but I still got all my thinkers and they working good too. Even now I don't forget much. Furthermore, I'll be 94 in October, not 95. She think I forgot about her making me a cake, but I didn't. I just don't want to sit around a lot of old folks talkin' 'bout nothin', and acting half dead. Man I wanna live till I die," Les said taking a dip of snuff from a tin container into his mouth.

"You were telling me about Foster," I reminded him gently.

"Yeah , this hoodoo woman got to him and messed him up. A couple months back she had him walking round talking 'bout he wanted to get hisself circumcised. Him damn near seventy years old talking bout getting circumcised cause he wanna' be like the chillun' of Israel. Nutty as a fruitcake. And about two weeks ago that fool started eating his food in the bathroom. He gets on my damn nerves, but Bertha put up with him. She a good girl, take care of things. She just keeps praying and believing Foster's going to get better and keep taking care of him just like was he a baby cause she love him. Though I don't see why. I believe that Bertha even know about that Hoodoo woman, but she just look the other way. I told Foster that one day Bertha was gonna get tired of his foolishness and leave cause she don't deserve to be two timed like that, but he don't pay me no mind. He have his good days and bad days but I don't think if he gonna never be right in the head again. Tell you somethin' funny though, when there is money involved Foster will act like he got some sense just the same as you or me."

Just then a nurse who looked to be in her early thirties passed by. and O.B. Lester called to her smiling,

"Hey little chicken, you got a wing for me?"

She smiled back.

"Mr Lester you ain't nothing but a mess."

"That's me, Les the mess," he grinned. "How is your Grandmomma doin' after her stroke?" he asked.

"A lot better, she's walking around a little now, thanks for askin'."

"You tell her that in a couple weeks when she feeling stronger, I'm coming over and I'm going to cook up some chitlins and greens and we're going to play some music."

"I'll tell her and I know she'll be looking forward to that," the young nurse responded. As she walked away, I smiled back and thought about a song by John Lee Hooker: "Big Legs, Tight Skirt Bout to Drive Me Outta My Mind."

"Her Grandmomma Marthy and me been good friends most of our lives, she from Waycross too. Buck knew Marthy, yeah he must have," Les said

He opened his tin and took out another dip of snuff.

"Anyway I was telling you about Foster and that damned Hoodoo woman

I don't know exactly how or why she did it, but I imagine Foster was messing around with her and they fell out. I only saw her one time when he asked me to go up to Mt. Vernon with him to pick up something, and I said OK. When we got there he told me to stay in the truck and that he would be back in a minute but when the minute turned into a half hour, I got curious and got out the truck and went up to the house. I peeped in through the window but I couldn't see nothing cause of this black cloth across the windows, but I heard sounds from inside sounded like grunting and panting. So I went on back and sat in the car and played the radio till he come back out about twenty or thirty minutes later smelling like a woman's privates and huffing mad. That told me everything I needed to know. Then just when he was about to drive off, she ran out of the house telling Foster to come back inside. He told her he wasn't coming back never again and she went crazy. Started cussing him and spitting on the ground and saying things in a strange language, I guess in her hoodoo language. Anyway it wasn't long after that, little by little he started losing his mind. Doing out of the way things like not getting up to go to the bathroom at night, pissing and shitting right in the bed and taking all his clothes off and walking around the house naked in the middle of the day. Calling people up from the telephone book cursing them out, and all like that. Truth is the only reason I let him stay is cause of Bertha. She a good girl. Sometimes when my arthritis acts up and I can't get around like I used to, Bertha looks after me, makes sure I'm alright. Cooks for me and washes my clothes too. You said the woman WoodHenry is living with sent you to see Foster, but I don't know nothing 'bout her, the only one I ever seen was his wife Paulette who died. She was a real smart girl too. Too smart for WoodHenry, but love is a funny thing."

"What kind of person is he?" I asked.

"WoodHenry, why, he in some kind of trouble?"

"Honestly I think he might be in danger, so I'm trying to find him before somebody else does."

"Anybody knows him will tell you WoodHenry ain't smart worth a damn. Fact is he's foolish, but he nice enough though. He was never the kind of boy to be in trouble. I never had too much to do with him, but we ain't never fell out or nothing. We just wasn't close. He was close to Foster though. Both of em liked playing the horses. Lots of times he would come by the house and they would go off to the racetrack together or he would come eat dinner and hang around and make up some songs and sing em for the kids. He's a good singer that boy. I always said. If he had took his music serious he'd have made a success of it I do believe. Anyway Foster's being crazy didn't seemed to bother WoodHenry. I used to laugh at 'em, two fools together."

"When was the last time you saw him?"

The old man thought for a moment and shifted his snuff to the other side of his mouth.

"Maybe bout two weeks ago."

"Was he acting any differently than usual?" I inquired.

"No, I remember he was in the kitchen talking to Foster about some gal he had met up at that hoodoo woman's place and I told him the same thing I told Foster before, that he better be careful foolin' around with hoodoo women, but he just laughed and went on without paying me no mind," Les said.

"Would you know how I might be able to contact this woman?"

"The hoodoo woman?" Les said.

"Yeah. You say I won't be able to get anything from Foster, but you've been to where she lives. Maybe she will know the woman that WoodHenry met," I said.

"I only went up there that one time and that was more than enough for me, but if you want to find her I can get her number. Foster got her number written down in his phone book. Her name is Minnie Patterson."

"Would you mind giving it to me?"

"I'll be back at home late this evening. You call me and I'll give it to you then," Les said.

"Thanks."

"Don't mention it, hey you like baseball?" he asked.

"Yeah. The Mets".

"Good, come by sometime, and I'll get Bertha to cook up some greens and cornbread and we'll watch some baseball. You eat greens and cornbread don't you?" Les said.

"Yeah love em."

"You wouldn't been no true grandson of Bucks' if you didn't. You know old Buck could play some baseball too."

"Really," I said thinking about how my being here and meeting O.B. Lester was just pure good luck. My father had always said, being in the right place at the right time made all the difference in a man's life.

Fifteen minutes later, I picked up Duke at the clinic's entrance and headed back to the bar. The doctor said the X-rays didn't show anything unusual but gave him some painkillers and recommended a hot bath and some vapour rub.

The BeBop Tavern was starting to fill up for lunchtime. Benny Sweetmeat was busy taking orders and Christine had her crew running things smoothly. I went into the back office and called the 28th Police Precinct and asked for Ross Lambert. He was the police lieutenant taking over while my friend lieutenant Al Mack was on vacation. Al said that he could be trusted so when Spongey told me what he had found I had called him.

"Anything on the murder last night?" I asked

"You were right on the money. NYPD found her dead in the apartment just like you said. Maybe we better meet somewhere because I got a lab report you might want to see," Lambert said.

"When and where?" was my answer.

"After work, I can come over to your place."

"Let's make it a bit more neutral just in case one of your colleagues sees you. It might raise questions, a blond guy looking like you hanging out in an uptown neighbourhood Harlem bar. Let's go for a sushi spot on 96th and Broadway called 'Kyoto'," I suggested.

"OK see you at six o'clock" he said and hung up.

Because of his back Duke was moving at half speed so I decided to take up the slack. Business had been very good over the summer months. The lunchtime crowd had gotten' so large that we had had to take on extra help. The big increase happened due to another one of Christine's brainwaves. She had come up with the idea of offering a free drink at happy hour to the customers who paid by company credit cards. As a result, lots of people who did business lunches returned in the evening to have a few drinks before going home.

"Boss, it's for you" Christine called from the end of the bar holding the phone in her hand.

"Hey Mr. Barnett, it's me Spongey, I'm ready to set up that meeting we talked about"

"OK, your call."

"I'm down in the Village, right across from the Pink Teacup, near Christopher Street in a bar called 'Skip's'" Spongey said.

"I know the area," I told him.

"Can you meet me at about four o' clock?"

I seemed to sense an edginess in his voice.

"No problem" I answered.

"Hey, can you bring the money with you?".

"What we agreed on" I countered.

"Oh, but, uh, I could really use an extra few bills cause I might have to get out of town for a minute. Plus I got something else to sell. This could be worth at least five hundred."

"See you at four" I said and hung up the phone. My watch read 2:36 pm. I had an hour and twenty four minutes to reach the village, which left me just enough time to finish off the lunchtime crowd and take the train downtown. As I continued pouring drinks, two things were running through my mind. One, why would a man like Tom Jerrod have waited for me to come along before he sent anyone to Elvira in search of WoodHenry's whereabouts. It would have been the first place I'd look if a man had four million dollars of my money. And two, Spongey had called me to report Elvira's murder and now he needed to get out of town. Who was he running from and why?

CHAPTER 10

SPONGEY WALKED INTO the bathroom of the small Greenwich Village bar. This had been the third time in the past half hour he had had to pee. His nerves were acting up something fierce and whenever this happened his bladder always got the news first. His wristwatch told him that it was. 2:41 pm. He was still trying to figure out exactly what to do. He had valuable information for sale. He had seen a killing, well at least knew who had done the killing which for his purposes was just as good. The thing that really worried him now was why suddenly out of the blue had he gotten a call from Bobby Jones. He had seen Bobby with the dude who killed Elvira in the Penny Bar, but he had made double sure that that Bobby hadn't seen him. Or had he? Naw. He was definitely sure he hadn't. Also, he hadn't told anyone what he had seen in Elvira's apartment except that Devil Barnett character who didn't even know Bobby, so he was safe there. Spongey tried to divert his mind with a game of pool but his lack of concentration would not even allow him to make the easy shots. After two games he gave up, then went to the bar and ordered another rum and coke.

"Wanna pay now?" Tim the bartender asked.

"No, run me a tab," Spongey said grinning to himself. He had plans for either Bobby or Devil Barnett to pick up the tab. Although he felt nervous he also felt very clever. At the moment he was the man. Even though he didn't know what Bobby wanted specifically he knew that the chances were good that he would pick up at least a couple bills for telling him something. Spongey had learned over his years as a nickle and dime informant only to give answers to the questions he was being asked. If people asked the wrong questions and got the wrong answers, it wasn't his fault. What the hell did Bobby want with him now anyway? The thought kept nagging at him, so he started another game of pool to try and calm himself. Three minutes later Bobby Jones walked through the door.

"Whassup brother" Spongey said and sank the eight ball with a one rail bank shot.

"Your eye is like an eagle, get you a few weeks in training and you'll be like Minnesota Fats in that movie 'The Hustler'," Bobby grinned.

Spongey stood up straight grinning from ear to ear. He was a sucker for the bullshit and Bobby knew it.

"What you want to see me about, must be important," Spongey said. "Word on the street was that you had something hot for me." Spongey had heard Bobby was looking for him about six hours after he had found Elvira and spoken to Devil Barnett.

"Yeah, I want you to ….uhh..." Bobby's voice trailed off as he looked around the bar. Because it was still early in the day, not many people were around, just a couple of gay guys talking at one end of the bar and two more guys playing the pinball in the back.

"Do we have to stay in here?" Bobby asked. "These gay motherfuckers make me uncomfortable."

Spongey looked around and shrugged.

"Let's take a walk" Bobby said.

"Let's just get a table in the corner, I'm waiting on a call" Spongey said

"Check it, you know when we made our little arrangement for me to meet up with WoodHenry," Bobby said and adjusted his glasses nervously before sitting down at a small table near the back of the bar.

"Yeah"

"We met for a minute and then we were supposed to hook up again but he never showed. I was wondering if you could hook me up again" Bobby said.

"That's going to be easier said than done, cause that day you saw him, was the last time I saw him too," Spongey lied.

Bobby sensed that Spongey was lying but couldn't be sure. Of course he could have put Brax onto him and within fifteen minutes he would have had all the information he wanted, but that wasn't the way he wanted to go about it. He didn't want Spongey dead, at least not yet. Besides Mr. Nicolli wouldn't look kindly on another dead body that the police could start asking questions about. Spongey needed to be worked smoothly and he knew just how to do it. Not only that, but he needed Spongey alive because he was going to be very important to his next set of moves. Flattery was Spongey's weak spot. Bobby had known that from the time they had met years ago. Back then Bobby was still selling drugs and Spongey was a runner. Spongey had always been a wanna-be. And even after the seven years Bobby had spent in prison, he saw that Spongey hadn't moved up in the world. He was still a nickle and dime wanna-be. But for Bobby's purposes Spongey was perfect because he would never see the big picture and therefore never see or suspect what he was really after with WoodHenry.

"Hey, you ever been to the Pepper Club?" Bobby asked.

"Shit, the damn drinks in that place alone is as high as giraffe's pussy, then on top of that, it cost fifty bucks just to get in. Since when did I start looking like the player of the year?" Spongey said frowning up his rat like features.

"You may not be player of the year but you certainly are a player. I got a membership and I can take who the fuck I want in as my guest, can't I?"

Spongey was trying his best to play it cool, but the thought of being invited to the coveted Pepper Club, where all of the top black players of the underworld came together overwhelmed him.

"Don't bullshit me now Bobby" Spongey said with a grin as wide as the Mississippi River.

"All you have to do is show up with this and you're in," Bobby said pushing the guest membership card into Spongey's top shirt pocket. "I think the time has come for me to introduce you to another level of the hustle. I mean we've been knowing each other a long time, plus I really appreciated the hook up you gave me with WoodHenry. When you come I got some top level hustlers I want to introduce you to. They looking for someone they can bring in on a major deal and I'm going to recommend you."

"How do I supposed to dress, I ain't got no fly suits and shit to be walking up in there with," Spongey said with the enthusiasm quickly draining from his face as he looked down at his new Nike sneakers.

"Here" Bobby said peeling off three hundred dollar bills from his bankroll.

Get yourself some player gear and meet me down there at twelve tonight. This is an investment," Bobby told him.

As Spongey watched Bobby leave the bar he fingered the three hundred in his pocket and thought about who he could borrow some clothes from for the night and keep the three bills. Spongey rocked his head to the music from the bar's jukebox as he looked around. He liked meeting straight guys in gay bars because it set them on edge and he could get what he wanted from them quickly. Spongey had the feeling that things had started to go his way. He looked at his watch. It was almost 4:00 pm. He fingered the three hundred dollar bills in his pocket again and smiled to himself.

"Hey Tim give me another rum and coke" he said as he started another game of pool. This time his hands were much steadier and he made all of the shots as easy as pie.

Spongey was still playing pool a half hour later, when the man he had met yesterday at Elvira's house walked through the door. He seemed somehow different than Spongey had remembered him. For a start he seemed more smooth and confident. Instead of the Ivy League suit, he now wore a well-cut quality pair of slacks and leather jacket that exuded a cool elegance. He seemed friendly enough, not the kind of person who tried to set you up immediately with the mind-fuck attitude of "I'm the big man and you ain't shit" kind of thing. There was something about the man that made you respect him. Maybe it was the way he never seemed to raise his voice and stayed focused on your eyes when he spoke.

"You said you had something else to sell" Devil Barnett said.

"For five hundred?" Spongey responded and sank the seven ball.

"That depends on how good the information is," the detective responded.

"Oh it's good alright," Spongey assured him and quickly sank two more balls in a row. "You said you wanted to find WoodHenry, right, well I know just where he is. That worth something to you?" he continued.

"If he is where you say he is, sure," Devil said.

"OK, I can do it tonight. Is it worth five hundred?"

"Yeah maybe. Any time after seven tonight is cool with me."

"Uh what about nine" Spongey said as he worked out the time it would take him to meet Devil, take a cab down to WoodHenry's place in Hell's Kitchen, have himself a nice soul food dinner at Jezebel's restaurant off 9th Avenue, then take a taxi up back up to the Pepper Club in Harlem.

"Can you meet me at this address?" Spongey said handing Devil a white piece of paper with an address on 148th Street in Harlem.

"It's my friend's place that I'm using for the moment. There we can sit down and go over exactly how we gonna make the move to walk in and surprise WoodHenry" Spongey said.

"Now about the other part" Devil said.

"What other part?"

"The part about the dead woman."

"Elvira, yeah man she was all fucked up, blood everywhere. Oh by the way did you bring the cheese?" Spongey asked.

Devil nodded and passed Spongey two one-hundred dollar bills which he quickly checked and jammed into his front left pocket.

"Did you see who did it?" Devil asked.

Spongey fought hard not to sound too forthcoming while still not sounding cagey. He had figured it all out before hand. He was willing to tell the man where WoodHenry was, which was one thing, but telling him about Elvira's killer was something else all together. Which meant there was more money to be made from this thing if he played his cards right.

"I didn't see her getting killed if that's what you mean, but I saw who came out of the apartment right before I went inside."

"Who was it?"

"I don't know his name but I know what he looked like."

"You know where I can find him?" Devil asked in a even voice.

"Wait a minute, before I say anything, how much is this information worth to you?"

"Two bills at least" Devil said.

"I was thinking more like three" Spongey interjected and watched for the man to react.

"Three huh?" Devil said.

"Yeah." Spongey said an sunk another ball.

"Just supposin' you give me the wrong information and when I check things out they don't add up, what am I supposed to do after you've got my cheese?" the detective asked.

Spongey searched his brain for an answer, but couldn't come up with one that he knew the man was willing to buy.

"I'm for real man" was all Spongey could think of to say.

"I have no doubt but if you can't give me a name then what? I'm just left with a description that I can't do anything with," the detective from Harlem said in his cool laid back way.

Spongey was searching for a way to reach the money that the detective was holding just out of his reach. He searched his brain for something that he could sell the man, something that the man could hold onto.

"Tell you what, how about I put you onto the dude who was with the killer just a half hour before I found the body."

"How would you know that ?"

"Don't matter how, but I know, and I'll give you the dude's name tomorrow.

"And you think that's his name is worth three hundred? Devil asked.

"Well, yeah" Spongey squirmed.

"No" Devil said shaking his head.

He could sense that Spongey was starting to lose his cool a little.

"I'd say that all you got to sell is worth nothing unless you give me the whole package at once. Remember you said that you were leaving town. What if tomorrow comes and you can't be found? I need the whole package," Devil said.

"What you mean the whole package?"

"Let's not dance around, OK. You know exactly what I mean. I want the name of the man who knows the guy that killed Elvira. When you tell me where WoodHenry is along with the name of this guy, then you get paid the eight hundred."

Spongey's mind was running and stumbling like a three legged horse in a four legged race. He suddenly thought that if he gave up Bobby's name and the man had to take Bobby out of action, that it would hurt his chances of getting in with the top level hustlers that Bobby had promised. On the other hand if he didn't, he would blow eight hundred in cash.

"It's your choice my man" Devil said.

"Well, uh OK, I'll meet you at nine tonight with both pieces of information," Spongey said going for his stock in trade position of "a bird in the hand".

"Now you must understand something" the detective said to Spongey.

"What?"

"If you take my money and your information turns out to be

wrong, you are going to have trouble with me," Devil said.

"Trouble, what kind of trouble?"

"Bad trouble," Devil assured him.

"You ain't gonna have no trouble with me, I deliver" Spongey said wiping a thin line of sweat that had formed on his top lip.

"You might think that you're a moving target and that I'll never be able to track you down, but you're wrong, because after I received your call last night about Elvira, I put some of my people on to you and they got back to me with this."

Devil pulled a piece of white folded paper from the inside of his jacket and laid it down on the pool table next to where Spongey was standing. Spongey unfolded the paper and looked at it with trepidation. At the top of the sheet of paper in neatly typed letters was his real name Aaron Johnson, his police record which included 6 months imprisonment in Rikers Island for selling drugs, his mother's address, his current as well as two former addresses, two old lovers with their names and addresses as well as four places where he hung out regularly. It also had the address where he presently worked.

Spongey was visibly shaken and had to sit down at a nearby table to steady his nerves.

"Give him another of what he's drinking and give me a ginger ale" Devil called to the man behind the bar.

When the man brought the drinks over a few minutes later, Spongey's eyes were still glued to the document.

"And this is just half of what I got. So don't make a mistake. If you don't have anything, I'll walk away and forget this meeting ever took place, but if you take my money you're on the hook," Devil told him.

Spongey felt a cold chill inside his stomach that seemed to curdle everything he had eaten for the past two days. It wasn't only what the man said but rather how he said it. Spongey sensed that behind the nice guy cool exterior, this man was very dangerous and that if he slipped up, he would get badly hurt. Sweat broke out on Spongey's forehead and ran down his rat-like face then settled in the crevices of his neck which he wiped away with his sleeve.

"I'm being straight with you" Spongey said.

"Now that we have an understanding, I'll tell you what I'm going to do. Just to show good faith I'm going to give you the three hundred for the man's name right now OK" Devil said and pulled a bankroll from his pocket.

" Right now?"

"Right now" Devil said then peeled three hundred from the bankroll and laid it on the table in front of him.

"OK OK" Spongey said lowering his voice, " the guy that I saw with the guy coming out of her apartment was Bobby Jones," Spongey said taking the money and cramming it down into the left front pocket.

Devil recognised the name right away. Honey's husband.

"How do you know him?" the detective asked.

"I used to work for him moving product and about a month ago I ran into him again."

"And you're sure it was him you saw last night?"

"Positive."

"So let's talk about how you came to know WoodHenry and Elvira"

Spongey felt a lump in his throat. "One night we was hanging out in a bar in Brooklyn and he met Elvira, I was there when they met."

"So would you say that you and WoodHenry are tight?"

"Oh yeah I'm his man, I mean the only reason I'm going to tell you where he's hiding is because I figure if that dude did that to Elvira then he probably looking for WoodHenry too like everybody else."

"So who is everybody else?" the detective asked.

"What?" Spongey blinked nervously as the sick feeling inside his stomach increased.

Shit. He had said the wrong thing. He shouldn't have said 'everybody else.'

"Who exactly do you mean by everybody else?" Devil Barnett repeated.

"Uh everybody, you know, people"

"Remember, you already took my money so now you're on the hook."

"I know, I know, but like I said...." Spongey stammered.

"I'm getting the feeling that you tryin' to fuck wid me." The detective's voice was soft but deadly like a cobra as he held Spongey in the grip of his hypnotic stare.

Spongey knew he had gone too far. A sudden impulse made him want to return the three hundred bucks, but he instantly put that crazy thought out of his head. Instead, in that split second he thought... what if he did tell every thing he knew about Bobby.... so what? He knew that Bobby would double cross him anyway if given half the chance. In fact he'd always thought that it was Bobby who had ratted him out to the undercover cop who busted him and got him sent away to Riker's Island. That as well as the fact that something about this detective dude scared the shit out of him, moved him to his next utterance.

"OK, Bobby Jones was the one I was talking about when I said everybody else. He was looking for WoodHenry too," Spongey said.

"Why?"

"He wanted to talk to him about a racetrack scam. You know WoodHenry knows a lot about race horses and he works on the horses that his boss Mr. Jerrod puts into races sometimes. I told him that WoodHenry was just a dumb country-ass "honest as the day is long" type country boy who wouldn't go for no scam, but he said he still needed to talk to him and he paid me, so I did it."

"Did what?"

"Set up a situation so he could meet and talk to WoodHenry."

"When?"

"Last Friday"

"How much did he pay you, if you don't mind my asking?"

"Two bills," Spongey said.

"Uh-huh, and how did you meet WoodHenry, originally?" Devil asked.

"At the place where he works. I supervise the cleaning crews that do the offices at night. I used to come in after the offices were closed and he would be there waiting for any late deliveries and we would get to talking. We discovered that we both came from Michigan. I'm from Saginaw and he's from Detroit so we started hanging out."

"So why is WoodHenry hiding?"

"I don't know, honest."

"He didn't talk to you about it?"

"No, like I told you when I called you on the phone, all I did was go up to his place to try to get his Momma's picture and his Daddy's watch-chain like he asked me to, and that's when I found Elvira. That's the God's truth Mr. Barnett"

"I believe you Spongey, I even believe you don't know why

WoodHenry is hiding," Devil said.

"I'm telling the truth," Spongey said.

"For your sake let's hope so" the detective said as he stood up to leave.

Spongey felt his stomach go weird again while he watched from the front door as the detective moved down the street and disappear around the corner.

No matter what happened, he was three hundred ahead of the game with the detective. He smiled at the thought that tonight he would pick up another five, not to mention what he might pick up with Bobby later at the Pepper Club.

His thoughts turned again to where he could borrow some fly clothes from so that he would look the part of a first class hustler when he stepped into the Pepper Club at midnight. He went back inside and put twenty dollars on the bar.

"Hey Tim, give me my regular again, take care of my tab and keep the change.

"You must be having a good day," the bartender said smiling.

"Yeah baby," Spongey said, "I'm moving up in the world."

As he sat sipping his rum and coke an idea the size of the grand canyon flashed inside his brain. The idea was so powerful that it sent adrenaline into his whole body. He stood up and walked out of the bar. He needed a pay phone. He didn't want to use the phone in the bar because this could be one of those heavy conversations. Excitement had caused him to walk all the way to the corner before he even realised it. If he could pull this one off, he would get not only the detective's money but maybe even add an extra thousand to his bankroll tonight. He dialled the number and waited. When the familiar voice answered he smiled.

"Hey this is Spongey, you'll never guess who I'm meeting tonight" he started.

CHAPTER 11

IT WAS ALMOST 5:30pm when I left Greenwich Village and took the Number 2 train to Broadway and 96th Street to meet Ross Lambert at the Kyoto sushi restaurant. Lambert arrived at 6:03pm with the autopsy report on Elvira. The report indicated that her nipples had been bitten off and her clitoris had been cut off with a knife.

"Some pretty nasty character huh?" he said.

"Yeah," I agreed.

"Lieutenant Mack told me when he went on vacation that I might get a call from you. Honestly, I didn't think you would call but at the same time I was kind of hoping you might. He said you were a top man, one of the best in the world," Lambert said lowering his voice and looking across the table at me.

I ordered Japanese tea for the both of us.

Ross Lambert looked about twenty two, with blond hair and green eyes. He was Al Mack's sergeant. On the surface he looked like he might be a rich kid from Westchester on leave from Columbia University, but he wasn't. He was twenty nine years old and a seasoned officer who on more than one occasion had proven that he was made from the right stuff. He had worked undercover successfully on two occasions and came up with the goods on a major drug dealing operation. For one assignment, he had been rewarded with a bullet in the stomach and for the other he had received a decoration from the department. Al Mack vouched for him and that was good enough for me.

"How are things at the Precinct?" I asked.

"Different now that Captain Varney retired."

"Different how?" I asked.

"With Varney there was a forty year history which left a lot of skeletons around. But with the new guy it's all spit and polish if you know what I mean."

"I do."

"Varney had his hands in a lot of dirty stuff, everybody in

Harlem knew that, maybe with the new guy at least we can take the department a few steps forward in the right direction," Ross replied.

We finished drinking our tea and I thanked Ross again for bringing me the inside info and then headed uptown towards 110th Street to check on Johnny Ray Slim who had returned my call and left a message that I should swing by and see him later. It was only 7:00pm, so I figured that I could make it to Johnny Ray's in fifteen minutes by taxi which would give me some time to catch up before I had to meet Spongey at 9:00pm.

Johnny Ray Slim was in his barbershop cutting hair when I walked through the door. He raised a hand that held a pair of clipping shears and greeted me with a wave. Johnny Ray and I were kindred spirits. We met at a Jazzcell picnic about two years ago in Central Park and hit it off right away. Both of us were jazz fanatics and he had a CD collection second to none I'd ever seen. Recently he had introduced me to some artists that I'd never heard, especially Brazilian jazz artists like Tom Ze and Dori Cayami, Elis Regina, and Airto.

He was also a great barber and his clientele were among the top people in Harlem as well as other parts of the city. It even included big entertainers and sports figures. On occasions he would fly off somewhere exotic to cut the hair of some celebrity who had decided that only Johnny Ray Slim could make them look the way they needed to look. He had even cut the heads of a few movies stars like Denzel Washington, Morgan Freeman and Will Smith.

Johnny Ray Slim had a very interesting personality in that he was the kind of guy people liked to tell their secrets to and trust with their confidences. As a result he was an invaluable resource and a treasure chest of information. But unlike Spongey his information was not for sale. Rather, he would use it to help people, and on a couple of occasions it had worked to his own good in a big way. For example he told me that once he was cutting the hair of the late black Wall Street tycoon Reginald Lewis who mentioned that one of his companies was going to be bought by a major conglomerate . The next day Johnny Ray borrowed five grand and bought the stock. A month later, he had enough money to open his own shop. On another occasion, word came to him that the daughter of one of Harlem's politicians was about to be kidnapped. Johnny Ray put the right word in the right place and probably saved the girl's life. Johnny Ray realised that his gift of having people open up to him was a rare one and he worked hard not to abuse it. Our friendship allowed me the privilege of asking him to look into certain things for me.

"So you hear anything?" I asked him as he draped the white towel around my neck as I settled into his barber's chair.

"Yeah" Johnny Ray said and turned up the volume of the radio on his barber stand up so that we couldn't be overheard by other people in the shop.

He started strapping his straight razor on the old fashioned black strap that hung from the side of the chair. When he got the razor just the way he wanted it, he lathered my head with hot foam and went to work. I had learned not to rush Johnny Ray when he had something to say. When he had shaved one side of my head he bent over close to my ear and started talking.

"I found out that your man WoodHenry has a price on his head. Not a killing price but a finding price. Five Gs,".

"Did they say who made the offer?" I asked.

"Nope, but it's real" was all he said.

A few minutes later, we started talking about going to a jazz concert at Carnegie Hall honouring the works of Duke Ellington and didn't say another word about WoodHenry and the reward. Didn't have to. When and if there was any more to tell, I knew that he would get the news to me as soon as he had it.

When Johnny Ray had finished shaving my head it was 7:15 pm. Only forty five minutes before my meeting with Spongey so I decided to stop in at the Tease Me Club which was owned by my Uncle Beans. It also gave me an excuse to see Honey who managed the place.

Melvin the senior bartender, was the first person to spot me when I entered. He was working along with two other people. In my place, people started coming in heavily on Thursdays and continued through the weekend, but with the Tease Me, every night was packed. The clientele was mostly professional and on the prowl. Beautiful young brown-skinned women in bikinis danced eye-popping sexy dances on various podiums placed strategically around the room. I recognised some of the people who waved their greetings as I made my way through the crowd.

Booney the bouncer knew me, so when I entered the

employees-only area leading back to where the offices were located, he let me through with no problem. My uncle's office was at the end of the corridor and Honey's was at the front nearest the entrance to the corridor. Her door was closed and I raised my hand to knock, but something stopped me. I kept walking until I reached the end of the corridor. My uncle's door was partially open and I could hear two male voices. I softly knocked on the door and peeped around the corner to find my Uncle and his long time friend Shelby Green having a drink and a cigar together.

"Beans look what the motherfuckin' wind blew in" Shelby said as a wide grin crossed his dark smooth features.

Shelby had the worse mouth in Harlem. My father had once said that if Shelby was around at the second coming he would curse Jesus himself. He just couldn't talk without cursing, but he was also one of the truest friends a man could have. Shelby Green, my father and my Uncle Beans had grown up as boys in Harlem together and the friendship between them had lasted for over fifty years. Uncle Beans was a successful Harlem politician and businessman and Shelby was a millionaire property owner with buildings all over Harlem.

"What you two old rogues doing, counting your money?" I joked.

"Money, I used to count my money, but you taking all my business with that damn jazz club you got," my Uncle smiled back.

"It's good to see you Tuffy, what brings you round? Every time I ask Beans about you, he told me you working your black ass off, making that business work. I came up there one day a couple weeks ago but you was gone somewhere. Man you fixed that goddamn place up nice, real nice. Booths in the back, music bandstand, nice sandwich bar, real nice Tuffy" Shelby said beaming proudly. "I wish your Daddy could see it with his cheap ass, I used to tell him, man spend some of that damn money you sitting on fix up the place."

Uncle Beans and I laughed.

"Boy and I seen some of those women that be in your place, not like these young skank ass broads Beans keep up in here to dance around just enough to get a niggas' dick hard then sell him a fantasy and take his money. No, in your place I saw some sure nuff fine ass real bona fide women. Tuffy, I bet they be just throwin' pussy at you don't they?. Aw boy, Ernest would just love it, wouldn't he Beans?" Shelby laughed and finished his drink.

"Aw yeah, Ernest would love it, no question" Uncle Beans agreed beaming proudly.

The interesting thing was whenever Shelby and Uncle Beans talked about my Dad they often talked about him like he was just away for a while and might be expected back any day. And in many ways, I realise that they had made me his replacement.

"Take a seat Dev" Uncle Beans said.

"Have a drink, kick your feet up," Shelby added.

"I wish I could but I got some business in few minutes."

"Oh I got cha'" Uncle Beans said with a knowing nod.

Both he and Shelby knew that from time to time I was taking on various cases, finding people, straightening out a problem here and there and they both were very supportive. Shelby was especially encouraging after I had helped a friend of his discover who had murdered his nephew. Before then he didn't know exactly what I did for the government. He thought I was just a paper pusher, but after I told him that I used to be a CIA assassin, he just looked me and said "Tuffy I got a whole building full of no-good motherfuckers that could do with a good killing, half of 'em don't want to pay the rent and the other half busy fuckin' up my place. If I could wipe 'em out, shit, I could go condo and make a couple million. You dust off your gun, and we'll go straight to the bank."

It made me laugh so hard that it brought tears to my eyes. Only Shelby Green could make a joke out of something so macabre.

"I just stopped by to say hey and to talk to Honey about something," I said.

"OK, talk on you later" Uncle Beans said

"Take it light Tuffy" Shelby said.

Honey's door was still closed. I knocked twice and her voice called from the other side.

"Who is it ?"

"Me, Dev"

"Come in."

She was sitting behind her desk going through a stack of invoices.

"Hey Youngblood," she greeted with a smile that made men

weak at the knees.

"I'm fine, just making the rounds to see what I can see."

I told her what Spongey had told me about Bobby and his knowledge of Elvira's killing as well as the fact that I was going to meet WoodHenry in a half hour. She just stared into space as tears started to well up in her eyes.

"I'm sorry." I said

"Oh it's not what you think, these tears aren't for Bobby. They're for our son. He deserves a lot better than he got for a father." she said.

"We don't get to choose our relatives." I said trying to soften the effect of my bad news.

"No we don't" she said and wiped the last tear away.

"Drink?" she asked.

"No, I think I'd better keep a clear head."

"If there is anything I can do?"

"Just sit tight and hope for the best" I said.

"With you on the case, I ain't worried," she smiled.

I kissed her on the cheek and left. It was 8:42pm. I walked towards the corner and hailed a cab. As the car made it's way east, I went over the case in my mind again. There were still too many unknowns and I felt now was the time to start covering my bets. I used my cell phone to make an out of town call.

"Hello," a female voice answered.

It belonged to Ginger Ferella, Jim Frazier's secretary.

"Hiya Ging, it's Dev,"

"Devil Barnett, how are you man?" her gentle Maryland accent purred through the receiver.

"I'm well."

"How's life on the outside?"

"Not bad, just doing the things that normal people do, going to work everyday, problems with the plumbing, trouble with women, you know the usual," I laughed.

"Jim said you were working as a detective these days."

"Yeah in a way."

"I know you called for Jim, but I'm sorry to tell you, he's in Brazil."

"Brazil?"

"He's visiting his brother who lives down there. He'll be away a least another month.

" Well anyway when you talk to him, send him my best. It's

good hearing your voice again," I said.

"You too, and listen just because you're not with the agency doesn't mean you don't still have friends here. Anytime you want you just call or come down, I'd love to see you, just to have a chat and catch up."

"Thanks, I appreciate that," I said.

Ginger had always been a nice person. Helpful and caring. I'm glad I had people like her and Jim in my life. Even if he was in Brazil.

Jim Frazier had been my partner in the field when I worked with the CIA. He was one of two people I knew I could trust with my life and depend on when the chips were down. I hung up and hesitated before I made the next call. I honestly didn't want to make this call, but felt I didn't have a choice. Jim was away and the only other person I knew who I could depend on to watch my back with no questions asked was the person at the end of my index finger. I thought about the phone number in New Mexico which I knew by heart and hesitated again. The hesitation came from a fear of ghosts. Ghosts that I told myself were resting permanently. For a while I had been successful in making myself believe that they were, but I also knew that making the moves I needed to make now would expose my delusion for what it really was. A lie. I felt the ghosts coming closer and closer so I put down the phone and pushed them back into the corner of my mind again. I needed to continue lying to myself a while longer.

I reached the address in Harlem that Spongey had given me. It was a five storey apartment building on a dingy block. I knocked on the door of the apartment for at least five minutes but there was no answer. My watch read 9:03pm. I went across the street and waited another five minutes. Still nothing. I decided that one approach might be to wait in the hallway in the shadows for a while to see if anyone came or went. As I started back towards the building, two New York City police squad cars pulled up in front of the building.

"Hey you, freeze," one beefy-faced black cop shouted at me from behind a loaded gun as I started to mounted the steps at the bottom of the stoop.

I calmly did as the man asked and watched as the patrolmen from the other car walked over to me with their guns drawn. Three were white and one was black. A green-eyed blond cop took the lead as his partner who was thin and lanky looked me over.

"Who are you and what are you doing here?" the green-eyed cop asked me.

"I could ask you the same thing" I said.

"Where have you just come from?" the lanky one asked.

"From across the street" I said.

"What were you doing there?" Beef Face said.

"I'm supposed to meet a guy."

"What's his name?" the lanky one inquired."

"Aaron Johnson," I answered sizing them up.

"Where is he?" the cop who hadn't spoken up to that time who had a hair-lip chimed in.

"He never showed," I said.

"Do you know where he lives?" Green Eyes asked.

"I don't know if he lives there but the apartment number he gave me is number 17," I said.

"Is that where you were headed?"

"Yeah"

"Let's go" the lanky one said giving the sign to his partner to keep a close watch on me. We all mounted the steps with the big cop in the lead. He knocked on the door for about three minutes and got no answer. An old woman stuck her head out from one of the doorways.

"Police ma'am" Green Eyes said in an authoritative way that was meant to intimidate.

"Do you know who lives here?" he asked her.

"No" she said and shut her door as quickly as she had opened it.

"Think we should go in? We don't have a warrant," Lanky asked of his partners.

"Yeah but we've got probable cause, don't we" Hair Lip answered.

The lanky one took out a set of lock picks and went to work. Within a few minutes he had the door opened and led the way inside with guns drawn.

The front door opened into a hallway. Off to the right was a living room. The lights were on and I could see a faded green sofa with matching curtains in a room at the far end of the corridor. The beefy-faced black cop pushed me towards the living room.

"Stay here" Green Eyes said as Beefy Face stood guarding me with his gun still unholstered. Already I had read the writing on the wall.

"In here Sarge," the voice of the lanky cop called out from the back.

There was a few minutes silence then the voice of Green-Eyes rang out.

"Bring him back."

Under the guard of Beefy-Face I made my way towards the back of the apartment. In the bedroom Spongey lay sprawled on the bed, as dead as they come. Someone had put a bullet in the back of his head.

"This the man you were planning to meet?" the lanky one queried.

"It was," I said looking down at him.

"At least the poor bastard wouldn't have to worry about trying to pay the rent next month. Luckier than some," Beefy-Face said.

"We're going to ask you to come down to the station with us," the green-eyed cop said.

"No problem" I said.

"Call homicide" someone said.

"I take it you already know who I am then, since you didn't ask me for any I.D" I said to the green-eyed cop.

He looked confused for a moment which told me a lot.

"No, we just got a call that there was a dead man in this apartment and that a guy fitting your description had just left his apartment."

"I see, mind if I show you my I.D?" I smiled.

"You're a pretty cool character. How do you explain your presence here?"

"As I told you earlier, I was only my way to meet this man but he never showed," I said pulling out my detective license.

"Mr. Barnett, were you up here before?" he said eyeing the license then passing it back.

"Yeah, I knocked like you did and no one came so I walked across the street thinking that he might be late and that I'd meet him walking down the street."

"Like I said we'd like you to come to the station with us" he said.

"Does that mean I'm under arrest?"

"No, I didn't say that. Why, do you think you should be under arrest?" he said trying out his junior cop tough-guy psychology.

"No problem officer" I said and walked back to the squad car under the guard of Beefy-Face who still had his gun in his hand.

The cops took me to the 28th Precinct where I was asked to wait in one of the offices while the cops went into conference among themselves. Five minutes later a black detective I'd never seen before walked into the room.

"Mr. Barnett my name is Lieutenant George Fredricks. I'd just like to ask you how you came to be in the vicinity of the dead man's apartment "

"You mean how did I come to be in the vicinity of the dead man's apartment along with half the other people walking up and down that street at that time of the night?" I responded.

"Yes but you admitted that you were on your way to see the dead man," Fredricks stated.

"And I was, but like I told your patrolmen, I went up, knocked at his door and no one answered."

"I hope you're telling the truth Mr. Barnett."

"You think I might have a reason to lie?"

"Why exactly were you on your way to see the dead man?"

"I had arranged to buy a piece of information from him and that's where he told me to meet him."

"You mind telling me what that information was?"

"You know I can't divulge that Mr. Fredricks, my clients might find it embarrassing," I said.

"I see" he said.

He didn't press the point so I figured that Fredricks had read me pretty well. He knew that unless he wanted to go ahead with a full court press based on hearsay, all they had was circumstantial evidence linking me to a crime which would be thrown out of court quicker than God got the news.

"If you don't mind, my Captain would like to have a word with you," Fredricks said and went out of the door. A few minutes later a middle-aged black man with a smooth-shaven face walked into the room.

"Barnett is it?" he started off. "I'm Captain Robert Curtis and I understand that you have some information that might help us in the investigation of a murder but you are refusing to co-operate."

"No I don't have any information other than I told your patrolmen".

"Mr. Barnett, since I came into this Precinct we have a perfect record on solving the murders that have taken place here. And I want to be the first to tell you that I mean to keep that record intact. Now if that means putting you on the spot or even getting your investigator's license revoked I will not hesitate to do it. Before coming in here, I did some research. I understand that you were an outstanding operator with the CIA which I must say is impressive, but that's as far as it goes. Now you're in my backyard and I believe you are withholding information that can lead to the solving of a murder that took place in my Precinct. So here's the deal Mr. Barnett, either you tell me what you know, and I mean everything that you know about this crime or I'm going to have your black ass in a jail cell. You've got twenty four hours to think it over. Have a good night Mr. Barnett, you are free to go," Curtis snapped and left the room.

As he spoke the words, I felt a surge of resentment and dislike for the man flow through me. I had never met this man before but I had met men like Robert Curtis at least a hundred times before. Having been one of a few black men in the CIA, I had been exposed to many other blacks in many different levels of law enforcement and I had seen enough to recognise Captain Robert Curtis as a type straight from Central Casting. The type that had started off as a bright recruit with a burning determination to succeed. That determination being so strong that it allowed him to withstand all the injustice and racism that the Department had thrown his way. As for the hurt, he had long ago learned to deal with that by pretending that it did not exist within him. After many years and many times being passed over despite his record of excellence he had hung in there until God decided to smile on him and he finally got his shot. He was the type that vowed if the time ever came, that he would set out to prove that a black man could do the job better than any white man had ever done before. So as a result Robert Curtis had decided that the only way forward was to become the best 'by-the-book' man that ever wore the badge. "By the Bookism" became his religion. His answer to the problems of the world were always to be found in the book, in this case the police manual. More work, more patience, more determination. More was always at the crux of the solution for guys like Robert

Curtis. He never questioned if what he was doing was right or wrong as long as it had the approval of the department manual. At least that the picture that he would present to the world. And he would go to the grave with his last dying breath trying to show the world that he, Robert Curtis was the shining example of everything good, and decent. The perfect by the book man which also meant being above showing any sensitivity to black people in any way, shape, or form. Because according to the book, it shouldn't have to work that way. He was the type who believed in the police manual like a priest believes in the Bible. He believed that for his efforts he would be rewarded with a place at the top of the law enforcement hierarchy. For this prize, his every action had to remain above reproach. He had to be sparkling clean, fair and firm, so said the book. Still deep in his heart he knew that the very same book he worshipped could suddenly at any time be used to proclaim him a heretic and have his balls cut off if he stepped out of line.

His greatest enemy was other blacks in positions of power who, according to the book, didn't measure up. Only his black superiors enjoyed his respect. Not because he admired them for their achievement but rather because he believed that they were his betters and had managed gain access to the magic formula that could tame the dragon of racism and defeat the monster of hate that he knew lay deep within the hearts of men. Men he worked with. Men who worked for him. Secretly he hoped that by becoming friends with these superior men he too would one day be given access to the magic formula so that he could rise even higher and show the world his greatness. That's why there would be hell to pay for any black person who got in his way or in any way threatened to commit heresy against his 'by the book' method of operating. In his heart Robert Curtis saw himself as a Supernigger.

As I walked away from the station my thoughts turned to the set up. Someone had called in to the station and sent the police around just at the time I was supposed to be meeting Spongey. Whoever killed him had made a mistake. They had locked the door on their way out. If the door had been unlocked there was a good chance that the police might have walked in and found me standing over Spongey's corpse. Anyway the whole thing was driving me to the place I didn't want to go to. I wasn't quite there yet, but I was definitely at the jumping off place, and the ghosts were in the corner smiling and waiting The ghosts knew that sooner or later that I would have to make the telephone call to New Mexico. And they were waiting. Waiting to be let out of their cage which lived in the darkest corners of my mind. They could afford to be very patient because they understood that I would always trust my instincts. And my instincts were the key that would unlock the cage. The same instincts that had kept me alive for fifteen years in the field as a CIA operative .

My grandmother had always taught me that your instinct was your first mind through which God was talking to you. And I believed her. Since my ghosts had been weaned on my instincts they knew that it was just a matter of time.

I got back to the bar and picked up the phone. The goddamn ghosts had won. I looked at the dial pad and almost cursed myself as I made the dreaded call to New Mexico.

"Hello" the female voice at the other end of the phone answered after the third ring.

"Hi Luz, this is Devil"

"Devil, como estas?" she responded.

"Todo esta bien, y tu?"

"Good, everything is very good," Luz said.

"Just the other day Francisco was saying how much he missed you and now you call. You have very good vibration my brother. We both miss you so much".

"I miss you guys too," I said not sure whether I had just lied or not.

"Momento, I will get Francisco, he will be so surprised and happy," she said.

I could hear her leaving the phone. A few seconds later Francisco's voice came on the line.

"Yes, hello?".

"Como estas me hermano," I said.

"Devil Barnett, what the fuck...Man how you doing?" Francisco said. I could almost see the wide grin spreading across his face

"I'm doing something here in New York that I could use your help on" I said.

"When?" he asked

"ASAP" I said in a flat tone.

"It's like that huh?" he asked.

"Yeah."

"I'm on the next flight out, expect me in the morning."

"Thanks"

"You know you don't need to say that right, we're family" Francisco said.

"I know."

"See you tomorrow" was all he said and the phone went dead.

Francisco was the best friend a man could ever hope for, or the worst enemy a man could ever dream of having. During my time with the agency Francisco and I had worked together. At first it was just a temporary assignment for a problem that was occurring in Argentina, but after our success, we continued working together. There is no question that the chemistry worked. The problem was it worked too well. We had the highest positive performance rating for any assassination team ever. Maybe it was a combination of our personalities or maybe it was just fate. Who knows.

The operation that changed the nature of the relationship and both our lives happened in Venezuela about five years ago. Our assignment had been to eliminate a member of the Venezuelan diplomatic corps who had compromised a network of American and Venezuelan agents by selling secrets to an unfriendly terrorist group in the middle east. The order came down from the office of a man named Tony Talbot, a man who had gotten his job as a result of political connections rather than merit. Talbot ordered the assassination of the diplomat as well as all members of his family who he decided were involved in the plot as well.

Only trouble was the only other member of the diplomat's family was his twenty- two year old daughter Luz, who was studying to be a nurse at the local college and knew nothing about her father's activities. We carried out our orders on the diplomat as instructed and then turned our attention to the next part of the assignment.

The big problem there was that prior to having discovered that the diplomat was a traitor, Francisco had met the man's daughter and fallen in love. Needless to say, our dilemma was beyond words. Against regulations, I made a decision. In direct contradiction to the orders I had received, I arranged for Luz to get a fake passport and escape to Costa Rica where she could establish a new identity. I told the office that we had lost track of her. On the day that I told Francisco what I had done he hugged me and wept openly.

That's when he told me that I would be his brother and that the bond between us could never be broken no matter what happened. At the time I thought it was all a bit melodramatic but as time passed I came to realise just how serious he was about his pledge.

When he quit the agency one year later and travelled to Costa Rica where he married Luz he still kept in constant touch. Often I would get a reminder from him with photos of him and Luz with Carlos their new little baby boy. He'd even send me photos of a group of community kids for which he and Luz had started a theatre company for New Mexico where they now lived under new identities. There'd be photos of Francisco changing the baby and driving the bus and photos of Francisco dressed up as Captain Hook.

Francisco had been born as simply Paco to a street prostitute in Mexico City some thirty-nine years before. He had lived on the streets with his mother. When he was six his mother was killed by a customer and he was taken to a Catholic orphanage in the countryside where the priests discovered that he had an extremely high I.Q. He took to formal education easily and by the time he turned sixteen and was ready to leave the orphanage, young Paco had become fluent in English as well as French. At the orphanage Paco was introduced to a father Francisco Gomez who became his mentor and arranged for him to go to University of Mexico. Unknown to young Paco at that time Father Francisco, a psychologist, was also an undercover agent for the CIA. He had long ago noticed a part of Paco's personality that allowed him to perform certain acts of cruelty without seeming to feel any moral consequence. The Father reckoned that it was the loss to him of everything he had ever loved at a very early age. By becoming the boy's friend and mentor, the priest realised that he could shape that part of Paco's personality into an instrument of destruction that could be very useful to the CIA. As a result Father Francisco began secretly grooming Paco for the Service.

During his second year of University, Father Francisco arranged for Paco to be recruited. Needless to say Paco immediately found his calling in the wet works department of the CIA which engineered the destruction and assassination of it's enemies. In honour of the man who helped him, Paco dropped his own name and adopted that of his mentor, Francisco Gomez.

When we were first assigned to work together there was nothing special between us, no camaraderie, no closeness, nothing to speak of that would distinguish us from any other team working together. But as time went by, we both found in each other a passion for our work that the other respected. I noticed almost immediately that Francisco could sense danger in the shadows as well as exploit areas of fear in a person's mind that they never even knew were there. He was the kind of person who could slice a man's neck so smoothly that the victim would never know he had been cut until his head dropped off his shoulders. He enjoyed the torture of his enemies, reveling in the knowledge that he played a part in a man's earthly suffering for his sins before sending him to God to suffer yet again. His style was brutal compared to mine but nevertheless very effective. We both truly believed that we were making the world a better place by ridding it of people who sought to disrupt the new world order as defined by our bosses who were the men at the CIA in brown offices and grey suits.

It comforted me knowing like Francisco had my back.

I remember on one occasion he scalded a man with boiling water and then skinned him alive because he refused to give up the names of terrorists who had bombed a bus killing women and children. Still I preferred him covering my back more than anyone except Jim Frazier who I had also worked with for a long time. With Jim it was a job, but with Francisco it was a burning passion. The passion is what made me uncomfortable. Most probably because I recognised and admitted that there was something within myself that shared Francisco's bloodlust and I didn't like it.

Nevertheless, it didn't disappear just because I found that part of my nature offensive. That part of me remained as ghosts. When I had left the agency I consciously decided to extinguish that part of my nature. Now my reconnection with Francisco made me feel as if I was walking around with a live grenade in my pocket. The ghosts with a taste for blood were walking the corridors of my life again. I had told myself time and time again that I had expunged that ugly part of myself. But like so many things in life, saying is one thing and doing it can be quite another.

I now felt that I was walking back into my past; a past that held secrets I was ashamed of, mingled with deeds that I swore I'd never think about again. Deeds done in the name of patriotism. Deeds that I wished I could somehow exorcise from my memory. Deeds as dark as the inner sanctum of a demon's soul.

CHAPTER 12

10:42 PM. "IT WAS SPONGEY alright. My cousin Jimmy who works on the ambulance just bagged him up. Said he recognised him right away," the male voice on Bobby Jones' cell phone told him.

"Motherfucker" Bobby said out loud and clicked off his call. He walked around the corner and inhaled deeply on the joint he was smoking. The smoke seemed to sour in his mouth as he thought about his present dilemma which seemed to be deepening with every step. Now his mind was on Spongey who had gone and got himself iced. Stupid fucker. Just when he was about to be of some use. Bobby had it all worked out. He had planned to pay Spongey for an introduction to Tom Jerrod. Even though Spongey only worked cleaning the man's offices at night, he still knew the man. He wasn't sure exactly how well he knew him but as long as it was well enough to make an introduction, that's all that mattered. Bobby figured that Jerrod was certainly smart enough to strike a deal with a man like himself who brought something good to the bargaining table. He had been thinking about it for the past two days. He didn't want to just walk into Jerrod's office out of the blue and make his pitch. But with Spongey to smooth the way it would have been be alright. Even though Spongey was basically an idiot and way down low on the importance scale, he nevertheless had a kind of a genius for putting himself into a position where he could pick up odd pieces of valuable information which he would always gladly sell . Everything would have been done in a smooth gentleman-like fashion. None of that back alley street deal shit. Bobby wanted to move up in the world and had hoped that this would be the deal that took him from being a small-time operator straight into the big-time.

He wished like hell Spongey was still alive. But like he used to hear the old folks say when he was a kid, "you could wish in one hand and shit in the other and wait to see which one gets full the quickest." He had to come up with another way of getting to Jerrod. A way to make him listen. He didn't have a choice. Getting to Jerrod directly was his only salvation, because he knew that Nicolli blamed him for letting WoodHenry slip away, and for that mistake he was a marked man. It was just a matter of time before Nicolli handed out his punishment. But for now Nicolli had to play it cool because he still didn't know where WoodHenry was. But the minute he did, Bobby knew that his goose was cooked.

As Bobby sat in Washington Square Park and looked across the small groups of night people passing by, his mind drifted back to the day that he had received the call from Brax telling him about a deal he knew about that make them both damn near rich. Brax took him to meet Nicolli who told them that a man had disappeared with a lot of money from a Wall Street brokerage firm where he worked. He then told him that if they helped him recover it, they would end up with two hundred thousand each.

Nicolli explained that he was allowing Bobby into the deal because he might have a way to make a connection with WoodHenry, the man who had the money, since Bobby knew him. When Bobby first heard the name he laughed out loud at the thought that country-ass WoodHenry would have nerve enough to even steal a piece of candy from a supermarket, let alone money from his job.

Two days later Bobby managed to contact Spongey. Together they hatched a plan. The plan was that Spongey would take WoodHenry to a bar and then Bobby would show up and he and WoodHenry would start talking about old times. Bobby had decided that even though he knew WoodHenry from before, he couldn't approach WoodHenry directly because WoodHenry knew about his criminal history and would automatically get nervous. It would look much better if the meeting was accidental and also if Spongey was present. They figured this approach would make WoodHenry feel more secure. Then in the middle of the conversation, Spongey planned to leave Bobby alone to talk with WoodHenry about a race track scam.

Everything had gone as planned. He, WoodHenry and Spongey had met up at a bar, had a drink and started talking about the good old days. WoodHenry asked about his son Harold and Bobby said that once he got himself together he planned to get in touch and do something nice for the boy in the way of securing his future. Spongey said he had something to do and would be back in fifteen minutes, then left the two of them drinking and talking. Then Bobby changed the subject from the good old days to horses. He knew that WoodHenry had worked with horses from the time he was a boy on his uncle's horse farm in Alabama..

As Bobby started to explain about a project involving a racehorse that could make him very wealthy, WoodHenry seemed to get excited. They agreed to hook up the following night to discuss the project in detail and to see some bloodline papers on this thoroughbred race horse Bobby had access to. Then it happened. That goddamned Mexican food that Bobby had eaten for lunch suddenly erupted like a volcano inside his stomach. He managed to make it to the bathroom with just seconds to spare before shitting his pants. He finished as quickly as he could then went back out to the bar only to find that WoodHenry had disappeared. Now the pressure was all on him. He had to pull a rabbit out of the hat.

For two days now Bobby had been thinking that he would get to Tom Jerrod and make his own deal behind Nicolli's back. He was thinking that he could find WoodHenry, get back the money, collect a big juicy reward and then maybe split the country. He had heard that Argentina was nice. He had picked up some rudimentary Spanish in the joint and was confident that if he got his hands on, say, a cool half million, he could disappear where Nicolli or Brax could never find him.

But that was something he couldn't think too much about right now. He had more important stuff on his mind. Like how he was going to meet this Jerrod dude then double-cross both Nicolli and Brax.

Ordinarily he might have felt a little nervous about such a daring plan, because he was by no means the courageous type. In fact most people he knew described him as a small time low-down dirty, cowardly, conniving son-of-a-bitch, and they were right. But this was different because this could be the big one. If this one came off, he would be over the hump forever. He took another deep drag on the stick of marijuana and felt uncharacteristically brave. Then and there he decided that there was only one answer. Like it or not he would have to go to see the man on a cold call, present himself and cut a deal. Feeling good about his decision he rose from the bench and began walking towards McDougal Street. The smell of food cooking drifted through the night air and turned his thoughts to where he might have a meal in one of the nearby sidewalk cafes. As Bobby moved through the crowd he was unaware of a dark skinned Mediterranean-looking man who followed him at a safe distance watching his every move.

CHAPTER 13

THE FIRST THING I did when I got back to the bar was to call Onion. It was 11:19pm. Onion is a top class computer hacker. Over the years he had worked for me getting classified information on people and institutions. He was at the top of his game and could come up with information on people that even government agencies couldn't get. I passed a name on to him and asked that he get back to me as soon as possible.

An hour later I was at home and in bed. But I didn't sleep too well, mostly because I was thinking that now with Spongey dead, how was I going to find WoodHenry. I got up and looked at the clock by my bedside. It was 3:37 am.

I put on a Sade CD, turned out the lights and let her sad voice float through the darkness toward me. When I woke again it was 7:30am. I had breakfast, then went in and opened the bar. There was a message from O.B. Lester and I returned his call.

We chatted for a few minutes and he gave me the address and telephone number of Minnie Patterson, the hoodoo woman who lived in Mt. Vernon. I called the number and told her I had been referred by O.B. Lester. Then I asked if I could stop by to see her about an important matter. She asked if I was willing to pay and I said I was. Without hesitation she agreed to see me in the afternoon.

Honey called at about 10:00am .

"See him yet?" she inquired.

"Uh uh, there's lot's to talk about"

"What about stopping by my place on your way home tonight, I'll be up"

I said I would.

At around 11:40am Hummingbird Moses came in. He ordered a ham on rye and a baked potato with a large Bud draft. After Benny Sweetmeat served him, he took his tray and moved to a back booth. Part of our deal was that he could take his meals at the bar for free as long as he was keeping a look out for me. When Moses saw me approaching he smiled and moved his weathered old straw hat off the table.

"Anything new?" I asked.

"Not since the other day, and I've been watching her from the time she leaves home going to work until she leaves work going back home," Moses told me between bites.

"Good, just keep doing what you've been doing and let me know if and when anything changes," I said and pushed a twenty dollar bill under his tray.

Moses nodded his agreement.

"Thank you Doctor" he said.

"No thank you" I corrected.

I worked through lunch, then made a mental note to call Jerrod. I wanted to see if he had gotten any word as yet on his missing four million dollar man. At 2:30pm I changed clothes and headed north towards Mt. Vernon.

To me the name Mt. Vernon always implied one of those small towns hidden away in the hills somewhere, but in reality it's just another urban town a little north of the Bronx. I found the address without too much trouble.

The house looked pretty much as O.B. Lester had described it, painted blue with dark curtains at the windows. There was a big black lazy-looking Labrador lounging on the front porch. As I began to approach the house, the dog started barking and a woman appeared at the door. I knew it had to be Minnie Patterson based on Les' description.

"The time I saw her she liked a scared me to death, I never seen anything like her. She looked like a bunch of who'd a thought it, wrapped up in a piece of damn your soul," he had told me.

She had one of those smooth ageless caramel-coloured faces that looked as if she could have been anywhere between forty-five and sixty-five. There were dark purple circles painted around her eyes and when she smiled she revealed that almost every tooth in her head was made of gold. It gave her the appearance of an insane clown in a carnival side show. Her head was wrapped in a black and blue cloth with orange and green bird feathers sticking out of the top. Around her neck she wore at least seven different necklaces. Some made from metal, while others appeared to be made from beads, wood and papier mache. Her hands were covered with what looked like thin lines of white paint that started as dots on her wrists and ran along the length of each finger until they reached her manicured bright gold painted fingernails.

When she opened the door to let me inside, I noticed that she wasn't wearing shoes and that her feet were painted a bright green with red designs.

O.B. Lester had been right. Minnie Patterson didn't look like anything that I had ever seen before either. The smell of incense inside the house was so strong that it startled me when I first crossed the threshold. It wasn't a stinking odour, but rather was a strange scent that seemed to go right through your nose directly into your sinuses like a Halls menthol cough drop. After a few minutes the smell seemed to settle and became kind of sweet and pleasant.

"Would you like some tea Mr. Barnett?" Minnie said in a clear and pleasant voice.

"No, no thank you" I said.

She must have sensed my apprehension.

"Oh don't be nervous, I can imagine that things may seem a bit strange to you at first but believe me, I wouldn't give you anything to poison you. Especially since you haven't paid me yet," and she laughed wide enough to show me her own Fort Knox again.

"Have a seat," she said opening her hand towards one of the two sofas in the semi-darkened room. After I had sat she curled up on the floor at my feet.

"It will be twenty dollars please," she said.

I paid her.

"Give me your hands Mr. Barnett," she said and extended her own hands towards me.

I did as she asked without hesitation. She took my hands in hers and looked at them for what seemed like a full minute before saying anything.

"You are a very strong man," she said and looked back up into my face.

I didn't say anything.

"How can I help you?"

"I'm looking for a man named..." I said.

But before I could say more she held up one hand.

"That's enough" she said.

I stopped in mid-sentence and she looked at me for another long moment then closed her eyes and began to rock back and forth. She suddenly stopped rocking, opened her eyes and called out.

"Albalita come in here"

Within a few minutes another woman appeared at the doorway of the room. She was younger than Minnie Patterson. The resemblance told me they were related. My guess was that Albalita was in her late twenties to early thirties. She was dressed in blue jeans and a white long sleeve top and had two long braids that hung down her back to her waist. Her bronze coloured face was smooth and almost glowing.

"Hello. I'm Albalita" she said.

"Hello, I'm Marcus Barnett."

Albalita looked in my direction through a pair of dark dreamy eyes.

"Over here" Minnie said who still sat at my feet.

As Albalita started to move across the room in small deliberate steps, I realised that she was blind.

"Here" Minnie said as Albalita reached the sofa where I sat and took a place on the floor next to Minnie who was still holding onto me and simply passed my hands over to Albalita.

Albalita's touch was gentle and warm as she looked up into my face with unseeing eyes. A slight smile appeared on her face.

"He's alive but he's not safe." Albalita said.

"She knows, that's her gift Mr. Barnett," Minnie said proudly.

"You've got to find him before they do. Otherwise they'll kill him for sure," Albalita said.

I wasn't sure what I should have said. First I wanted to make sure we were all on the same page.

"Who exactly are you talking about?" I asked.

"WoodHenry Taylor of course, that's who you're looking for isn't it?" Albalita said with the innocence of a child.

Suddenly I felt light-headed.

Not because I necessarily thought that I had just experienced something supernatural because I realised she could have known about me looking for WoodHenry from a number of sources, maybe Les or even Foster. But it was more something about the way she said it. Something unexplainable moved inside of me. I decided not to ask her how she knew, but rather how could I find him.

"Do you know where he is?" I asked.

"I see it but I don't know how to get there. He's in a room, a little room. Just a little plain old room, and he's scared, real scared."

Then the sound of the dog barking diverted my attention.

"Must be those children picking at him again" Minnie said jumping up from the floor and walking towards the noise. She opened the door, peered out and whistled. The black dog appeared at the doorway and walked lazily inside. It was then that I felt the drops of water on my hand. I looked back to see tears running down Albalita's smooth bronze face. She squeezed my hand gently.

"You'll find him won't you Mr. Barnett?" she said.

"I'm going to try" I said.

Without speaking, Albalita slowly got to her feet and walked back into the part of the house she had emerged from.

"My sister has the gift for finding people you see. If you want to find him, I can help you but it's going to cost you."

"How much?"

"One thousand" she said

I didn't respond.

"You can afford it," Minnie said looking at me.

"Frankly I can't" I admitted.

"But there are people who can" she said.

My mind immediately flashed to a picture of Tom Jerrod in his mansion with it's pastel walls.

"Yes there are" I said.

"Mr. Barnett, you will find that I am not a quack as many people would have you believe. What I do is a very old art that has been practised for centuries. When I held your hand I could see for example that you are a man with a strong sense of good inside you, but I also see that you are a man with a very dark side. I can tell you many other things as well, things that will help you find WoodHenry, but first you have to pay me," she said.

I walked away from Minnie Patterson's house with mixed emotions. A thousand dollars was a lot to pay for information, but not if a grand would get you four million. And especially not if you were Tom Jerrod and a grand was nothing to you but chump change.

CHAPTER 14

WOODHENRY LOOKED AT the newspaper and read the story for the third time. He still couldn't believe his eyes. But there it was as plain as day and in black and white. Two murders, two pages apart, two people he knew: Elvira and Spongey. Suddenly he wished that he could have moved back the hands of time. If only he had it to do all over again. WoodHenry felt so bad that he wished he were dead. Well almost. Suddenly he fixed all the blame on Missy Free. It was all her fault. How could she do this to him? Treat him like this after all he had done for her. He looked up at the clock for the third time in the past two minutes. If she was coming, she was late, a whole damn three days late. But he knew better. She wasn't coming. Not tonight. He felt like walking down to the store on the corner and getting another bottle of whiskey to calm himself down. He had drunk a whole fifth of scotch in the past 36 hours. But now with everybody getting murdered he was so nervous and messed-up inside his head that he didn't think he could make it to the store and back without getting killed himself. Plus what if she came while he was out? Man Oh Man Oh Man Oh Man. To him Missy Free was all of the love songs that had ever been written and also every blues song that had ever been sung. Damn. How could he ever have gotten mixed up with her in the first place. He should have listened to his conscience when he first laid eyes on her at Tom Jerrod's employees party, flashing that Hollywood smile and wearing that low cut dress with her breasts standing up like soldiers at attention. Something in both the back and the front of his mind had told him that she was nothing but trouble. But did he listen? Hell no. His little head was doing all of the thinking and now he was in the shit for sure.

Now two people were dead and most likely because of him. Maybe Missy Free didn't even love him at all. Maybe he had seen her for the last time. Maybe she wasn't ever coming back again. Maybe she was somewhere lying dead too. No, no, no. He couldn't even allow himself to start thinking like that.

Because that kind of thinking would drive him over the edge for sure. If he started thinking like that he might just go out and do something really insane like walking into the police station and telling everything he knew from start to finish. He had even thought of going to his minister, but what would he say? He couldn't tell him the truth either. If only she would send a message or something. It had been three whole days and not one peep from her to see if he was still alive or dead. For all she knew he could be dead locked up in this one room like a prisoner in Sing Sing. WoodHenry thought about praying to God for help, but then figured that God wouldn't be too interested in listening to him after what he had done. Just when it felt like his head would burst open, he ran outside and down to the liquor store. He bought a pint of whiskey and rushed back to the room.

He sat down on the bed and took off his shoes and socks then looked at his toes for a good ten minutes with melodies and crazy thoughts flying through his head like a raging fire. He drank and drank, then he got out his songwriting notebook and began to write his thoughts down. He hoped that writing down his emotions might somehow help keep the ugly thoughts away, or at least slow them down when he mixed them with melody, but it still didn't seem to help much. As he thought about Missy Free, the song just continued to flow.

Music Track #4
ON and ON and ON

Oh sugar baby I love you so
I gotta testify so that the whole wide world will know
When we make love I'm on fire
What you do keeps takin me higher
I need you baby I need you bad
You are the best woman I have ever had
And I want you from the bottom to the top
The way you make me feel I won't ever stop

MY LOVE IS GOIN ON AND ON AND ON AND ON AND ON AND ON
MY LOVE IS GOIN ON AND ON AND ON AND ON AND ON AND ON

MY LOVE IS GOIN ON AND ON AND ON AND ON AND ON AND ON AND ON
MY LOVE IS GOIN ON AND ON AND ON AND ON AND ON AND ON AND ON

Some people say you got a spell on me
But I don't care please just let me be
The one that you come home to, baby so I can love you
When you walk it's such a beautiful sight
Heads be turnin left and right,
I have no eyes for others you are the only one
And my love is forever like the circle round the sun

MY LOVE IS GOIN ON AND ON AND ON AND ON AND ON AND ON AND ON
MY LOVE IS GOIN ON AND ON AND ON AND ON AND ON AND ON AND ON
MY LOVE IS GOIN ON AND ON AND ON AND ON AND ON AND ON AND ON
MY LOVE IS GOIN ON AND ON AND ON AND ON AND ON AND ON AND ON

Don't cha break my heart don't go away
I need you here so I can love you night and day
If I was lost in a raging storm
All I would need to find my way home is your love to keep me warm

MY LOVE IS GOIN ON AND ON AND ON AND ON AND ON AND ON AND ON
MY LOVE IS GOIN ON AND ON AND ON AND ON AND ON AND ON AND ON
MY LOVE IS GOIN ON AND ON AND ON AND ON AND ON AND ON AND ON
MY LOVE IS GOIN ON AND ON AND ON AND ON AND ON AND ON AND ON
(I love baby can't get enough I love you baby I love your stuff)

He wrote and drank and then drank some more, hoping that the whiskey would at least keep the blues away, but it didn't. When there was no more to drink WoodHenry started to cry. He couldn't think of anything else that could possibly feel as bad as he was feeling. He thought about the reasons for which Missy could have abandoned him. There was only one argument, just one, that he could remember ever having with her. It had something to do with her wearing her dresses so tight that it showed every curve that God had given her. He didn't blame her though, not really. It had been his jealousy talking but nevertheless they had argued about it. Not even a big argument. Just a few words really. But the longer he lay alone on the bed the more his mind tortured him with his shortcomings as a companion and deserving lover of his angel. Thoughts and melodies. He tried to sleep but couldn't. All he could do was think about that little argument and blame himself and continue to write in his music notebook. More thoughts and melodies He allowed his muse to lead him into a deep deep hurtful place. His voice found the expression for what was taking place inside him.

Music Track #5
I DON'T BLAME YOU

I DON'T BLAME YOU FOR HURTIN ME
I DON'T CLAIM THAT FOR CERTAIN
I WAS IN THE RIGHT
I DON'T BLAME YOU FOR HURTIN ME
I DON'T CLAIM THAT FOR CERTAIN
I WAS IN THE RIGHT

If I have offended you please send me a clue
Just tell me the truth baby
Why are you acting strange and playin games and pretendin to
I'm aggravated, so frustrated I don't know what to do

I wanna know why you're sleepin and keepin yourself so far away.
I wanna know why you're sleepin and keepin yourself so far away

I DON'T BLAME YOU FOR HURTIN ME
I DON'T CLAIM THAT FOR CERTAIN
I WAS IN THE RIGHT

I DON'T BLAME YOU FOR HURTIN ME
I DON'T CLAIM THAT FOR CERTAIN
I WAS IN THE RIGHT

Without you, I can not find my piece of mind
I feel my whole life is ruined
Tell me what did I say to make you stay
away from me so long without so much as a hello
how are you doing.

I wanna know why you're sleepin and keepin yourself so far away.
I wanna know why you're sleepin and keepin yourself so far away

I DON'T BLAME YOU FOR HURTIN ME
I DON'T CLAIM THAT FOR CERTAIN
I WAS IN THE RIGHT
I DON'T BLAME YOU FOR HURTIN ME
I DON'T CLAIM THAT FOR CERTAIN
I WAS IN THE RIGHT

Can't work it, like a short circuit ,
Can't connect I'm a nervous wreck,
I wake at night and realise I'm calling out your name
I keep tellin myself, that you gonna come back
I keep tellin myself that I'm on the right track
I keep tellin myself, I keep tellin myself
I keep tellin myself, I keep tellin myself

I DON'T BLAME YOU FOR HURTIN ME
I DON'T CLAIM THAT FOR CERTAIN
I WAS IN THE RIGHT
I DON'T BLAME YOU FOR HURTIN ME
I DON'T CLAIM THAT FOR CERTAIN
I WAS IN THE RIGHT

.....After what seemed like an eternity WoodHenry's muse evaporated and he almost drifted off to sleep. Almost but not quite. Even though the muse had left, the monster of loneliness still dominated the room. The giant demon loomed over him more hungry and powerful than ever before.

CHAPTER 15

MISSY FREE ROLLED over and looked at the body lying in bed next to her. She reached out with a soft tender touch and rubbed the strong muscular thigh, then leaned forward and kissed the forehead. How beautifully the morning sun enhanced the image of her loved one sleeping peacefully. She took a deep breath and snuggled closer to the warm body. She felt that she was the luckiest woman in the world. Soon she would have all that she had ever wanted. She had the love, now all she needed was the key to her freedom. Freedom sweet freedom. Freedom was just a half hour's train ride away in a dumpy rented room in Hell's Kitchen. The thought of WoodHenry lurking in the corners of buildings wearing that ridiculous wig almost made her laugh out loud.

"Hmmm", the voice beside her stirred and turned over.

Missy Free gently moved forward towards the delicate parted lips that now vibrated gently with deep breaths only inches from her own sumptuous mouth. She leaned forward and planted a loving gentle kiss. A kiss sweet enough to wake a sleeping fairy princess, and that's just what it did. Catherine's eyes batted twice, opened and looked directly into the eyes of Missy Free.

"Morning baby" Missy Free smiled and kissed the young woman again.

"Morning," Catherine responded in a velvet voice.

"You sleep well?" Missy inquired.

"Yeah" Catherine replied and returned Missy's morning kiss.

"What you want for breakfast, baby?" Missy asked as she watched the morning sun combine with the brocaded curtains and make a dancing pattern of light across Catherine's beautiful dark features.

"I want you for breakfast," Catherine smiled as she pressed her pelvis into Missy Free's.

Missy responded to the cue and moved her hand between the young woman's legs. Missy sighed and felt excited that

Catherine was already wet.

"I want you inside me" Catherine said and bit Missy's shoulder.

Missy strapped on the dildo that was fitted to a belt that she girded under her legs and around her waist. Then the two woman began to make love. Not just any kind of love either. This was the kind of lovemaking that could shake the leaves from the trees.

Catherine's smooth young face seemed to glow as she looked up lovingly at Missy.

"Harder," Catherine moaned as she synchronised her body movement with Missy Free's.

"Yeah, yeah, ooh yeah baby," Catherine grunted then suddenly arched her back and pushed upward with her pelvis. Missy felt Catherine's body spasm under the force of the orgasm. Then she went limp. Missy unhooked the dildo and began to kiss Catherine's smooth athletic body from head to foot. They made love for another half hour until they both fell asleep in each other's arms.

It was like a giant hand reached out from the darkness and savagely shook her by the neck. Missy Free awoke with a start and looked at the clock on the nightstand. 11:06am. Shit. She had decided to meet WoodHenry this morning. She never told him when she was coming but she figured that whenever she turned up he would waiting, just like always. Missy had never seen such a sap before. But he was just what the doctor had ordered, a fool in love. For the past three days she had been busy celebrating Catherine's twenty-fifth birthday. During that time she hadn't given much thought to WoodHenry. To her he was just the fool who was going to give her the life that most people could only ever dream of. During the past three days Missy Free and Catherine had stayed in Martha's Vineyard walking through the woods and making love under the stars. She smiled and wondered what WoodHenry would say if he knew that she had a woman lover.

Because of his religious beliefs and standards of morality, WoodHenry would put sleeping with the same sex in the same category as being a mass murderer or a child molester. The thing she hated most about the situation was having to fuck WoodHenry to keep him on the hook. But she had long decided that it was worth the trouble because he was such a rare find. A perfect patsy for a perfect plan. Now all that she needed for the plan to work was the natural passage of time. The more time went by, the more he would believe that she was in love with him. Love was her weapon. Just part of her toolkit. Besides it was only a job. Their relationship had rules. Rule number one, she would always contact him. He had no way of contacting her, so he was at her mercy just the way she wanted it. Rule number two, she was running the show.

She had told him point blank that if he ever tried to violate the rules, she would never see him again. That was the same day that she bought a potted plant with which they pledged their love. They read a passage from the Bible and she had said something stupid like "may our love grow like this flower in springtime." She had just made it up on the spot, but that fool WoodHenry had started to cry because he said that she had been the first woman since his wife died to show him any real love.

It had been three days since she last saw him, but that didn't worry her.

She had left him with more than enough money for food, drink and rent. The agreement was that she would keep him supplied with money enough to stay in hiding until the second part of the plan could be worked out. He had begged her to get a cell phone so that he could make contact in case of an emergency, but she had vetoed the idea. Now she had him just how she wanted him, dependent on her for everything. She played the tune and he did the dancing. She was confident that WoodHenry's infatuation would keep him waiting even if she was a whole year late going to the room.

As Missy Free took her shower, she thought about what new lies she would tell WoodHenry about her absence. Absentmindedly she sang the old Ike and Tina Turner song "You just a fool and you know you in love, ohh, ohhwooah ohhh."

The cool breeze of the Indian summer danced in her hair as Missy walked confidently down 42nd Street. She had already put herself in the right frame of mind to make love to WoodHenry. To make it all palatable she played a game with herself. While she was with WoodHenry she thought of herself as a film actress performing a role. A role that would make her very rich. She had even given herself a movie star name, Joyce Dashwood.

It was Joyce Dashwood who would be fucking WoodHenry not Missy Free. After all these years, she was finally on her way. Almost at the finish line. All she had to do now was hang in there just a little while longer. She thought about all the changes she would make in her life. After the second part of the plan came together, maybe she would buy a nice little villa in someplace like Italy or France. Somewhere where people would only know her as Missy Free, the rich American woman rather than Denise Williams from the projects of Chicago. Once and for all money would put her beyond the reach of the bullshit she'd always had to put up with. To make sure nobody would ever reach back into her past and uncover things that could taint her future, she had paid a cop in Chicago ten thousand dollars to erase any infractions with the law from her records. Back in Chicago when she was hustling, she had always dreamed of being free. Free from the day-to-day bullshit that is the normal part of a ghetto existence. Freedom sweet freedom. Back then she thought that moving to New York would give her that freedom. But she thought wrong. She soon found that New York was just the other side of the same coin. She had almost given up on her dream of being free when fate stepped in and WoodHenry Taylor appeared on the scene. He would be her ticket to freedom. Then Denise Williams aka Missy Free would be as free as she had always wanted to be. Free to love who she wanted to love. Free to have what she'd always wanted. Free to be Missy Free. She would prove all of her bloodsucking relatives wrong. They had always said that she'd never be anything but a doormat for some handsome man to wipe his feet on. Soon they would all see.

She stopped at the Duane Reade drugstore on the corner and bought a box of condoms and then proceeded north towards 49th Street. With each step she got more into character. The lovely and vivacious Miss Joyce Dashwood.

At 1:34pm, Miss Joyce Dashwood climbed up the grimy stairs of the apartment and screwed up her nose. The smell of stale urine that was as much a part of the place as the dirty blue paint barely clinging to the walls. She opened the door with the key and let herself in the room. She was half expecting to find WoodHenry asleep but what she actually found almost made her heart stop. There was a note on the small wooden dresser. It read:

Dear Missy Free,

I love you so much that I can't live without you. I know now that you don't really love me and I just have to face it but I can't and that's why I'm going to kill myself.

Love you forever,

WoodHenry.

The blood rushed to her head so quickly that she felt ready to pass out. The thoughts scampered amuck inside her head like a bunch of cockroaches in flight when suddenly exposed to light. The truth hit her like a ten ton Mack truck. She had over-played her hand and left the fool alone for too long. She had allowed her emotions for Catherine to cloud her view of reality. Shit.

She had to find him. Before he killed himself. She sat down on the dingy bed and lit a cigarette. As she smoked, the jangled thoughts in her head seemed to organise themselves. She knew two places he might go to. One would be his church. The other would be his cousin Foster's house. But what if he'd gone straight to the river and thrown himself in. Then the second part of the plan wouldn't work at all. The thought sent a shiver through her body. The next thought was equally disconcerting. Now she would have to let the man at the top of this elaborate scheme know that she had blown it.

What would he say? Missy Free sat on the bed, smoked two more cigarettes and a joint before she got the courage she needed to make the call to the man.

She knew exactly where the man would be. Today was Tuesday and the man made it a habit of not going into the office until late in the afternoon unless he had an important appointment. She almost wished that he was out, but she knew better.

"Hello", she spoke into the cell phone.

"Yeah" the man's voice came on the line.

"It's me, Missy, we've got a little problem" she said trying to make it sound as abstract as possible while keeping any emotion from her voice.

"OK tell me" the man said in a flat even tone. He was used to problems.

"WoodHenry is missing" she said and held her breath.

"Missing?"

"I came back here and he was gone."

"Do you think he'll be back?"

"I don't think so, he left a suicide note," she said and held her breath again.

The laughter from the other end of the phone was the last thing that she had expected.

"What's so funny?" she wanted to know.

"Read it" the man ordered.

Missy read the note verbatim.

"He's still alive" the man said

"How can you be sure?" she wanted to know

"Because he believes in heaven. And he knows full well that if he commits suicide his chances of getting into heaven are zero. He left that note for your benefit. He's just feeling heartbroken. I thought you were supposed to be taking care of him and making sure that he felt all warm and cosy until I could finish making my moves."

"I did but...." she started weakly.

"But my ass," he cut her off. "If I knew that you couldn't handle it, I would've made other arrangements."

"But......" she started to add.

Then Tom Jerrod's voice cut her off.

"But nothing. Just do what I tell you to do," he said. His voice was not angry just stern like an irritated father talking to a child.

Missy Free felt scared, hurt and angry all at once. She tried to stifled a cough that had welled up inside her throat. She used every ounce of energy she had to try and stay calm. Saying the wrong thing now might upset the whole apple cart. She had come too far to turn around now.

"OK, I'll find him, don't worry" she said in a last ditch effort to bolster her self- confidence that had all but faded.

"I hope so," he said still in a cool even tone.

"I love you Tom" she said.

"And I love you too" Tom Jerrod said then hung up the phone.

She didn't understand what Tom was doing, but Tom was not a simple person. Whatever his mystery plan was, she had screwed it up. Missy Free felt truly bad because Tom Jerrod was the one person in the world she never wanted to let down.

As Tom Jerrod started out of the room, he encountered his wife coming through the doorway.

Greta Jerrod said "who was that you were talking to on the

phone dear?" She was trying to mask her suspicion with nonchalance.

"Just a business call" Jerrod smiled.

Greta Jerrod looked away quickly from her husband as she felt the tears of jealousy welling up in her eyes. She hated it when he patronized her. Tom Jerrod picked up the Wall Street Journal that was lying on his desk and walked past his wife through one of the many pastel- coloured rooms towards the swimming pool.

Before meeting Tom Jerrod, Greta had never thought of herself as a jealous woman but after marrying him she had come to realise how love, hate and jealousy, all walked hand in hand .

CHAPTER 16

THERE WAS SOMETHING about the way Albalita said WoodHenry's name that made me understand. It was the same way I had once said Amanda's name. Before she had been killed. Maybe it was the same way that I had heard Sonia say my name. I'm not sure. Anyway it was enough to drive me back to the little house in Mt. Vernon the following day. I had parked and waited patiently across the street under a tree away from view of the window. I was trying to decide how to approach Minnie without the thousand dollars she had demanded upfront when Albalita came out of the front gate being led by the black Labrador. The pair turned north and began up the street. I decided to follow on foot. She walked to the corner where she expertly crossed the street and then turned right towards the park. She reached the park and sat on a bench while the dog sat obediently at her side. I took a place on the bench next to her.

"Nice day isn't it" she said.

I said "yes it is," and watched the expression on her lovely features change.

She was quiet for about a minute then finally spoke.

"Hello Mr. Barnett," she said.

"Hello."

"I knew you would come back."

"What made you think that?"

"Because I could tell that you're the kind of man who is not easily fooled."

"You mean the story your sister gave me about not knowing where WoodHenry was?"

"Uh huh, that's part of it."

"What's the other part?"

"You don't have to ask that Mr. Barnett, otherwise you wouldn't be here."

"So can you tell me something that you weren't able to tell me yesterday?"

"Yes and no."

"How is that?"

"If you want to know if I can tell you where WoodHenry is, I can't. But I can tell you that he is still alive."

"Are you saying this from first hand knowledge or is this other-wordly information?"

She started to laugh. I guess I was startled because her laugh didn't sound like I thought it should have. Rather than being sensitive and gentle the way I pictured her, it was a strong hearty laugh imbedded with a kind of edge that I would have associated with a woman who had lived longer and harder. She scratched behind the dog's ear and cocked her head in my direction.

Albalita said "move closer Mr. Barnett."

The dog looked up at me curiously and then turned his attention to a group of children playing with a frisby.

"You don't believe I'm for real do you?"

"What do you mean?"

"The second sight thing, you think it's all a con game don't you, be honest."

"Well let's say I still have my doubts until I see some conclusive proof," I said.

She smiled again.

"Give me your hand Mr. Barnett, your right hand."

She placed both her hands around mine. I was surprised how warm they were. Even in the cool breeze, her hands were as warm as when she had been inside the house. She closed her eyes and began to sway gently back and forth as she made small circles in the palm of my hand with her fingers. Then she stopped moving and held my hand tightly. She then turned her face toward mine.

"You are a violent man Mr. Barnett, you have killed many times in the past. I'm seeing the number 39. But this is your past. You have tried to submerge that part of your life. You say you are a detective but I see that you also run some kind of business. It has to do with people eating and drinking, maybe a restaurant or a bar. I also see a man coming into your life who is as violent as you are. This man is not from this country. This man loves you deeply, like a brother. And you care for him too, even though you are reluctant to admit it. Together you and this man are extremely dangerous." Albalita opened her eyes again. "You believe me now?"

I was too stunned to speak. These were things she couldn't have known. I had never told anyone about Francisco or the number of men I had killed in the line of duty. She was right. There had been 39 exactly.

I stuttered. "OK, lets say that you can see into the past or the future. What does that do, or how does that help me?" Her words were still ringing fresh in my ears.

"Not so fast Mr. Barnett, let me explain something so that you will understand.

I know what I told you was the truth and you know it too. These are things I couldn't have possibly known because these are things that you keep locked away deep inside yourself. But because I am able to see these kinds of things in people's lives, as you imagine I can make people very nervous. That's why I try not to get involved with my sister's business because, well lets say if I see something in someone's life, I will warn them so that they can either help themselves or avert disaster. I do this for free because that's my nature, but Minnie, on the other hand is driven by money and oftentimes we are in direct opposition."

I was unable to hold my curiosity any longer.

"So this power you have...." I wasn't exactly sure what I really wanted to say.

"In the same way some people are born with a gift for music or art or science, some people really are born with a gift for seeing things. In my case I can see into other people's lives. I've always had it. As a child my parents discouraged me from talking about it. As a result of our powers, they moved from the city to a small town. My father became a professor at a small college in Mississippi so we wouldn't be bothered by lots of people and so we could be educated at home away from the prying eyes of society who would have made us into novelties."

"You say we?" I interjected

"Yes me and my sister are both psychic, but I'm much more powerful that she is. I have the power to see things in the past and find people too, but she is by far the better showman and businessman," she smiled.

"So how much of what she says about finding WoodHenry for me is true?"

"Oh it's true alright she could find him, but the only trouble is I'm not going to let her. I know how to block her visions, so that she can't see."

"And why wouldn't you want me to find him, especially if he's in trouble?"

"Because if you did, I'm afraid he might get killed."

"By whom?"

"The people who he was involved with to steal that money."

"So you know about the money, the four million?"

"Yes, about the money and the woman too" she said.

"What woman, his common law wife, Elvira?"

"No, the other woman."

"What woman is that?"

"The one that made him crazy."

"Do you have her name?" I asked

"He just calls her Missy"

"Did he tell you he stole money?"

"He didn't have to, I held his hand like I held yours and saw it. But it wasn't like you think."

"How do you mean?"

"I can't say anymore about it. I promised WoodHenry that I wouldn't."

"Do you know where he is?"

"I can't tell you that"

"You can't or you won't?" I responded.

Her face was still calm and looking out blankly towards the park as the wind caught strands of her hair and blew them up gently across her face.

"Then can you tell me if he is alive?"

"Yes he is." Her voice was calm and steady.

"If you won't be of any assistance in helping me find him, then I don't know what else to say," I said.

"There's nothing to say."

"What about the money he stole?"

"What about it?"

"It was wrong to do, don't you think?"

"I think it was, but then again you don't know WoodHenry. If you knew him you would understand. WoodHenry is a very good man Mr. Barnett, but he has been a very lonely man since his wife died and sometimes loneliness can drive you to do foolish things. But if you had ever heard some of his songs you would know that he is far too sensitive to ever be capable of something like that."

"You're the second person whose told me about his musical abilities."

"Yes he's a very gifted songwriter. Someone touched by God's spirit with his kind of talent doesn't have the spirit to be a killer Mr. Barnett. Both spirits can't live in the same soul. Right now I just have to do things my way. All I can ask is that you trust me."

I was sure that she was totally convinced of what she was saying.

"I'd like to, believe me I would" I said. "Something else you should think about. If I was able to trace WoodHenry to you and your sister, don't you think other people might too?"

"Oh yes, I've thought of that, but..." she let her voice trail off.

"One man who was going to help me find WoodHenry turned up dead you know"

"Really." There was real surprise in her voice. "Who?"

"A man named Spongey. Someone put a bullet in his head, the same day he was supposed to set up a meeting for me with WoodHenry. Maybe WoodHenry knew something about that."

I was looking real hard for some trace of a reaction.

"I don't believe that anymore that you do, Mr. Barnett. You're just trying to get me upset and worried that WoodHenry isn't the person I know he is, but that doesn't bother me because it's your job to create doubts in peoples minds so that you can use their fear to your advantage. You are a very clever man Mr. Barnett, but WoodHenry couldn't hurt anyone. About that I'm positive." she said.

"OK, let's say I believe you, and for the sake of argument let's also say WoodHenry is being used by this woman, where will it all end?"

"I wish I knew, but I will say this, WoodHenry is safe for the moment but he won't be for long, especially if these people who are after him find him. I've tried talking to him but he's all upset now. What you've got to do is find these people before they find him."

"When did you last speak to him?" I asked.

She went quiet again.

After about another minute she spoke. "Sorry I can't tell you that. He made me promise not to."

"Suppose because you're not telling me what I want to know, these people will catch WoodHenry and kill him, how will you feel then?"

Her jaw tightened. She sat for a few minutes in silence then folded her hands into her lap and sighed.

"I'll tell you what, give me two days and by then I will have something worked out."

"Two days is a long time especially in the life of a man with a price on his head." I was hoping to strike a chord, but all I seemed to be doing was striking out.

"Two days," she repeated and held her face straight ahead as if she were looking across the park.

I said "OK, see you in two days." I didn't really have a choice.

"Thank you," she said then smiled.

"Mind if I ask you something else?"

"Sure, go ahead" she said and turned her unseeing eyes towards my face again.

"How does Foster fit in to all this? I was told that he and WoodHenry used to come up here to visit. I thought maybe Foster might have told you or your sister something that could be helpful to me finding these people."

She thought for a moment.

"WoodHenry may be naive but he isn't stupid. He wouldn't have told Foster anything about the money because he knows how Foster is. He wouldn't have trusted Foster with any information that was important."

"What do you mean by how Foster is. Exactly how is he?"

"Have you ever met him?"

"Yes, once at his house" I said

"How did he seem to you?"

"He seemed odd," I admitted.

"You're being kind. Foster is crazy, pure and simple The other thing is, Foster loves money."

"So why do WoodHenry and a crazy man come to see you and your sister?"

"Foster comes to see my sister for sex."

"Sex?"

"Maybe I shouldn't be saying this, but both my sister and Foster have, let's say, unusual sexual tastes. They find satisfaction with each other. As for WoodHenry, he comes to see me because we're good friends. Not sexual friends either."

"Do you love him?"

She stiffened a bit. "What made you ask that?" Her voice

kept the same even tone.

"From the way you're protecting him. That's the reason I came back. When I was here yesterday I sensed that there was something special between you and him."

"Do you have anyone special in your life Mr. Barnett?" she asked.

"Well not really, not girlfriend-wise," I said.

"What about this friend that you're helping to find WoodHenry for? You're putting yourself on the line for this woman because there is something special about her that touches you, right?"

"Yes I guess you could say that, in a way."

"Would you say you loved this woman?" she asked.

I said "no I wouldn't say that, well….." I stammered as her words opened up a can of worms I wasn't prepared to deal with.

"Sometimes we feel things that we can't admit to ourselves for whatever reason, but nevertheless the feeling remains," she said.

To be honest her words had jarred me and I suddenly wanted to get the hell away from her before she made me start thinking about things that I didn't want to think about.

"O.K, two days," I said again.

"Thank you Mr. Barnett, you're a good man," she said as I got up to leave.

"Thank you," I said still recalling her words about my feelings for Honey Lavelle.

"And oh yes," Albalita called out as I walked away, "don't allow these bad people to destroy all the good work you've done on yourself."

"Myself?" I responded automatically both amused and puzzled.

"Don't worry it will come to you in time," she said.

This young woman had done two very interesting things. Firstly, she had cleverly side-stepped the question about whether or not she was in love with WoodHenry by turning my question back on me and secondly, she had reached inside me with her own sensitivity and touched something that I had secretly hoped no longer existed.

I went home early that night and slept soundly. When I woke it was almost 3:10am. I put on Marvin Gaye's classic Let's Get It

On CD, and made a cup of hot chocolate.

"Pretty little sexy Momma you sure do love to ball, pretty little sexy baby you sure love to ball." Marvin's voice was so cool and relaxing. It made me think of being in bed with my ex-girlfriend Sonia. I drifted back off to sleep and woke again at 6:00am.

Years of practice had allowed me to pre-program myself so that I was never dependent on an alarm clock. At 7:15 am I was on the road, ten minutes from LaGuardia Airport. The plane landed at 7:39 and at 7:50 am I embraced my friend Francisco Gomez.

"You look good, married life agrees with you" I told him.

He stepped back, took a long look at me and laughed. Francisco looked exactly the same as he had the last time I'd seen him, two years before. Still fit. Still deadly.

He said, "yeah, it's good, but sometimes I admit I do miss the excitement of the old days."

As we made our way back towards Harlem, he filled me in on his new life in New Mexico and I filled him in on the situation with WoodHenry.

CHAPTER 17

AFTER I GOT Francisco settled in at my place, we went over to The BeBop Tavern.

"Nice place" Francisco said looking around.

"I've been working on it little by little" I explained.

"So do you miss it?" He was still looking at the décor but his mind was moving in another direction.

I knew exactly what he was talking about.

"Sometimes I guess. I did a lot at first, but I made up my mind that was a part of my past and I try to keep it there. Most times, I think I've been successful, but then at other times..."

"I've done the same thing. The wife and the kid. Sometimes it seems like that's the only life that I've ever known. At other times, the old urges keep trying to find their way through and honestly I'm not sure what to do about it. Is that why you got into the detective business, to keep in touch with the thing that was a part of you for so long?"

I could have lied or tried to bullshit myself, but Francisco was too smart for that. We had seen each other in the worst of times. Two steps from destruction and three seconds from hell. When you are that close to a person, the truth will expose a lie as quickly as a match burns a hole through tissue paper.

"I guess so," I wasn't terribly proud of my answer.

We both let the meaning of our words float somewhere in our shared memories. Memories that neither one wanted to voice out loud. We both knew we were trapped in a violent past that sometimes called out to us like a beautiful but deadly siren. Ghosts. We had been ghosts. Human monsters sanctioned to kill by the United States of America. Ghosts. The name given to the assassin operatives by other members of the CIA. Ghosts. We lived in the shadows and became the unrelenting terror that filled the nights of our enemies. The ghosts that civilized society doesn't want to admit exists.

"Hungry? It's almost lunch time," I asked.

"I ate breakfast on the plane but it smells so good in here, I got to say yeah," Francisco smiled.

I put my arm around his shoulder and led him to the counter where Benny Sweetmeat was setting up the sandwich bar. His eyes lit up like a child at Christmas as he watched Benny slicing off thick chucks of meat from a huge side of corn beef.

"How about one of those with mustard" Francisco said and pointed at the meat.

"You heard the man. And a tuna on whole wheat for me," I said.

"Coming right up" Benny smiled and served us quickly.

We took our food back to my favourite booth which put us mostly out of earshot from the customers at the bar. As we ate I filled Francisco in on my conversations with Albalita and the history of Bobby Jones.

"So you think the blind girl is hiding him?" he asked.

"If she's not there's no doubt that she knows where he is or how to get in touch with him if she needs to."

"Mr. Barnett" the voice came from behind me.

The voice belonged to a young black face, dressed in a police patrolman's uniform.

"My captain would like to see you right now sir," he said.

I looked him up and down. He tried to look authoritative but we both knew that he was just a pawn caught up in the game of being Curtis's errand boy. Poor bastard.

"OK," I said "but can I finish my lunch first?"

"I guess so" he replied. The poor guy was caught in the middle and I didn't want to make it worse so I told him to go order a sandwich and drink on the house. Which he seemed glad to do.

"Shall I take my car or do I go with you?" I asked the cop when we had finished eating.

"He didn't say sir" the young patrolman said and blinked uneasily.

"Can he come too?" I asked nodding towards Francisco.

"He didn't say sir, I guess it would be OK," the young patrolman answered.

Francisco and I rode in the back of the squad car to the precinct. When we reached the station house, the patrolman escorted us back past the detectives' desks towards the Captain's office. On the way I looked over to see Ross Lambert's desk empty. Curtis was in his office sitting behind his desk looking self righteous when Francisco and I entered.

"OK Barnett, let's get right to it, you know why you're here," Curtis said looking disdainfully at me over the top of spectacles that sat on the bridge of his nose.

"I told you before I don't know who killed the man."

"You know more than you're telling me though. Who is your client and why were you meeting the dead man in first place?"

"I told you before, I was there to buy information, but that's all I can tell you."

"You think I'm playing around with you don't you?" the Captain said hunching over his desk.

"Not especially, I just think you're a man desperate for answers."

"And who is this, your lawyer?" he asked looking at Francisco.

"No, just a friend from out of town in to visit for a few days."

"Well friend, you're going to have to do your visiting at another time because Mr. don't-know-nothing Barnett here is going to jail," Curtis said looking up at the patrolman who stood behind us. "Book him for withholding evidence and if he don't come up with some new information in a little while we'll see if we can't add suspicion of murder."

"Knock yourself out, if it makes you feel better Captain," I said.

Curtis' jaw clenched. I was exactly the kind of person he hated, a black man with a law enforcement background that didn't believe in doing things by the book.

"When you're ready to talk maybe I'll be ready to listen, just maybe Mr. Smart Ass" Curtis said.

"Onion will have the answers. Ask Christine at the bar for his number," I told Francisco as I passed out of the room under the patrolman's escort. Francisco turned and headed towards the precinct exit as the cop led me towards the finger printing section.

Thirty minutes later I had been mug shot, fingerprinted and booked. The holding cell that they placed me in was in the basement of the precinct.

Counting me, there were seven guys inside the holding cell. All black. Three of them looked to be in their early twenties, one in his late sixties and wearing a suit with dried blood stains on the lapels and another was in his mid thirties and built like a weightlifter. The seventh man who looked to be in his early forties paced back and forth talking to himself.

The only thing decorating the cell besides the cold pale walls was a stainless steel toilet and a wash basin. There were no benches or beds to sit on so the men hunched down against the wall or sat on the floor. I took a place against the wall and listened to the other prisoners talk about their busts. The three young men in their twenties had been caught in a drug raid and the weightlifter said that he was in on an armed robbery beef which he claimed was a case of mistaken identity. The elderly man with the blood on his suit sat in one corner with his head hung not talking to anyone.

"What's your beef?" one of the younger men asked of him.

"Me?" the man in the suit looked up awkwardly. "They charged me with assault"

"Assaulting who, the police?" the young man responded.

"My cousin attacked me with a meat cleaver and I uh, stopped him."

"Did you kill him?" one of the other young men asked.

"No but... no, I..." the old man stammered.

"What happened?"

"He's in a coma," the old man in the suit answered. "He was trying to rob me."

"Yo dog , I don't blame you. Relatives be doing shit like that don't they," one of the young men said.

"You better hope he don't die though " the weightlifter chimed in, then turned to me.

"What you in for?"

"Withholding evidence," I answered

"Evidence of what?"

"Murder."

"Did you do it, yo?"

"No."

"But you know who did I bet?"

"No" I answered again.

"Don't worry you'll walk, they can't make that kind of shit stick. Them motherfuckers always trying to do that shit, harassin' the brothers. They brought me in on suspicion about four months ago cause there was a robbery in my building. I was beefin with some dumb bitch who lives there. She told 5-0 that she saw me hanging out with the cats that broke into her apartment. But that was bullshit. The only reason she said that was because she wanted me to let her buy my shit on credit cause I be selling some smoke. She really got mad cause I started going with her cousin. She was a cutie and knew how to treat a brother so I was hooking her up with some free product and the bitch got jealous. They brought me in for withholding evidence and I was back on the street within twelve hours. All my lawyer had to do was come down and next thing you know I was walking cause they knew it was bullshit. Circumstantial. They was just trying to wipe the books clean and shit," the weightlifter explained.

While the weightlifter chatted and played the role of the jailhouse lawyer I settled down into the corner of the cell and thought about all the pieces of this WoodHenry puzzle.

"Must be almost lunchtime," the weightlifter said as he saw one of the guards pass the cell with a tray of sandwiches.

"What we got?" the sickly looking old man asked when another guard stopped at the cell door started handing sandwiches and coffee in through the steel bars.

"Veal" the guard responded.

"Don't shit ever change do it, damn" the weightlifter asked.

"For some it do, for some it don't" the guard remarked.

Everybody grabbed a sandwich from the tray except me.

"You ain't eating?" the old man in the bloodied suit asked with one eye on me and the other on the sandwich tray.

"You can have it, I ate just before I came in," I responded.

"Thanks Mister," he said and quickly took another sandwich and the cup of coffee from the tray.

As he turned back into the cell, he stumbled forward and almost fell over his own feet.

"You OK?" I asked.

"Yeah, thanks" the old man said, then retreated into a corner.

Comments and noise from the other cells along the corridor drifted down towards me.

"Give me a match"

"I want me some pussy"

"Who got a cigarette?"

"I got somewhere I gotta be, what time the judge going to be in this motherfucker?"

Everybody inside the cell I was in seemed pretty calm except the pacer who was constantly looking around and spitting comments. He looked crazy, like maybe he had a bad drug habit. A few of his comments were aimed at people in the cell but most were aimed at imaginary beings.

Through various comments he made, I picked up that he had done jail time before and I also got the impression that he was a bully who was used to having people look up to him. He told everybody that his name was Percy Rock. After lunch he seemed to settle down a little.

As it was starting to get chilly during the evenings, I was wearing a fleece windbreaker which I pulled off and rolled into a ball to use as a pillow. Others who had chosen to lay down after lunch had taken off one of their shoes and propped it under their heads, while other used simply their arms. I was dozing when awakened by a sharp noise.

"Motherfucker I should kill you," the voice boomed over me like a loudspeaker.

It belonged to Percy Rock who now stood over the old man in the blood stained suit.

"What's up?" one of the younger men inquired.

"This motherfucker stopped up the toilet. Now we have to smell his shit all night, cause they won't send nobody to fix it till tomorrow," Percy bellowed and held his fist ready to pound the old man.

"No I didn't, it was stopped up already," the elderly man protested.

"Yeah I think it was fucked up already," agreed one of the younger men.

"Who the fuck asked you anything? Shut up," Percy growled at the young man.

Percy was like a wild animal marking territory, trying to make himself the king of the cell. Because he was big and burly Percy towered over the old man in the suit like a giant. While the old man cowered under his threat, Percy looked around the cell to see if his intimidation was working. The weight lifter was quiet and the younger men had moved away from the commotion. Then his eyes rested on me.

"What the fuck you got to say about it?" he asked.

"I think you're about as full of shit as that toilet if you want to know the truth," I looked him straight in the eye. Percy knew I had left him nowhere to go. Either he would have to show his hand or back down and show everyone that he was just a loudmouthed punk.

"I'll fuck you up" Percy said.

I felt the first demon inside my head escape. Shit. Instinct took over.

As Percy turned his body in my direction I raised up on one knee. Being the dirty fighter he was, Percy had never planned to give me a fair chance. He rushed toward me and lifted his foot to kick me but I was way ahead of him. When his leg went back to kick I threw a right uppercut straight into his balls. His eyes grew wide as he lost his breath. As the shock of the blow bent him over I stiffened my middle finger and pushed it like a blade into Percy's right eye. He make a squealing sound and fell head first and hard onto the concrete floor.

As he gasped for air the other people in the cell came alive. The weightlifter and the young men moved forward to get a better view. When Percy tried to gasp for air, I pinched his nose hard with my thumb and forefinger and then forced my forearm up against his mouth until I was sure he couldn't breath. He spasmed a couple times as his eyes almost popped out of their sockets. I bent over him and put my mouth very close to his ear.

"You ready to die?" I asked softly as I released just enough pressure so he wouldn't suffocate.

"P-p-please..." he managed to splutter, like a car engine trying to ignite but failing to find the connection.

I released his nose and he almost collapsed from lack of oxygen. Percy Rock turned over and lay motionless on the concrete floor covering his face. I went back to my place on the floor and left him lying there. The old man stood up and stepped around Percy and came over to where I was sitting.

"Think he'll be alright?" he inquired under his breath as he sat down next to me.

"More or less" I shrugged.

I knew that the blow to Percy's scrotum would leave him pissing blood for at least a week and that he'd never see properly out of that right eye again. At least not without an operation. But that was the price he'd paid for being a bully. Fucking ghosts.

The old man in the suit watched as Percy stirred and started to crawl slowly towards a corner of the cell with his hands still covering his face. Nobody in the cell spoke for a while. Not in words anyway but eyes and expressions were talking just the same. And the chorus was unanimous. Fuck Percy Rock. He got what he deserved. The weight lifter broke the ice as he started talking to the young men about all the women he knew. Every now and then he's glance in my direction hoping to get me into the conversation but I wasn't interested. I had decided that the weightlifter was probably a snitch that the police had planted in the cell.

"My name is Kelly, James Kelly, what's yours," the old man asked offering his hand to shake.

"Barnett" I said shaking his hand.

"Thanks" Kelly said.

"No problem" I said.

"Your first time in here?" he asked.

"Yeah, what about you?"

"Mine too."

The old man told me the story of his cousin who was geeked up on crack and tried to rob him when he was closing up his hardware store. He said the cousin pulled a knife, held it to his throat and demanded money. Fear for his life made him push the cousin to the floor and start beating him with a flashlight. Now the cousin was in a coma. I gave him the name of a lawyer friend of mine and wished him the best. Then we agreed to watch for each other as we slept just in case Percy Rock got crazy again.

Funnily enough, anxiety was not part of my emotions as I drifted off to sleep. On the contrary I was comforted by what I sensed was taking place in a quiet house somewhere during the middle of the night.

CHAPTER 18

CAPTAIN ROBERT CURTIS was a careful man. A man of order. All through his life he had prided himself on being careful and orderly. It was that sense of order that had finally got him promoted to Captain. Robert Curtis closed the financial report that he had just finished reviewing and gulped the last swallow of his Hennessey double malt that lingered at the bottom of the glass. It was almost 1:30 am and he was tired. Tired but happy. Happy because he had become a success in his profession. As a New York City police captain he could comfortably afford to live in a nice home and send his son to a prestigious private school. He had a respectable bank account and was not worried about his future. His life was in order. His orderly wife Doris Jane had gone upstairs to bed an hour ago. Curtis turned off the lights, checked the doors, then climbed the stairs of the five bedroom two-storey home located in Long Island. He looked in on his eight year old son Matthew who slept peacefully. Doris Jane was snoring as he climbed into bed and he drifted off almost as quickly as his head hit the pillow.

The bedside clock was reading 4:19 am when Doris Jane woke to use the bathroom. She walked out of the bedroom into the hall as she did every night. Just as she sat down on the toilet she felt a sharp pain in her neck. The man moved with incredible efficiency. He pulled Doris Jane over his powerful shoulders as easy as if she had been a toddler and eased his way down the stairs. The man could see from the layout of the house that he could easily escape if he had to make a fast getaway. But escaping wasn't in his plans. He knew exactly where the orderly police Captain slept and he also knew that if had wanted to kill him while he slept, he could do it easily. The man thought of the young boy lying safely in his bed. At least safe for now. The man turned his mind back to the task at hand as he carried Doris Jean into the garage area that was connected to the house. He didn't worry about their electronic alarm system because he had expertly disabled it earlier when he had arrived. The man made his movements with the alacrity and stealth of a hunting cat. No sound, very little motion. Total concentration and precision. The man lay Doris Jean on the concrete floor of the cold garage. She didn't stir an inch. She was out cold. The man looked at her long legs that stretched up to her naked pubis. Doris Jean was in her late forties and still an attractive woman. Not overweight and still solid in all the right places. A specimen that no doubt gave the good Captain a run for his money between the sheets.

The man went to work by the moonlight that shone through the garage window. As he worked, he kept a sharp ear out for any sound that came from inside the house. He was ready in case anyone tried to surprise him. He could have knocked the Captain out earlier, but he preferred to do it this way. It gave him a certain thrill to know he was courting danger. It had been a long time since he had worked in this way. Doing this awakened his razor sharp instincts. Within ten minutes he had prepared Doris Jean in exactly the manner that he wanted. Afterwards he slipped back up stairs into the boy's bedroom. He could hear the Captain still snoring gently. Three minutes later the man slipped out of the same garage door through which he had entered earlier in the evening when the police Captain and his Mrs were attending a cocktail party.

The man was dressed in black from head to toe. He walked along the manicured tree-lined street carefully blending into the shadows. His presence in the night was like a whisper in a hurricane. Totally undetectable. A half mile away, the man climbed into a rented car and looked into the rear view mirror. The face of Francisco Gomez smiled slightly as he pulled off his black skullcap and started the engine. It felt good to be back in the game that he loved. What was even better was that he was back in the game with and on behalf of his best friend, a friend who had saved his life and had helped him obtain the love of his life, a friend that he would kill for without a second thought, a friend that he affectionately called El Diablo Negro: the Black Devil.

The scream shot through the Captain's mind like a blinding white- hot fire. He sat straight up in bed. Panic seized his heart and intestines. The scream came again as he swung his feet to the floor. His young son came running into the room looking anxious and confused. At the same moment they both looked at the empty space in the bed. The space where Doris Jean was supposed to be. Oh my God.

"Mommy," young Matthew cried as a third scream from downstairs sent terror bolting through his father's mind like a raging runaway stallion.

Curtis' instincts were torn. His orderly mind told him that whatever kind of monster had his wife in it's clutches might want his son too. He instinctively grabbed his police revolver from under the mattress and turned to his son.

"Go back into your room son. Don't question me now, do as I tell you," Curtis said trying to make the statement in his most stern and orderly voice.

He didn't wait for the boy to respond he just hoped that he would obey and moved rapidly towards the top of the stairs. The scream came again. The pain and anguish of a thousand nightmares penetrated Curtis' skull. He stumbled down the stairs with the gun pointed straight ahead of him. The sound of whimpering was coming from the kitchen and he could see that the door leading from the kitchen to the garage was open. It should not have been. He was sure it was closed when he went to bed.

The Captain held the revolver in front of his body using the standard double handed police grip. He thought of calling for backup. But the thought boomeranged almost as quickly as it had left his mind. THERE WAS NO BACKUP. He was the cavalry to the rescue. A lone avenger against forces of evil. Time to do or die. Sweat popped out on his brow and bile come into his mouth. The Captain knew he wasn't a street fighter. He was a man out of his element. He had long ago realised that his best weapon was his brain and his patience. With each inch towards the open garage door a sense of dread accompanied his movements like a thousand pound weight. His mind reached for order. But there was none. Order had deserted him. Only alarm and panic remained in its place.

What he saw when he stepped through the open door almost physically knocked him off his feet. He opened his mouth to scream but their was no sound. Only tears instead. Tears because he had not been able to protect her.

Doris Jean's lovely features were distorted into a mask of wide-eyed horror as what looked like blood cascaded through her very expensive hairdo down onto her face. He could see that she was butt naked and tied up. A closer look and he could see that her body was covered with some kind of substance. A brown substance. The Captain moved closer but really he wanted to shut his eyes, turn back and run the other way. Then the smell hit him like a gunshot. He knew the smell. He had been raised on a farm. Unmistakable. Pig shit. Who the fuck in this world would have the nerve to smear his wife with pig shit. Pig shit and pig's blood. The Captain was repelled by the smell as much as he was by the sight of his precious Doris Jean struggling helplessly against the ropes that bound her hands and feet. She was caught like a mouse in a trap. As Curtis moved towards his wife, her eyes met her husband's. For the first time in his life he felt totally helpless and ashamed.

First Captain Curtis examined his wife's body for marks of puncture. When he was satisfied that she hadn't been stabbed or shot he began untying the knotted rope which matched the knots of confusion in his brain.

"Mommy..." The sound of his son's voice came from behind him.

To Matthew, his mother looked like a stinky slimy space monster that might have escaped from an extra terrestrial's spaceship. The Slime Queen.

"Matthew." The Captain tried to sound stern and orderly but his voice caught somewhere between his mind and vocal chords.

The boy started towards his mother who was gasping for air like a fish out of water. Doris Jane screamed again at the sight of her son. The Captain realised that she was in shock. Then his eyes fell on the area around her. There were photographs taped to the floor and on the door and window of his new Land Rover. At least fifteen of them. Eight by tens. Black and white. As he focused on them he found his voice.

"Matthew, stand back goddammit," he screamed so loudly that it brought Doris Jean back to herself, well at least almost.

Little Matthew who had never been cursed at by his father started to cry. The Captain wanted to tell his son that he was sorry. Sorry for not being strong enough to protest him from this horror. Sorry for not being strong enough to protect their orderly way of life. But his mouth couldn't find the words. All he could think about were the photographs and his wife who had been defiled by some debased animal.

"Baby, baby," Curtis whispered to his wife as he brought her close to him in what he hoped was a reassuring embrace. But she was still thrashing around like some wounded creature fighting death.

He tried to hold her still but she continued twisting and turning for what seemed like an ice age. She finally calmed down enough for Captain Curtis to finish untying her restraints. The pig shit now covered both of them as Matthew continued to cry from the edge of the garage. This was not the orderly life that the Captain had made for himself. The sight of her son crying seemed to steady Doris Jean's nerves a bit. Then her eyes focused on her husband's ashen face staring in disbelief at something on the garage floor. The Captain quickly tried to cover her eyes with his hands, but in one quick move Doris pushed his hands away and saw what her husband had been staring at. She let out a scream filled with so much pain that it would have made Satan himself proud. Then she fainted in her husband's arms.

As Captain Curtis carried his wife back into the house past his weeping son he started to cry as well. Robert Curtis put Doris Jean into the bath tub and filled it with warm water. He was still thinking about the photographs. They were lying like a million open sores on the garage floor. Taunting. Threatening. Though Curtis was shaking from shock and rage he managed to steady himself enough to wash the blood and faeces from his wife's body. He dried her with a fresh towel from the linen closet and carried Doris Jean back into the bedroom. The water brought her back to a conscious state, but she still had not uttered an intelligible word. As soon as his wife and Matthew were safe in bed, Captain Curtis went back to the garage with his gun in hand. But it was too late for that. The photographs had already done their damage. Even as he burned the hated photographs in the fireplace, the black and white images of his precious wife Doris Jean sucking the penises of different men seared the Captain's mind. It made him feel as limp inside as a greasy over-used dishrag. With all his heart he had believed that he had concealed that part of their past forever. He had been so orderly and careful in erasing all traces of Doris Jean's former life. When the pimp she had been working for was killed in prison he was sure that all traces of her former life had been erased forever. But now, somebody was using their secret to turn his orderly life upside down.

When those photos were taken, his wife had been Doretha Jeanette Palmer, a hooker and porno actress. A naive Doretha had gotten tricked into prostitution by a pimp named Hollywood Freddy who had enticed her into a sordid life with the promise of getting her a job paying five hundred dollars a week dancing in a Broadway show. Instead she wound up turning tricks for show business wannabees for twenty bucks a pop and working in no-budget porno films made by Hollywood Freddy Productions. The Captain was still a vice cop when he busted Hollywood Freddy. That's when and how he had met Doretha. After a long conversation with her, he discovered like him, she had been raised on a farm in Georgia. After more conversations they discovered that they were kindred spirits.

She was the only woman he had ever met who understood his overwhelming need and drive to become a success. She also understood and accepted that he was not a quick-witted intellectual man capable of great charm but rather appreciated that he was a serious hard working man who believed in order, to make his life better. She accepted his limitations like no one else had ever done before. Besides, she too craved a life of order. A life free from hurt and ugliness. Robert Curtis helped Doretha get a job in a New Jersey dress factory where she learned to become a seamstress. Soon after that they began dating. After three years of orderly courtship they were married in a small civil ceremony where the only witness to their matrimonial bond was a man neither of them had ever met before. During the early years of their marriage she was uncomfortable and ashamed to show her face at police functions for fear that her chequered past might one day surface to hurt her husband's rise to prominence. She even convinced her husband to allow her to have plastic surgery and changed her name from Doretha Jeanette to Doris Jean which she thought sounded more sophisticated.

As he started to rise through the ranks it became necessary for Doris Jean to appear at certain police functions with the other wives and socialise more. To Doris Jean's credit she had gone for counselling to help shed her former life. The psychiatrist had assured her that everyone had things in their past that they were ashamed of and that she was no different. So after thirteen years of marriage, a nose job, a name change, six years of psychological counselling and the death of Hollywood

Freddy, together they had buried the life of Doretha Jeanette Palmer forever. The birth of Matthew also helped to make her former life a thing of the past. But the bogey man that they had banished to the abyss of dark secrets was now back with a vengeance.

The Captain looked down at the brown envelope that he held in his trembling hands. On the outside of the envelope three words were written: Attention Captain Curtis. The last fifteen minutes had shaken a world that had taken him over thirty years to build. Now he shuddered to think what was inside the envelope. He got up and poured himself a scotch. As he gulped it, he caught sight of the dawn peeping over the tops of the houses in his suburban neighbourhood. He had the urge to pitch the envelope into the fire, but he knew better. After a few more agonising moments he stood up and mustered up the courage to look inside.

Printed on a white piece of paper were another three words that sent his mind into a spin. I HAVE MORE.

What the fuck did that mean? More of what? Suddenly a pain shot through his body that weakened his legs. He collapsed into the nearby chair and remained there until the sun had risen.

The wall clock told him it was 6:07am. Normally he would be waking in exactly 43 minutes to begin his day. But today was different. At 6:11am, the phone rang. The Captain answered on the second ring and a man's voice spoke.

"Let Devil Barnett go now, or else there will be much more information about you and your wife that the world will know about."

The Captain drew in his breath and the phone line went dead. A combination of hate and fear surged through the Captain. He hated the thought of someone having the balls and evidence to blackmail him. Even though he was a by-the book-cop now, he was nevertheless still a cop with a past. As a result, there were still one or two skeletons lurking around in his closet.

There was that snitch he beat to the point of brain damage when he was a vice cop twenty five years ago. There was that fifty thousand dollars cash in drug money he had shared with another cop when they walked in a Brooklyn apartment and found one of the big pushers of the day murdered. There was the prison guard in Sing Sing he had paid five thousand dollars to make sure that Hollywood Freddy never left prison alive.

The possibilities of disaster hung above him like a bolt of lightning poised in the sky waiting to blow his world apart. The smell the pig shit on his clothes made him remember how as a child he used to help his father who was a tenant worker on a pig farm in Georgia clean out the pig pens. The Captain felt weak and alone as his hand moved to the phone and dialled.

"Hello, this is the Captain," he spoke into the phone authoritatively when the patrolman answered.

"Yes Captain" the voice answered.

"There's been a mistake. Release Barnett immediately" he said.

"Yes Captain," the voice said and hung up.

The Captain replaced the phone and breathed a sigh of relief. He wanted to but didn't dare think of retaliation. The Captain reasoned that whoever the hell this Devil Barnett really was, he was far more dangerous than he had ever imagined.

CHAPTER 19

WITH SPONGEY SIX feet under, Bobby hadn't figured out any other way to do it. That's why he was sitting in the reception area of Fidelity Trust Brokerage looking at the paintings of six old white men in black suits. They all had that constipated look. These were the original founders of the company back at the turn of the twentieth century. Bobby fidgeted in his chair and picked up the Wall Street Journal from the coffee table. Using Spongey's name as a reference he had called the man's office directly and to his surprise was told to come in right away. The secretary came out.

"Mr. Jerrod will see you in a few minutes. Would you like coffee or a soft drink Mr. Jones?"

Bobby said "coffee please, black no sugar," and then adjusted his glasses and smoothed the top of his hair with the hand as she was walking away.

Five minutes passed. Bobby sat wading through the unintelligible language about stocks and bonds and take over bids in a financial magazine. He was wondering how he could strike a deal that would keep his life safe as well as put some real cash into his pocket.

"You can go in now," the secretary said.

When Bobby walked into the room, Jerrod greeted him.

"Have a seat Mr. Jones. Sorry about you having to wait. Now exactly why did you want to see me?"

Bobby adjusted his glasses and sat up straight, thinking somehow that the glasses made him look more respectable and intelligent.

"Um, I don't know quite how to say this but I happen to know that you are looking for someone that I know, a WoodHenry Taylor."

He watched closely for Jerrod's reaction but was disappointed. Jerrod looked back at him with cool blue eyes that said nothing

"I think I might know where he is," Bobby said.

"OK, but I'm not exactly sure that I'm looking for him, why should I be?" was Jerrod's answer.

"Because I was told that he had something that belonged to you," Bobby replied.

"OK" was all the Jerrod said.

"The reason I'm here, is to find out if you want me to help you to get it back."

Jerrod was still as cool as a cucumber. He lit a cigar, leaned back and started puffing. Without warning, a sense of nervousness swept over Bobby and left him feeling uncomfortably exposed.

"One pretty lady has already had some serious problems over what you've lost," Bobby said.

"Why, what happened?" Jerrod asked.

Now Bobby could sense a different level of interest.

"Dead as dogshit."

"Dead, how?"

"Brax killed her."

"Who's Brax?"

"Somebody you wouldn't want to meet, believe me. He does whatever his boss tells him too. Brax and his boss are both very dangerous men" Bobby said feeling more confident with every word.

"His boss?" Jerrod said this time the interest coming through as clear as day. Bobby pushed back his shoulders, lit up a cigarette and relaxed a little now that he felt things were starting to go his way.

"Yeah his boss is an ugly little white man named Nicolli, a foreigner. He does investigative work. He's looking for WoodHenry Taylor too," Bobby said with a smirk.

"I see, so what's your proposition Mr. Jones?"

"I think I can find WoodHenry before Nicolli does, and when I do I'd like to be able to disappear without having to worry about money for a while. A long while," Bobby explained.

"How much money are we talking about?"

"I was told that WoodHenry walked with two million of your dough and to help find him, my share would be 250 g's,"" Bobby said.

"I'm afraid to say that you'll be a bit disappointed to know that the figure he disappeared with was actually four million" Jerrod said, watching Bobby like a cat watching a bird.

"Four!" The words shot out of Bobby's mouth before his brain could get into gear.

Jerrod just smiled and sat back in his expensive chair and he sucked on the fat cigar and Bobby felt that all the while Tom Jerrod was calculating his next move like some grandmaster chess player. There was something about the man that Bobby found disconcerting, almost like the man knew the very next thing he was going to say.

"How did you come to get involved in this affair?" Jerrod asked.

"Through Nicolli first, then Spongey who is or was a friend of WoodHenry's. Nicolli found out that I knew WoodHenry because he used my name on his job application so he told me and the guy that killed the prostitute that if we could arrange for him to meet with WoodHenry then we would walk away with a lot of gold dust," Bobby told him.

"So you knew WoodHenry?"

"Yeah, his wife and my ex-wife used to be close," Bobby explained.

"So how did this guy Nicolli come to know that I was looking for WoodHenry?" Jerrod inquired.

"I don't know for sure, I just know that he does special investigations for people. From what I've been told, the man has his hands in a whole lot of shit" Bobby said.

"You ever work with him before?"

"No."

Jerrod turned his chair towards the window and looked out of his tenth storey window towards New Jersey. Without talking he smoked the cigar halfway down before turning back to Bobby.

"Tell you what, if you bring in WoodHenry, you're looking a half million in cash in addition to a plane ticket and passport in any name you wish to any part of the world," Jerrod said.

Bobby drank in the sweet sound of the financial man's words.

"That sounds cool," Bobby said grinning.

"Another thing, I want to find out how this Nicolli guy learned about the missing money."

"That might not be too easy, we don't have exactly what you might call a friendly kind of relationship," Bobby said.

"Nothing's easy in this life, Mr. Jones. That's why I'm willing to pay you a million dollars," Jerrod said looking him straight in the eye.

"OK, I'll see what I can do"

"Call me when you find out anything" Jerrod said as he quickly scribbled a few numbers on a on a business card and passed it to Bobby. "That's my cell phone number."

"Sure thing" Bobby said and placed the card carefully into the inside pocket of his sports jacket.

"My secretary will show you out" Jerrod said as he pressed a button on his large mahogany desk.

Before Bobby could stand up, the young white secretary with short dark brown hair had opened the door.

Mr. Jones is just leaving," Jerrod said and immediately turned his attention to some papers on his desk as if Bobby had already evaporated into thin air. Arrogant cocksucker Bobby thought. But what did he care what personality defects the man had as long as the man was going to make him rich.

Within two minutes Bobby was in the elevator and walking out into the lobby at the street level entrance. Suddenly Bobby felt smarter than he had for years. He had planned it to the T. He had even lied to fake Brax out with a story that he was meeting a woman in a hotel just so that he could get space to operate. Now he was on his way to becoming a millionaire.

The building was in the financial district at the bottom of Manhattan so he decided that he would take a walk and consider his new arrangement with Jerrod. As he walked along he thought about what he would do with a million bucks. One thing for sure, he would use it to get a million miles away from Brax and Nicolli. He grinned to himself in the plate glass mirror of the store he passed and thought about what his new name might be. Since he had a pretty good ear for languages he even toyed with the idea of learning French and passing himself off as a prince from some part of West Africa. With a million in his pocket he could be anyone he damned well pleased.

He felt hungry again and decided that he would walk around until he found an interesting-looking restaurant. He wasn't due to meet with Nicolli and Brax for another six hours yet, so he decided just to chill out and enjoy the rest of the day. He chose a small but expensive restaurant frequented by Wall Street executives. As he enjoyed his meal of sirloin steak and mashed potatoes he was again unaware of the very average-looking dark olive-skinned man that had followed him from the time that he had left his hotel room. The olive-skinned man positioned himself in a place where he could keep an eye on Bobby without being seen then proceeded to make a call on his cell phone. When the other voice came on the phone the olive-faced man began to speak in Turkish.

"Mr. Nicolli, he went into one of the financial buildings down in the financial centre. The log book said he went to the tenth floor which is occupied by the Fidelity Trust Brokerage Company. He stayed for about twenty five minutes," the man reported.

"Good, you can let him go now and I'll call you in the morning," Nicolli responded in his native tongue. Nicolli put down the phone and bit into the stuffed vine leaf. He wiped the juice that flowed from the corner of his mouth with the back of his girl-like pink hands. Then he smiled at the thought that there were people around he could really trust. As Nicolli lit his third cigarette in twenty minutes, he began to plan how he would get the best use out of Bobby Jones whom he now knew was trying to double cross him. Yes, he would plan a nice little demise for Mr. Jones, and the nicest part of it was that his killing would be carried out by Brax, Bobby's own partner in crime.

CHAPTER 20

JERROD DIALLED MISSY Free's cell phone number and waited, but there was no answer so he hung up. He sat at his desk with both thumbs hooked under his chin, palms together and fingers touching as he thought about things. If Bobby Jones really knew where WoodHenry was, it certainly made sense for him to play along. Then he figured that if someone else was also looking for WoodHenry, especially somebody dangerous like this guy Brax and his boss then Missy Free might be in danger if word got out that she had been asking around. There was a lot to think about. Still he wasn't very worried because thinking was his strongest asset. His experience had shown him that he could out-think most people. Then Tom Jerrod started to think about his wife Greta, the woman behind the throne. The woman who stayed in the background. He had long ago decided he had to get away from her in order to keep his sanity. She made him cringe whenever he touched her. This woman who held him captive because of her bank book and her controlling interest in Fidelity Trust Brokerage Company. He walked down the corridor to his wife's small office. He used his key to enter. He carefully locked the door behind him and then removed a framed photograph of a pastel flower arrangement from the wall. He then used a special electronic instrument that he had bought from a high class burglar to unlock her wall safe. He was careful not to upset the contents or the arrangement of the safe. It only took a few minutes before he found what he was looking for. The item was a small leather address book which held all of Greta's important telephone numbers. Under the letter N was written in her neat hand writing the name Nicolli-Private Investigations, Missing persons, Insurance. and a telephone number. He took an index card from the inside pocket of his custom made suit and copied the information. He then calmly closed the door to the safe, replaced the framed photograph and walked back to his office. He called Missy Free's number again, but again no one answered.

Bobby turned the rented car into the driveway at exactly 14 minutes before 8:00pm. He still felt the elation of his deal with Jerrod earlier in the day. He got out of the car and entered the house through the front door with his key. Brax was stretched in front of the television watching wrestling with a half-eaten Big Mac and a large drink on the arm of the chair. Nicolli was in the kitchen.

"Hello fellows" Bobby said as he crossed the room.

"Hey Lil Nigga" Brax mumbled between mouthfuls of the burger and immediately turned his attention back to the wrestling match.

He momentarily saw Nicolli moving catlike from one side of the kitchen to the other with a dish in his hand. Two seconds later Nicolli emerged from the kitchen with a plate of olives and hard cheese.

"Mr. Jones, you're right on time" he said smiling as he headed for the sofa.

"Yeah," Bobby said as he lit a cigarette and flopped down in the chair across from where Nicolli sat.

"I heard you had a hot date last night" Nicolli said.

"Oh yeah, she was a hot one alright" Bobby said and grinned dutifully.

"You know I've had a lot of women like most men I guess, but the one thing I've never had is a family."

"You know what they say, it's never too late," Bobby said trying to sound attentive. In reality he thought that if Nicolli had ever impregnated a woman that at best the poor child would most likely come out half human and half gila monster.

"You have a son in college, what I wouldn't give to have that. What did you say he was studying?" Nicolli asked.

"Computer science."

"Computers, well there's no doubt it's the way of today as well as the future. I mean for all practical purposes we are dinosaurs. Even criminals who use computers are in a position to make more money without half the risk guys like us take. I really admire young people who go after their dreams with an eye on the future," Nicolli said and stuffed a piece of cheese into his mouth. "You know, I've never really been one to donate to charity, but I would like to do something for someone like yourself who I admire. Would you mind if I make a gesture?"

"What kind of gesture?" Bobby asked.

"I hope you don't take this amiss but I would like to make a donation to your son's education, just a small token maybe just five thousand as an anonymous gift to help him through."

Bobby opened his mouth to say that it wasn't necessary but before he could get the words out Nicolli jumped in again.

"I would really take it as an insult if you wouldn't let me at least make such a small gesture," Nicolli said looking Bobby straight in the eye. "He's at the University of Connecticut right?"

"Yeah" Bobby said.

"That settles it then, when I get around to it, I'll send a donation and make sure it gets to him. That would be a good thing, don't you think?" Nicolli said.

"Sure why not," Bobby said and adjusted his glasses nervously. Interference into his family life was the last thing Bobby wanted or needed from Nicolli, especially now that he was getting ready to get his million bucks and then get the fuck into the wind. But what the hell could he do except listen to this man's shit? After all he was living off the man's money, so he just got up and poured himself a large drink from the bottle of Johnny Walker Black Label that sat on a tray near the TV and settled back down into the chair.

Bobby couldn't quite figure what angle Nicolli was trying to play, but whatever it was, he figured it couldn't compete with the deal that Tom Jerrod had put on the table. A cool million bucks. He had put the word out in some places he knew around Harlem. He still had a few more tricks to play, furthermore some people on the street still owed him some heavy favours. Yeah he was getting ready to get rich. All he had to do was track down WoodHenry. Bobby savoured the taste of the scotch and watched the ugliest man in the world chew on a piece of cheese like a giant white rat. He also created visions in his mind of gorgeous tanned naked women waiting on him hand and foot on some deserted beach in some beautiful and safe corner of the world. The imagined beautiful women and the thought of being a millionaire gave him courage.

Simultaneously Nicolli gnawed on the cheese and pretended to watch wrestling as he thought about Bobby's attempt to double-cross him. He figured that maybe Bobby had already found out where WoodHenry was and was holding out on him. He also figured that he had probably found out from his ex-wife who WoodHenry would have most likely called if he was in trouble. Wasn't that what friends were for, to call on each other in times of need? He decided for the moment to play dumb and wait. He could afford to, because he had a couple other cards up his sleeve that he had not played yet.

CHAPTER 21

FRANCISCO WAS WAITING for me on the morning I was let out of jail. First thing I did when I reached my house was call Christine at the bar.

"You alright? I tried to call you last night but didn't get an answer," she said. There was genuine concern in her voice.

"Everything's cool, just a little business I had to take care of" I said.

"You must have had a hot date last night for you to have disappeared off the face of the earth. You didn't even take your car. It was parked the same place it was yesterday"

"Did I get a ticket?"

"No you're cool. Hey you had better not let Sonia find out about it or she'll be sniffing around trying to find out what's up," she joked.

"I know that's right. Listen, hold down the fort and I'll see you in a couple hours," I said and hung up.

After I had taken a shower, we sat down to coffee and Francisco told me all about his activities on the previous night at the Captain's house. Nothing surprised me. That kind of intimidation was a normal part of the stock in trade of the profession when I was an agent. I had done similar kinds of things many times before myself. Even worse. I guess that's why I kind of actually feared bringing Francisco into my new life and environment. The same way that some people seem to be magnets for money or misfortune, Francisco and I together had always seemed to be magnets for death. Anyway Onion's research had led him to the information he needed to make the previous night successful.

The phone rang.

"Hey brother," Johnny Ray Slim said in his rich baritone when I answered. In the background I could hear Miles Jones playing "Sketches of Spain".

"Whassup?" I asked.

"Something came my way last night that I think might

interest you. When can you get over here?"

I looked at my watch. It was still only 8:30 am.

"How about eleven?" I said.

"In a minute" Johnny Ray said and hung up.

"What do you think about this Jerrod character?" Francisco asked.

"I know he's not telling the truth. That much is obvious."

"What exactly are you hoping to find when you finally do come upon this WoodHenry Taylor?"

"I don't really care Cisco, I got into this for the sake of a friend so if I find him alive that will be good enough for me. Which reminds me of something I need to do"

I dialled Honey Lavelle's number and on the third ring she answered.

"Hey Youngblood, how you doing baby" she cooed with sleep still in her voice.

"Fine I just called to check on you."

"Thanks."

"You busy?"

"If I was busy at 8:30 in the morning then you would be interrupting, now wouldn't you?"

"I guess so" I laughed.

"Why?"

"A friend of mine just came into town and I'd like to stop by and introduce him to you."

"Had breakfast yet?" she asked.

"No, just coffee."

"How do pancakes sound?"

"As sweet as a Lester Young solo."

"How long will it take you to get here?"

I said "about twenty minutes?" I could almost taste the pancakes already. I knew from first hand experience that Honey could really cook.

"See you then."

Five minutes later Francisco and I were in a gypsy cab headed for Lennox Terrace Apartments where Honey lived.

"Did you bring the bracelet?" I asked Francisco.

"Yeah right here," he said pushing a small box into my hand.

"You must really be hungry," Honey said when she opened the door. "You got here in only fifteen minutes."

"You got that right. This is my friend Francisco from New

Mexico, he's visiting for a while."

"Hello Francisco, I'm Honey," she said shaking Francisco's hand.

He gave her a smile that I had seen only a few times before. That was the thing about Honey, she had a positive effect on almost everybody she met, even the people in the Tease Me Club where she had to throw the odd customer out for misbehaving. They protested a bit but never seem to take their anger out on her. But that was all part of the package that made Honey Lavelle a very special woman.

The pancakes were light, fluffy and tremendously delicious.

"Girl, you got some serious skills with the pots and pans" I said.

"Oh don't you even go there" she laughed.

Francisco finished of a sixth pancake and relaxed back into his seat and patted his stomach.

"You want more Francisco?" Honey asked eyeing his empty plate.

"Then I'd have to roll him down the street," I said.

Francisco held up his hand to Honey shaking his head and started to laugh at my comment. I started to laugh too. At that moment it seemed like the past three years had never taken place. It was just like it used to be. Me and Francisco cracking jokes on each other, and finding camaraderie among the sharp ugliness of life's prickly thorns. Despite all of the danger and uncertainty, the friendship we forged in those days somehow kept us from going off the deep end. We had been there for each other in the worst of times. I guess after all is said and done that's why I had called him. I knew that he would do whatever it took to make sure no one would put a knife in my back if I happened to be looking the other way.

"Here" I said extending a small box toward Honey.

"What's this?" Honey asked.

"It's something I want you to wear for a while."

She opened the box and took out the bracelet from inside.

"It's nice."

"It's got a homing device inside."

"You think I'll need this? I got a cell phone you know."

"This ex-husband of yours is a pretty bad character and I don't know exactly who or what I'm dealing with yet, so this is just a precaution."

I purposely hadn't told her about Elvira or Spongey turning up dead.

"Our experience has been that it's always good to cover your bets," Francisco added.

"OK if you say so" Honey said.

"Thanks" I said.

"You guys want some coffee?" she asked as she turned on the pot.

"That would be great" Francisco answered before I could.

At that moment my cell phone rang.

"Just checking on you Doctor, I saw you going into Honey's place about a half hour ago, everything alright?" The voice belonged to Hummingbird Moses.

"Yeah, everything is cool, how you keeping?"

"OK, heard about your troubles over at the Precinct."

"Word travels fast," I quipped

"This is Harlem, you know how it is," he said.

"Indeed I do."

"Anyway I'm still on the case. I'll catch you later."

"Good man" I said and hung up.

"Everything alright?" Honey asked.

"Yeah everything's cool," I said glancing at my watch.

"You on the run this morning?" she asked

"Yeah, sorry."

"Don't sweat it Youngblood, you still got a standing invitation" she said and winked in Francisco's direction.

We thanked her for breakfast and left. The weather was starting to warm up.

We took a cab back up to the Be Bop Tavern. I said my hellos all around and then picked up my car.

"That's some woman you got there" Francisco said.

"Yeah she is, only problem is, she ain't mine, not in that way. We're just friends."

"If she ain't then she should be" he shot back. "A blind man can see that she's on you like white on rice brother, and when you look at her you feel something too don't you. That's what brought me to town wasn't it? You helping her out?"

"Yeah that's why I asked you to come" I said and continued driving south towards 110th Street to meet Johnny Ray Slim.

With just a few words, maybe Francisco had managed to articulate what I had been afraid for my heart to say. Maybe my fear was the fear that if I really loved someone as beautiful and full of life as Honey then maybe I would eventually destroy her with my uncompromising commitment to playing detective. And she would wind up miserable in an unfulfilled relationship with me the way Sonia was.

Maybe it was something that went even deeper. I just knew for me whenever love takes the lead, hurts always seems to follow close behind. Maybe there were a thousand reasons that I didn't tell Honey how special and wonderful I thought she was though I was sure she already knew. Anyway I hoped she did. I wasn't even exactly sure how to define my feelings for Honey, I just knew that emotions between Honey and myself were always on the verge of sparking something. I guess that's what Francisco saw so plainly.

When we walked into Johnny Ray's place Francisco had to do a second and then a third take. Johnny Ray Slim's was one of those Harlem barbershops of legend. It was a place where young men could hear stories, jokes and lessons on life and women. It was also a place and where old men heard the latest music, picked up on the newest street slang and even once in a while could catch a quick peek at some pretty young woman who happened to be hanging around waiting for her young man to be properly coiffured. The decor could have been right out of Bad Housekeeping Magazine with it's tacky orange walls and poster calendars of young girls in bikinis mixed in with photographs of Johnny Ray posing with entertainers and sports figures. Some of photos were icons like Muhammed Ali, Joe Frazier, Sammy Jones Jr, Quincy Jones and Marvin Gaye. Everybody in Harlem knew about Johnny Ray's place. Even though it was small with only four chairs, from Thursday through Saturday you could only get in by appointment.

Though Johnny Ray was an ardent jazz fan, he catered to the tastes of the people who made the shop a success. Therefore his CD player put out a constant mixture from the latest black pop music like Jay-Z and Dr. Dre to the cool old crooners like Nat King Cole and Johnny Hartman. He also played the jazz greats like Miles Jones and Theolonius Monk.

Johnny Ray's barber's chair was nearest to the back of the room next to his office. He was just finishing up a customer and smiled as we took seats near his chair while he dusted his customer off with talcum powder.

"So how you been making it, man?" Johnny Ray greeted as his customer left.

"I'm cool. Let me introduce you to a friend of mine from New Mexico. This is Francisco," I said.

"New Mexico, man I drove through there once on my way to California about eight or nine years ago, I remember it was a beautiful place. Hot but beautiful," Johnny Ray said shaking Francisco's hand.

After a few more exchanges of small talk Johnny Ray led us into his office at the back of the shop. Adorning the walls were more photos of Johnny Ray with celebrities. The piece de resistance was mounted in a glass and mahogany frame. It featured Johnny Ray as a teenager with his father standing next to a young, clean-shaven Malcolm X.

"You ever heard of a chick named Missy Free?" Johnny Ray asked as we sat down in front of his old beaten up wooden desk.

"Why?" I said.

"She's been looking for your man."

"WoodHenry Taylor?" I said

"The very same, and from what I understand she's offering serious money for whoever finds him."

"How much?"

"Five grand."

"She must really want to find him."

"Yeah, the story she got working is that one of his distant rich uncles died back in Detroit and left him a whole lot of money, so she's trying to find him. Not only her but another dude is looking for him too.

"Know his name?"

"Bobby is all I was told. Didn't say why he was looking though."

"Did you see either one of them?"

"No, I just heard about them from my people."

"Do you think you could set up a meeting with the woman?" I asked.

"No doubt, when you want it?" Johnny Ray responded.

"As soon as you can. There's been some ugly stuff happening and I want to check out what end of the street she's really working," I said.

"I'll get the word out right away."

"Thanks."

"Oh yeah I knew there was something I wanted to show you," Johnny Ray said opening his desk drawer and pulling out a small blue booklet.

"You ever heard of this place?" he asked pushing the booklet across the desk towards me.

"Sao Paulo, Brazil, yeah," I said, "it's about four hours from Rio De Janeiro driving."

"A musician friend of mine told me that he was down there last year playing in this Jazz Festival that they have there every year."

"The Free Jazz Festival" I said.

"So you know about it?" Johnny Ray looked surprised.

"Yeah, I've always wanted to go."

"I hear it's supposed to be the bomb, all kind of great artists from all over the world and some knockout women too."

"I heard the same thing" I said grinning across the desk at him.

"I've been there once, Sao Paulo reminds me of New York with all the hustle, Rio is more laid back like L.A." Francisco chimed in.

"Sounds like the place to be. We just missed it for this year but we can definitely be on the plane for the next one, give us something to look forward to," Johnny Ray smiled.

"I'm down" I said.

Johnny Ray looked at Francisco.

"I would love to go, but my wife would never allow me in Sao Paulo without her glued to me. Too many beautiful women in Brazil," Francisco smiled.

"OK, so it's on right?" Johnny said looking at me.

"It's on."

We slapped palms to seal the deal.

"Sao Paulo, here we come," Johnny Ray grinned.

He was still grinning when we left the shop five minutes later.

Back in the car as we were heading back towards the bar, Francisco turned to me.

"So what do you make of this Missy Free person?" he asked me.

"Don't know for sure but if she's willing to spend five grand to find him, she probably knows that he's not dead, at least not yet."

CHAPTER 22

WOODHENRY WASN'T DEAD yet, even though he felt that he was right on the verge of death. The pain of love had wrapped itself around his heart and was squeezing the life out of him like a giant anaconda. With each breath he took the fear of being caught grew and grew. At any moment it felt as if he would suffocate to death. Even when he was sleeping his fear reached out and rattled his subconscious. Sometimes the dreams came in the form of dark creatures waiting at the end of a long corridor ready to devour him and at other times they came in the form of musical nightmares like the one he was having now where Missy Free had betrayed him and as result he was in a mental institution.

Music Track # 6
MESSIN' WID ME

YOU BEEN MESSIN' WID ME BABY
I WANNA KNOW WHATS ON YOUR MIND
YOU'RE ABOUT TO DRIVE ME CRAZY
WON'T YOU PLEASE GIVE ME A SIGN

I am feelin' confused,
And my thinking is obtuse,
so I wanna know
Why my head is screamin
Why I'm actin this way,
my doctor can't say
what's the matter
He thinks I maybe
having myself
A first class nervous
breakdown, disorder
I'm on the border-line
of losing my mind

But he says he thinks
I may be getting better
But why am I wearing
my trousers over my head
like a sweater

YOU BEEN MESSIN' WID ME BABY
I WANNA KNOW WHATS ON YOUR MIND
YOU'RE ABOUT TO DRIVE ME CRAZY
WON'T YOU PLEASE GIVE ME A SIGN

Hey Jack
give me the prozac
I'm a fiend for ya thorazine
I need it to keep my
head on straight
It is early, is it late
Why do I keep walkin
The floor in a figure 8
People say my neurotic side
is in overdrive just because
I got a special friend named Mr. Cockroach
who lives inside the ceiling
He crawls down and he talks to me
about what you been
doing and feeling and it ain't
too appealing, what he's tellin me
about you.

YOU BEEN MESSIN' WID ME BABY
I WANNA KNOW WHATS ON YOUR MIND
YOU'RE ABOUT TO DRIVE ME CRAZY
WON'T YOU PLEASE GIVE ME A SIGN

My mind is jumpin'
flippin grinnin', spinnin',
Am I goin', or comin'
Hey Doctor, give me some medicine
Ain't it time to watch David Letterman
More water please nurse
I swear I swear, I won't

wet my bed again.

Pickin' my nose, playin with my toes
As well as other parts of myself,
but the Doctor don't like that
kind of behaviour, says its bad
for my health.
But I can't help it, cause I'm obsessin'
and stressin' cause you are messin'
With my brain …girl
My body's on fire desiring
to rendezvous with you
it's true girl,

YOU BEEN MESSIN' WID ME BABY
I WANNA KNOW WHATS ON YOUR MIND
YOU'RE ABOUT TO DRIVE ME CRAZY
WON'T YOU PLEASE GIVE ME A SIGN

Missy Free had hurt him so badly by abandoning him, that it seemed to blank everything else out in his life. It even blanked out the small little dingy little room at the back of the blind man's house where he was living. The place had been arranged for him by Albalita who seemed to be his only true friend in the world. He had left the room in Hell's Kitchen accepting the fact that Missy Free cared about as much for him as she did for a dog turd laying in the street. At first he just wandered around Manhattan in his wig and black suit disguise for awhile. He had thought of jumping off the Brooklyn Bridge. Then he had thought about throwing himself in front of an oncoming subway train but somehow and somewhere between those thoughts he found his feet making their way toward Mount Vernon. The reason he went to Mount Vernon wasn't altogether clear in his mind. Maybe he just went there to talk to somebody he could trust. Albalita. Maybe he went there because he thought that the sound of another woman's voice might somehow ease the pain caused by Missy Free playing him for a chump. Albalita. Whatever it was, it had apparently kept him from killing himself, at least for the moment. Albalita had always liked him and he liked her. But just as friends

His eyes strayed from the faded cream-coloured wallpaper with a flowered print to the old scarred chest of drawers where Albalita had neatly placed his clean underwear. The chest of drawers were next to a small sink under which the blind man had placed a can of rat poison. For a moment WoodHenry found himself thinking that he could just take the poison and end his misery all at once. But if he did that, he knew that Albalita would be mad with him, and he cared too much for her to cause her any pain. So he just curled up on the bed and started to think about how he had gotten himself in this whole damn mess in the first place. It had all started with that damn Spongey. If only Spongey hadn't taken him to that damned party at Tom Jerrod's house. It was at that same damn party that he had met Missy Free. And if he had never met Missy Free... he would have never fallen in love... and if he had never in fallen in love.... he would have never agreed to stealing all those bonds that Tom Jerrod had asked him to deliver as a favour. He couldn't believe what a fool he had been to believe Missy Free. She said that they were going to sell those bonds to somebody she knew and they would get enough money to disappear and live happily ever after as a rich couple on some villa in sunny Spain. What a chump. He wanted to kick himself right in the balls whenever he thought about it. How could he have been so damned stupid. Then he thought of another time just after Paulette died when he had gotten mixed up with a woman named Janey who had almost gotten him killed. She had been strung out on crack and kept coming to him for money. She had told him that it was for re-hab, but when it became evident that she had no plans to get straight he tried to finish the relationship. Janey got mad and got one of her junkie friends to try and rob him as he was coming home one night. Luckily had able to see the flash of the man's knife in time enough to hit him and run away.

"Stupid stupid stupid,." he said to himself. By the third time he said it, his muse had joined him.

Music Track #7
STUPID

You were livin' fat but today you're broke,
Tryin' to borrow money for a burger and a coke,
I know what you're sayin', heard it all before
When you get down and out I see you at my door.
But the gravy train is off the track,
So don't you bother even comin' back, baby
Cause you're stupid,
STUCK ON STUPID WITH SUPERGLUE.
(I don't know how you could be so stupid)
STUCK ON STUPID, STUCK ON STUPID WITH SUPERGLUE

Girl, the man that you've been thinkin' was ripe,
I'm tellin you, he's been sellin' you out and you been buyin' the hype.
But I say you should get your money where you been spendin 'your time,
Cause he's so cheap he wouldn't give you two nickles for a dime.,
STUCK ON STUPID, (Stupid Stupid Stupid)
STUCK ON STUPID WITH SUPERGLUE.
(I don't know why you so damn stupid)
STUCK ON STUPID, STUCK ON STUPID WITH SUPERGLUE

Hangin' out, stayin' high 24-7,
your looks are starting to go and your mind is goin' too,
now you wanna kick it with me all over again,
But uh, uh, baby I ain't even hearin' you.
15 times you came to me and I took you back in
And 16 times you went away and you did it all again.
If you lookin' for a fool, you'd better look elsewhere,
I ain't even tryin' to get with you, it's over girl I swear,
because you're stupid. (Stupid, Stupid, Stupid)
STUCK ON STUPID WITH SUPERGLUE
(I ain't hearin' you) STUCK ON STUPID
STUCK ON STUPID WITH SUPERGLUE

At times he thought that maybe he could go back to Tom Jerrod on his hands and knees and give him the key to the locker that held the bonds and everything would be alright. But it was too late for that. Then he thought about Spongey. Then he reasoned that Spongey was probably dead because he might have somehow found out about the stolen bonds. He also figured that Elvira was dead because she knew Spongey who might have told her. Then he reasoned that Tom Jerrod had killed them both. In WoodHenry's mind there was no doubt what would happen to him if Jerrod ever caught up with him.

Then like a lightening bolt out of hell the most ugly thought that he could have ever imagined flew into his mind again. He had been trying to suppress this ugly notion for more than two days but without success. It was so terrible it made him start walking the floor and talking to himself. Damn Damn Damn. What if Missy Free hadn't come to him because she hadn't been able to. What if Missy had really loved him. What if she had been killed too. What if she had been killed because Tom Jerrod found out their plan.

He looked at the small potted plant that he and Missy Free had bought together. It was the same plant that Missy had made a pledge of love on after reading a passage from the Bible. As WoodHenry thought about all of these things, emotion welled up inside him and the tears flowed down his sad face.

The only thing he could think of to make himself feel a little better was Paulette, his dead wife. Why did God have to take her away from him? All those years together. From the day they'd met in the lunchroom in high school until her dying day, Paulette had always been there for him keeping his mind, body and soul together. He had tried to tell himself that he had gotten over her death. He had tried to move on. But it was just too hard. He had prayed to God that Missy Free would help fill the empty space created by Paulette's death.

Then he thought of his friend Honey Lavelle again. She was a true friend. He was sure that Honey would help him, even hide him and get him out of town. But how could he involve her. Suppose the same people who killed Spongey and Elvira found out about her trying to help him. They might try to kill Honey too. Paulette would never forgive him for getting her best friend killed. Besides what would he say to her? How could he tell her that he had allowed a fine woman with a nice shape and sweet face to talk him into stealing four million dollars in bearer bonds from his job. No, he could never tell Honey that. She knew him, really knew him. Telling Honey would be too much like telling Paulette. Even though he knew that she would understand that loneliness drove him to do it, he would still be too ashamed.

WoodHenry was emotionally adrift laying on a single bed in a room at the back of a blind man's house. He waited for Albalita to come. She had told him that she wouldn't be able to come to him often because she would be too easy to follow, just in case anybody knew that he had come to her for help. So all he could do now was wait and pray. Albalita said she was working things out for him. He hoped so. Lord knows he hoped so. He sent up a prayer that no one would find out about Albalita helping him because he didn't want her hurt either.

Suddenly the thought crossed his mind that he should just get up, walk out of the blind man's house and disappear. Though his mind wanted to leave, his body kept him glued to the bed curled up in the foetal position. His eyes were closed tightly as he breathed in the hot air he had created under the covers pulled up over his head. He tried to lose the pain in his heart by saying another silent prayer. He asked God to deliver him from the evil that dogged his misdeeds and wished that he was somewhere way off in space. Way off in a place too far for the emotions of this painful life to ever touch him again.

CHAPTER 23

THE PHONE RANG at the Be-Bop Tavern while I was helping with the after lunch time clean up detail.

"Hello, may I speak to Mr. Barnett." I recognised the voice immediately.

"Mr. Jerrod, how are you?" .

"I was wondering if you had you found out anything" he asked.

"Not much more than before honestly, except that a man named Spongey who was a cleaner for your company has been mysteriously murdered, but that wouldn't be relevant to your missing person I'm sure." I was trying to see if he would take the bait in any way.

"Yes, I heard about it the day after it happened. It was in the papers. It's a shame really" he said.

"Did you know him well?"

"Not well but we had spoken a few times. He came in sometimes as I was working late and we would talk about sports. Often if I'm around I talk to some of the guys about sports. Actually it was Spongey who introduced me to WoodHenry."

"How did that come about?"

"Horses. I was telling Spongey that I was having trouble training a couple of my horses and he told me that there was a man who worked for me as a messenger who knew more about horses than most people, so I asked him to make the introduction," Jerrod said.

"I see, well I'm sure you didn't call me just to chat."

"That's true, is there any chance you can get into see me at my office today?" Jerrod asked.

"Depends."

"On?"

"On how much you think my time is worth," I said.

I figured that he hadn't found WoodHenry, otherwise he wouldn't have called.

"What about five hundred, to show?"

"What time are we talking about?"

"It's 3:15 now. In an hour?" he said.

I decided to drive down town where his office was located. Francisco and I drove down together. I left Francisco with the car in a parking lot south of Canal Street and made my way over to the Wall Street Financial Centre. I found the Fidelity Trust Brokerage firm on the building directory, signed in at the security desk and took an elevator up to Jerrod's floor. Jerrod's secretary escorted me into his office.

"Would you like anything to drink?" she asked.

"No thank you."

"Mr. Jerrod will be with you in a few minutes" she said and gave me a little nervous smile. Just as she turned to walk away, a woman's screaming voice came through the walls.

"You bastard, I'm not having it anymore." The voice was high and stressed. The secretary's eyes met mine in an embarrassed flurry as she hurriedly left Jerrod's office and closed the door behind her. The woman's screaming voice kept penetrating the room.

"I know what you're up to with her. I know it, and I'm not having it anymore. I love you Tom. I'm not as young and pretty as her but I love you too goddammit."

Then there was about two minutes of silence. I half expected the secretary to come back in to tell me that Jerrod had an emergency appointment and couldn't see me but she didn't.

Jerrod stepped into the room followed by the artificially tanned woman I had seen at his pastel-walled mansion. The same woman who had introduced herself to me as his wife.

"Greta just cool down, we'll talk about this at home," Jerrod said

Tears were streaming down the woman's face. Neither one of them seemed to notice me standing in the corner of the room.

"Tom I'm damned sick of it, I've given everything to you and still you don't give one damn about our marriage" she said.

"Dammit, chill, just chill the hell out will you Greta," Tom Jerrod said grabbing her by the shoulders and shaking her the way an angry parent might shake a misbehaving child.

The woman dropped her head and suddenly stood still as the tears continued streaming down her face and dripping onto the expensive carpet.

"Please Greta" Jerrod said in a softer tone.

The woman turned slowly as if in a deep hypnotic trance and walked out of Jerrod's office without another word. After she had gone Jerrod turned to face me.

"Sorry about that. My wife is a very emotional person" he said moving towards the large mahogany desk that dominated the middle of the room. He sat down heavily and opened one of the desk drawers.

He looked straight at me and took a letter sized envelope from the desk drawer.

"Mr. Barnett I'll get right to the point," Jerrod said passing the envelope to me.

I glanced inside to see five one hundred dollar bills.

"I'm very concerned about a friend. I'm concerned that someone might be out to do her some harm. I'd like for you to try and find out something about a man who might be interested in harming her." He handed me an index card. In neat hand-written letters I read the words Nicolli. Private Investigations, Missing Persons, Insurance along with a telephone number and address.

"Would your friend be somehow connected with the disappearance of WoodHenry Taylor?"

"No, this is a separate matter altogether."

"Why would someone want to hurt your friend?"

"Let's just say that my friend is very naive and may have taken a very wrong turn without realising it."

"Do you want to give me anymore, maybe like the name of this friend?"

"Not just now, for the moment I'm more concerned about the man whose name is on that index card."

Like a lot of guys with money Tom Jerrod was arrogant. He believed that his money would buy him all the secrets in the world. I felt like getting up and walking away, but I didn't. There were still a few questions that I needed to answer for myself.

"The five hundred only bought you my presence, my co-operation is going to cost you another five hundred a day, plus expenses" I said.

"No problem," he said then called his secretary in.

"Clair, make out a check for two thousand to Mr. Barnett please."

The woman disappeared from the room again.

"I'll report every three days whether I find out anything or not," I told him.

"Good" he said and reached for a cigar.

There was something about Tom Jerrod that bothered me. Something that wasn't fitting together in my head. It didn't bother me that he was a rich arrogant son-of-a-bitch who was obviously lying to me, but rather something else. Something that I couldn't quite put my finger on. Nevertheless I sensed it, like the lingering residue of a scent in the air that you can't quite identify. The secretary returned with a check and then I left.

When I returned to the car I called Onion and gave him the information on the card, and received some information from him that I had inquired about the day before. That was one piece of the puzzle solved. I now knew that WoodHenry was alive and where he was hiding. Onion had hacked into the phone company records coming from Albalita's house and had traced a number that she had been calling more than usual during the past few days. That number was traced to a man named Granger Hobbs who lived a few blocks away in Mount Vernon.

I still needed to find out who had killed Spongey and tried to set me up to take the fall by calling the police to the scene when they knew I'd be there to meet him. As Francisco and I drove north towards Harlem I was getting some new ideas about how to get the rat into my trap.

"You mind if I get out around midtown and take a look round for a few hours?" Francisco asked, "it's been a long time since I was in New York and a lot has changed."

"Knock yourself out. If you need me, I'm on my cell phone," I said.

"Cool."

Francisco jumped out at 9th Ave and 42nd Street. On the way back uptown, I consciously tried to get a fix on what was bothering me about Tom Jerrod, but by the time I got back to the bar, I still wasn't any closer to the answer.

CHAPTER 24

MISSY FREE WAS sitting in a bar having a drink near 154th and Amsterdam Avenue. She was still mad at herself for not having paid more attention to WoodHenry and allowing him to get away. Now all she could do was to ask around in Harlem to find out if anyone had seen him. The money she had offered as reward was sure to bring some news but she also knew that it might attract the kind of bees to her honeypot that she didn't need or want. She had to find him. Tom Jerrod had instructed her to go home and not try finding WoodHenry. But she wasn't that kind of person. Her sense of duty and responsibility to herself was stronger than that. She had screwed things up, so she felt the least she could do was to find out if WoodHenry was somewhere in Harlem. She felt she at least owed Tom that much. Besides she really loved him, more than anyone in the world, even more than her lover Catherine. She didn't like the thought of letting him down, not after all he had done for her.

That was exactly why she was in a Harlem bar waiting to meet a man who told her he could lead her to WoodHenry. The man's name was Hummingbird Moses. She had asked around Harlem about him. According to her sources, Moses had a reputation for knowing a lot about what was going on, so chances were he had something worth her money. She waited twenty minutes before Moses showed up with another man. This man had a dishevelled appearance, seemed slightly drunk and looked to be in his sixties. Moses introduced him as Foster, WoodHenry's cousin.

Since Foster was supposed to be WoodHenry's cousin Missy Free realised that she had to adjust her story from that of money left by a dead relative to something else.

"Want a drink?" Missy asked the pair.

"I'll take a Bud," Moses said.

"Make mine a G and T. Gordon's. A triple if you don't mind" answered Foster grinning directly at her with glowing eyes that looked as if they had been lit by a fire inside his skull.

Missy Free nodded the order to the bartender then looked back at the two elderly men. Even though Moses was somewhat ragged she could see the sparkle of intelligence in his eyes. Whereas with Foster she only saw the gleam of madness momentarily contained.

"So WoodHenry is your cousin?" inquired Missy Free.

"Yeah, so who is this relative you say left him some money cause if they kin to him then they gotta be kin to me too. Me and WoodHenry, we first cousins," Foster said hungrily eyeing the drink that the bartender was preparing.

"It wasn't really a relative but a man who knew his Momma when she was a girl. That's who left him the money," Missy said. "But that's not the point. The point is I'm willing to pay you good money if you can tell me where WoodHenry is."

"Good money," Foster echoed.

"Five thousand cash," she said to emphasise the point. "So now do you know where he is or not?"

"I surely do. Can lead you right to him, right?" Foster grinned toward Moses and took the first sip of his drink.

Hummingbird Moses nodded in agreement.

"Can you take me to him tonight?" she asked.

"Uh huh, when do I get my money?" Foster wanted to know.

"When I see WoodHenry."

"So why you doing all this for him?" Foster asked.

"He's my boyfriend."

"Boyfriend?" Foster squinted in her direction.

"Yeah, we been going together for a couple months now. He may have mentioned me. My name is Missy Free."

"Uh-huh. Uh-huh you the one alright. Yeah he done told me bout you. The high class gal, yeah, why he run off from you then?" Foster asked taking another long swig of the triple gin and tonic.

"Cause I wanted him to leave his wife."

Foster wrinkled his brow in confusion.

"His wife is dead," Foster said matter of factly.

"Not that one, the other one."

"You mean Elvira. She dead too."

"I heard."

"How did you know?" Moses asked Missy.

"From the papers like everybody else. She was a resident of Harlem before she moved down to the Village, wasn't she. It was in the Harlem local newspaper."

"Sure was," Moses agreed.

"When can you take me to him?"

"When can you show us the money," Moses said.

Missy Free opened her purse and held it so that Hummingbird Moses and Foster could see a fat wad of bills inside.

"You satisfied now?" she asked looking in Moses' direction.

"I'm satisfied alright, you satisfied?" Moses said turning to Foster.

"Don't you two old farts think that you're going to gang up and rob me either, cause I'm carrying a gun and as God is my witness, I'll kill you both dead if either one of you try anything funny."

"OK" Moses said.

Foster just grinned stupidly.

"So where we going?" Missy Free asked.

"You driving ain't you?" Moses asked Missy.

"No, I took a cab."

"So did we," Moses said.

"We can take a cab there together can't we, I'll pay for it," Missy said.

Foster stood up from the bar stool. He was weaving slightly and staring into space as they left the bar.

Moses put up his hand for the gypsy cab that was near the corner of the street. The cab pulled up to where the trio stood and stopped.

"Mt Vernon" Hummingbird Moses said.

"Let me see some money" the driver said. He was a fit handsome-looking black man in his mid thirties. He wore a black skull cap and was chewing on a toothpick hanging from the side of his mouth.

Both Hummingbird Moses and Foster looked in the woman's direction.

Missy Free pouted again and took out a twenty from her purse and held it up so the driver could see it.

"Mt. Vernon it is " the driver said and pulled out into traffic.

As they drove along, Foster looked at the lights that sparkled from various storefronts. He smiled as the gin continued to idle his brain and adjust his level of reality from a stark disconcerting buzz to a comfortable mellow hum.

"There it is" the driver said as they passed a street sign that read YOU ARE NOW ENTERING MT. VERNON NEW YORK .

Missy Free adjusted her body in the seat and rolled down the window because Foster's gin breath had started to turn her stomach.

"How much further we got to go?" Missy barked at Hummingbird Moses who sat in the front seat of the taxi.

Moses called over his shoulder "not far. At the next street, take a right," Moses told the driver.

"Where we going?" Foster blurted

"Thought you said you knew where we were going" Missy free shot back angrily.

"I didn't say I knew nothing, he did" Foster retorted flippantly.

Missy Free turned and pinned Foster with a look that would have frozen the face of death itself, but he wasn't paying her any attention. He was way too drunk for that.

"Stop here at this little white house" Moses said to the cabbie.

"You want me to wait?" the driver asked.

"Yeah that might be a good idea," Moses said.

"How long you gonna be? Really I should keep the meter running."

"Fifteen minutes" Moses said.

After fifteen minutes, I'm turning on the meter," the cabbie yelled as the trio paid him and turned to walk away.

Moses led the way up the walkway to the house and rang the bell with Missy Free and Foster in tow. He rang twice and then waited. A few minutes later, an elderly brown face showed halfway through the curtains at the glass panel of the door.

"What you want?" the man asked through the window.

"I'm the police, we want to see the man you have in there with you. His name is WoodHenry Taylor" Hummingbird Moses said in the deep authoritarian tone he usually reserved when reading his street corner Shakespeare recitals.

"You got the wrong house Mr., ain't nobody living here by that name, it's just me in here," the old man said with a noticeable unsteadiness in his voice.

"We're serious Mr. Hobbs, we know he's in there, and if you don't open this door we're going to have to break it down. Then you're going to be in trouble for harbouring a dangerous fugitive from justice," Moses announced.

The old man showed the remainder of his face through the curtains. The pupils of his eyes were a milky white and stared into nothingness.

"OK," the blind man said deep in his chest like someone had a lead weight pressing down on his body and cutting off his breath.

With expert fingers he undid the locks and held the door open.

"I didn't know he was no criminal" Hobbs said. "I was just doing a favour for a friend" he said in the direction of the man behind the sonorous voice.

"You're not in any trouble yet, just tell us where he is," Hummingbird Moses said. He was enjoying the role.

"In the back, straight through" Mr. Hobbs answered.

As they started towards the back of the house Missy Free ran to the front of the group.

"Baby, it's me baby, your Missy, it's me baby sweets" she started yelling at the top of her voice towards the back of the house.

WoodHenry thought that he was dreaming. But the voice was so real.

"Baby sweets" the voice called out again.

He was sure that God was punishing him, maybe even calling him into hell for what he had done. That was the only way that he could reconcile why he was smack dab in the middle of this vivid nightmare. The door to his room flew open and WoodHenry sat up in bed. He still couldn't be sure he wasn't dreaming. But then he saw her face. His very own Missy Free was there in his room. WoodHenry still couldn't quite believe his eyes.

"Baby I love you so," Missy moved towards him with arms open wide. WoodHenry still sat on the bed looking dumbfounded.

The force of her body combining with his weight on the old single bed proved too much, and as a result, there was the sound of cracking lumber as they both toppled to the floor.

"I thought you…." WoodHenry tried to say, but Missy wasn't wasting any time.

She was all over him, hugging and grabbing and planting kisses on his face like she was a sex machine gone amuck.

"I...I.... Baby..." WoodHenry tried to get a few words in amid the fast flurry of wild kisses.

"I thought you had left me" he finally said barely managing to catch his breath.

"No, Baby sweets, never, never, never in a million years," Missy said.

Suddenly WoodHenry was aware of other people standing in the room.

"Why are they here?" WoodHenry said looking apprehensive.

"They helped me find you" she told him as she rubbed her manicured hand over his head.

"But how did you know where I was?" WoodHenry said to Foster.

"Don't look at me, he brought me here" Foster said pointing to Hummingbird Moses.

"They the police," Mr. Hobbs' voice said from somewhere beyond the doorway.

"Where's the money?" Foster said to Missy Free. He was already thinking that the sooner he got his money, the sooner he would be able to get himself over to Minnie Patterson's place. The place where he could get himself some of her Hoodoo love.

But WoodHenry thought that Foster was talking to him. WoodHenry felt relieved that the police knew about the money. He figured Missy must have told them and now everything was alright. He was happy to have the chance to unload his burden to anyone, even to Foster.

"I ain't got it on me but...."

"Shut up". Missy told him.

"But...." WoodHenry started to say

Before he could get another word out, Missy Free slapped WoodHenry in the mouth so hard that he saw stars. But other than the stars he didn't seem to notice much. They say love is blind, maybe it numbs the senses as well.

"Don't you hit my first cousin you bitch" Foster blurted. He tried to take a threatening step forward toward Missy but lost his footing and tumbled head first on top of her and WoodHenry who were already on the floor.

Suddenly Missy Free looked around for her purse but it was not where it was supposed to be. When the bed broke the purse had fallen behind the bed. She spotted it and quickly grabbed it from the floor.

"I don't want no trouble with the police that's the only reason I let 'em in WoodHenry," Mr. Hobbs said.

"Police?" WoodHenry said looking up at Moses.

"He ain't nobody," Missy spat.

"I'm the somebody that got you here, so I want to be paid," Foster said to Missy Free as he struggled to rise to his feet.

"That's right" Moses echoed.

Missy quickly struggled to her feet. She turned her back to Foster and Moses and dug inside her purse to fish out the roll of money that she had separated previously for the occasion. But when she turned around to hand the money to Moses she was startled that the cabbie was now standing in the room.

"What the fuck you doing in here? You supposed to be waiting in the cab, motherfucker" she growled.

"You keep talking to me in that tone and I might forget to be a gentleman," the cabbie said. Missy started to size him up.

There was something threatening about the man. He didn't seem scared or nervous in any way. She felt that even if she had pulled the gun that she kept in her purse and aimed it at his heart, the cabbie would have been ready for anything, including hurting her. The cabbie hadn't said two good words, yet something about the man had taken over the room.

"You OK WoodHenry?" the cabbie inquired.

"Yeah I'm OK, who are you, the law?" WoodHenry asked.

"No."

"Lets get out of here" Missy said as she quickly pushed a wad of dollar bills into Foster's out-stretched hand.

But WoodHenry hadn't moved. He was still confused by everything.

"You have some very good friends who are worried about you" the cabbie said to WoodHenry.

"Who?" WoodHenry was more interested now that he realised that he may have more friends in the world.

"Friends? He ain't got no friends, except me," Missy Free was quick to interject. "Ain't that right Baby sweets?"

"You got a lady friend who knows you from Detroit, don't you WoodHenry" the cabbie said.

WoodHenry immediately knew who the cabbie was talking about.

"Yeah I do," he said.

"My name is Barnett" the cabbie said. "Your friend Honey Lavelle is a friend of mine too. She sent me looking for you."

WoodHenry looked Devil straight in the eye. His friend Honey must have known about his troubles. He started to feel ashamed already.

"Listen," Missy said with irritation in her voice as she eased her hand inside the purse.

"No you listen, if you go for what's in your purse I'm going to hurt you. I may even kill you so if I were you I would put that bag down and step over here while I talk to Mr. Taylor," Devil said raising his right hand from behind his thigh slightly to reveal the Baretta he held.

"She don't mean no harm, Mr. Barnett she just got kind of a tough way about her, that's all," WoodHenry said apologetically as Missy dropped the bag on the bed.

"As long as you're alright I'd like for you to make a call to our friend. Why don't you step over here and walk out in the next room, in case you want to talk privately," Devil suggested.

"Privately" the word exploded from Missy's delicate mouth. "He ain't got no private, I'm all the private he got and all he needs to have," she screamed as WoodHenry reached for Devil's cell phone.

Missy 's screeching stopped WoodHenry's arm in mid-air. He turned and looked at her like a lost puppy torn between life and death.

"Can I go now?" Foster interrupted turning to Devil and raising up a fist full of money. "I got what I came for."

"Don't you go getting amnesia on me now brother cause half of that money is mine," Hummingbird Moses chimed in.

Foster frowned at Moses. "I know, I know," Foster said as he started to count out Hummingbird Moses' half of the money.

"Speaking of money," Devil said turning to WoodHenry.

"I know, and I meant to give it back."

"Shut the hell up WoodHenry," Missy said then turned to Devil. "He don't know nothing about no money Mr., do you Baby sweets?" she said turning back to WoodHenry and trying to put the softness back into her voice, but it was too late. WoodHenry had started to wake up from the awful nightmare he had been living for the past few weeks. He just wanted it to all be over.

"I'm sorry sweet cakes, but I know that this is the right thing to do" he said turning to Missy.

"Goddamn fool" she said.

WoodHenry looked at her with sad eyes for a moment then he took the phone from Devil Barnett and walked out into the hallway.

"I'm gone like a turkey through the corn," Foster grinned. He handed Hummingbird Moses his share of Missy's reward money and stuffed the rest of it down into his pants pockets.

"You mind if I ask you for a favour?" Foster said turning to Devil, "I just need to get to my friend's house."

Devil's scornful expression answered in full.

"Never mind I'll walk" Foster said as he moved past the blind man towards the door.

"Hello, Honey this is WoodHenry, yeah baby, I'm still alive and kicking girl, yeah, thank you for worrying about me."

Missy frowned at the pleasure in his voice.

"There's been a little trouble, but thank the good Lord and your friend Mr. Barnett, it's all over now," WoodHenry said.

"Ain't that a bitch," Missy spat twisting her mouth into a scowl.

She wanted to grab her gun but didn't dare for fear that the cabbie would shoot her dead. Instead she stood in the corner of the room blowing angry air through her nostrils like some frustrated dragon that had lost it's ability to breathe fire.

Three minutes later, WoodHenry finished talking and passed the phone back to Devil.

"Yeah," Devil spoke into the mouthpiece with his eyes still glued to Missy Free. "Don't worry, I'll see you soon" Devil said and clicked off the call.

"So, what's it gonna be?" Devil Barnett said looking straight at WoodHenry.

"Baby sweets", said WoodHenry turning to Missy.

"Baby Sweets my ass. Don't you baby sweets me nigga, don't sweet talk me, I paid good money to find you and protect you, now you're deserting me, what kind of way is that to treat somebody you supposed to love" Missy said.

"But you didn't come to me, for three whole days. I thought you forgot about me" WoodHenry countered weakly.

"I couldn't I was too sick and in the hospital, I fainted on the street cause I'm pregnant. With your baby, man, " Missy told him.

"Really?" WoodHenry said. His face sprung to life.

"And don't you say nothing more about no money WoodHenry. You could go to jail you know" she said.

"But he won't be going alone will he?" Devil added.

"What the hell you talking about Mister?"

"Bonds, four million dollars worth," Devil said and looked at WoodHenry who seemed to melt under Devil's accusatory glare.

"Missy I can't lie no more, I got to tell him, I reckon he knows anyway" WoodHenry pleaded.

"He don't know shit, he's guessing," Missy insisted.

"Tom Jerrod, the man you stole the money from isn't guessing," Devil said.

Suddenly Missy was as confused as hell. The last thing she expected him to say was Tom's name.

"What about if I give him a call" Devil said.

"Do what the hell you like. I'm leaving" Missy said as she started to walk out of the room.

"Baby sweets, don't go, please don't go," WoodHenry pleaded.

"Either you coming with me or you're going with him. 'Cause if I walk outta' here after busting my ass to find you, I guarantee you will never see me again in this life. And you ain't going to never see your baby either. I'll make damn sure of that," Missy threatened.

WoodHenry looked as if he was ready to cry.

"Go on with her" Devil said to WoodHenry's surprise.

"Don't you worry Mr. Barnett, I'll call you first thing tomorrow. Me and Missy just got to straighten a few things out, but don't worry I won't disappear again. I'm going to straighten everything out you'll see," WoodHenry said.

"You take care of yourself WoodHenry" Devil said.

"Albalita ain't gonna like this at all," Old Man Hobbs said turning his face in the direction of WoodHenry's voice.

"I'll call her to explain things" WoodHenry said.

"Who the fuck is Albalita?" Missy wanted to know.

"Just a friend of mine. When I thought you left me, I came to her for help and she got me this room," WoodHenry explained like a child trying to talk his way out of a whipping.

"Man if you want me back, then you're going to have to show me something," Missy pouted.

"Like what?" WoodHenry asked.

"Like you won't run off again."

WoodHenry turned to Devil looking confused.

Devil wore a blank expression.

WoodHenry was a man torn between the devil and the deep blue sea of love.

"Where you two going?" Mr. Hobbs asked.

"Where we going?" Missy replied indignantly "We grown. We don't have to tell you a goddamn thing, you ain't nobody in authority."

"That's right," Devil said then turned to WoodHenry. "So what you want me to tell Albalita?"

"You know Albalita too?"

"Yes."

"She's a fine girl Miss Albalita, she gon' be real disappointed" Mr. Hobbs said.

"Yeah she sure is" WoodHenry agreed.

"Fuck her whoever the hell she is," Missy said.

"She tell you where I was hiding?" WoodHenry said ignoring Missy.

"No, I found out through somebody else" Devil said.

"Who?" Missy jumped in

"Don't worry about it. You found him, that's all you need, right" Devil remarked.

"Come on WoodHenry" Missy said and grabbed him by the hand.

"Don't worry Mr. Barnett I'll call you first thing in the morning. I'll straighten out this whole mess you'll see," WoodHenry promised as he was being pulled towards the front door.

Missy Free and WoodHenry walked along the street in silence until they reached the corner of the street. WoodHenry was glowing and walking on air. He was going to be a Daddy. Missy Free used her cell phone to call a taxi. The call was answered quickly and five minutes later WoodHenry and Missy climbed into the cab and headed back towards New York City.

Both Missy and WoodHenry were unaware of a blue car that followed the taxi at a safe distance.

Once back in New York, Missy Free stopped in at Smilers Deli on 54 and 7th Ave. She bought two sandwiches of hot roast beef and a large container of potato salad, dill pickles and three

Hershey candy bars. She also stopped at a nearby liquor store and bought a fifth of Johnny Walker black. Then the pair checked into the Warwick Hotel. While they ate WoodHenry tried to explain what had happened and what made him run away, but Missy said she wasn't interested. She told him that she was so glad to have him back that it didn't matter. That statement put a smile on WoodHenry's dumb features the size of the Mississippi river. After they had eaten and showered, Missy made sure that WoodHenry drank almost half of the scotch. Then they made love until WoodHenry was exhausted and dropped off into a deep coma-like sleep with a smile still on his face. As soon as he was snoring Missy Free got up, put on her clothes and went down stairs to the lobby of the hotel. She called Tom Jerrod on his cell phone at home. It was 3:42 in the morning

"Yeah" he answered drowsily.

"I found him," she said.

"How?" Tom Jerrod's voice was suddenly awake.

Before Missy could answer, Greta stirred next to him.

"Who is that Tom?" she asked.

"Just a call from overseas. Go back to sleep" he said. He then pulled himself out of bed and padded on bare feet into the next room still holding the cell phone to his ear.

Missy Free told Tom everything about finding WoodHenry including how the man named Barnett disguised as the cabbie got WoodHenry to talk on the phone to a woman named Honey who had been looking for him too.

Tom Jerrod took a seat on the sofa, stretched and took a deep breath.

"That's all very good baby, but we can't afford to let him start talking. If he starts telling everything he knows then both our boats are going to be sunk," he explained.

"l can take him out of town I know a place where nobody could find him and I won't let him out of my sight this time I promise," Missy said.

"No baby, I don't think you understand," Jerrod said purposely keeping his voice as low as possible. "I'm talking about something a little more permanent. I'll have to work things out in a way that no one will suspect. I'll get back to you and let you know how things should be done."

"OK" she said then hung up the phone.

Tom Jerrod kicked his bare feet up on the sofa and reached for a half smoked Cuban cigar in the nearby ashtray. He lit it and began to blow smoke rings in the air as he thought up the next part of his plan

"Who was that?"

The voice lanced his bubble of solitude and concentration.

His wife stood in the doorway watching him with a strained look on her face.

"Who was that Tom?" Greta Jerrod demanded again.

"I told you it was a call from overseas, England. Go back to bed," he said trying to keep the growing irritation from his voice.

"It's almost four in the morning, it was that woman wasn't it?"

"Stop being jealous of nothing Greta" he scolded.

"Are you having an affair Tom? Please, just be honest with me," she pleaded.

"No Greta, now go back to bed."

Greta Jerrod turned and without another word went back into the bedroom. Once back in the bed, she thought about Tom Jerrod, the man she loved in the arms of another woman and gently cried herself to sleep.

CHAPTER 25

BOBBY JONES WAS dead to the world when his cell phone rang. He turned over in his bed and looked at the clock by his bedside. It read 4:10am.

"Who the fuck could that be?" Bobby said to himself as he reached for the phone. He had only gone to bed an hour before. It had to be some woman.

"Yeah" he answered roughly.

"Can you talk?" was all the male voice said.

"Who is this?" Bobby answered.

"Tom Jerrod."

Bobby struggled to sit up in bed and clear the sleep from his head all in one motion.

"Uh, not really," Bobby said thinking about Brax in the next room and Nicolli who was asleep down the hall in the third bedroom.

"Can you listen then?"

"Yeah" Bobby whispered.

"I want you to get to a place where you can call me back on my cell phone as soon as possible, like in five or ten minutes."

"OK" Bobby replied and the connection went dead.

Bobby eased out of bed and dressed himself. As he pulled on his jacket he decided that that he would take everything he needed to travel just in case he had to leave suddenly because of Tom Jerrod's conversation. He filled his pockets with car keys, wallet and the three fake identification cards he always carried. He smiled to himself and thought of being one step closer to a cool million bucks.

Bobby approached the doorway of his room and stood quietly for a while listening for any other sounds in the cabin. All he could hear was snoring coming from down the hall in Nicolli's room. Then he strained his ear in the direction of Brax's room and there was total silence. Like a thief walking on eggshells he crossed the room and slipped out into the night. When he had walked down the gravel pathway that led up to the cabin he took a left turn and went towards the woods about twenty yards away. He checked over his shoulder to make sure no one had heard him go out, then he called Tom Jerrod's cell phone number.

"Yeah Mr. Jerrod" Bobby said.

"Listen I've got a problem, WoodHenry Taylor has turned up" Jerrod said.

Bobby didn't know what to say. Fuck. His cool million had just gone up in smoke.

"Why is that a problem? I thought that's what you wanted," Bobby countered.

"That was then and this is now. Things change. All you need to know is this. I don't need him walking around talking to people, so I'd like to arrange to have him........"

There was suddenly silence on the line.

"You mean you want him dead," Bobby said.

"Yes."

"That's a tall order Mr. Jerrod, I mean that kind of thing is not exactly what I do."

"Would another let's say half million make a difference?"

A million and a half. Damn, Bobby thought.

"I'll give you a down payment tomorrow and the rest when the job is completed. But I want you to do this thing exactly as I tell you to so nothing points back to me," Jerrod said.

"Yeah, no sweat." Bobby was thinking that WoodHenry was already a dead man.

"I'll call you around 11:00am tomorrow to fill you in on the plan. Be at a place where we can talk without interruptions."

Bobby said "OK" and clicked off the call.

"A mil and a half," Bobby said out loud and grinned.

Maybe he would ask for a hundred grand in his hand, tomorrow. Bobby suddenly felt a jolt of adrenaline shoot through his body like he had just sniffed some first rate cocaine. For a mil and a half, he would figure a way to make an excuse for not being there when Brax and Nicolli woke up in the morning.

"Fuck 'em" he thought as he looked towards the rustic cabin at the top of the gravel driveway. Every light was still out. Last night he had been the last to arrive back at the cabin, so the car he had rented was nearest to the road. He figured that he would take the emergency hand brake off and silently roll the car back into the street until it was well away from the house before he started the engine. Bobby fingered the car keys in his pocket and walked in a slow and easy motion back towards the car. He unlocked the door on the driver's side and bent over the seat to release the emergency hand brake.

"Where you going Little Nigga?" The voice assaulted him like a red hot knife in his side. He jumped up so quickly that he banged his head hard against the sill of the car door. Automatically he reached under his jacket for his snub nosed 38 pistol.

But his motion was stopped when a strong hand grabbed his arm. The hand squeezed it so hard it paralysed his movement. When he gained his bearings, he realised that Brax was standing in front of him.

"Nigger, what you doin'?" Bobby protested as Brax loosened his strongman grip enough for him to wriggle free.

"Where you goin'?" Brax inquired.

"I wasn't going nowhere," Bobby said catching his breath and rubbing the pain in the top of his head .

"I heard something out here, I thought I'd better come see," Brax said.

"We'll it's me Goddammit, I couldn't sleep and I forgot my cigarettes," Bobby said

"Oh."

When Bobby got back into the cabin he was surprised to see Nicolli sitting on the sofa wide awake. He was in his dressing gown.

"Thought we heard a burglar" he said crossing his skinny pink legs on the cocktail table and looking slyly at Bobby.

"Sorry about that, I didn't mean to wake you guys up," Bobby said.

"How about some coffee" Brax said.

Nicolli just looked impassive and smoothed his dark hair back over his skull with one of his girlish hands.

"Yeah," Bobby said. We would have agreed to anything not to be in the same room with these two crazy low life bastards. In the kitchen Bobby started running water from the tap into a saucepan.

Bobby called from the kitchen "Instant OK?" He was thinking about making his great escape. Tomorrow he would be on his way to being a rich man. Rich and far away from Brax the psycho and the monster with little girl's hands.

"Sure," Brax replied.

"Tell me something Mr. Jones," Nicolli said with sleep still in his voice.

"What's that?" said Bobby trying to sound as normal as possible.

"Tell me about your progress on looking for Mr. Taylor," he said.

"Mr. Nicolli, we went over that already tonight, remember?" Bobby said raising his voice enough to travel into the other room as he placed the saucepan full of water on the burner and turned the flame to the high position.

"I do but I thought maybe there were some things you may have forgotten, you know it's always better to go over these things again and again. Sometimes the smallest overlooked detail can lead to something," Nicolli called back.

Bobby yelled again "I went over everything, honest Mr. Nicolli."

"You didn't tell us what you talked about when you spoke to your wife" Brax said sitting down at the kitchen table.

"I told you that before," Bobby said belligerently.

"I know what you told us, but you didn't tell us about the fun part" Brax leered.

"What fun part?"

"About how y'all plan to get together and burn the sheets up," Brax laughed.

"Man you crazy, it's all over between us, has been for years," Bobby said.

"So you say, but that's kind of hard to believe. Man if I ever had married me a fine woman like that, and especially if I had a kid with her, you can best believe that I would still be sliding my dick up inside of her until she cried from pleasure and pain, hah hah," Brax laughed tauntingly.

"Well you ain't me OK, stupid motherfucker" Bobby spat before he realised it.

"Who you calling stupid motherfucker" Brax said glaring in Bobby's direction.

"I told you what happened, so why you keep going over the same shit," Bobby said. He purposely changed his tone and tried to make what he was saying sound apologetic. The last thing he needed was a fight with a psychopath. Bobby could tell from Brax's demeanour that he was about two minutes from wanting to fight.

Brax was thinking about giving Bobby a jab in the mouth when something happened inside his head. He suddenly decided that he would enjoy annoying Bobby more by playing with his mind than he would by kicking his ass. All the while Nicolli sat listening in the other room like a bloated gila monster soaking up the sun.

"Tell you what I think Lil Nigga, I think you must still be in love with her," Brax started again. Bobby pretended he was engrossed in getting the cups from the cupboard and the spoons from the cutlery drawer.

"What makes you think that?" Bobby said trying hard to maintain his cool.

"'Cause every time I talk about fucking her you get upset," Brax said.

"I ain't getting nothing, I just told you what happened that's all, and you keep……"

"Keep what?" Brax interrupted.

"Come on man just drop it" Bobby urged.

"I ain't droppin' shit, all I said was, I sure would like to fuck your ex-wife who you ain't suppose to have nothing more to do with, so why should you care," Brax grinned pinning Bobby with his psycho jailhouse bully grin.

"I don't care, it ain't my business," Bobby said turning his attention to the saucepan of water that had just started to boil.

"OK, if you don't still love her and if you don't care then why don't you make a call and arrange for me to meet her. I betcha' she would like a big long dick like I got," Brax said.

"Man you talking crazy, you ain't hardly her type," Bobby laughed

"What that shit supposed to mean?" Brax said.

"It just means she goes for a different type of man that's all."

"You mean a man like you huh? A man scared to get his hands dirty, a man scared to take chances, a man scared to kill a motherfucker even when they fuck wid you. That the kind of man she like, a pussy man? I think she might like a fuck from a real man wid real balls," Brax chided.

"What she likes is a man with a fucking brain, OK."

"Motherfucker you think you so much smarter, let's see how smart you are when I kick your ass," Brax said suddenly standing up.

"Gentlemen let's keep this professional" Nicolli said. He was standing in the doorway to the kitchen now watching the pair. He looked at Brax the way a disapproving parent looks at a child and accordingly Brax sat back down in the chair.

"I believe Mr. Braxton may be feeling somewhat annoyed because he thinks that you might have been holding out on us Mr. Jones. Would you be kind enough to make mine with honey rather than sugar please" Nicolli said all in the same breath.

"Holding out how?" Bobby said.

"You look all dressed to go somewhere tonight, maybe there's something you forgot to tell us" Nicolli said.

"I told you everything that happened and if you don't believe me, what can I do."

"Don't you back talk Mr. Nicolli nigga. You just lissen when he talkin to you," Brax growled like a junkyard dog.

"What about today around lunchtime, what did you do?"

Shit, Bobby knew he was trapped. Even before he got his mouth ready to lie he could feel the beads of nervous sweat forming at the top of his head.

"What do you mean?" Bobby said licking his lips and adjusting his glasses.

"Someone said they saw someone who looked exactly like you in the financial district in the Wall Street area. In fact I believe it was in the very same building where Tom Jerrod has his offices."

Fear suddenly flashed through Bobby's mind like a bolt of lightning. His next move was automatic. His hand reached for the pot of boiling water. From the corner of his eye he saw Brax leaning forward, ready to move towards him, but fear of dying had given his movement precision. Before Brax could stand up Bobby flung the scalding water into his face.

"Ahhhh......." Brax fell backwards crashing into the wall. At the same moment Bobby bolted forward straight towards Nicolli. The surprise of the impact knocked Nicolli to the floor and caused Bobby to stumble and trip as he made his way towards the front door.

He desperately twisted the doorknob, but it was locked. He turned the latch that secured the door and flung it wide open when he heard a sharp crack. The sound coincided with a hot flash of pain at the back of his neck. Bobby tried to move forward but couldn't. It was as if he was suddenly moving in slow motion. He managed to lift his foot. He was still moving forward when another crack sounded. This time the pain flashed in his back. Bobby stumbled outside and fell forward.

Lying in the driveway fighting to catch his breath, Bobby Jones sensed images from his life flashing through his mind. So many images. Him as a little boy. His mother walking with him on the first day of school. Playing basketball and scoring the winning basket as a teenager. Making love to a woman in the backseat of a car. Meeting the young beautiful jazz vocalist Miss Honey Lavelle. The birth of his son. Snorting cocaine. The police taking him from the courtroom. His wife and mother crying. Sitting in a jail cell. Watching the killing of a prostitute. Then nothingness.

Mr. Nicolli slowly walked out of the cabin door onto the circular gravel driveway. Brax stumbled out behind him still holding his face. Nicolli looked down at Bobby on the ground. He pointed a gun at Bobby's head and pulled the trigger three more times.

"I wish I had killed him," Brax growled peeping through his fingers which he still held tightly against his burning face.

"Dead is dead Mr. Braxton" Nicolli simply said and turned back towards the house.

"Motherfuckin' traitor" Brax cursed and spat on Bobby's corpse. Brax dropped to the ground still clutching his face in agony as the burning sensation seemed to re-ignite inside his flesh.

"We'll need to get you to a doctor. I'll make a call to have Mr. Jones' remains taken care of," Nicolli said as he re-entered the house.

Brax didn't hear him fully. The pain had all but blocked out the cognitive part of his senses.

"Well, well, well, it seems we have a small problem" Mr. Nicolli started talking to himself in a small almost inaudible voice as he began pacing the room.

Pacing and talking to himself was an old habit he had started as a boy when he had been forced to live as a fugitive in the hills of Turkey. He would talk to the wind. As he talked things would seem to get clearer in his head.

"It was unfortunate that Mr. Jones had to die in such an inefficient manner. I'm sure just a small bit of torture would have been so much more effective. Still all is not lost. He still has an ex-wife that I'm sure knows something worth knowing. Maybe they were even in the plan with Tom Jerrod together. I mustn't worry because there are many ways to find out these things," Mr. Nicolli said to himself.

CHAPTER 26

I ADMIT I FELT good about finding WoodHenry. Maybe that's why my mood was so upbeat when I took the elevator up to Honey's apartment.

I had been thinking about the private investigator that Jerrod had asked me to check out. I figured that it probably did have something to do with WoodHenry but that he wanted to play that part of it close to his vest. Anyway I had done what I'd set out to do which was finding WoodHenry.

I figured that I would check out this Nicolli guy, tell Jerrod what I found but then tell him I wasn't interested in continuing on the case.

I still had Jerrod's money in my pocket, so I figured that I was ahead of the game.

I knocked on the door and waited for about a minute before Honey answered.

"Congratulations Youngblood, and thank you" she said and hugged me as I entered the room.

"You don't have to thank me, I was just doing a friend a favour" I said handing her the flowers and bottle of wine that I was holding behind my back.

"Wow, I should be the one giving you flowers, you did all the work."

"Yeah, but it was you who,,,"

"Me who did what?" she cut me off and smiled.

"Well it was you who caused him to be found and probably saved his life."

"You think whoever it was that set him up really wanted to kill him?"

"Yes, I think they probably still do."

"Then congratulations isn't exactly what we should be talking about then?" she said as a worried look crossed her face.

"No, I think he's alright for now."

"Where is he?"

"With his girlfriend in the Warwick Hotel."

"Think he's safe there?" she asked.

"At least there I can have someone keep an eye on him. Francisco is there."

"He's so crazy about her that he would follow her anyplace huh?" Honey asked.

"That's about the size of it " I confirmed.

She sat down on the couch and crossed her legs under her. I sat next to her.

"So what's the next move?"

"I'm just going to let the other side make their move and see how it plays."

"So in other words you let WoodHenry go with her because you want to use him as bait."

"Yeah."

"Don't you think that kind of thing could get him killed?"

"It could, but if I tried to keep him from that woman sooner or later he would run off looking for her and then we would be right back where we started. Then there would be even more chance of them getting to him," I explained.

"What do you think she plans to do?"

"I'm not 100 percent sure but I have an idea, or at least I think I do."

"I hope you're right about all this."

"I hope I am too."

"Did he say anything about the money he was suppose to have stolen?"

"He wanted to, but his woman wouldn't let him."

"Which means she knows about the money too."

"Exactly. My feeling is if she knows about the bonds then she may know who killed Spongey and Elvira too. The unfortunate thing is, when the news about this money comes to light, WoodHenry is going to be a prime suspect in the death of Elvira" I said.

"Why?"

"As the common law husband, the police are going to figure that Elvira may have known about the theft and maybe was threatening to tell somebody, and to keep her quiet WoodHenry might have put her out of her misery."

"But you don't think...."

"No, WoodHenry's not a killer, not for money anyway," I said glibly.

"What do you mean by that?"

"For love maybe, but not money."

"You think he could kill for love, you think he loves this woman that much?" Honey asked as her face drew into a scowl.

"Yeah I do" I said.

"So how long do you think it's going to be before the theft comes to light?"

"It should have happened already, but it hasn't."

"And why do you think that is?" she asked

"There could be a number of reasons," I said.

"That you don't want to elaborate on?"

"Not just yet, but I should have a pretty good idea in the next day or two."

"So you think until then WoodHenry will be safe with this woman?"

"I think he'll be OK. Besides if she makes a move for the money, Francisco will see that too."

"All this money doesn't seem to phase you, anyone else I know would be hungry to make WoodHenry tell so that he could get to the money first."

"I'm not saying four million doesn't sound good, but the money wasn't the reason I got involved in the first place. So I feel a lot more comfortable just sticking with things the way they started."

"You came this far OK, Youngblood, so I guess whatever you're doing is working. Anyway I trust you," she said.

"Thanks."

"Oh by the way, I heard something that I thought you might like so I bought it for you" she said and walked over to the CD player in the corner of the room.

She pressed a few buttons and smiled at me over her shoulder. As she walked to the centre of the room, Randy Crawford started to sing "Rio de Janeiro Blue."

"You like Randy Crawford?" she asked.

"I love Randy Crawford. But you knew that already, right?"

"Yeah" she laughed and started to sway back and forth to the music.

"Come on" she said holding her arms open.

"What?" I said feigning ignorance of her intentions.

"Don't play dumb with me, you know what I want. Come on

dance with me."

"Honey, I don't dance."

"What?" She stopped moving.

"I don't dance," I repeated

"Why not?"

"Well...I..." I felt like I was about eight years old.

"Well what?"

"The truth is, I never learned, I've got two left feet."

"Have you ever tried?"

"Not really."

"Well it's never too late you know, come on" she said then took my hands and started to pull me towards her.

"OK, I'll try, but don't laugh."

"Okay just put your arm here" she said guiding my arm around her firm waistline. "Don't be afraid man, get close, I'm not trying to seduce you, you know. I'm just showing you how to dance, that is unless you are just faking. I wouldn't put it past you."

"No I just never learned, honest" I said still embarrassed.

"Just relax and follow me. One, two, one, two, just feel it and flow with it Youngblood. I bet you've broken lots of hearts in your day with that cool elusive way of yours," Honey said.

"Don't think so, but maybe I could have if I had known how to dance," I quipped as I swayed awkwardly to the rhythm of Randy's smooth delicate voice.

"As much as you love music, how is it you never learned to dance?"

"Guess I just never got around to learning the steps" I admitted.

"Youngblood you keep surprising me," Honey grinned as she eased my body into the proper flow of the music.

"Tell you what, you give me lessons in how to play chess and I'll give you dance lessons" she said.

"You think that's a fair trade? You might need a new pair of feet after I finish stepping on them" I told her.

"Don't worry about me, I can handle myself, even with a clumsy man."

"Why is it that I believe you?" I laughed.

I stumbled forward suddenly as I felt the music change.

"What's wrong?" she asked.

"I think I lost the beat." I stammered.

"Don't tell me you're getting all hot and bothered over an older woman like myself Youngblood" she smiled.

"Listen woman" I said feeling embarrassed again, "I'm going to sit myself down on that couch and have a glass of wine before I make a complete fool of myself."

Without another word she simply followed me back to the sofa and started pouring the wine. We spent the next half hour talking about WoodHenry, about Sonia, about her job, about her son Harold.

"Harold was the only good thing that came from me and Bobby's union. I do hope he grows up to be a serious man like you Youngblood," she said.

"That's one of the nicest compliments I've ever been given."

"I've been around men all my life, she said "all kinds of men and I can say without a doubt that special guys like you only come along once in a deep blue moon."

CHAPTER 27

THE DARK OLIVE-SKINNED Turk waited at the end of the computer science building walkway. He watched the students file past and checked their faces against the photograph of the young black man he obtained from the woman who worked in the college administration office. She had given it to him after he had flashed his fake I.D. and told her that he was a plain clothes detective working undercover in the drugs unit of the State Police Department.

He had also told the woman that if she refused to co-operate and told anyone of his request that he would see that the political powers that be would made sure that she lost her job. Needless to say she provided him with everything that he wanted including the off campus housing address and phone number where the young man lived. She even provided the names of his friends with whom he played on the college basketball team. The olive skinned man recognized the face on the photograph when the young black man exited the building. When the young man headed for home, the olive skinned man followed at a safe distance. He was masterful at following people.

When the young man reached his residence, the olive-skinned man called his boss and spoke in Turkish. He reported that all was going according to schedule.

Ten minutes later, he walked up to the young man's residence. The person who answered the door was not the young man the Turk wanted but rather the young man's roommate.

"I'm looking for Harold Jones" the Turk said in his most official voice.

"Just a moment," the roommate said.

When Harold Jones appeared at the door a few seconds later, the man flashed his phoney identification again.

"My name is Sergeant Kurkesha from the state drug enforcement agency. Do you have a classmate named Fred

Jackson?" the olive skinned man asked.

"Yes, we're on the basketball team together," Harold replied.

"It seems that Fred Jackson was beaten up pretty badly today. We suspect that some drug dealers on the campus might have been responsible. We have an eyewitness to the beating who might have I.D.ed one of the men running from the scene of the crime. We would like you to come down to the station and look at a few mug shots to see if you might have seen any one fitting the description of two men we think might have done it. We think they also may have been selling drugs on campus. We're hoping that maybe you've seen some of these men around campus. All of this will be kept confidential of course," the Turk said.

"Sure just give me a minute" Harold replied and disappeared from the doorway.

The man lit a turkish cigarette as he waited.

Within a minute or so young Harold was back at the door wearing his autumn jacket.

"I'm sure your friend Fred will appreciate this," the Turk said as Harold followed him around the corner to a side street where he had parked his car.

As Harold walked to the driver's side to get into the car he didn't notice the man reaching under his jacket. Just as Harold bent down to seat himself in the car the Turk swung a five pound sap that connected with the back of Harold's head. Harold stumbled forward as the Turk pushed him through the open passenger's door.

The Turk quickly checked that young Harold was unconscious and then walked coolly around to the driver's side of the car. Within minutes he was driving south down the Merrick Parkway. His destination was a place in Harlem where he had been ordered to go. The Turk figured that the young man on the passenger's side wouldn't come around for at least another hour. He called his boss again.

"I got him" the Turk said.

"Was there any trouble?" Nicolli asked.

"No."

"OK , I'll see you within the hour."

During the next hour Nicolli read the newspaper and thought about what he was going to do. Between the sports and the financial pages a thought came to him. He used his cell phone to dial the person who had brought him into this situation.

"Hello" Nicolli said when the woman's voice answered the phone. "Mrs. Jerrod, it's Nicolli can you talk?"

"Yes I can."

"I wanted to see if there has been any news from your end."

"It seems that's a question that I should be asking you," she said with irritation.

"I think I'm very close to finding something."

"Something like what?"

"The missing money of course," Nicolli said.

"And the woman?"

Nicolli was silent.

"Well Mr. Nicolli?" Greta Jerrod said sharply.

"I haven't had much luck in that area" he stated.

"That's an understatement isn't it. You came highly recommended but up until now the only thing I've had from you is excuses. I hired you to do two things; to find out who my husband was having an affair with, and two to find the person that stole those bonds from my family's company."

"I understand fully Mrs. Jerrod. Please try to be a little patient and we will have something for you shortly," Nicolli said.

"Let's hope so, otherwise, I'm going to hire someone else."

Nicolli put down the phone and started to ponder his dilemma. He had come up with a blank on any woman Tom Jerrod was involved with. Both his office phones had been illegally tapped and he had been followed for the past two weeks and not the slightest trace of any secret woman in his life. Only problem was, Jerrod's cell phone calls went unmonitored because he had bought his cell phone through a special company that charged a premium to make sure it's clients cell calls both incoming and outgoing remained untraceable. Though he had struck out on the love angle, Nicolli did feel he was getting closer to the money. The only other way was to grab Tom Jerrod and torture him until he told all that his wife wanted to know. If it came to that he was prepared to do it.

A few minutes later his Turkish henchman called on the cell phone to announce his arrival. The Turk drove into the warehouse and pulled the young man who was still unconscious from the car.

"In there," Nicolli ordered as the Turk flung the young man over his shoulder like he weighed little more than a shoulder bag.

The Turk took Harold inside a small room equipped with only a small iron bed and two chairs. Nicolli held smelling salts under the young man's nose until he came around.

"Listen we didn't bring you here to hurt you, that is unless you choose not to co-operate. What we want you to do is to call your mother," he said extending the cell phone towards Harold.

Harold took in the small ugly features of this stranger who smoked a cigarette as he spoke. Right away he noticed that the man's hands didn't seem to fit with the rest of his body. They were young and delicate like a girl's.

"My mother?" young Harold Jones said.

"Yes," Nicolli said.

"But why?" Harold said. At that moment the Turk stepped into the room and closed the door behind him.

"I'll tell you why" Nicolli said and nodded to the Turk.

Without a word the Turk stepped forward and slapped Harold across the face so hard that blood started to pour from his nose.

"There's going to be a lot more of that if you keep asking questions," the smallish ugly white man assured Harold as he handed him the cell phone.

Harold's mind was full of fear and confusion as he dialled his mother's number.

"Hello" he said when his mother's voice came on.

"Mom," Harold said in a strained voice.

Nicolli took the phone from him.

"Miss Lavelle, Miss Honey Lavelle?" Nicolli said.

"Yes," Honey answered.

"We have your son with us. At this point he's safe, but he won't be in another hour if you don't do exactly as I say. I want you to go downstairs right now and stand in front of your building. Within a few minutes a man with a white bandage covering part of his face driving a black Lincoln Town Car will be there to bring you to where your son is being held. Needless to say if you alert anyone, like the police or even your friend Mr. Barnett, then I will kill your son, do you understand?" Nicolli said

"Yes I understand," Honey said

CHAPTER 28

IT WAS ABOUT 8:30pm and I was relaxing at home when the phone rang. It was Hummingbird Moses.

"Hey Doctor you know you told me to keep an eye out on your pretty young lady. Well I was doing just that, when she came downstairs and got into a black Lincoln Continental Town Car with a guy who has his head rapped up in a bandage. She looked worried" he said.

"How long ago?"

"Just two minutes ago. I'm in a cab following them now. I called her on her cell phone but she don't answer. I can see her up ahead though."

"OK stay in the cab behind them and I'll catch up with you." I said jumping up to put on my jacket.

Sounded like somebody was making a move. I called Francisco who was at the Warwick Hotel and told him what I had just been told. Then just to be on the safe side I told him to bring WoodHenry with him to meet me. I didn't want to chance losing him again. I called Honey on her cell phone but just like Moses said she didn't answer.

*****

Charles Glenhaven sat in his squad car in South Brooklyn thinking about the birthday party he would have for his five year old son. This was his third year on the New York City police force and he was planning to take the detective's exam within the next six months. He prided himself on being alert and insightful, all of the qualities he believed would make him a good detective. He wished his father could see him now. His father had been a cop too, and had always wanted him to be a cop but young Charles like so many other sons growing up had turned away from his father's profession.

After putting in twenty-three years on the force, one day Charles Glenhaven Sr. was pulling traffic duty of all things when he was killed by a hit and run driver who was high on PCP. The next year Charles Glenhaven Jr. signed up for the Police Academy. Maybe it was his wanting to make his old man proud.

Glenhaven noticed the black Lincoln Town car being driven by a man that had his face half covered by what looked like a bandage. Maybe it was his natural detective's instinct that made him start his engine and pull into the traffic behind the Town Car. He routinely called in the license plate number and found that the car had been rented. Through the back window, he could see someone on the passenger's side. A woman. He pulled to the side of the Town Car and looked over. The man behind the wheel didn't notice him. How could he, the left side of his face was covered. Charles Glenhaven decided that he would pull the guy over to caution him. The cop reasoned that the driver had a blind side which could result in running someone down the same way someone had run down his old man.

He flashed his lights and told the driver of the Town Car to pull over. The Town Car slowed and pulled over into a small side street. Charles Glenhaven ever mindful of his police training got out of his squad car cautiously. He had the strap to his revolver holster undone just in case he had to pull out his gun.

"Sir, may I see your license and registration?" Officer Glenhaven asked.

The last thing he was expected was what happened. The man reached inside his jacket, pulled a gun and shot Charles Glenhaven twice in the face.

*****

I had almost reached Brooklyn Bridge when my phone rang.

"That crazy fool who picked up Honey just shot a cop," Hummingbird Moses said.

"You still see him?" I asked.

"No, he got away. The cab driver was following him but after he shot the cop the taxi driver got scared and stopped. But I saw the car pull into the Old Brooklyn Navy Yard. There is no way out from this direction, so he's still inside, but there are lots of places he can hide" Moses said.

"Thanks, I'm almost there" I said then called Ross Lambert at the Police Precinct up in Harlem.

"Ross, I just heard about a cop being shot near the Old Brooklyn Navy Yard, the shooter was driving a Black Lincoln Town Car plate number TG99846"

"Thanks, how'd you hear about it?" he asked

"One of my people was following the car and saw it happen."

"Think he may be willing to talk to us?" he asked.

"One hand washes the other," I said

"Good, so what can I do for you?" Ross asked.

"For the moment, just follow up and tell me anything you can find out about the car."

"I'll get back to you," Ross Lambert said and clicked off.

I called Francisco and asked him how things were going.

"Just about to do it now" he said.

*****

Francisco adjusted the bellboy's jacket on his body. It was a very snug fit but it would have to do. He had managed to steal the jacket from the laundry cart of the hotel supply room. He walked into the hotel kitchen and picked up a fruit basket from one of the large steam tables. No one questioned his action because he looked like just another one of the many Latino workers going about their chores. He took the elevator up to the fourth floor and knocked on the door of room 428.

"Who is it?" a woman's voice called.

"Hotel management" Francisco answered.

A few seconds later Missy Free answered the door.

"Compliments of the management Ma'am" Francisco said making his Spanish accent distinctively heavier and placing the fruit basket in front of him.

As she opened the door and extended her hand for the basket, Francisco quickly stepped into the room and hit her squarely in the jaw. Missy Free fell backwards and stumbled to the floor. But before she could recover, Francisco grabbed her head and expertly held a cloth filled with chloroform against her nose and mouth. In less than two seconds she was unconscious. He carried her over to the bed and pulled up the covers almost over her head. Missy's cell phone was on the night stand. Francisco picked it up, pressed a button to make the number of the phone appear on the screen. He then copied the number down into a notebook which he pulled from inside his shirt pocket.

From the bathroom he could hear a male voice singing. WoodHenry's muse was working overtime.

Music Track # 8
WONDERFUL LIGHT

There was a time that I felt so low,
I had nowhere to go,
I was barely holding on,
All of my hope was gone.
Then you came, turned my world around
Then you came, helped me put my feet back on the ground
With your love inside of me, everything is right,
Now that I am walking in your light.
WALKING IN YOUR WONDERFUL LIGHT
WALKING IN YOUR WONDERFUL LIGHT
WALKING IN, TALKING IN, LIVING IN AND LOVING IN,
WALKING IN YOUR WONDERFUL LIGHT

Deep, deep in my soul, my spirit broke, my heart said no,
The smile was always running from my face.
Life was a gloomy place.
Then you came, opened up the door
Then you came, you convinced me there was something more
With your love inside of me everything is right,
Now that I am walking in your light.
WALKING IN YOUR WONDERFUL LIGHT
(you made me love somebody)
WALKING IN YOUR WONDERFUL LIGHT
(Yes you did)
WALKING IN, TALKING IN, LIVING IN AND LOVING IN,
WALKING IN YOUR WONDERFUL LIGHT

I was confused, I was searching for
An open door to escape the pain inside my heart,
Didn't know where to start.
Then you came and opened up the door
Then you came, suddenly you were that something more,

With your love inside of me everything is bright,
Now that I am walking in your light.
WALKING IN YOUR WONDERFUL LIGHT
WALKING IN YOUR WONDERFUL LIGHT
WALKING IN, TALKING IN, LIVING IN AND LOVING IN,
WALKING IN YOUR WONDERFUL LIGHT

From the cracked door Francisco could see inside the bathroom. WoodHenry was taking a shower. Francisco stepped inside and pulled back the shower curtain.

"Wahhh" WoodHenry screamed, jumping back and nearly slipping off his feet.

"Don't worry everything is OK Mr. Taylor, I was sent to get you."

"Sent by who?" he asked suspiciously.

"Mr. Barnett sent me to get you because your life as well as the life of your friend Honey Lavelle might be in danger."

"Danger, where's Missy?"

"Asleep," Francisco said, then added "I'll explain things to you on the way but we have to leave now. Right now."

WoodHenry quickly dressed, careful not to wake Missy. He kissed her gently on the forehead then grabbed his songwriting notebook and followed Francisco out of the hotel. As Francisco steered the car through the night WoodHenry thought about Missy Free and how much in love he still was with her despite what she had done to him. He figured that they could stay together if only he could prove to her how much he loved her. His plan was to convince her that even if they did give the money back and he just worked a regular job that they would never have to worry about anything. Security, that's what he figured she really needed, like most women. Since he had always been able to express his feeling better through song, he decided that he would write it all down and present it to her at the right moment. He then fished out a sheet of paper and pen from his jacket pocket. As always his old friend Euterpe, the daughter of Zeus and the muse of music and lyric poetry was available for him inside his head. She breathed and musical vibrations began to flow through WoodHenry onto the paper as if by magic.

By the time the car reached 23rd Street WoodHenry was absentmindedly tapping his fingers against the his knee and singing a soulful tune to himself.

Music Track # 9
NEVER WALK OUT ON YOU

I'LL NEVER WALK OUT ON YOU
I'LL NEVER WALK OUT ON YOU
I'LL NEVER WALK AWAY
I'M HERE TO STAY SO BABY
RELAX AND ENJOY THE RIDE
CAUSE THIS IS A REAL BONIFIDE
LOVE RELATIONSHIP AND I AIN'T GONNA SLIP

(dancehall rap)

We've had our ups and downs but I'm still here,
My actions speak for me, let's make it clear.
You are my woman I made a vow
The love we got is here and now.
The past is gone so why you bother comparin me,
Cause I ain't your baby father, (no no no no)

I'LL NEVER WALK OUT ON YOU
I'LL NEVER WALK OUT ON YOU
I'LL NEVER WALK AWAY
I'M HERE TO STAY SO BABY
RELAX AND ENJOY THE RIDE
CAUSE THIS IS A REAL BONIFIDE
LOVE RELATIONSHIP AND I AIN'T GONNA SLIP

All of the he-say and the she-say that's been going around,
I don't buy it don't you try it
I ain't gonna let that get me down
Your skanky girfriend's been lyin' and I got her sussed,
She's just jealous of what we got
That's why she's tryin' to start some shit between us

(dancehall rap)

No, No, No, No, No, No No No
No, No, No, No, No, No No No

I'm here to stay so baby
No, No, No, No, No, No No No
No, No, No, No, No, No No No
I'm here to stay so baby

I'LL NEVER WALK OUT ON YOU
I'LL NEVER WALK OUT ON YOU
I'LL NEVER WALK AWAY
I'M HERE TO STAY SO BABY
RELAX AND ENJOY THE RIDE
CAUSE THIS IS A REAL BONIFIDE
LOVE RELATIONSHIP AND I AIN'T GONNA SLIP

I was on the telephone with Ross Lambert.

"Mr. Barnett you're right on the money, the ambulance is picking up the shot cop now. Thanks. The car you wanted was hired from a company in Long Island under the name of Arial Insurance Investigations. The guy who signed the credit card for it was a M. Nicolli," Ross said.

"How's the cop?" I asked.

"Critical. He took it in the neck and head. We got an APB out on the asshole shooter for attempted murder. As soon as he can talk, if he is ever able to talk, we'll work up a face on the perp. Anything else you need?" Ross asked.

"Not for the moment thanks."

"Any idea where the perp might be headed?" Ross added.

"My man saw him turn the car around so my guess would be Jersey, at least that way he would be out of New York's jurisdiction," I said deliberately lying.

He said "thanks" and clicked off the call.

I met Hummingbird Moses near the Navy Yard and waited for Francisco to show. I had stopped not far from where the shooting of the cop had occurred. The area around the crime scene was blocked off but in the distance I could still see the police conducting their investigation. While I waited I felt that old thing returning. That old unmistakable feeling. I had known it so many times before. The demons of death. Moving inside me like a cat easing it's way towards a bird's nest at the top of a tree, thirsty for the taste of blood. Somebody was going to die.

A few minutes later Francisco pulled up with WoodHenry.

"You got the sensor?" I asked referring to the bracelet we had asked Honey to wear, just in case something like this should happen.

"Yes" Francisco said. He turned on the tracking device and starting looking at the direction of the signal. It was coming from north of Manhattan which meant when she left the house she wasn't wearing the bracelet.

Suddenly my mood turned from hope to depression. Shit. I had planned for almost everything, but obviously something had happened that made Honey forget to wear the bracelet.

"You think she's here?" Francisco asked.

"Yeah, lots of old warehouses around here though, she could be in any one of these buildings." I said

"We could try to get some of Honey's clothes and get a bloodhound," Francisco suggested.

"I know something better than a bloodhound," WoodHenry chimed in.

"What?" I growled. My mood was growing blacker by the second.

"Albalita" he said.

CHAPTER 29

BRAX WAS SCARED, not because he had shot a cop and had a whole police force looking for him, but rather because he had shot a cop on an errand for Mr. Nicolli. He had panicked because his driver's license had expired two days before. He had figured that with his bad driving record plus the load of unpaid parking tickets he had accumulated during the past few months, he would most likely have had to spend the night in jail. But no doubt about it, Mr. Nicolli would be very upset. Before Brax had left to pick up Bobby Jones' ex-wife, Mr. Nicolli had taken special care to explain to him that he wanted him to come straight back to the warehouse with the woman.

"Don't stop, and don't get delayed," had been his exact words.

It was the strange combination of those words and the images that he had in his mind of Mr. Nicolli putting out a killing contract on him that had caused Brax to lose his head and shoot the cop.

He could tell that the woman was scared stiff after what she had seen. There was no way Mr. Nicolli was going to let her walk away alive. Even if she told where WoodHenry was, she would still have to die. She knew too much.

As Brax eased the car towards the freight elevator he could see the Turk coming towards the driver's side of the car. Brax figured that for the time being he wouldn't tell Mr. Nicolli about the cop, thinking that his boss would find that out soon enough anyway. By then Brax hoped he'd have his payoff money in his pocket and be far enough away from Mr. Nicolli so he wouldn't have to feel the wrath of his displeasure. But what if he asked the woman, or if the woman said something? Shit. What was he going to do?

"Everything go OK?" the Turk asked him.

"Yeah" Brax said as he got out of the car. The Turk opened the door nearest to where Honey was sitting.

"Where is my son?" Honey asked..

The Turk answered "He's safe, you're going to see him now."

With the Turk on one side and Brax on the other Honey entered the freight elevator that started to crawl slowly downward.

*****

Normally I would have thought WoodHenry was talking out of his ass, but now my back was against the wall. I remembered how Albalita had amazed me in the park by telling me things that no one else could have known. As I sat in the car watching shadows in the Old Brooklyn Navy Yard, old O.B. Lester's words came back to me. I remembered him saying that there were a lot of real things in this world that we don't yet understand. Maybe Albalita was one of them.

I asked WoodHenry to call Albalita. Albalita wanted to know if I had a piece of clothing or jewellery that belonged to Honey. I told her that I could get a jacket or some article of clothing that she kept at her job. We agreed that she would pick up Honey's jacket from the Tease Me Club on her way down from Mount Vernon.

As I waited I went over and over in my mind the mistake I had made. The more I thought about it, the more the demons whispered in my ear. I could tell that Francisco had been hearing them too.

Forty-three minutes later the taxi with Albalita pulled up.

"Thank you for coming," I said to Albalita

She looked in the direction of my voice and smiled. WoodHenry walked over to her. He hugged her but didn't say anything.

"Don't worry Mr. Barnett, you're not wasting your time with me," she said sweetly.

"I never thought that" I defended.

"I've already been picking up your friend's vibrations from this jacket. I'm ready."

"Moses you wait here" I said.

"She's close by" Albalita said.

"Told you," WoodHenry blurted out like a proud kid in a playground who had just won a bet.

"Is there a group of buildings over there?" Albalita asked pointing north.

"Yes," I said and checked to make sure my small utility bag was fastened securely around my middle.

"Let's walk in that direction if you don't mind," Albalita said.

Albalita, WoodHenry, Francisco and I moved towards the building. With each step forward I felt that I was slipping backwards into an abyss. An abyss of death. With each breath, the demons screamed louder and increased my bloodlust. No doubt about it, I was a man on a mission, going to commit mayhem.

*****

Honey was naked and tied to a small iron bed.

"It's too bad that you don't know anything Miss Lavelle because if you did, you wouldn't have to be put through this terrible ordeal," Nicolli said.

"Just don't hurt my son, please" she said.

He walked out of the room without answering.

Brax grinned down at Honey like some great Monster in heat. His penis was erect and throbbing as he unconsciously rose on the balls of his feet to let air coming in from the vent above caress his naked body.

"I'm gonna fuck you then I'm gonna carve you up and throw you in the water, piece by piece. I bet when I cut off your clit and eat it, it's gonna taste as tender and sweet as some of that melt in your mouth chicken my Momma used to make," he grinned and licked the serrated blade of the hunting knife.

Honey's face was frozen, not from fear, but rather from emptiness. The cold from the dampness of the basement on her nude body had already numbed her senses. Her legs were spread open and strapped to the iron bed posts so tightly that she couldn't feel her feet anymore. She was helpless and knew it. She closed her eyes and decided that she would block out all conscious thought as she waited for death to come. In the recesses of her consciousness she wished she had telephoned her friend Devil Barnett before she had run out. But she had panicked. So much for hindsight. She could feel her skin crawl with disgust as Brax's hot breath came closer to her beautiful face. Brax mounted her and began moving inside her.

"How you like that pretty lady?" he asked.

As Brax moved up and down Honey silently prayed that death would come quickly and that God would somehow be merciful enough to spare her only son.

*****

As we walked towards the warehouse I saw three large rats making their way towards a rubbish pile. The noise of us approaching gave them pause but they didn't run. They simply sniffed the air and went back to their task of hunting for food.

"I feel her close now. She's in here," Albalita said as we stopped at the door of what looked like an abandoned warehouse.

Francisco expertly picked the lock and we were inside within two minutes. It was dark inside. The only light was from two long florescent tubes that ran the length of the huge room throwing a weak beam of light throughout. It was enough light to allow me to see the Lincoln Town Car parked against the far wall. From somewhere, we could hear faint voices. The voices of two men talking in a foreign language that I couldn't readily identify. It sounded old and eastern like Arabic. Maybe Turkish or Persian.

"OK," I whispered to WoodHenry. "Take Albalita back to the car and tell Moses that I want everyone to wait for me at the small diner at the corner of the street. And tell him to be sure and keep his phone on."

"OK Mr. Barnett," WoodHenry said as he took Albalita by the hand and started moving back towards the door.

"Be careful Mr. Barnett" Albalita whispered over her shoulder.

"I will."

When WoodHenry and Albalita were out of the building, Francisco and I started moving towards the voices. We could see that there were steps leading to the lower level. Francisco and I pulled our guns and attached the silencers. Francisco went first into the stairwell. Once at the bottom of the stairs he shone a penlight against the wall to let me know that no one was in sight and that all was clear to come ahead.

On the lower level I heard the voices growing louder. They were coming from a room down the hall. The voices mixed in with what sounded like noise from a space heater. We both knew that whoever was in that room doing the talking was going to get shot, no questions asked. Francisco took up a position on the opposite side of the wall and we eased down the long dark corridor like big cats stalking our prey.

Along the corridor were a succession of doorways. The first door was cracked slightly. I stopped to look in. Nothing. Francisco peered in through the second doorway and nodded back to me over his shoulder then moved to the opposite wall to cover me while I looked in.

Against the wall was a bed. On the bed a young man was lying face down with his arms tied behind him and a gag in his mouth. From where I was standing he couldn't see me but I recognised the face. It was the same one on the photograph in Honey's house.

Without a word I moved past the door closer towards the sounds of the voices. I gave the signal. Then with syncopated movement that had been practised and made precise over many years, Francisco and I both stepped into the doorway. I went in high and Francisco went low. In an instant we took in the room and the two men standing facing each other. One was smallish, white, about fifty five, ugly with a swarthy complexion. Before the smaller could turn to get a good look at me I shot him through the shoulder. The bigger one reached under his jacket but all for naught, because the second his hand moved, Francisco shot him through the left eye.

Both men fell to the floor.

"Where is she?" I asked the one I had shot as I pressed my gun into his mouth.

He shook his head. Then with all of my strength I hit him in the mouth with the barrel of my gun. After he had finished choking and spitting bloody teeth, he managed to tell me that she was in the room at the end of the hall. Francisco stayed with him as I made my way down the dark corridor alone. As I grew closer to the door I could hear sounds of grunting.

"Yeah is that how you like it, you filthy bitch," a male voice growled.

I moved closer and closer to the voice.

"I'm gon' kill you just like I done those other ones. First I'm gonna bite off your pretty little nipples and make you scream. Then I'm gonna kill you slow. I done killed six bitches just like you and they all screamed before they died, and you gon' scream too pretty lady just you wait and see," Brax bragged.

The door was open and from the hall I could see what was

taking place. A big light-skinned man was lying on top of Honey who was tied to the bed. My heart leaped into my mouth as the venom of my hate boiled up inside of me.

"Hey," I said. The sound came out more like that of a demon than a man.

The man turned to meet the sound. When he saw it wasn't someone he recognised he paused.

"Your friends are dead, and you're next," I said.

Suddenly the man jumped up and started to fix his huge hands around Honey's throat. But before he could get a grip, I shot him in the groin.

He doubled over and groaned loudly and stumbled forward toward me. I advanced into the room as he tried to straighten up. I could have shot him again and finished him off, but I suddenly had another idea.

I let him stumble forward and hit him on the back of the head with my gun. He tried to reach out towards me but I side-stepped and drove a kick into his knee that broke his kneecap. He went down to the floor and didn't move.

Honey's eyes were still closed when I walked over to her. I bent down to touch her and she opened her eyes. I felt like I wanted to die and hold her all at the same time. I gently untied her, dressed her in her clothes that were lying in a heap on the floor and carried her in my arms down the hall to the room where Harold was being kept.

I quickly untied him and without another word went back down the hall to check on the big yellow-skinned naked rapist that I had shot. I approached the room with my gun poised and ready for anything, but he was still lying on floor where I had left him. I tied his hands and legs with the rope they had used on Honey and walked back to the other room where Francisco was minding the wounded ugly white man with the strange pink little girl looking hands.

"Let's leave him for 5-0" I told Francisco.

Within seconds Nicolli's girlish hands were handcuffed behind him. Then Francisco tore off a piece of the ugly man's shirt and stuffed it into the open wound so that he wouldn't bleed to death. He then lashed Nicolli securely to a pole.

"Help me in here," I told Francisco.

Together Francisco and I carried the naked rapist up the elevator and across the warehouse out through the door. It had gotten dark by then.

"Where you taking me?" Brax managed to groan and I hit him again with the butt of my gun in his eye. He slumped over in pain and groaned some more.

I immediately saw a place that suited what I had in mind. With Francisco's help I dragged the big man to a place near where a heap of uncovered garbage lay in the open. I used nylon cord that I carried in my utility bag to secure the man tightly onto a portion of the dock near the waters edge. I made sure that he was tied so tightly that he couldn't move. Not even an inch.

"Please," Brax started to beg.

"Just like those women you raped and killed, they pleaded too didn't they" I said.

"I'm sorry," Brax cried.

I made several small cuts on his naked chest and legs. When the blood from the flesh wounds started to trickle I stuffed his mouth with a handkerchief gag. Then I backed away to watch his twitching body blend in with the moonless Brooklyn night.

CHAPTER 30

I MADE SURE that Honey and Harold were situated comfortably in my car. As I started to get in Honey spoke up.

"I'm sorry, I know I should have called you but I panicked."

"Forget it, you're safe now, that's what counts," I said.

"Where are you going?" she asked me.

"To take you and Harold home."

"Is WoodHenry OK? You'd better make sure he's out of danger, I'll be alright if Francisco takes me home."

"You sure?"

"Yes."

"There's a few things I need to clear up but as soon as I do, I'll come over, OK?"

"Do what you gotta do" Honey said.

Francisco drove my car off into the night as I started towards the diner on the corner where WoodHenry, Albalita and Hummingbird Moses were waiting.

"Honey and Harold alright?" WoodHenry asked.

"No" I said wishing that I was driving her back home rather than Francisco.

We sat in the diner and WoodHenry ordered a hamburger, cherry pie and a tall glass of milk. Albalita had a salad and Moses and I had coffees.

"So let's get down to it," I said looking at WoodHenry.

"Oh yeah I know what you mean," WoodHenry said looking up at me "About the money you mean?"

"Yeah." I was tired and anxious to go check on Honey but I knew that now was the best time to get it all out in the open.

"It's hidden," he said.

"Where?"

"In a locker."

"You got the key?"

"Yes."

"So where is this locker?"

"In a fitness club near Madison Square Garden."

"Does anyone else know that it's there?"

"Only Missy, in fact she borrowed the key from me to take some of the bonds and sell them so I could have something to live on. But she gave it right back."

"You realise that what you did is a felony and that you're facing jail time if Jerrod decides to prosecute," I said.

"I know," he said solemnly.

"But he didn't mean to do it, he was tricked," Albalita defended.

"Tricked, how?" I asked.

"Bamboozled. He was set up. Tell him WoodHenry," she stated.

"I didn't know I was going to steal the bonds when I did. It kinda' just happened."

"Explain."

"You see I was doing this favour for Mr. Jerrod. The deal was I was supposed to take these bonds over to this clearing house but on my way out the door I run into Missy and she was asking me to go with her and I told her I couldn't at the moment cause I had to take the bonds over to the clearing house and then she started crying saying that I didn't love her, and didn't want to be with her on her birthday after she had spent all her money to get dressed up pretty just for me. She even said that she was going to do away with herself 'cause I didn't love her enough just to go and have one drink. So…."

"So you went and had a drink with her?" I asked.

"Just one, well it started out as just one 'cause I told her that I had to go and deliver the bonds and that I would be right back but she said she couldn't stand to be away from me even for a minute on her birthday. I guess I must have had one drink too many 'cause the next thing I remember I was in a hotel room and she was butt nak... I mean...you know…." he stopped himself and jerked his eyes in the direction of Albalita who was listening intently.

"Well, no clothes on, you know what I'm trying to say Mr. Barnett," WoodHenry continued.

"I do, and you still hadn't delivered the bonds. Correct?" I said.

"No sir."

"How did you get to the hotel room?" I asked.

"I don't know, honest. I just woke up and was there. And

then the next thing you know Missy started talking about how poor she was when she was a child growing up down south and how they was so poor her mother had to sell herself to white mens just so they could have enough money to feed her brothers and sisters. That was after her Daddy was killed by a the police in a case of mistaken identity."

"And you felt sorry for her, didn't you?" Albalita said starting to pick at her salad.

"I did, I imagine most anybody with a heart would, don't you think?" he said turning to me as he jammed a fork full of cherry pie into his mouth.

"She dropped something into his drink, that's obvious isn't it Mr. Barnett, and she had help too, otherwise how did she get him into the hotel room?" Albalita said.

"Did you leave the table anytime when you were drinking, maybe to get other drinks or go to the bathroom?" I questioned.

" No I don't think so except the time I went up to the bar to get Missy some red devil hot sauce for her potato chips. The bartender had to go back into the kitchen for it."

"So how did the bonds get into the locker?" I wanted to know.

WoodHenry explained. "Well like I say she started telling me all this stuff and the next thing you know she was crying and I guess I was too. Then she started talking about what a beautiful life we could have if I had the money from all the bonds in the suitcase. She said that we could go away and live happy and never be heard from again and that the insurance company would give Mr. Jerrod his money back so nobody would really be hurt. She said insurance companies got it figured so that even if a company like Mr. Jerrod's lost ten or twenty million they still come out on top."

"And you believed her," I quipped sarcastically.

"Well yeah I guess I did, she a real smart girl. She been to college and everything," WoodHenry said and stuffed in another forkful of pie.

"So the money…?" I said.

"I told her that it was a crazy thing to talk about, let alone try and do, but I guess after a while, I guess she kind of convinced me that it would be alright."

"She seduced him Mr. Barnett," Albalita said.

"And then she suggested that you go put the bonds in a

locker, right?"

"Yeah she said that it was better to keep them in the locker because if for any reason the police caught up with us then I could claim that while I was walking across the street I got knocked down by a car and lost my memory with amnesia. And I could say that I didn't know what happened to the bonds. That's the other reason she said I should go into hiding, so that if anybody ever got wise I could say I lost my memory and I didn't even know who I was no more."

"And that made sense to you?" I said in disbelief.

"I guess it sounded like a good idea at the time. Plus Missy said that by now Mr. Jerrod had already probably reported the bonds missing and that the police was probably already looking for me."

"And then together you and Missy took the bonds to the locker?"

"Yeah, and she said that she knew where she could take some of them to get them cashed in, so I could go into hiding while she could make plans to get me a false passport and a new identity. You know, everything so we could leave the country," he said sadly.

"Can't you see Mr. Barnett, this woman had this all set up from the beginning," Albalita said.

"But she couldn't have known that I had the bonds, didn't nobody knew I had them except Mr. Jerrod," WoodHenry said finishing the last of his pie.

"Did you ever think that maybe her and Jerrod were working together?" Albalita asked him.

"Naw, I don't think so."

"Where did you meet her?" I asked him.

"At Mr. Jerrod's house but she didn't know him. She was there with Spongey."

"Spongey?" I said.

"Yeah she was helping him out 'cause he was doing the DJ-ing that night for the employee party. You know he used to go around sometimes doing D.J. work for parties. Well when we got to the party, Missy showed up and Spongey said that she was a friend of his."

"And that's when you two got tight?" I asked.

"Well we became friends, well I guess you could say she really liked me and she told me so right away. It was the first time a woman as pretty as her had ever come right out and said anything like that to me."

"Did you take her home that night?" Albalita asked

"No, but we started seeing each other that same week. But we never did no foolin' around or nothin', we was just friends, well until that time in the hotel."

"How long ago was the party ?" I asked

"About six weeks ago now," WoodHenry said.

"Did Spongey say how he knew her?"

" Naw, but Spongey knew lots of different people, sometimes I know he sold reefer and so he was always meeting people," WoodHenry said.

"Got the picture now Mr. Barnett?" Albalita said.

"Yes, crystal clear."

"So the money is still in the locker as far as you know?"

"As far as I know Mr. Barnett" WoodHenry said.

"I'd be real surprised if it was," Albalita remarked sarcastically.

"But the question I keep asking myself is, if she had access to the money then why didn't she just take it and leave. Why did she still need you? She could have reported you to the police or even killed you after she got the money, if that's all she was after," I said to WoodHenry.

"I know Missy can be a little head-strong at times Mr. Barnett but she ain't the type of person that would ever kill nobody, " WoodHenry declared.

"WoodHenry," Albalita said without looking up. "There's a lot of people laying in the cemetery that said the same exact thing."

"So what now?" he asked innocently.

"For the moment I think you'd better go home with Albalita."

"But what about Missy and my baby? I just can't abandon them," WoodHenry said.

"If that woman is pregnant, then I'm a chinaman," said Albalita.

"You don't think she pregnant then?" WoodHenry said.

"She lied just to make you leave with her. Your trouble is you don't know who to trust. When you going to start trusting somebody who cares something about you," she replied.

"I trust you, that's why I keep all my song notebooks in that trunk at your house. Cause I trust you," he said defensively.

"I know " she said.

"And I trust you too Mr. Barnett" he said looking at me.

"Then keep trusting us until Mr. Barnett can straighten this thing out," Albalita said.

WoodHenry just looked blank.

All this time Moses hadn't spoken a word. He reached over the table and put his hand on WoodHenry's shoulder.

"She telling you right son," Moses said.

"Can you keep him safe Albalita?" I said.

"You mean can I keep him away from that woman?" Albalita asked.

"Albalita, I know Missy can take care of herself, and I trust you and you brought me through, so I'm going to take your advice and give things a little rest between me and Missy for a while. I need time to think things out. Besides I'm in enough trouble already."

"You can say that again," Albalita stated.

"I know it was all my fault. I shouldn't have listened to her in the first place" WoodHenry said.

"Don't worry, I got something in mind Mr. Barnett. He'll be safe with me," Albalita said.

Albalita had all my confidence now, after leading us straight to Honey with her magnificent powers. If she had told me that there were green men from the moon living in the back of the diner I would have believed her.

"And where's the key to the locker?" I asked WoodHenry.

"Right here" he said and pulled the key from his pocket and placed it into my open hand. While the trio finished eating I decided to take a little stroll. There was still a couple things I needed to do before I left the area. One was to call Ross Lambert and tell him where he could find the man whose hired Lincoln Town Car had been involved in the shooting of the cop.

CHAPTER 31

THE YOUNG MALE had been travelling alone since yesterday. He had been kicked out of his family because he had become too big to share the food that was brought in for the rest of the group. Now he was on his own, fighting to survive among the other young males. In recent times pickings in the area had grown scarce. There had been lots of changes in the area brought on by the big, hard, shiny, noisy things that tore down the places where they'd once lived. The big noisy things also brought famine because when they came tearing down buildings they caused more and more families to be displaced. Which meant now more families poured into other territories in search of food. This caused fights and even killings. At present, things were very bad. Usually there were a few scraps here and there to be found among the garbage containers or the mud in the Old Brooklyn Navy Yard but not now. The increased competition for food meant that he might have to fight or kill if he wanted to survive.

Suddenly the wind changed direction and he smelled something. He sniffed the air again to make sure that he was certain of what he thought he had smelled. Yes, he was sure now. The unmistakable scent of blood. It was coming from near the docks. He moved closer to the smell and waited. Instinct told him that if he smelled it, then there might be others nearby who had smelled it too. The wrong movement at the wrong time could prove fatal. He didn't want to go rushing into a situation and find himself facing a hungry gang. That could be very dangerous. In times like these cannibalism was not unusual. Therefore he moved intently but cautiously along the bottom of the building making sure to stay in the shadows that blended in with the moonless night.

Then there came a sound. The sound would have normally scared him and sent him scurrying in the other direction, but not tonight. He was too hungry to be frightened. He hadn't eaten anything for two and a half days. His sharp eyes picked up movement about twenty yards ahead. The low sounds emanating from the thing had the same low pitch as those creatures he had often heard when playing with his brothers and sisters in the place where they used to live before all the big shiny noisy hard things came. He had always been taught to fear these creatures because they had terrible instruments of torture and death. As he moved closer, the smell became stronger and sent hunger pains to his stomach.

Closer and closer he moved. The smell was so strong now that he felt he was even willing to chance going out in the open. He moved closer, inch by inch.

The creature thing on the ground didn't move much except for a twitching motion. He decided to take a chance. Besides, what choice he have. He ran forward towards the moaning thing and quickly put his mouth to the ground. He quickly licked up a droplet of fresh blood. The thing made terrible sounds but he was too hungry to care. Now there was no turning back. He went closer and saw where the blood oozed from an open place on the living thing. A place that smelled warm with food. He moved forward sniffing for danger. Then suddenly all fear was gone. His survival lay before him. In one fast motion he bit into the place where the blood flowed from and tore off a piece of flesh.

The thing groaned loudly. He retreated back into the shadows, a safe distance from the creature and started to chew. He gobbled the warm bloody flesh and suddenly felt himself becoming bolder. He started back towards the twitching thing again. But just as he stepped from the shadows he saw two more just like him. Two hungry males that had smelled the creature too. Normally he would have felt fear, especially in hard times like these. But tonight was different. The warm flesh inside his stomach had given him courage. He gave the two just like him a look of confidence and boldly ran back to the creature thing and tore off another piece of flesh.

This time he didn't run back to the shadows but stood boldly near the groaning thing as he gobbled down the flesh. Then he stood up on his hind legs in a gesture for the other males to join him. The thing groaned and twitched and made horrible sounds but it didn't matter. The young male did not move. He just took another bite of flesh and gobbled it down.

When the other two just like him saw what he did, it gave

them courage too. Following his lead they ran forward and bit off chunks of bloody flesh from the groaning creature the same way he had done. They looked at him admiringly and nodded approval. Nothing more needed to be said. There was enough for everyone. Within a few minutes the young male was joined by ten others and then a gang of about twenty arrived. The creature thing continued to make horrible sounds but no one paid any attention. The feast was on. Group after group came. Many disappeared inside the groaning creature thing as they discovered it's tasty softer inner organs. No one was interested in fighting now. Everyone was too busy eating. The young male ate and ate until he was almost too stuffed to walk. And then he ate some more. When he was too full to move he sat down on his haunches and looked at the miracle taking place before his eyes. Now there had to be at least five or six hundred just like him swarming over the creature. But the creature no longer groaned. Some like him were covered with the blood of the creature thing as they continued to eat. No one fought or argued. They just ate and ate and ate. A couple of inviting females had offered to mate with him as his name was now circulating as the one who had found the creature thing. One of the older ones came up and told him that it was the first time he had ever seen such a thing and that this event as well as his name would go down in history. The young male felt proud. This would be an event that he would be able to tell his grandchildren about. And maybe for generations to come they would talk about him as the one who found the thing that caused the big feast and saved many families from the famine. The young male felt proud that his name would be associated with the big feast. The big feast where everyone was welcome.

Suddenly there was a ray of light from a distance that gave everyone pause. For a second panic seized the gathering as everyone looked up at the light and instinct took over. They prepared for flight. But suddenly the light went away and everyone went back to the feast. Devil Barnett stood in the distance watching the rats swarm over Brax's bloody corpse. He replaced the high beam flashlight in his pocket then turned and started walking towards his car satisfied that the rats had done exactly what he had wanted.

CHAPTER 32

WHEN MISSY FREE woke up and found WoodHenry gone she thought she was dreaming. She walked around the room looking for him in the oddest places; behind the curtains, in the closet and even in the dresser drawers.

"This just don't make no sense. How could the same damn thing happened to the same damn person, two damn times in a row?" she said out loud.

She called Tom Jerrod on his cell phone but he didn't answer. She waited five minutes then called again but he still didn't answer. Then she called his office. The secretary told her that Mr. Jerrod wouldn't be coming back until the following day. And he didn't leave a forwarding number. As Missy wandered around the hotel room she was suddenly seized by a panic attack that seemed to grab her by the throat and cut off the oxygen to her brain.

"Tom," she cried out loud.

Then suddenly the voice of panic spoke to her.

"Tom might be dead," the voice stated.

"No," she answered back.

"Never know, a lot of funny things are happening" the voice of panic replied.

Missy Free didn't even take time to look in the mirror to fix her makeup or brush her teeth. All she had on her mind was seeing Tom Jerrod alive. She marched straight out of the Warwick Hotel and over to 10th Avenue where she rented a car. She didn't wait for the man behind the counter to tell her about all of the special discounts that were being offered. She just rented the car quickly and asked if he had a map that showed the way to Westport, Connecticut.

*****

I walked into the building for my meeting with Tom Jerrod at 5:20pm the following evening. "Mr. Barnett, I'm glad you were kind enough to meet me here," Tom Jerrod said as he led me into a large room of the private club where he was a member. It was right out of a Charles Dickens novel. A proper gentleman's club. The men were younger than in the films but they wore the same kind of conservative dark suits and stodgy appearances as in the Dickens novels. They sat behind newspapers smoking silently and drinking snifters of brandy and glasses of whiskey served by elderly silent waiters. A large sign above the entrance to the room a sign read WHEN ENTERING PLEASE TURN OFF ALL CELLULAR PHONES.

"I'm very pleased that you finally found WoodHenry and that he's safe," Jerrod began as we took a seat.

"And let's not forget about the money" I said.

"No."

"One of the things I've always been curious about is why you never reported the theft to the insurance company since I'm sure your company is insured against theft."

"Oh I did, but as I explained before one of my big concerns was the timing of it all. If I had reported it too soon then my Board would have become aware of what had happened, which would have caused trouble inside the company. But to answer your question, I knew I would eventually have to report the bonds missing. In fact I told them two days ago."

"And the insurance company said...?"

"They didn't want to pay of course."

"And you told them about WoodHenry disappearing with the bonds?"

"Unfortunately I had to."

"And presumably they will be suggesting that you press charges."

"I'm afraid so, which is very unfortunate, because he was doing me a favour," Jerrod said dropping his eyes sadly.

"The man Nicolli that your wife hired, he's in police custody now. It seems that he was part of a gang whose idea of investigation included rape and murder"

"Why my wife would hire someone like that is beyond me."

"You think she knew about the loss of the bonds?"

"She must have, it would be the only reason for her hiring an investigator, but when I told her, she didn't say she knew about the missing bonds. But she could have discovered it and chose to use an investigator rather than confront me," he said.

"That's an interesting theory" I said.

"The problem is, my wife was born into this business but she's not a business woman in the true sense of the word. In fact she isn't very capable of making difficult decisions all at. Like so many rich people she has been sheltered from the real world all of her life," Jerrod said as he reached down into his side jacket pocket and pulled out his gold horsehead lighter.

"Well, what's the next step in the process as you see it?" I asked as Jerrod lit his cigar and then replaced the lighter into his side jacket pocket.

"From where I sit it's up to you. If you want to tell the police where WoodHenry is hiding you can, but between you and me I wouldn't be opposed to helping him get away, because from what you say he was pretty much a victim of this woman," Jerrod said.

"Yes, but I think that he should pay the price for having stolen from you, especially when you trusted him. The way I'm thinking now, I'd like to tell the police where he is," I said.

"I understand. By the way do you have any idea of what happened to this woman.... what did you call her, Missy?"

"Missy Free," I said.

"Yes Missy Free."

"Unfortunately she got away clean, but I'm going to put the police onto her as well," I said.

"As far as I'm concerned you've done a very good job, I'm sure that these terrible men my wife hired would have never been brought to justice if not for you. And I'd like for you to think seriously about forgetting about WoodHenry and this woman he was involved with." He then pulled a check from his inside pocket and passed it over to me.

I looked at the sum. It read ten thousand dollars.

"This is very generous, thank you," I said pocketing the check.

"Think of it as a bonus. You say you don't believe WoodHenry's story about the bonds being in the locker. Just for a moment, lets consider this. What if he really was telling the truth?" Jerrod said.

"You mean if he really did put the bonds into a locker" I said.

"Yes."

"Mr. Jerrod, this is the key that I got from WoodHenry last night but I knew he was lying so I decided why waste my time with a wild goose chase," I said, holding up the key to show him.

"What if you went to the locker and found the missing bonds?" Jerrod said.

"You mean if they mysteriously turned up, well that would certainly get WoodHenry off the hook" I replied, "but why should they turn up...?"

"There are still some questions that could come to light which could be damaging to me, Mr. Barnett. I'd rather this whole thing just dry up and blow away as quickly as possible. WoodHenry being arrested will only drag things out. Besides I just spoke with someone this morning who located the bonds on the black market and for a certain, lets us say, consideration, I can arrange to have the bonds turn up in the locker WoodHenry rented. That way, nobody's hurt."

"I see what you mean," I said.

"And as I said, I still feel responsible in a way for having asked WoodHenry to do me the favour that led to his troubles. If WoodHenry were to take a little vacation until this thing blew over, let's say in some part of the world where no one would ever find him, I think that would be better than him going to jail. For me as well as for him. Besides he's a man who made a mistake for love, but he's not really a criminal" Jerrod said. "Have you ever been in love Mr. Barnett?"

"Yes."

"Well weren't there some things that you may have done under those circumstances that you would have never done otherwise?"

"I guess you're right. I never thought about it quite like that" I said.

"What I like about you Mr. Barnett is that you're a smart man, as well as a practical man. And let's not forget, you're ahead of the game moneywise on this deal."

"I can appreciate that too. Tell you what, I'll talk to WoodHenry. What length of time would you suggest for him staying away?" I asked.

"At least ten years, but don't worry I'll make sure that his new lifestyle will more than compensate for his sentimental loss," Jerrod said.

"I'll run it past him and see what I can arrange," I said winking at Jerrod.

"Good that's settled then," Jerrod said and stood up.

"You know I've read about places like this but I've never been inside one, it looks like something right out of the history books," I said looking around. "Would it be too much trouble if you could show me around a little, I'd really would like to see what some of the other rooms look like," I said.

"No problem," Jerrod said. We walked side by side along the corridor and he began to give me the history of the place.

Twenty minutes later I walked out into the street. It had been an interesting little visit. I had always known that Jerrod was as wrong as two left shoes but what I didn't know was why he was playing things the way he was playing them. I also knew that the woman had played a part with Jerrod too, but exactly what part I hadn't quite figured yet. That's why from the minute I walked into his fancy club I had decided to play Jerrod. I figured that his ego was so big that I could use it against him. Anyway it had given me the opportunity to get my hands on something that would clear up a major question I had.

After I had gotten back into my car I reached down into my jacket pocket with my fingertips and gently lifted out Tom Jerrod's golden horse head cigarette lighter. I had picked his pocket during our little tour of his club. Picking pockets was just a part of the tradecraft that I had learned and used on occasion when I had been an agent with the CIA. Gingerly I placed the lighter into a white handkerchief, and my cell phone rang. It was Onion.

" Dev I got something interesting on Fidelity Trust kkkkkk ssssss sshh crackle-crackle."

"What?" I can't understand you, the reception is bad, I'm in the car."

I could hear him say the words Fidelity Trust something, but the connection was breaking up.

"I'll be back at the bar in two hours, call you back then" I said.

"Co...ol," I made out through the crackle and hung up.

Walking towards my car, I felt my demons again. They were fully awake again. I hated that. Still in some strange way it was a comfort to know that they could be called upon to serve when needed. With this feeling of duplicity ruminating in my soul I started the car and headed towards Harlem. I had an appointment with New York City police detective Ross Lambert.

CHAPTER 33

THE CLOCK IN the rented car read 8:30pm. "What cha gonna to do now bitch huh, huh, huh?" the voice of panic was saying to Missy Free from inside her head.

She drove faster and turned up the car radio to drown out the voice but it didn't work. That damn voice just kept singing and messing with her mind.

"What cha gonna do now bitch, huh, huh?" Missy Free was still listening to the voice when she pulled up to the gates of Tom Jerrod's Westport Connecticut Mansion.

"You really have lost everything now and you may have lost Tom as well," the voice of panic sang to her as she rang the bell.

A man's voice coming through the metal box answered "Yes?"

"My name is Missy Free. I need to see Mr. Jerrod" she said.

"Do you have an appointment?"

"No but I work for Mr. Jerrod, I have an emergency message for him."

"Just a minute," the voice said.

She felt that maybe she had just blown the biggest opportunity she had ever had. With WoodHenry gone the second time what was she going to tell Tom Jerrod now. The first time it happened she could hardly bring herself to tell him, but now this was just too much.

"Dumb ass bitch" the voice of panic said. She felt she was really starting to freak out.

"Shut up," Missy Free said out loud.

"I beg your pardon?" came the response of a female voice through the metal box.

I'm sorry, I was just talking to myself. I've got to see Tom Jerrod, I know he's not here, but it's an emergency, please," she begged.

"What's your name?" the female voice asked.

"Missy Free."

"Come in" the woman's voice answered as the gates started

to slide back.

When Missy reached the mansion she was greeted to her surprise by a middle aged white woman.

"Hello, my name is Greta Jerrod, I'm Tom's wife, won't you come in?" Then Greta led the way through two rooms of pastel walls into an atrium filled with plants, paintings of nature scenes and a wide screen television.

Ordinarily Missy would never have dared to come here, as Tom had always made it plain that his house was strictly off limits unless she were invited for a party like the time she had come with Spongey. But this was different, this was an emergency.

"Ohhh stupid bitch you really in trouble now, coming up here and meeting Tom's wife." The voice of panic still wouldn't leave her alone.

"Have a seat," Greta said looking at the pretty youngish bronze-skinned woman and suddenly feeling that she was not half as attractive to her husband as this young black woman, even though she was a million times more rich and powerful.

"Is there anything that I can get you?" Greta asked as she studied Missy Free's features and remembered that she had seen this same woman a few months before at one of Tom's garden parties.

Greta recalled that on that night, this same woman was locked in what looked like a personal conversation with her husband, and she remembered not liking the feeling.

"No I'll just wait for To... I mean Mr. Jerrod," Missy Free corrected before completing the final syllable.

"OK, he's expected soon," Greta Jerrod said suddenly feeling a wave of jealousy.

Greta quickly walked out of the room as she didn't know what else to do. Now she was thinking how she would confront Tom Jerrod when he came home.

"The nerve of him allowing one of his sluts to come into our home," she thought as she walked upstairs towards her bedroom.

She didn't know what else to do so Greta sat at her dressing table and started to comb her hair. As she combed and combed she started to cry. The tears that ran down her ageing cheeks were full of lost hope. She had never loved a man the way she had loved Tom Jerrod. Her tears were full of the old hurts. Old hurts of a strict Protestant upbringing full of sterile rules and proper behaviour, but devoid of love. This was the tradition inherited from her grandfather who had founded Fidelity Trust Brokerage and her father who had been president of the company. Her father had been a rich philanderer who drove her mother to an early death with his infidelities, vile moods and strict disposition. Combing her hair, Greta thought about her mother. Her sad unfortunate pathetic mother who died of a broken heart. If only she could have done something to help her. She had been only twelve years old when her mother had died. In that same week, her father packed her off to boarding school where she remained until graduation. Then it was off to University and Europe and one empty relationship after another until her father died. She then inherited his business, and the emptiness had continued and continued until she met Tom Jerrod.

She knew Tom was far from perfect, but he allowed her to be herself. He didn't mind if the walls were the colour of spring flowers all the year round. He allowed her to express a part of her nature that no one ever acknowledged or even dreamt existed. To the world she had always just been plain Greta but with Tom she was a woman and a wife who deserved to be loved. In exchange for his validation of her, she overlooked his arrogance and insensitivity. Sometimes she even suspected that at times he put his horses on a par with their marriage. Still he was her Tom. But now with this young woman sitting downstairs she didn't quite know if she even deserved to be loved by Tom anymore. Maybe she didn't even deserved to be loved by herself anymore.

A few minutes later she heard Tom's voice downstairs. She started to go and tell him that there was someone waiting, then she then decided that she was just being oversensitive and silly about the whole thing. Greta took a valium to calm her nerves, freshened her makeup and decided to go downstairs to greet her husband.

As Greta reached the top of the stairs, she was stopped. Not by a physical force but by a force a million times more powerful. Jealous outrage. That woman and her husband Tom were hugging and she was crying on Tom's shoulder.

"I'm so sorry Tom," the young woman said whimpering.

"Don't worry about it baby, everything is going to be alright.

I've made some other plans, it'll all work out just the way I said it would when we began this thing, its OK baby " Tom said and hugged the woman tightly.

Greta didn't say a word, she just took her hurt and receded back into her room. On her dressing table she looked at her father and mother's photograph. She fixated on her mother's sweet face and seemed to hear her mother's voice crying. Then from nowhere something miraculously came into her head. A plan. A plan that would help manage the rage and hurt she was feeling. A plan that would help to ease the pain and humiliation that her poor kind-hearted mother had suffered. Greta picked up the cell phone and dialled the number to the land line phone downstairs in her own house. She allowed the phone to only ring once, then she ended the call.

Tom had walked to the other side of the room and the young woman named Missy Free was no longer crying now.

"Tom, Tom," Greta's voice preceded her into the room a few seconds before her arrival.

Tom Jerrod looked up.

"Tom" Greta called again almost out of breath as she reached the middle of the staircase.

"What is it?" Tom said with irritation written on his features.

"I just had the strangest telephone call from the stables," Greta said and left the sentence hanging in the air like a gentle mist.

"What?"

"Someone just called and said that you needed to get over there right away because that stallion you bought was having some kind of convulsion."

Without another word Tom Jerrod started across the room. Halfway out of the door he turned around say something to Missy Free but Greta was there to accommodate his worried expression.

"Don't worry she'll be fine, we'll just entertain ourselves until you return," Greta said with just the proper amount of wifely dutifulness in her voice.

"I was just going," Missy said.

"Don't worry," Greta said to Missy as Tom bolted out of the door. "You look like you could use a cup of tea. You sit yourself there, Tom will be back in a moment. No need for you to rush off," Greta said in a caring tone. "How do you like your tea, with sugar or honey?"

"Honey please" Missy Free said and relaxed back into the folds of the comfortable sofa as Greta walked towards the kitchen.

"While Tom's is out attending to his horses you and I can relax and have a chat," Greta said with the kind of smile that her etiquette instructors at Finishing School had often told her to practice, a smile that was designed to win friends and influence people.

CHAPTER 34

AN HOUR AND a half after my meeting with Jerrod I sat having a cup of coffee with Ross Lambert in a little café near the police station.

"I've got some friends in the FBI who owe me a few favours, I can have word back on these prints in a couple hours," Lambert said as he placed Jerrod's gold horse-head cigarette lighter into a plastic container.

"Any word on the cop that was shot?" I asked.

"Yeah, he died about three hours ago," Lambert said.

"Did they catch the guy who did it?"

"Funny you should ask that," Ross said. "An anonymous caller phoned in to report that the guy who had rented the same Lincoln Town Car you told me about was tied up in a nice little bundle and waiting for the police. A guy named Nicolli."

"Imagine that," I said.

"There was another man they found too. He had been tied to the docks, well he used to be a man but when the cops found him, most of him had been eaten by rats. Wonder how that could have happened," Lambert said looking directly at me.

"The world is a weird and interesting place. Shit happens," I said as I started to move towards the door. I headed back to the bar hoping that it wouldn't be long before the big question that had been plaguing me was finally answered. Then I remembered that I still needed to talk to Onion.

The bar was about half full. A few of the regulars like Po Boy and Goose were watching sports on TV as Benny Sweetmeat and Duke Green were swapping stories about the old days in Harlem. Christine was talking to one of the suppliers who had dropped by and waved to me as I entered the bar. In my office there were three messages on the answering machine. One from Shelby Green who wanted to know if I wanted to fill in as a substitute in a long-running poker game that met regularly at his after-hours club on Wednesdays because Ed Fredricks one of the regular players dropped out. Another was from Hamp, my adopted 12 year old son. Well let me put it another way. Hamp was my son in as much as I was one of three Uncle-Daddys who had agreed to provide fatherly guidance for Hamp's upbringing. It was kind of a weird set-up but it worked out well because all three of us were responsible guys. Hamp wanted to know when I planned to take him to a baseball game and the last caller had been my ex-girlfriend Sonia who asked if I wanted to come by her place for a romantic dinner next week.

I dialled Onion.

"Yeah" he answered after the fourth ring, out of breath.

"What the hell you doing?" I asked, knowing that Onion was a paraplegic who was confined to a wheelchair.

"Chasing my wife around the bedroom if you don't mind. Brother, did I hit pay dirt today. You're gonna love what I found out about Mr. Tom Jerrod" he said.

*****

Missy Free pulled the rented car beyond the gates of Tom Jerrod's mansion and headed back towards the Merrick Parkway. The meeting with Tom had gone well. He wasn't angry like she thought he would be. What an amazing man. He had prepared for all eventualities and even WoodHenry's second disappearance had not altered his master plan. She would still become a rich woman. Tom had assured her of this and she believed him because he had never lied to her yet. Not in all the years she had known him. That's why she loved him unlike anyone else in the world. Even when she acted stupid, he was supportive and loving. Missy pulled the car onto the Parkway towards New York. The serenity of the full moon hanging so beautifully in the deep blue sky matched the calmness that she felt now. The voice of panic inside her head had gone silent too. Tom had killed the bastard off. Now the only sounds ringing inside her head were from the sweet sounds of the cash register clanging as she imagined spending all of the money that she would make from this deal. And the best part of it was that she would never have to sleep with WoodHenry again. That in itself was a blessing. Now she could spend all the time she wanted with Christine.

Funnily enough she hadn't even thought much about Christine during the past twenty four hours. Not since she had found WoodHenry last night. But soon she would be able to think about her all the time. She imagined herself and Christine lying on some Italian beach in a little town on the Mediterranean.

As she drove, she dialled her cell phone. She realised then that she was tired. The strain of it all must have caught up with her.

"Hello" Christine's voice answered.

"Hi baby, it's me" Missy Free said.

"You OK? I've been worried about you."

"I'm OK, I just ran into a little trouble but everything is fine now. I'm on my way home. I should be there in about an hour."

"I've missed you," Christine said.

"I've missed you too. Have you had dinner already?

"No I've been too worried about you to eat."

"I'll pick something up."

"Don't worry, I'll cook something and run you a bath" Christine told her lover.

"That sounds beautiful. OK see you soon, love you," Missy said and clicked off.

For the first time in her life she felt truly worthy of her name. Missy Free. Now with her new found wealth and freedom she would be free to do what she damned well pleased. Free to love. Free to live. Free to be.

As these thoughts of loveliness danced in her head pulling her homeward a shock jolted her as a pain as violent as anything she had ever imagined shot through her abdomen. The next instant her vision blurred and her muscles collapsed like they were made from jelly. She fought for control of the steering wheel but couldn't negotiate it. Then in one sudden motion the pain came again and blackness closed in on her image of a perfect life.

The car flew out of control, hit the guard rail and rolled over and over towards the middle of the highway creating giant sparks until finally it skidded and started to roll down the small ravine that bordered the highway. When the car slammed into the trees at the bottom of the ravine, the fuel tank ignited and the car burst into flames. All at once the life that had once belonged to Denise Williams from Detroit who called herself Missy Free was just a sad burnt memory.

CHAPTER 35

AT 10:26AM THE following day I made my way up the Merrick Parkway again. Francisco lit a cigarette and blew the smoke out of the window.

"Thought you had given up those things," I said glancing quickly in his direction.

"I had until two days ago."

"All the activity huh?"

"Must be" he smiled, taking another deep drag of the cigarette and relaxing back into the seat.

"You ever think that certain people are meant to do certain things or be a certain way in life?" he asked after about ten minutes of silence.

"Destiny?"

"Exactly," he said.

"What brings about this sudden philosophical outpouring?" I asked. But I knew the answer already. What was inside our heads was so alike that we could have been thinking from the same brain. We both thought that we had escaped. Escaped being the men that had been before. The men we liked being. Men of action, men of violence. Ghosts. We had both taken steps to erase those men that it had taken us years to become. Over the past few days we both realised that the erasure process was at best only a temporary measure. An ugly fact neither one of us really wanted to accept.

"So what are you going to do about it?" Francisco asked.

"Nothing, I guess I just have to learn to live with it, like you."

"And hope that the need to activate that side of your personality never gets too overwhelming huh?"

"Something like that," I said.

"I honestly thought that with Luz and the kid I had gotten rid of that part of me. I thought that I had gotten it all out of my system especially the part about enjoying it."

"We all have crosses to bear," I sighed.

"Tell me about it," Francisco said and threw the remaining

part of his cigarette out of the window.

We drove in silence for about the next twenty minutes as we communicated our mutual pain to one another telepathically.

"And how is the sickle cell?" he asked.

"Recently I've been fine. Haven't had an attack in over a year not since that time I got shot in London."

"You gotta keep a close watch on that thing you know. I wouldn't want to lose you to something I couldn't take any revenge against," Francisco said.

"Me neither."

Francisco was right. I was a sickler and my disease was as deadly a killer as any gun knife or poison we had ever faced. But the doctors said if I continued keeping my health together and avoiding extremely stressful situations, the chances were I could live a normal life without any major complications, at least for a while anyway.

The Connecticut estate of Tom Jerrod loomed before me as I pulled the car to a stop.

I spoke into the metal box at the outside gate: "Marcus Barnett for Mr. Jerrod, I have an appointment."

The gate opened right away and I drove along the path towards the mansion. Oscar, the servant met us and showed us through the pastel rooms back to where Tom Jerrod and his wife were sitting in the pool area.

"I didn't expect to see you again so soon Mr. Barnett," Tom Jerrod said.

"This is a friend of mine, Mr. Gomez".

"A drink gentlemen?" he offered.

"No thank you" I said. Francisco also declined.

"So what brings you here Mr. Barnett? I thought our business was concluded. When you called and said that you had to see me right away I admit I was quite surprised."

"This is kind of personal Mr. Jerrod."

"I'm more than happy to help if I can" Jerrod said as we sat down next to him on chairs near the pool.

"Should I leave dear?" Greta asked.

"No, please don't Mrs. Jerrod this is something I think you might be interested in also," I said.

Jerrod's face showed curiosity, but he was playing it cool.

"You said it's a personal problem, I don't really see how I need to hear this, especially when I don't even know you" Greta

Jerrod said.

"I know but if you would just indulge me for a few more minutes I'm sure you'll find what I have to say interesting," I said.

Greta Jerrod sat back in her chair as Tom Jerrod now more interested sat up straight.

"To come right to the point, I don't like being set up and played for a fool" I said.

"How do you figure that?" Jerrod asked.

"Let's start at the beginning shall we. When I first came to you inquiring about WoodHenry you told me that he was doing you a favour by taking the bonds in secret to make a deal behind your Board members' backs," I said.

Suddenly Greta Jerrod was all ears.

"You see Mrs. Jerrod I thought this part might interest you especially since you are the Chairman of the Board of Fidelity Trust Brokerage."

"Anyway go on Mr. Barnett, I told you already that all this would come to light eventually" Jerrod said confidently.

"Yes, you brought me in so that you could show that you had made private inquiries just in case anyone got hip to your plan. That way you could always say you had hired a private investigator, but in truth you never wanted me to find WoodHenry."

"That's not true."

"Otherwise why did you arrange to set WoodHenry up to have the bonds taken off him by a young woman named Missy Free?"

"Did WoodHenry tell you that?" Jerrod asked.

"Yes he did."

"Well he lied. It's as simple as that" Jerrod said.

"And he also told me that Missy Free took the money to a locker. Now I admit what you did was very clever and to be honest, I wouldn't have cared much if your whole plan had worked except for a few mistakes that left two people dead and me holding the bag for a potential murder rap."

"Dead?" Greta said.

"The first was Elvira Benson, WoodHenry's common-law-wife and the other was Spongey."

"I don't know what you're talking about" Jerrod said still as cool as can be.

"You or somebody under your direction killed Spongey and then tried to set me up for the murder," I said.

"How do you figure that?" he asked.

"Somebody did, and you have the most to gain so why not. I also believe that you most probably threw a few hundred dollars Spongey's way to set up the original meet between WoodHenry and Missy Free. "

"That's just supposition Mr. Barnett and you know it" Jerrod quipped confidently.

"Maybe, but I've been doing a little checking, and one of the things I found out was that you didn't just meet Spongey when he was working as a cleaner in your offices. You knew Spongey from back in Saginaw Michigan which made him the most dangerous person around. One word from him and your whole house of cards would have come tumbling down. Maybe Spongey got a little too clever so you decided that it would be better to have him done away with. But then you figured since I was around asking questions you could frame me for his murder by calling the police just at the time you knew I would be meeting him. That way you could kill two birds with one stone."

Jerrod was a different man now. He sat up and the colour started to drain from his face.

"Back in Michigan about fifteen years ago, you were known as one of the best con men around. I bet most people would be very surprised to know that you aren't white at all but rather that you were born in Chicago Illinois to a black mother and father. People gave you the nickname White Tommy because when you were playing the con you would often pass for a white man."

"This is preposterous," Greta said jumping from her chair.

"Totally incredible" Jerrod smiled nervously.

"You can lie Mr. Jerrod but your fingerprints can't. The other day when I met you at your club, I took your golden horse-head lighter and had your fingerprints checked. That's right, and they came back as those of Thomas Jerome Williams, aka White Tommy, a master con man who served sixteen months in prison for fraud in Saginaw Michigan."

Tom Jerrod turned pale.

"Don't look so surprised Mr. Jerrod, I've had my doubts about who you really were from that day when I came to your office and your wife was upset. You were upset too but you didn't want me to know it. I remember when your wife was crying, you told her to "chill the hell out". I couldn't put my finger on it then but after a while it hit me that I had never known any white person of your generation to use that phrase before. That phrase somehow just didn't match the persona of Tom Jerrod the conservative business stockbroker. I had only heard black people use the phrase in that way before. When I put that suspicion together with the lie you told me, things started to fall into place."

"What lie?" Jerrod asked.

"Remember when I first met you and you gave me that bullshit about you needing the bonds to use them as collateral to buy stock in a company called Amalgamated Bio-Products? Well guess what, I checked that company out through a computer friend of mine and there is no such company. Interestingly enough though that same friend was able provide me with documents of your recent large purchases of Fidelity Trust Brokerage stock."

"What is this man talking about Tom? This is outrageous," Greta asked.

"Ludicrous," Tom Jerrod insisted.

"Now this part is especially for you Mrs. Jerrod. You see your husband and Missy Free arranged to take the four million in bonds from Fidelity Trust, but they didn't want the money to disappear for good. They just needed it for a short while to use as part of their bigger scam."

"My head accountant told me about the disappearance of the bonds from the vault the day after it happened and that's why I called in an investigator. I thought maybe one of the other executives had done it and I didn't want to worry Tom with it since I know how much he worries about share prices falling. That's why I called in that Mr. Nicolli to investigate," Greta said.

"Where did you get all this information?" Tom Jerrod shouted at me.

"I got it from a very reliable source who also explained to me that recently a great deal of Fidelity Trust Brokerage stock was purchased with a highly leveraged method. I think the correct term is call options."

"Call options?" Greta said.

"As you probably know a call option is a financial instrument that allows it's owner to buy a specific stock at a predetermined lower price in the future if and when the price of the stock falls. As I understand it, it's a high leverage move because the owner of the call option only risks the price of the call option premium. It's a way to make huge profits if you make the right moves at the right times. Especially if you know that the price of a certain stock will be falling."

"I'm still confused" Greta said.

"Let's say for example that I bought some call options for $10.00 per share in a pharmaceutical company that made a certain medicine. And let us say that this pharmaceutical stock is presently selling at $100.00 per share. This call option I just bought then gives me the right to buy that pharmaceutical stock at the price of let's say $25.00 per share at some time in the future when and if the stock price of this company ever drops to $25.00 per share" I explained. "Now let's say five days later, I decide that I wanted to cash in on my call options and buy this stock at the option price but that the market isn't falling fast enough for me. So I decide to take a few of the company's products from the supermarket shelves and poison them. As a result a few people become ill or die. Naturally the holders of that company's stock will lose faith and want to get rid of that stock, so they would all sell and drive the price down. Let's say that the panic selling drives the stock price of this company from $100.00 down to $25.00 per share at which point I could exercise my option and buy the stock in this pharmaceutical company at $25.00 per share. And in the end all I would have spent would have been the cost of the $10.00 call option."

Jerrod fidgeted in his chair. The colour had drained from his face.

"That's called using leverage of the call options to take control of your wife's company isn't Mr. Jerrod?"

"You got your facts wrong Mister," Jerrod said curtly but trying to control his anger.

I ignored him and turned to his wife.

"Tell me Mrs Jerrod about the share price of your company during the past few weeks."

"It's been going down steadily" she said matter of factly.

"I'm not surprised. Some cleverly placed information with certain institutional investors about four million having gone missing from First Fidelity Trust as a result of shady dealings would certainly make it's shareholders nervous enough to start selling and drive the stock price down."

"This man is talking pure rubbish" Jerrod spat.

"Am I?"

"This can't be true, can it Tom?" Greta asked turning to her husband.

"Oh it's true alright. Here," I said passing her some papers that I took out of my inside jacket pocket. "In fact he's been buying the shares for almost a week now. If you look where it says new owners registration, you will see a Company headquartered on the island of Jersey in England called Freedom Corporation that now owns most of your company's stock Mrs. Jerrod. If you look at the owners of Freedom Corporation the two principal owners are a Thomas Williams and a Denise Williams. Denise Williams by the way, is the real name of Missy Free. According to this report, the stock they own now represents 68% of your company's shares, but the best part is still to come," I explained.

Greta Jerrod was speechless and trembling by now.

"This is bullshit, get the fuck out of my house" Jerrod said jumping up from his chair red faced.

"Wait brother don't fly off the handle, 'cause I'm not finished yet" I said coolly.

"Yes you are" Jerrod said as he started across towards me, but Francisco stepped in front of him and stopped him with a short right uppercut in his stomach that took his breath away and bent him over.

I turned to Mrs. Jerrod. "Now as I was saying the most interesting part of his plan was that the money that he set WoodHenry up to disappear with was the same money he used to buy the call options with. So in effect Mr. Tom Jerrod here stole four million in bonds from Fidelity Trust Brokerage and then used that same money buy the call options. Then he started leaking rumours about the failed financial dealings of First Fidelity Trust which made the price of your stock start to fall and then Mr. Jerrod simply exercised all of his call options he had bought to buy your company's stock at a cheap price. Slick, very slick, I have to admit, but then again the word from Michigan police department is that White Tommy wasn't just any old con man. They said that he was highly intelligent and a perfect actor, that's why he could pass for white and play the big white con."

Greta Jerrod started to cry, and I turned back to Jerrod.

"The part that always confused me was why you were willing to make sure the four million in bonds would eventually show up in the locker, after they went missing. When you told me that bullshit about wanting to help WoodHenry, I acted like I believed you, but I knew that there had to be another reason. But once I found out about the call options, it made perfect sense. You needed to have the bonds show up again so that then you could explain the disappearance of the money as an accounting error. This little explanation would be all that you would need to restore investor faith in your company's stock again and get the price of the stock to start rising again. When this happened then you and Missy Free would not only be in control of the company but also become very rich.

Greta stood up and started to walk the floor.

"I'm glad I did it, I'm so glad Tom," she cried. "I killed that bitch."

Jerrod looked up at his wife puzzled.

"Killed who, what?"

"That's right, you wouldn't know about it yet, because you went to sleep early last night, but I heard it on the news. She crashed her fucking car going down the Parkway and burnt to a fucking crisp. I'm glad I did it too. hat's right, I lied to you and said someone wanted you down at stables when your little whore was visiting you yesterday. It gave me the chance to slip an overdose of my sleeping medication into her tea. I knew it would kill her. I knew it would. That's why I did it. You and that bitch together. Never. I swore you wouldn't do to me what my father did to my poor mother never. I swore never, never."

Jerrod looked up at me helplessly.

"It's true brother, the lady known as Denise Williams aka Missy Free died in a car crash yesterday. The police told me this morning" I explained.

"Bitch," Jerrod said jumping toward his wife. He raised his hand to strike her but Francisco stepped in between them.

"I begged you not to leave me, but you were going to leave me for her I know it. I saw you hugging her. I never cared about the money. You could have had it all. I just couldn't stand for you to leave me for her. Not the way my father had left mother," Greta cried.

"Bitch, Missy Free wasn't my lover, she was my sister. My little baby sister," Tom cried in anguish. He fell back in the chair as the tears began to roll down his face. His body began to shake from the shock of what he had just heard. Greta looked at me in horror with her mouth wide open utterly speechless.

CHAPTER 36

"SO UNTIL THE NEXT time huh?" Francisco said as he stood at the entrance to the departure area of La Guardia airport.

"Yeah."

"I gonna try to do something and I want you to do the same" he said.

"What?"

"Our demons, lets try to keep them sleeping. Because as good as it sometimes feels to wake them up, it doesn't do a lot of good for the soul if you know what I mean."

"Yeah I know just what you mean," I agreed.

"Promise?"

"I've never known you to be worried about people's souls before."

"You're not just people, you're my brother, that's different."

"OK, I promise then" I said.

We hugged each other and without another word Francisco turned and walked towards the plane.

By the time I had reached my car in the short term parking lot, I was missing Francisco already. I knew where I had to go next. Not that I didn't need or want to go, but I guess I felt guilty about showing my face.

I entered the building behind a lady with a load of shopping. I rode the elevator to the floor I needed and walked out into the corridor. My feet seemed to get heavier as I got closer to the door. I stood for at least two minutes not knowing what to do or say before I rang the bell.

"Hello Youngblood" Honey said looking as beautiful as I had ever seen her.

I walked in and stood in the middle of the room awkwardly.

"Have a seat, want a drink?" she asked.

"Maybe some juice" I answered.

"I have a nice one, a mango and apple combination."

"Yeah that sounds good."

My throat suddenly felt as dry as scorched sand.

"So what have you been up to, since I saw you last?"

She was acting as if what had taken place at that warehouse in the Brooklyn Navy Yard two days ago had never happened.

"Just finishing up with this WoodHenry thing, you know." Then I told her about my confrontation with Jerrod.

"So what do you think will happen to him?" she asked.

"To be honest I don't know. I know the Security and Exchange Commission is probably going to prosecute him for insider trading, but I think that's going to be a small price to pay when you measure it against losing his sister and probably his wife. I'm sure he must have really loved his sister. He had always taken care of her from the time their parents died. She was twelve years old then. Also she was the only family that he had," I said.

"Why do you think Jerrod didn't kill WoodHenry once he had the money?" Honey asked.

"Because if someone ever found WoodHenry's body there would always be more of a chance that the police would discover his scam because of the murder investigation. Remember, Jerrod needed to carry out his plan without arousing suspicion, and a murder investigation could have raised embarrassing questions and caused someone to look more closely at the company books. But with WoodHenry still alive, all Jerrod and Missy Free had to do was keep WoodHenry under their influence until they had pulled off their plan. I think they planned to kill him off later and no one would connect the two events," I explained.

"You ever figure out who called, threatening you?"

"No, but my bet would be Bobby."

"He seems to have just disappeared, you think he's dead?" she asked.

"It wouldn't surprise me."

"Me neither," she agreed shaking her head sadly.

"I checked the call list from the cell phone number that Francisco took from Missy Free's hotel room and found that she and Spongey had talked a few times on the day he was killed."

"So you think she killed him?"

"Either her or Jerrod."

"And WoodHenry almost suffered the same fate. All because he fell in love with that evil woman," Honey mused. "Loneliness can be a terrible thing. It's a shame ain't it?" She sat down next to me on the sofa.

"Yeah it is," I said.

"Well at least this whole thing put WoodHenry in touch with someone who really cares about him," Honey said.

"You mean Albalita?"

"Yeah, WoodHenry called this morning and told me that they're getting a place together. I think she's just what the doctor ordered for him."

"Maybe, I hope so, for his sake," I said.

"She loves him, there's no doubt about that and I've found that you can never discount the power of love. It's worth a lot more than most people realise," Honey stated and sipped from her glass.

I sat quietly not knowing how to say what I wanted to, or even where to start.

"I'm really sorry about what happened, I mean about the guy raping you and..." I started then stopped.

"Yeah I am too, but at least I'm still alive and Harold's not hurt. It could have been a lot worse."

"Yeah I suppose it could have, but still I shouldn't have shifted my concentration from you not even for a moment."

"You couldn't have possibly known what was going to happen Youngblood, and anyway, if you hadn't had Moses looking after me, I would be dead now, not to mention Harold too. You have nothing to be sorry for, in fact I consider myself a very lucky woman that I had you on the case. Anyway the past is the past." She smiled and placed her glass on the cocktail table, and pulled her feet up on the sofa under her. She relaxed down into the seat and placed her head on my shoulder.

"Too bad about one thing though" she chuckled

"What's that?"

"That you're so afraid of older women, maybe you could learn a thing or two from someone like me," she smiled.

"Maybe."

"But don't sweat it, maybe one day you'll wise up, maybe" she laughed and snuggled closer to me.

"Maybe," I said still thinking about how Honey might have been killed and how I almost lost one of my best friends. After a few minutes I could hear her short shallow breaths. She was fast asleep. I sat there thinking about Honey's courage and spirit and maybe she was right. Maybe love was worth a lot more than most people realised. Tom Jerrod had realised it the hard way.

Maybe when you get right down to it, love is the only thing that holds the world together in a funny way. People loving each other, making mistakes, and then being strong enough to forgive and continue loving each other the next day. Maybe love was one of those truly indefinable and priceless things like the feeling of closeness that I was experiencing at the moment for my friend. It felt beautiful. Kind of like a baby's smile or even like the beauty of a John Coltrane saxophone solo.

THE END

Other songs from WoodHenry's songwriting notebook

Track # 10
TOUCHIN' YOU IN THE MORNIN

I LOVE TOUCHIN YOU IN THE MORNIN
I LOVE TOUCHIN YOU IN THE MORNIN
I LOVE TOUCHIN YOU IN THE MORNIN
WHAT A GREAT WAY TO START MY DAY

Of all the things that I adore
like walkin on the shore
Playin with the babies on the floor
The thing that I love most
is holdin you close and feelin your body
as warm as toast,
It helps my potential, it's part of my essential, well being
Mind freein helping me through day,
so I just want to say that..

I LOVE TOUCHIN YOU IN THE MORNIN
I LOVE TOUCHIN YOU IN THE MORNIN
I LOVE TOUCHIN YOU IN THE MORNIN
WHAT A GREAT WAY TO START MY DAY

On my business trips, I'm starting to slip
and feel I'm losing my grip, because of the pressure.
I know it's just a reaction ,cause I need to get home
to my satisfaction.
The thing I really dread to the bone
is going to bed alone and waking up
in the middle of the night on my own
I can't stand it, I feel so stranded
That's why I' m willing to drive straight through the night
on the turnpike, that's alright
It's worth every minute every mile every inch
To reach what- has- been heaven sent
to me, there is no higher degree of
intimacy I have ever achieved
than the one I have when the sun comes up
and I feel you in my arms girl yeah.

I LOVE TOUCHIN YOU IN THE MORNIN
I LOVE TOUCHIN YOU IN THE MORNIN
I LOVE TOUCHIN YOU IN THE MORNIN
WHAT A GREAT WAY TO START MY DAY

My heart is jumpin must be somethin'
Extraordinary and necessary
You authenticate me, you motivate me
Resuscitate me, emancipate me
Sun starts over the horizon
And my hand starts massaging your thighs and
Birds start singing, my body's tingling
Hormones are flowin, our love is growin

I LOVE TOUCHIN YOU IN THE MORNIN
I LOVE TOUCHIN YOU IN THE MORNIN
I LOVE TOUCHIN YOU IN THE MORNIN
WHAT A GREAT WAY TO START MY DAY

Track # 11
BEEN GOOD TO YOU

Ooh baby love the way you make me feel
Ooh sugar you sure know how to keep it real
Can't deny I'm turned on by, watching you dance nude
(sexy sexy momma)
You wreck my head when we're in the bed
with the things you do
What you give me I never had before
Won't let go so sensual I need it more and more
What you got me baby it's a crying shame
I toss and turn and sweat and burn and I call your name
Baby..baby Ohh…oooh baby, All night long baby)

I BEEN GOOD YOU YOU,
SO DO WHAT I SAY DO,
BABY'S GOT SOMETHING TO HELP YOU THROUGH
I BEEN GOOD YOU YOU,
SO DO WHAT I SAY DO,

BABY'S GOT SOMETHING TO HELP YOU THROUGH

Ooh baby love it all night long
(Just don'y stop, don't stop baby)
Soak n wet four thirty in the morning we still goin strong
O0h baby I can understand
(I love this thing you do)
how the stuff you use can turn a boy into a man]
Ooowee sugar unplug the phone
(girl, I don't want to talk to nobody)
Make me do what me to til I scream and moan
Ooh baby you are number one
(I don't want nobody else)
What you got is a helluva lot make me talk in tongues

I BEEN GOOD YOU YOU,
SO DO WHAT I SAY DO,
BABY'S GOT SOMETHING TO HELP YOU THROUGH
I BEEN GOOD YOU YOU,
SO DO WHAT I SAY DO,
BABY'S GOT SOMETHING TO HELP YOU THROUGH

Track #12
YOUR HEALER

Let me share your hurt let me share your pain,
We can make it through the pouring rain,
standing strong together.
I know you've been let down badly in the past,
but better days are coming, the dark don't last forever.

LET ME BE YOUR HEALER,
LET ME BE THE ONE TO HELP FIND A BRIGHTER DAY
LET ME BE YOUR HEALER,
LET ME KISS IT BETTER AND CHASE YOUR BLUES AWAY.

.

Rely on me to always be respectful of your feelings
I want to be your confidant your soul-mate and your lover.
I understand that even though I do the best I can
that human beings aren't tailor made and fitted to each other.

LET ME BE YOUR HEALER,
LET ME BE THE ONE TO HELP FIND A BRIGHTER DAY
LET ME BE YOUR HEALER,
I WANT TO KISS IT BETTER AND CHASE YOUR BLUES AWAY.

Everybody faces rough times in life, times when you might be feeling a little insecure or you might not believe in yourself enough or feel strong enough to take the next step alone. I know what you're feeling because I've been there too. I'm not saying that I'm some kind of magic man, but I'm just willing to give you the best that I have, so that maybe together we can discover something better and more positive than we have alone. I'd just like to try and be there for you as much as I possibly can and with all of my heart.

Truth can be an empty word, it's one no doubt you've often heard,
I make to you no promises but I have got the notion,
that I can help you find the key to unlock a sweet melody,
in which we can find harmony and long lasting devotion.

LET ME BE YOUR HEALER,
LET ME BE THE ONE TO HELP FIND A BRIGHTER DAY
LET ME BE YOUR HEALER,
LET ME KISS IT BETTER AND CHASE YOUR BLUES AWAY.

LET ME BE YOUR HEALER,
LET ME BE THE ONE TO HELP FIND A BRIGHTER DAY
LET ME BE YOUR HEALER,
LET ME KISS IT BETTER AND CHASE YOUR BLUES AWAY.

Track #13
NEXT TO YOU

(rap)
I got that feelin you wanna get right down to it,
You got problems, don't worry baby we'll get through it,
baby it's alright, cause we're gonna do it tonight.
Don't worry bout what your friends are sayin
They don't understand a single thing about us, naw,
Ah baby, just let me make love to you tonight.

All I WANNA DO IS GET NEXT TO YOU.
All I WANNA DO IS GET NEXT TO YOU.
All I WANNA DO IS GET NEXT TO YOU.
All I WANNA DO IS GET NEXT TO YOU

This is no fantasy I am not a dragon slayer,
I'm tellin you girl I'm no player
Baby it's alright I wanna make love to you tonight.

I know you want it, something you can feel good about
(you want some lovin)
The kind that turns you inside out.
Babe I guarantee I have got just what you need

(rap)

Tonight, Tonight Tonight
All I WANNA DO IS GET NEXT TO YOU.
All I WANNA DO IS GET NEXT TO YOU.
All I WANNA DO IS GET NEXT TO YOU.
All I WANNA DO IS GET NEXT TO YOU

Track # 14
OBSESSION

My love for you is a raging fire
Out of control growing higher and higher
You are my soul's insatiable desire
Right here is where I want to stay
I would not have it any other way
Got to have you- Got to have you with me every day

OBSESSION, POSSESSION
SOMETHING YOU GOT GOT A HOLD ON ME,
LIKE VOODOO WHAT YOU DO
WHAT YOU GOT JUST WILL NOT LET ME BE
I SWEAR ON STARS ABOVE
I GOT AN OBSESSION WITH YOUR LOVE.

Sometimes you make me want to cry
I want to stop this thing but I'm too afraid to try
and don't wanna even understand the reason why
At night I wake up in a sweat (girl, yes I do)
Realisin that you I never forget (always on my mind)
Never in my whole life had my whole so upset (what I got for you is).

OBSESSION, POSSESSION
SOMETHING YOU GOT GOT A HOLD ON ME,
LIKE VOODOO WHAT YOU DO
WHAT YOU GOT JUST WILL NOT LET ME BE
I SWEAR ON STARS ABOVE
I GOT AN OBSESSION WITH YOUR LOVE.

The other novels in the Devil Barnett series are:
Blood Red Blues
Dead By Popular Demand

devilbarnett.com
email: devilbarnett@hotmail.com